The Boundaries of

TWILIGHT

*Czecho-Slovak Writing
from the New World*

Edited by C. J. HRIBAL

Many Minnesotas Project Number 6

NEW RIVERS PRESS 1991

Copyright 1991 by New Rivers Press
Library of Congress Catalog Card Number 90-61092
ISBN 0-89823-121-3
All Rights Reserved
Book Design by Gaylord Schanilec
Typesetting by Peregrine Publications
Front Cover Photograph by Jan Frank
Editorial Assistance by Paul J. Hintz

The editor would like to thank Darrell Fike, for his editorial contributions as first reader for a number of manuscripts, and for his insight and enthusiasm; Josef Škvorecký, for putting him in contact with a large number of the North American Czecho-Slovak community of writers; Bohumil Krcil, for presenting the portfolios of Czech photographers in exile; Zdenik Sadlon, for his consultations and advice; Joseph Rothschild, for his book; Krystyna Kornilowicz, for her editorial assistance, patience, faith, and advice; Bill O'Donnell, for going to bat for him; the many contributors who made this project possible; and Katie Maehr and Bill Truesdale, for their endurance and good humor in making this book a reality.

Special thanks also to Memphis State University, which supplied Faculty Research Grant funds that allowed for the editing of this collection, and to Marquette University, where the collection assumed its final form. An editorial error in compiling this collection resulted in an accepted manuscript, "Two Voices" by Bronislava Volková, not being printed. The editor apologizes for the omission.

The Boundaries of Twilight: Czecho-Slovak Writing from the New World was published with the aid of grants from the Arts Development Fund of the United Arts Council, the Beverly J. and John A. Rollwagen Fund of the Minneapolis Foundation, Cray Research Foundation, the Elizabeth A. Hale Fund of the Minneapolis Foundation, the First Bank System Foundation, Liberty State Bank, the Star Tribune/Cowles Media Company, the Tennant Company Foundation, and the National Endowment for the Arts (with funds appropriated by the Congress of the United States).

New Rivers Press books are distributed by

The Talman Company   Bookslinger
150-5th Avenue   2402 University Avenue
New York, NY 10011   St. Paul, MN 55114

The Boundaries of Twilight: Czecho-Slovak Writing from the New World has been manufactured in the United States of America for New Rivers Press (C. W. Truesdale, Editor/Publisher), 420 N. 5th Street/Suite 910, Minneapolis, MN 55401 in a first edition of 2,000.

To Krystyna, as always

CONTENTS

Introduction

IRONY, TOLERANCE, AND MEMORY

"The music is playing, cheerfully from afar."
— Josef Sudek,
Czechoslovak photographer when
the right image greeted him inside his viewfinder

THIS BOOK IS BORN from the hyphenation of a hyphenation. When Thomas Garrigue Masaryk cajoled the Western powers after the First World War to create the political, if not culturally homogenous, entity known as Czechoslovakia, he did it partially by enlisting the support of numerous Czech-American and Slovak-American associations, and to a certain extent based the validity of his arguments for such an enterprise on the enthusiam and support of those associations. He even went so far as to allow the North American groups to write some of the laws to which the Czechs and Slovaks in Czechoslovakia would be subject.

That perversion of the statute-making process didn't last, of course. But the country did. Not that it was an easy alliance. In the words of Joseph Rothschild, in his *East Central Europe Between the Two World Wars,* Czechoslovakia had "the dubious distinction as ethnically the least homogenous of all the new states of Europe." In addition to internal separatist movements during the years of the First Republic (Czechoslovakia came into being from the merger of Bohemia, Moravia, parts of Silesia, Ruthenia, and Slovakia, bargained for from the Great Powers meeting in Versailles following the First World War's conclusion) there were the political and military pressures on them from Germany, Poland, and the Austro-Hungarian Empire, which claimed the territories now comprising Czechoslovakia. Yet during the period between the wars, Czechoslovakia was the most prosperous and politically stable of the Eastern European countries, and this was at least partly due, according to Rothschild, to the more ethical/intellectual bent of its leaders, as compared, at least, to the political/military bent of its neighbors.

One wonders, of course, if Czechoslovakia as we now know it would have existed at all if not for the shrewd politicking of its leaders, who seemed particularly adept at making the sand castle of their dreams hold together. It is true, however, that while politically ambitious, Czechoslovakia's leaders were not militaristic. Even during the Depression, Rothschild writes, Czechoslovakia remained "committed to constitutional parliamentarianism while all around her neighbors were succumbing to totalitarian, military, or royal dictatorships."

Twice since its founding Czechoslovakia has disappeared as an autonomous entity – following Munich in 1938 (in the years of the Nazi Protectorate Czechoslovakia was dismembered and only a "rump" state was allowed continued existence), and following the Communist Putsch in 1948. Twenty years later came what Josef Škvorecký calls the "armed ambush" of August 21, 1968, which ended the Prague Spring in a bloody reaffirmation of Russian hegemony over its reluctant and resisting satellites. (There is an old joke, going back to the days of the Czar, that for a Russian the only secure border is one with a Russian on either side of it.)

Yet the country has proven to be surprisingly resilient. The nation that was a unified state as the medieval kingdom of Bohemia, now Czechoslovakia's largest province, when not only Germany and Italy, but even France and Spain were still disunited and internally fragmented, the nation that was one of the few in Europe to avoid the bubonic plague (only to fall victim, centuries later, to a political one) is reasserting itself as a democratic entity. I write this introducton on a day in June 1990, just after Civic Forum and Public Against Violence have won a majority of seats in their parliament in the first free elections to be held in Czechoslovakia in forty-four years. And the country's president, Václav Havel, (a playwright!), is being compared to Thomas Masaryk, whose succinct motto "Truth will prevail" Havel has updated, given the contingencies under which he's operating, to "Truth and love must prevail over lies and hatred." Still an imperative, but an imperative cognizant that what must happen doesn't always happen – a qualification reflecting, no doubt, a half-century's worth of actions to the contrary, and a knowledge of how fragile moral imperatives can be.

＊ ＊ ＊

What does this brief historical overview have to do with a book compiled from the writings of some fifty North Americans of Czechoslovak descent? It is this: One of the typical outgrowths of coming from a small country with a proud but benighted history is a strong sense of irony coupled with an amused tolerance of what goes on around you (and to you). Like Poland – another crossroads for armies from just about any direction in Europe – Czechoslovakia is not a strong country. Its pride lies elsewhere. It has to. History has steamrollered it. And both the inhabitants of and the immigrants from steamrollered countries tend to have long memories.

Acknowledging weakness in the face of superior strength is not a bad tactic when you think about it. For one thing, it buys you time to undermine the strength of those above. In a perverse reversal of Orwell, it is not ignorance but weakness that is strength. "They pretend to pay us and we pretend to work," goes the old joke in countries suffering from micromanaged central planning. Kundera, Hašek, Čapek, Kafka – all show in their works the possibilities, and the limits, of such weakness. If Hašek with his Good Soldier Švejk (Westernized as Schweik) demonstrates how successful cheerful subjugation can be – Švejk's greatest triumph being the moment he is captured by his own troops – then Kafka reveals the dark side of the same notion. Over and over in his books Kafka chronicles the painful stories of people unable to come to terms with a baffling, pervasive bureaucracy except through capitulation. And yet the center of such stories is an equally fantastic, pervasive, and bleak humor. Milan Kundera reports in *The Art of the Novel*, "When Kafka read the first chapter of *The Trial* to his friends, everyone laughed, including the author."

Let's go back to resiliency for a moment. In David Byrne's film *True Stories*, the mayor of the imaginary town of Virgil, Texas tells the story of how God labored for six days creating the earth, and towards the end of the sixth day He got around to Texas, but just as He was getting started it was time to quit, and after taking the seventh day off all that half-finished land had hardened and baked dry. And God, in His infinite wisdom, decided not to start over from scratch but instead said, "I know, I'll make a bunch of people who'll like it here!" People adapt – to history, circumstance, fate – and reinvent their lives in the process. Sometimes they adapt and reinvent through flight. They escape their known tyrannies for the possibilities of the unknown, carrying their histories inside them, inside the elastic yet fragile shell of their memories. Everything they encounter in the new world first filters its way through that shell of memory.

Not that there aren't major losses, memory and otherwise, for each immigrant. There is the loss of the original holders of the cultural heritage, for one thing. People die, to put it plainly. Links are severed. We lose our connections to our past because our forebears' knowledge is not our knowledge and never can be. They learned one thing, we learned another. And it is a combination of joy at one's possibilities in the new homeland and the sad knowledge that the old homeland is forever lost that causes immigrants, no doubt, to procreate with such startling and rapid frequency, scaring the bejesus out of the more staid and financially secure WASPs who have been here long enough to fool themselves into thinking they have some kind of divine right over the continent.

For the new immigrant, and the immigrant community, assimilation itself is a kind of death. The substitution of cultures – the kids of immigrants speak a kind of pidgin Czech, the grandchildren not at all – is a process in which the richness of one culture is invariably lost, or overwhelmed, by the richness, the diversity, of the adopted culture. Sometimes all that remains is the names of the food. Jiternice, kolachke, all the varieties of homage done to the potato and the cabbage in clean, cramped kitchens smelling of fat and steamed vegetables – these are the tangible artifacts of our cultural heritage. The filtering shell of memory is empty. For example, by the time I was growing up and was told of my heritage – I was Bohemian on my father's side, both of my grandparents having come from a small town just outside Prague (I was told where Bohemia was much later) – I thought that to be a Bohemian meant to be one of a select number of a small Indian tribe, and looking in a mirror at my blonde hair and green eyes, was amazed that such a thing could be possible. I thought this because my German relatives called us Bohunks (they good-naturedly/viciously told Bohunk jokes I didn't understand – they all possessed punchlines in which mushrooms figured prominently) and told stories of how our ancestors on the German side of the family had fought Indians coming across the Plains. I made the erroneous connection that the perjorative "Bohunk" referred to those historical enemies. Little did I realize the animosities were of more recent vintage. That I later volunteered to *be* the Indian in all our stupid childhood games of Cowboys and Indians perhaps marked my future course as believer in lost causes and rooter for majestic losers, the dispossessed at plenty's table.

I became a Cubs fan.

* * *

You will find in this volume a number of stories and poems about sex, about death, about sustenance – physical, psychological, moral – about the irretrievable past. Sex and death, death and sex. Inextricably, obliquely, the procreative act is linked to life's cessation; it is the obliqueness that no doubt fascinates writers. Family histories (and novels) are frequently chockfull of stories about such and such a child being born on the anniversary of or the actual day of death of a grandparent or great uncle, as though for any one family a certain number of souls are allotted and strict accounts kept. If you cannot duplicate yourself or the past, you strive to create an approximation. This is true equally of writing and children. It's the same with the other great themes of existence. You connect with your past through those things that gave you sustenance. Things which are passing away. Even the food, which I mentioned earlier. My wife, a first generation American via Poland, worries with her siblings that once her mother, who came to this country in the mid-fifties, is no longer able to make the traditional meals at Easter and Christmas, they will be hard-pressed to recreate those rituals that for over thirty years have bound them to the country of their origin. The food will still be there, but not quite the same, not quite right. And it's not something you have any control over.

Nor should you. The danger in writing about your forebears is that they tend to get lionized. In writing about the past, everything tends to be seen through a rose-colored wash. Truth gets obliterated by good-intentioned, well-meaning revisionists. The writing here avoids that. The various forebears and fictional selves presented here are not presented as icons, calcified in their purity and goodness, nor are the various pasts invoked here invoked for their nostalgic simplicity. Rather the people are presented as the stubborn, foolish, bewildered survivors and louts humans usually are. And the past is the past, not some revered holy land of perfect time. Saints are not endearing. People rife with foibles are. And you do more to honor what's been lost or left behind by presenting not what is noble and heroic but what is tragic and enduring. The writing here bears witness to the complexity, the contrariness, the inherent contradictions of being human. The horror and humor of the everyday nightmare married to a deep and abiding willingness to believe, with tolerance as the maid of honor and skepticism as the best man – this is what is at work here, this is what these writers have lovingly, painstakingly achieved.

* * *

A proposition: If there is a Czechoslovak national character on display in these pages, it is to be found in the whimsical epigraph I've borrowed from Joseph Sudek. There is joy in that little sentence, yes – the music is most certainly playing. But no small amount of irony, either – the music is far away; you can barely hear it. But you tolerate distance because the music is cheerful, and because you remember it from when it was near.

– C. J. Hribal
March 1991

C. G. Hanzlicek

PRAGUE, LATE NOVEMBER, 1989

ONE QUARTER OF A million people are gathered on the square. After seven hundred lost battles for Czech freedom, they can feel in the air that the time may have come to win one. They light candles at the base of the statue of Wenceslas on horseback; candles, like ardor, burn even in this cold. The tricolor, which must only be flown side by side with the Soviet flag, waves all across the square in sudden solitary dignity. When Alexander Dubcek appears on a balcony and throws out his arms in an embrace that enfolds an entire nation, a giddiness rises among them, as if they are breathing laughing gas. They chant, "Jakes to the garbage, Jakes to the garbage," and then, "Dubcek to the Castle, Dubcek to the Castle." The Party twitches, but it is dead. Privilege is dead. The professor who has been stoking boilers on the night shift for twenty years may teach again. A man who closed down his newspaper in '68 is passing out free copies of today's revived edition. A voice over a loudspeaker calls for attention, and the crowd instantly falls silent. There is an urgent message: a nine-year-old boy named Honza has become separated from his mother. "Be brave, Honza, be brave," they chant. No Czech can be truly free until Honza finds his mama.

CEMETERY IN
DOLNI DOBROUČ, CZECHOSLOVAKIA

Over the stone wall, an old man
Cuts hay with a scythe, stacks it
With a wooden rake.

A diamond in the dark
Is poor as this old villager,
But birches shivering in the sun of Bohemia

Are pure silver.
Rodina Hanzlikova.
Family Hanzlicek.

My people,
Ashes;
The unburned shards of bone

Are diamonds in the heavy loam,
Unlit beneath geraniums.
The old man's work is done.

The logs of his cottage
Were hewn two hundred years ago
By people whose names are still spoken.

He will lie back against his wall,
Sigh and take the sun,
Drink an amber glass of cool beer.

Rodina Hanzlikova.
No given names; there could be two or
twenty turned into the soil.

My work is done.
I will return to my forty-year-old house,
In a country where

No one can pronounce my name,
But I was here a while,
Silent in the sun shivering the birches,

Among my people,
Nameless,
Ashes.

PRAGUE WREATHS

You never have to walk far
To find a silver foil
Wreath with its marker,
Yet they always come as a shock:
Against a wall
Beside the gentle sweep of the Vltava,
Near an apartment entrance
On a busy street
(There must have been a hundred witnesses),
Over the buttons to a freight elevator
In a department store.
All about the city,
Men forced to find a way
To be more than men
Were executed on the spot
By Germans.

I can hardly imagine myself
In that place.
Maybe I'm talking,
Maybe a book lies open on the table,
Maybe my hands
Move beneath an eiderdown
To map a body,
And in an instant the thought,
The word, the caress,
Whatever the search,
Is halted
By a gunshot in the street . . .

In front of a wreath at the gate
To my favorite park,
A blue titmouse
Couldn't care less which fool
Inspires my politics.
It's morning, he woke hungry,
So he flits down from a maple
To eat the crumbs of a breakfast roll
From my open hand.
Forty years ago,
Some hungrier distant relative of his
Saw the fall, the blood,
Right here,
Of Karel Zbiral (1897–1945),
A creature
Who could not be tamed.

ADRIFT

We're all having such a good time,
Alone yet not alone,
And then the projector jams:
There is a yellow and red blossom,
A white, brown-rimmed center
Flows to the edges in seconds
Until the whole screen
Is a blinding sheet.
There is a moment,
After the auditorium falls totally dark,
When the blackness feels like release.

Like that dream where you are dangling,
Way up there,
And you have to drop
One hand to protect something,
Heart or crotch or eyes, maybe all three,
It's a nightmare after all,
And you twirl there
Like a blue-stamped carcass of beef
Watching the milliseconds stretch to hours,
And then the last of you is gone,
And you simply straighten your aching fingers,
And it turns out to be not at all as bad
As you thought it would be,
Letting go,
Adrift.

DEBT

A row of mulberries is heavy
With the clatter of starlings
Preparing for evening.
Their Latin name says they're vulgar,
But everything alive must flock,
Chatter, sleep,
Eat and all that follows.
Past the mulberries,
Past the path worn to a powder,
The steel gate
Needs a loud slam to set its latch.
Hundreds of pigeons veer off in unison,
And the sun is thrown
From their wings
As if from a turning mirror.
I see myself
In the horse's slow eye.
He noses my forearm
And doesn't seem to mind
I have come empty-handed,
Though he's grazed his field
To stubble.
I admire him
Because he is a mild creature,
He is by nature loyal,
Silent,
Attentive to caresses,
And he couldn't care less about money.
I owe very little,
Yet I feel indebted to everything.

Deborah O'Harra

LITOST

> *Litost is a Czech word with no exact*
> *translation . . . The first syllable,*
> *which is long and stressed, sounds*
> *like the wail of an abandoned dog.*
>   – Milan Kundera

The woman has no eyebrows:
Her eyes are houses without roofs.
Therefore, she is never shocked
By the incidental brutality of
The drunken soldier, the fearful poet.

She cannot knit her face into confusion
When her child asks her
If angels are invisible.
The child, accustomed to her blankness,
Walks away without his imagination.

She smiles at the doctor before
He inserts the tube that will suck
Someone's life from her, but the smile
Is a mystery, a picture without a frame:
No irony, no wistfulness, no cynicism.

She lives in a nation without eyebrows:
When the foreigners stole them, the nation
Could not raise its eyebrows in disapproval,
Shoot its eyebrows up in shock,
Gather them in pain; could only smile

At the memory of its own face:
Surprised, but wise; could only sigh,
Not unable to see the irony, reflected by
Halos of spring sunshine on black tanks.
Calling passionately for the angels

Of revenge, the nation paints eyebrows
Upon itself, visible only to those who know
How laughter and vengeance, defeat and longing
Can copulate, giving birth to the litost
Of a lost nation, keening of an ageless orphan.

BOHUNK LOVE

for Jim Hazard and Whiting, Indiana

We're coming off the Grapevine careening
Through the curves on the road to the Bohunk
Side of the family: the uncouth, my Swedish grandmother says.
We're all drunk – Dad on scotch, Mom
On fear and us kids on impending drama.

Dad honks the horn in the driveway and the whole house
Comes running out, shouting. We are hugged and kissed, tossed
Half in the air. They shove another drink into Dad's hand
Before we even get to the porch
And we kids open presents out there on the gravel.

My sisters and I get new nightgowns: pastel blue, pink and green
With angel sleeves. We run inside and put them on, take
Turns standing on the toilet to see in the medicine chest mirror.

At once the men begin: "Goddamn Republicans!
Goddamn Ronnie Reagan!" They praise the Teamsters, curse
All pipefitters, pound their fists on the table,
Where I sit, eating Grandpa's salsa sauce straight
From a coffee cup. "She's a real Bohunk, that one," someone says
And suddenly it erupts. Grandpa wants to go

To the Elks or the topless but Dad says,
"Goddamn it, we just got here" and then Uncle Don says
"Let's stay home, Dad," and Grandpa says, "What do you know, you
sorry sonofabitch, you voted for Reagan for governor," and then
Dad is saying, "All you kids in the car" and we are whisked

Outside by Aunt Patsy, who hides us in the bushes. She says
"Shhhh!" while Dad's yelling, "Where in the hell
Are those goddamn kids?" My brother and I giggle;
My sisters hold their breath and each other's hands.

I lift my arms and spread my sleeves, pretending I am
Invisible, pretending I can see inside
The house, even though I'm standing out
In the bushes, nipples hardening in the chilly dark.

Dad and Uncle Don are fighting and Mom and Grandma are screaming,
"Stop or we'll call the police! Chuck, the neighbors will hear!"
Grandpa is putting his lard belly and his straight-line mouth
Between them and they almost hit him, but they stop
And he's shaking his finger at them, turning his back,
Gesturing them away with a closed hand.
Then Dad starts to cry and Uncle Don says something funny
And Grandpa cackles and they're all hugging each other.
Back in the bushes, I laugh and twirl, arms out, catching

Handfuls of cold air. My sisters glare, appalled at my glee,
Afraid to walk back into the house. But Aunt Patsy knows
It's time, downs her Coors, tosses the can in the bushes,
Wipes her mouth with the back of her hand. "Let's go."
My sisters glide sideways toward the door, but
I fly ahead. The men are laughing and
Crying, hugging each other, saying "sonofabitch."
They draw me into their circle and close it. I cry, too,
Alive with their terrible love.

Laura Pappano

THE MARTHA IN MY RED DRESS

I MARRIED MY WIFE because I became entranced with her small waist. I would see her traveling the elevator in my office building with the sash of her red print cotton dress wrapped tight around her slender middle. When she wore that dress and others that framed her so well, I felt the urge to capture her delicate shape in my arm and draw her inside my open, seersucker lapels.

I used to have such thoughts. Standing behind her in the elevator car, I would imagine resting my two curved hands in the perfect cricks of her waist. And I would imagine how light she would be if I then lifted her, laughing, to see some rare sight above the crowd. I worried, though, that in my excitement, I would lift her too high and she would become the star, casting her radiance on the crowd and leaving only a hard shadow for her pedestal.

For the longest time I never spoke to her. I would only stare. I fixed my eyes on her waistline each time she pressed her hips against the heavy glass doors of 254 Walnut Street. I followed with my gaze as she moved through the marble lobby to the bank of brass-doored elevators. I doubt she ever noticed me then, just one more man in a suit eager for the elevator car to reach his floor. She tells me now she knew me from the others, but I don't believe her. She could have married any one of them and probably never known the difference.

Her name is Martha B. Morris. She took my name when we married almost twenty-six years ago, leaving her name, Jindrulik, to be an abbreviated reminder of her foreign youth. She was twenty-three then. Now, when I look at her, after three children, after three great swellings that have left her skin tired and loose around her middle, I sometimes cannot believe she is the same woman. I have never told her this. Always, I have told her she is as beautiful now as when I first saw her. She closes her eyes and smiles when I say that. Her expression is deep and confident like someone well-satisfied with her life.

She wears her long, gray-streaked hair casually pulled away from her face and wound in double nests above either ear. She has a deep voice for a woman. And when she laughs it is so hearty and powerful like a man's that I feel embarrassed to hear it in the company of others. When we are with friends and she laughs like that I glance towards her and touch my fingers discreetly to my lips. She curtails her laughter, clamping it in her throat obediently because she likes to please me. But she frowns as she does it, as if to tell me "you have no right, but I will stop because I love you."

* * *

"Martha," I say to her. We are alone in our grand white colonial house with green shutters. She has made stuffed chicken with carrots and we are eating our delicate portions in the sun room, now wrapped on three sides by the vague darkness of a summer night. Absently, I fix my eyes on the yellow lamps posted on either side of the outside door. I see them reaching into the dark, hoping for some object on which to pour the color of their light, but there are no trees or fences nearby, only the hungry night air which takes in the glow and gives nothing in return.

"Martha," I say again. I want to talk to her, to tell her something. I stop eating, and try to grasp at this thing I need to tell, but I fail. "Martha, this chicken is lovely."

"It is good, isn't it," she answers. "They have a new meat man down at Packard's. I think he really makes a difference."

* * *

I have never learned to talk to Martha, the way I want to talk to her now. I don't mean that we don't have conversations, because we do. When we returned from a dinner party at the Clarks' about two weeks ago, we talked for a full hour. It was playful talk, laced with laughter. It was the kind of talk that builds and falls and builds again, that would look like the shape of a mountain range if you could draw it. And like mountains, each story bred another, slightly more wicked and childish than the one before, until stopping, I realized we were far from the seed that started it all.

That night it started when Martha said she didn't think Winston Pildner's jokes were funny. I said the only thing funny about Winston was the way he looked when Bonnie Mills accidentally brushed his face with her stacked hairdo as she twisted to pass the mustard sauce. Her hair was organized so carefully, Martha said laughing, that she worried it would fall right there on Winston – the ribbons and pins and faux braids. I laughed, and she laughed again as we undressed. We jabbed fun at the way Lloyd Spencer kept calling Dolly Patterson, "Polly" because somehow he got it into his head that that should be her name.

And when I absolutely ripped apart Bert Clark's toast to his guests and his wife's floral dress that made her look like the sitting room sofa, I felt so attracted to Martha. I felt flushed seeing her standing in her underwear near the window, her mouth covered with both hands to mute the sound of her deep laugh. But when the laughter ended, we were worn out and naked, each on our own side of the room. Martha took a tissue from her bedside stand and wiped the tears from her eyes.

"I haven't laughed like that in a long time," she said.

"I haven't either," I said.

"You were very handsome tonight," she said.

"It was the tie," I said, and she smiled, happy that I had worn that gift from her.

I got out my robe and draped it over the chair, as I do every night before bed. Martha let her hair down, putting the hairclips on her bedside stand. She combed out the day's tangles, as she does every night. Then we each climbed, naked, into our own sides of the bed, which is big enough so our skin does not touch in the night.

For a month I have not crossed the line to her territory. She has crossed to mine only once. That time, about three weeks ago, she moved close to me, molding her body against my back as I slept on my side away from her. I remember feeling her soft, warm skin drawing close to mine, and I thought of the way we used to sleep, always touching. Then I felt her tongue gliding in a circle on the smooth skin of my back. When she used to do that, I would shudder inside and turn around, eager. But that time, I pretended I was so deep in sleep that I could not be woken. She traced the pattern one more time, but I could not bring myself to move. Finally, she kissed my right shoulder and rolled back to her side. I heard her crying softly, and I felt sad, but I could not make myself respond.

Our youngest child, Anna, left four years ago. She took with her the clamor and the clutter of family life. I am still getting used to the sounds that for so long have been masked by rock music, running feet and the shrill of voices yelling up and down the stairs. Now, in the evening, the sounds of Martha preparing dinner visit me as I relax in the sitting room. First I hear grinding and chopping, the snarl of the electric grater or the firm sound of a heavy knife against a wooden cutting board. Then I hear the hiss of cold food tossed in a hot pan. And lastly, the clatter of Martha searching for the right lid to cover and contain our meal.

On Saturdays now when I read the paper, I can hear Martha's footsteps upstairs. I hear her as she gathers the laundry from the hall hamper, carries it downstairs, and stops in the kitchen for soap before traveling to the basement.

There are other changes, too. When we go out to the store or for a trip now, I pull the car out of the garage and only Martha is there, waiting at the edge of the drive to get in. Sometimes when I see her there, her mint green cardigan sweater pulled over her shoulders, and her arms hanging down in front with her two fists wrapped around the handle of her white vinyl summer purse, I want to drive past. I want to drive down Route 37 to the city, and turn onto Walnut Street. I want to stop at the tall office building at number 254 and wait for that woman to come and press her hips against the heavy glass door.

When I married Martha I told her I had plans, that I was going to be some-body. Whenever I told her that, she stared me in the eyes and said, "You already are." "I know, but you know what I mean," I said back. "No," she said sternly, and held on to her expression.

When she got like that, stern and sure of herself, I would place my two hands on either side of her face and kiss her until she softened. I would kiss her so deeply that I could not tell where her lips ended and mine began. Those times, I would close my eyes and think of every small thing I was feeling so that when I was away from her I could close my eyes again and reassemble the parts of her smells and her breathing and her movements.

I have not abandoned my plans, but I don't talk to her about them anymore because I know she disapproves. I can tell because when I mention my plans and my fears about failing, she folds her arms across her chest, her neck muscles erect, and tells me she married me for who I was and that she doesn't want anything more.

* * *

I tip my head against the window of the sun porch and stare at the yellow lamps. Large-winged flies hover around the torch-shaped cage of light. I see them land and take off again, lured by the light but repelled by the heat it generates.

Martha picks up my plate and hers and walks them to the kitchen. She leaves the water running, and returns to shake the crumbs from the placemats and napkins. She rolls the table dressings together and stuffs them under her left arm. With her free arm, she uses a sponge to wipe the crinkled glass tabletop, brushing the food crumbs into the cup of her wet and waiting left hand.

"Pour some whiskey?" she asks. She smiles furtively and makes one last sponge round of the table.

"Good," I say. I speak to her back because she has turned toward the kitchen, her cupped hand of crumbs held carefully away from her body.

In the evenings after dinner, we sometimes play Scrabble. Tonight, Martha has already taken the game out of the hall closet and placed it on the low mahogany table in the living room. It is her signal.

I get up from the table and move into the living room. Martha redecorated the room a month ago in what I call "hunting colors" after more than twenty years in the soothing shades of cream and white. The walls are now painted a deep, strong red. The beige sofa has been reupholstered in a brown and red floral print and she has even stained the oak floors a deep walnut brown. The change, she says proudly, is her artistic statement. "I wanted you to see my talents. And besides, I think we need some life in here," she said to me when she mentioned her plans. I take my only comfort in knowing that the old room still exists beneath the layers of paint and fabric and stain.

I open the Scrabble box and give us each a wooden letter holder in order to shield our strategies from one another. Next, I turn the small wooden letter squares into the top of the box, which is worn on two diagonal corners from being passed back and forth between us. I am not very good at this game, but I play it because Martha likes it. I think she only likes to play because it is an excuse to drink whiskey. I told her that after a game once, and she looked at me with a hateful expression. She said marriage to me was excuse enough. Later, she cried and said she didn't mean it, that she had only said what she said because she'd been drinking.

I am terrible at this game. So, as a safety measure I plant the letters I need in strategic places around the box top. I put an "A" upside down in the corner most worn from handling; an "E" in the next closest corner, and an "X" and a "U" in the other two corners. Along the edges I place other letters crucial to survival: S, T, N, R, I, and O. I have done this for so long that I think Martha must know, but she's never said anything.

"Whiskey?" Martha has brought the bottle and two shallow glasses. It is our ritual drink with this game. She places the two glasses on the table and hands me the bottle to pour. She unties the thin belt of her cotton print dress and reties it, letting it hang looser around her middle before sitting on the sofa in front of the game board. I am in my green stuffed chair – the only piece of furniture in the room she didn't change.

"Okay, draw," I say, pouring the whiskey. Obediently, but with careful consideration, she picks up eight wooden squares from the box top and places them in her letter holder. I put a glass of whiskey on a bamboo coaster in front of each of us. She takes a sip while I pick my letters.

She starts simply. "C-H-I-L-D." We drink. I study my letters. I have a "V" that will fall on a triple point square. I spell "L-O-V-E," from her "L," see

I have an "R" and add it. "L-O-V-E-R." She looks at me and smiles. She is like that. She takes small gestures and interprets them for herself.

She spells "V-O-L-U-M-E" from my "V." I cannot compete. I spell "M-I-S-S" from the "M." On my next turn I put "T-R-E-S-S" on the bottom, but she stops me as I start to count the letters for my score.

"That is not how you spell it," she says. Her tone is harsh. She takes a long drink from her glass and pours some more. After a few turns of three and four letter words, she smiles then boastfully spells out "S-O-I-L-E-D" from my earlier "S." "There," she says, and counts her score.

"Very nice," I say.

I take a drink and look at my letters. None seem to go together. "Martha," I say, touching my hand to her arm. "Do you really want to play?"

"Why?" Her voice is light and hesitant. She lifts the glass to her lips. "I just thought we could talk instead," I say.

She touches her fingers to the loose nests of gray hair on either side of her head. "If you want to talk, we can talk," she says, bringing her hands to rest in her lap. She is silent, now, waiting for me. I feel the weight of the house and the room pushing on my shoulders and my back. I take a drink and sit back in my chair and let my head sink into the worn green head cushion.

"You know, I've been meaning to tell you, I really like how you've done the room," I say, my eyes facing the far corner of the room where the red wall and white ceiling are bridged by a wide piece of corner molding.

"I'm glad," she says, her eyes fixed on me, even as she lifts her glass to take another sip.

"I like the red. It's very rich, very strong . . . it reminds me of that dress you used to wear."

"I don't remember," she says.

"That red dress," I say. She realizes the one I mean and she frowns. "It's funny you liked that. I wore it as my last choice. It wasn't me."

I take a drink. It feels like a lit match traveling down my throat. "You know, dear, I thought I was the luckiest man on earth, marrying you. Whatever made you marry me?"

"I don't know," she says. She turns her face away to take a sip. "I could tell you a lot of things, but I really don't know."

I take another sip. I can feel the rims of my eyes burn. They feel as if they are pulling away from my face. I don't know if it is the whiskey or hearing Martha's voice so unwavering. I had expected her to say something else.

"Dear," she says, drawing my attention with the power of that word. "What did you want to talk about? Not about that dress?"

I look toward the window at the far end of the living room, through the new gold drapes. My eyes are stopped at the glass. Martha has turned off the outside lights and the night air now looks thick and dark and finite, pressing against the windows of our house as if it were solid. There is nowhere else to go.

"Martha. This thing. I have to tell you," I say. I pause and I wonder why I feel compelled this way. Finally, the words escape my lips. They are small and helpless when they reach the air, in such contrast to the weight they have carried all the times I have repeated them over and over to myself practicing for this moment.

She looks at my mouth as I speak. I know because I cannot see her eyes looking at mine. She does not smile, but closes her lips together. When she opens them to speak, she does not look at me. "And how is that?" she asks. "How is it that you love me, now?"

When she finally lifts her deep brown eyes to meet mine, they are dry and stronger than I imagined they would be at this moment. I am suddenly afraid to realize how calm she looks. She has known for years.

Mary Kolada Harris

GIRLS IN YUGOSLAVIA

The girls in Yugoslavia,
he said, and he should know,
mold themselves to beds
like flowers pressed in books,
eternally fresh and fragile.
They exude yeasty aromas –
homebaked bread and musk.

Serbian girls are loyal,
willing to die for love or less,
and he's danced on enough graves
to quell my doubts. Slavic girls
are exquisite, wearing nothing
but bronzed olive skin. They
perspire scented oil and never shave.

He married a girl from Yugoslavia,
of course. Numbed by his litany,
I had already left, escaping
the country of his obsession.
His wife speaks no English and
has a downy black mustache.
How could I possibly compete?

Josef Škvorecký

FEMININE MYSTIQUE

Translated by Paul Wilson

WE WERE SITTING in the warehouse waiting for Kadeřábek. From the church on the square came the sound of the organ and the wailing of the old women:

> *Joyously we greeeet thee,*
> *Mother of Our Loooooord...*

I tried to imagine Marie in her May dress, which was dark blue with a pattern of white flowers on it, and with a blue ribbon tied around her hair so that it cascaded down her back like a waterfall of gold. When she first showed up in school with her hair that way, Lexa told me a pony-tail was a phallic symbol. According to him, it meant that my chances with Marie, which had up till then been practically non-existent, were about to improve. But I hadn't yet read *Introductory Lectures on Psychoanalysis* (I was in line for it after Lexa, who'd borrowed it from someone's library) so I asked, naïvely, what a phallic symbol was. Lexa guffawed out loud, the teacher interpreted this as a deliberate disruption of his math class, and a chain reaction took place, the climax of which came when Lexa was asked about integrals, as much a mystery to him as they were to me: both of them – teacher and student – maintained a three-minute silence, then Lexa received an "F" and and an official reprimand, noted in the record book, for disturbing the class.

During break, Lexa explained phallic symbol.

I stared at the golden waterfall undulating and sparkling a few paces ahead of us as we promenaded through the halls. "But that's dumb," I told him. "It sure doesn't look like one."

"But it's called a pony-tail, don't you see? 'Tail' is a homonym for 'cock.'"

"Synonym," said Berta, who as usual had done his homework.

"But it's just a word. It doesn't look a bit like the thing itself," I said.

"Words can be erotic symbols too," said Lexa. "Like, Freud says that when you dream about a room, it really means a vagina."

I thought about that for a moment, and then remembered a dream I'd had the night before, about how I was in church with Marie and – I quickly suppressed the rest of it and said, "Bullshit. If that were true almost all of our dreams would be – " I stopped, and then said, "I'm always dreaming about being in some math class with a teacher trying to prove I'm a mathematical idiot. Where's the vagina in that?"

"It's in the word," said Lexa. "In German, the word for woman is *Frauenzimmer* – in other words, a female chamber. And a chamber's a hollow space, like a vagina."

"Then it's a linguistic problem, gentlemen," said Harýk. "Only Germans can be surrounded by cunts in their dreams. And maybe inhabitants of the *Ostmark*."

"Why?" asked Benno. It was generally recognized that Benno was a little slow.

"What about 'boudoir,' maestro?" said Harýk, turning to him. "Could that be a synonym for woman?"

"Depends on what a synonym is," replied Benno.

"Or a homonym?" said Lexa.

"Boudoir and woman are not homonyms," said Berta firmly.

My conscience was assuaged. Dreams of Marie in church were not immoral after all. Not in Czech, anyway.

And Marie was certainly in church right now. Her superb contralto voice was somewhere in all that wailing. I tried to pick it out but the church was too far away.

You are a jeeeewel in God's heavenly crown . . .

sang the old women.

"Which one are you thinking about now, dreamer?" I heard Lexa say. Quickly I returned to the warehouse. Přema was standing in front of me, and he handed me a sheet of paper.

"Can you check my spelling, Danny?" he said. "Make sure I didn't make mistakes."

I took the document. *Brothers!* it began. *We haven't forgotten the events that happened one year ago at the Charles Univercity, when the student Jan Oplétal got shot –*

I corrected the mistakes and then said, "You should add 'Sisters'."

"What?" Přema said.

"Trust Smiřický to think of the *Frauenzimmers*," said Lexa.

"You mean I should start it off 'Brothers and Sisters'?" asked Přema. "I don't think that's such a hot idea. Resistance isn't for girls."

He took his fiery appeal, which amounted to an invitation to kill the

Germans on sight, and went over to the corner where, in a box from the First Republic marked "Czechoslovak Tobacco Board," he had hidden a small stenciling machine.

"So how come we told Kadeřábek to go ahead?" Nosek asked.

"That's different," said Přema. "Gerta has got serious reasons."

Someone rapped out the pre-arranged signal on the warehouse door. Přema went to open it. Kadeřábek slipped into the room and sat down on the crate that Přema had just got up from. The murky light from a single bare lightbulb that hung on a wire from the ceiling made his features stand out. He looked like the mannequin in the window of the Paris Fashion House that Berta always dressed in a tux for the winter season, when there were a lot of formal dances in town. But Kadeřábek's masculine beauty was marred by a puffy lower lip, which he hadn't had when he'd gone off into the woods on his assignment. My lewd imagination placed its own interpretation on the puffy lip, and I found myself silently agreeing with Přema: women had no place in a resistance movement.

"Well?" said Přema.

Kadeřábek coughed.

"Will she or won't she?"

"I – uh – " said Kadeřábek, " – no."

"What do you mean – no?" asked Harýk.

"She – uh – " said Kadeřábek, and again he coughed uneasily, as if to clear his throat.

* * *

We had decided to drag Gerta Wotická into our resistance group because she'd had some trouble with Leopold Váňa, and Leopold Váňa didn't want anything to do with the resistance. Or perhaps he wanted to join but his father wouldn't let him, just as he wouldn't let him have anything to do with Gerta. That was what the trouble was all about.

Like everyone else, Váňa tried to make out with girls, but whereas my efforts along those lines came to nothing for reasons that were not clear to me (in the past year this had happened twenty-two times, each time with a different girl), the reasons why Váňa had the same rate of success were as clear as day. He was, as one girl put it, boredom in trousers. (Precisely what she had in mind, or precisely what it was about him that bored her, she didn't say. Lexa professed to be morally outraged by her metaphor, if that's what it was.) But Irena told me that among the girls he'd tried to get anywhere with – and so far Váňa had tried it with only three, including Irena, so she spoke from personal experience – there was a general consensus that bordered on the telepathic. In addition, Váňa didn't look too good: he was as fat as Benno, but he didn't play an instrument, and he wore glasses with wire frames that hooked behind his ears.

But in the end he succeeded with Gerta, which wasn't really very surprising when you thought about it. Gerta was no Rachel, although both of them were avid swimmers. Gerta was good at high diving and Rachel was the district champion in the breast stroke, both in and out of the water. But Rachel was a real beauty; she reminded me a little of Paulette Goddard in *Modern Times*. Gerta was a skinny girl and as far as breasts went, Benno – as Lexa put it – was two sizes bigger. She had pretty black eyes, but they were separated by a caricature of a nose – like the ones in the cartoons Rélink, the painter, started publishing just after the Germans established the Protectorate of Bohemia and Moravia. Rélink called himself an anti-Jew, an expression he'd obviously made up: right after we were annexed to the Reich, Czech was widely purged of foreign words, and I guess Rélink thought the expression "anti-Semite" was too un-Czech. At the time, Lexa set up a club of pro-Jews, but it never got anywhere because Benno – who, as he said himself, was a half-Jew – refused to be president. Also, it soon became clear that anti-Jewishness wasn't a joke the way the painter Rélink was a joke, so we quickly forgot about the club. Mainly, as a matter of fact, because of the trouble Gerta got into.

Anyway, Váňa finally made it with Gerta during the winter vacation in the Krkonoše Mountains in 1938, when Gerta saved his life. Váňa was a terrible skier. He couldn't go more than a few meters without falling and no one would ever go out on the slopes with him. One day while he was out alone, he fell and broke his leg, and of course he couldn't move. It happened in a ravine, right near a waterfall, so no one could hear his cries for help. A fog came down and the rest of us retreated to the chalet. No one missed Váňa until Gerta noticed he wasn't at supper because there were dumplings left over. Meanwhile the fog had dispersed and the slopes were sparkling in the starlight. We lit some torches and set off to look for him. It was the first time we'd ever been on skis at night, and with torches, at that. Lucie applied her torch to the seat of Harýk's pants, making him yelp, then we all started fooling around with the torches and forgot about Váňa again. Marie was pointing up in the sky at Venus with exaggerated interest, with a finger gloved in pink wool, and I was just looking up at the planet of love when I caught sight of a flickering flame quickly descending into the ravine by the waterfall. Gerta. Perhaps they were destined for each other.

But they weren't. Though it seemed that way at first, both socially and sexually. Mr. Váňa and Mr. Wotický owned the two biggest textile stores in Kostelec; one of them had an only son, the other an only daughter; the daughter was no Aphrodite and the son was no Adonis, more like Hephaestus (particularly after his skiing accident, which gave him a limp). It looked like a serious relationship – a little premature, perhaps, since Váňa was only in the sixth form and Gerta in the fifth, but that was hardly exceptional. That summer one of Gerta's classmates, Libuše Nováková, who also was no Aphrodite, got married a day after she turned sixteen. Not that she had to, but her father, Dr. Tannenbaum, was pushing eighty and was afraid he wouldn't last till the plums ripened. It was an open secret in Kostelec that Mr. Novák, the head-waiter of the Beránek Café, wasn't Libuše's father, although he purported to be, just as he wasn't the father of her older sister Teta, who'd gotten married the year before, a day after she graduated from high school – nor of her eldest sister, Kazi, who had to wait a full year after graduation before Dr. Tannenbaum finally managed to get her hitched. In her case, of course, he wasn't in any hurry; at the time he was only seventy-five and still took part in the Christmas polar-bear marathon swim in the Vltava River. And it was obvious to everyone in Kostelec that the head-waiter hadn't built his villa below Černá Hora, designed by a famous Prague architect, from the money he made on tips. Even if there were people gullible enough to believe it, they might well have wondered why all three of the girls with pagan names were as ugly as night, when their father was an elegantly handsome man with a Clark Gable moustache and their mother, now in her early forties, looked like an eighteen-year-old model from Rosenbaum's fashion salon in Prague. The gullible, had they wondered, might have explained it as a freak of nature, but the rest of us knew why: the President's Master of Ceremonies, Dr. Tannenbaum, looked like those paintings of troglodytes in anthropology textbooks. As well as being the author of a famous manual of social etiquette, Dr. Tannenbaum had written a work called *The Mores and Customs of Czech Paganism*, which explained why he'd named his daughters after women from old Czech legends. It was also whispered that he had accumulated his fortune not as a famous man of letters or from his salary as Master of Ceremonies, but as a marriage-broker for the old Austro-Bohemian aristocrats.

So a serious relationship between a girl from the fifth form and a boy from the sixth was more a rule than an exception at the Kostelec high school. We had some shining examples in the band. Benno had been going with Alena since the third form, but it was Harýk who had broken all the records of this odd tradition. In the spring of '38, after the municipal physician, Dr. Eichler, conducted his annual check-up of the students, he summoned the architect, Mr. Hartmann – who was Lucie's father – to his office. When Hartmann came home, Lucie's brother told us, he took a belt to her without a word of explanation and then put her under house arrest for three months, which was, of course, too late to save her virginity. The reason didn't remain a mystery for long because Dr. Eichler's son, who was studying Latin and was bored to tears, had heard Mr. Hartmann through his father's office door lamenting his daughter's fate, and of course he couldn't keep such sensational news to himself. At the time, Lucie was in the second form and Harýk in the fourth.

* * *

Gerta and Váňa had a serious relationship, but whether it was true love or not was another matter. It looked more to me like making a virtue of necessity. Although I wasn't really capable of understanding something like that – since of course all twenty-two of my attempts had been made when I was in love, at least while the attempt lasted – I knew such things existed, because people aren't all the same, except insofar as they're all after that one thing. So I supposed it wasn't passion that kept them together, but simply the fact that Váňa couldn't get anyone else, that and Gerta –

That was another one of the open secrets of the Kostelec high school: of all the girls who had fallen for the magic of Kadeřábek's mannequin beauty, Gerta had fallen the hardest. And if all the victims were suffering from color-blindness, Gerta was living in a permanent fog – or rather, in the heart of a Babylonian darkness. From the third form on, Kadeřábek had been fast friends with František Buřtoch, despite the fact that Buřtoch was ten years older. Buřtoch's father, a butcher, had disinherited his son when, upon completing his butcher's apprenticeship, František had set up a business in antiques and *objets d'art* using money left him by a bachelor friend. So the thing was obvious, but not to those color-blind girls, who secretly, with hard-won money, bribed a photographer to sell them studio portraits of Kadeřábek. In short, love had blinded them, or perhaps they'd been raised so correctly that the truth about Kadeřábek's preferences had simply eluded them, though I knew them too well to really believe that.

Kadeřábek was indeed a perverse Adonis. Instead of playing tennis, he was a shot-put ace for the Kostelec Sports Club, which was also why athletics suddenly became so popular with the girls that Kostelec had the largest club of young female hopefuls in the entire district, and also the best, because otherwise there wasn't much competition in women's athletics. The only girl who drove herself around the cinder track because she really liked doing it was Irena, but she was perverse about it too. Otherwise the girls would jog around the soccer field or leap into the long-jump pits for reasons that were clear, if not low and immoral. Marie, unfortunately, was not one of them, although I'd have loved to see her in shorts. Perhaps her boyfriend had emotionally neutralized her.

Gerta had done high diving since she'd been a little girl and now, having succumbed to the magic of Kadeřábek, she took up the high jump and eventually broke the junior women's record. But it didn't do her any good. The day when she made a name for herself came later: the heavy shot slipped out of Kadeřábek's hand and fell behind him, and Gerta rushed out of the crowd of admiring girls, picked the shot up, and ran to return it to the astonished athlete.

It was as clear as day.

But whether this was passion or not, in the autumn of '39 Gerta didn't come to school for two days, and when she finally showed up her beauty carried another blemish: her large nose now glowed like a peony and there were big red circles around her pretty black eyes. Váňa stopped waiting for her after school, and on Saturday he came into the Beránek alone for the tea dance and tried to dance with Alena, but he stepped so hard on her shoes that she cried out, and he then sat by himself until the end of the dance, glowering into his lemonade.

Because we weren't very fond of him, and because Gerta looked so miserable, we went over to his table during the *Jauzepause* and Lexa spoke to him:

"What did you do to her, you murderer?"

"Nothing. I stepped on her corns. It could happen to anyone."

"I'm not talking about Alena. Don't tell me you don't know who I mean!"

Váňa said nothing.

"Well, sir, are you going to explain yourself?" said Harýk.

"It's not my fault," said Váňa.

"She gave you the gate, right?"

"No, she didn't."

"Then how come you ditched her? You were just stringing her along, weren't you?"

"No, I wasn't," said Váňa.

We looked at each other and shook our heads.

"Okay, then. If she didn't come across, that's your fault. You had a year and a half to work on it. But that's still no reason for you to shit on her."

"I didn't shit on her."

"So how come you're not going out with her anymore? Can't you see the poor girl's suffering?" said Lexa.

Váňa was silent again.

"What lies are you concocting now, sir?" asked Harýk.

Suddenly Váňa blurted out: "She's a Jew!"

We were floored. That was when we realized that all this anti-Semitic stuff wasn't a joke any more. But how could Váňa be such a jerk?

"You hardly seem a zealous enough Catholic, sir, to object to the religious affiliation of your bedmate," said Harýk.

"It's got nothing to do with religion," wailed Váňa. "You know what this is all about."

"Do we know what this is all about, gentlemen?" asked Harýk, looking around at us. We all shook our heads.

"It doesn't bother me a bit, seriously," said Váňa quickly. "But my old man – "

There are some fools in the world who obey the fourth commandment to the letter so their days may be long on this earth. Their thoughts should be on heaven, but they're not. We couldn't get Váňa to budge. Probably he had nothing personal against Gerta. But he wanted his days to be long on this earth, just like his old man.

＊ ＊ ＊

So Kadeřábek was queer, but otherwise he was ready for any mischief. The students of Moses' faith still went to the high school, but from the way things were going it was pretty clear that even the Jews in the eighth form wouldn't make it to matriculation. Soon after Váňa ditched her, Gerta had to sew a yellow star on her negligible breasts, but that was after her second, and worse, disaster. Then Mrs. Mánesová began wearing a star, and Rachel too, except that by the end of 1938, at least according to Father Meloun's records, she was married to Tonda Kratochvíl. For the longest time only Father Meloun knew about it, because it had been a secret wedding. Why it was secret when the parish records said it had taken place in '38, back during the First Republic, wasn't clear. The explanation came in '41 when we were rehearsing at the school revue, but that's another story. Benno kept attending school even after the stars started appearing, and so did his sister Věra, because they were only half-Jews. I began to like Věra more and more, but I didn't try my luck with her a second time (although otherwise I had nothing against second and third and sometimes even fourth and fifth attempts, and, in the case of Marie and Irena, I'd lost track because there were no computers in those days). But not for the same reason that Váňa had dumped Gerta. Even people of mixed race were beginning to feel the heat now, because at any moment the Germans could up the "racial awareness" ante, though God knew when. And I didn't want Věra to think I was exploiting the situation or taking an interest in her as an act of mercy, or that I was trying to silence a bad Aryan conscience, since I was, well, an Aryan. I didn't know. I wasn't sure why I was so reluctant. I was just a jerk. But a different kind from Váňa.

I also can't remember who first got the idea. Whoever it was, he got it after Kaderábek, of all people, came up with the notion of starting a resistance movement. It's hard to say which idea was more stupid. When I told Přema about it, he swore me to silence and then told me that they already had a resistance movement, of people in trades, and that he, Přema, was the leader. Přema had originally been a student at the business academy, but after 1939, out of pure patriotism, he'd refused to learn German. In fact, the teacher couldn't get a single word of German out of him, so the principal quickly expelled him from the academy. In his own interest, he went to explain it personally to Přema's father, Mr. Skočdopole. At first Mr. Skočdopole, as a former legionnaire, was somewhat crusty with him. But then, as an alcoholic, he pulled out a bottle of home-made slivovice, a gift from his brother in Moravia, and they both got drunk under a portrait of President Masaryk, from which Mr. Skočdopole had removed, for the occasion, a picture of Bozena Němcová with which he'd covered up Masaryk when the Protectorate was declared. Finally they both agreed that Přema had it coming to him, and then they fell asleep. Now Přema decided that we should combine the groups so we'd have connections with the intellectuals as well as ordinary people, and one idea led to another until finally someone said we should also have connections with the Jews, who happened to have the best reasons for getting mixed up in a resistance movement, and as a final idea, someone said, "Gerta."

"We can rely on her," said Nosek. "In a way, she's already been hit by the German laws."

"But she's a girl," objected Přema.

"Well – " said Lexa, and he was going to continue, but then stopped and said, " – as a matter of fact, she is."

"Girls are timid," said Přema.

"Sure they are!" said Harýk. "Look, would you have the guts to dive off a thirty-foot tower?"

"I can't swim," said Přema.

"Lord!" said Harýk.

We were silent. Then Kaderábek said, "In a democratic state girls are equal. And according to physiological reseach, they can stand more punishment than men, relatively speaking."

This sounded strange coming from him. The short sleeves on his elegant shirt were not enough to cover his bulging biceps.

"But not emotionally," said Lexa.

"Bullshit. Look at Joan of Arc," said Nosek.

We were silent again. Then I said, "A girl who's not afraid to dive from a thirty-foot tower must have a pretty good set of nerves."

In the end we decided that Gerta, girl or not, must have nerves like Tarzan, and that furthermore, because of that jerk Váňa, she'd been the first in the school to suffer the consequences of Nazism, so she had better reasons for doing this than we did.

The next question was who would talk to her.

"Wee Daniel, of course," said Harýk. "He's the champion talker."

"But he's not the champion persuader," said Lexa. "At least not of ladies."

By this time my embarrassing reputation had ceased to bother me.

Then came the final idea, the most brilliant of all, and I was the one who had it. "I have someone better in mind."

"Who? Berta?" asked Lexa. Berta involuntarily twitched and blushed.

"No," I said. "Květomil."

Květomil was Kadeřábek's first name. An appropriate name at that. Flower-lover.

"Gentlemen – " Kadeřábek was clearly taken aback. "I'm not – I mean, that kind of thing's not my – my cup of tea."

"This is politics, not erotics, sir," said Lexa.

"Besides that, you're the chairman," I said. "Or I mean the commander."

"And Gerta's always had a crush on you," said Harýk. "Remember the time she brought you back the shot-put?"

"Go ahead and have your fun," said Kadeřábek. "I don't mind. But it's not my cup of tea."

"I repeat: it's a matter of politics, not erotics," said Harýk.

"Or of politics through erotics," I said, "and the end justifies the means."

Because we were a democratic resistance movement, we put the matter to a vote, and decided that Květomil would be the one to establish contact with Gerta.

※ ※ ※

He tried the next day during the lunch-break. That morning an embarrassing situation arose during the first lesson, which was German. Ilse Seligerová stood up and asked Miss Althammerová to make Gerta sit in the back row. Ilse had been sitting beside Gerta since the first form. She was German and preferred speaking German to Czech. Miss Althammerová was a German too, but even so she asked Ilse, *"Warum den?"*

"Sie wissen doch, Fräulein Doktor," replied Ilse icily.

Miss Althammerová turned red, took a deep breath, then let it out again and said, in a quiet voice, *"Na gut – wenn Gerta nichts dagegen hat."*

Gerta burst into tears and ran to the back row where the overweight Petridesová sat. The classroom was as silent as a tomb. I saw Petridesová give Gerta her handkerchief.

Petridesová was walking through the halls beside Gerta during the lunch-break when Květomil joined them, perspiring. Petridesová played the fifth wheel for a while, then discreetly went off to the girls' washroom. With a shiny face, Květomil promenaded around the halls with Gerta, speaking to her while she raised her red-rimmed eyes to him. When the bell rang, I saw that the shot-put champion was smiling.

"So, what happened?" asked Harýk.

"Well – I established contact," said Květomil.

"And – is she for it?"

"We didn't get that far. I have to sound her out first, don't I?"

"Oh, Lord. And how did you 'sound her out'?"

"Well, we talked about movies and – "

"And what?"

"And so on," said Květomil.

"And then?"

"And then the bell rang."

So the first contact was just reconnoitering.

In the week that followed, Květomil must have discussed the entire history of the cinema with Gerta, because he couldn't think of anything else to talk about. Gerta's gaze became more and more amorous. He could have talked to her about bowel disease, or even about the resistance, and Gerta wouldn't have minded. The red circles around her beautiful eyes vanished, and her nose regained its accustomed whiteness. But they never got beyond what Květomil called "sounding out." Finally, at the end of the week, he said "I can't do it in school. I'll have to invite her somewhere."

"You should have done that long ago, you jerk," said Lexa.

"Take her to the movies," said Harýk.

"That's even worse than school."

"Make a date to see her in the woods," I said. "No one will hear what you say there."

And so Květomil invited Gerta to meet him in the woods in a small meadow called By the Cottage – although the cottage, which had once belonged to a shepherd, was in ruins. The meadow was overgrown with aromatic moss – not long before, I had tried to intoxicate Irena with its perfume. In vain, of course.

From the window of Mánes' villa we watched as Květomil – in corduroy trousers and one of his elegant shirts, beneath which his cultivated muscles rippled – strode into the forest. After ten minutes Gerta walked across the bridge to the brewery. She was wearing a Sunday dress.

* * *

Later we sat in the warehouse and waited for Květomil, and possibly for Gerta, if he'd managed to persuade her. Time dragged and this didn't augur well. Or perhaps it did. Finally Květomil himself showed up and said, "I – uh – no."

"Wait a minute," said Harýk. "What do you mean, no?"

"She –" said Květomil – and delicately, he touched his tellingly swollen lip, which I had misinterpreted.

So I don't know. I guess we made a mistake. We chose the wrong tactics. We were young and stupid. We held the glories of this world in contempt, but we had no antennae. Three years later – where did Gerta end up? Back then, she could probably think things through more clearly than I could, than Lexa could. Everything. The resistance and love. Anyway, our resistance group faded away too, and for all I know it may have had something to do with Gerta. Only Přema stuck to it, probably because at the time he hadn't understood anything at all. Přema wasn't much for the girls, though for different reasons than Květomil. He was naturally shy, he didn't understand girls and was even afraid of them. I wasn't afraid of them, but did I understand them? It had been my dumb idea to use her queer idol to persuade her to join us. So I didn't understand girls worth a damn either.

* * *

We could still hear the old women singing in the church.

The jewel of all the heaaavens thou aaaaart...

I no longer tried to make out Marie's sweet voice in that infernal, or perhaps heavenly, wailing.

"She what?" asked Harýk.

"Well," said Květomil, "I didn't want to come right out with it, so I began to – " He stopped.

"Don't tell me," said Lexa. "You talked about movies."

"No, about athletics. Then about swimming," said Květomil.

"Wonderful," said Harýk, looking at his watch. "God, how can swimming and the shot-put take up four hours of anyone's time! That must be a district record. Maybe even a world record!"

"We talked about literature too," said Květomil.

"Now that could only have taken you five minutes," I said. I knew that the only printed matter Květomil ever read was the illustrated sports weekly *Start.*

"And then about politics," said Květomil.

"And did you tell her what you were supposed to?" asked Harýk impatiently.

"I began slowly so I wouldn't frighten her, right?" said Květomil. "I said I'd been watching her for a long time, and that of all the girls at school she'd always seemed to me kind of – "

"Kind of what?" said Harýk.

"Kind of – the most mature. And – the most interesting."

I could imagine them there in the tiny meadow, sitting on that aromatic moss that almost, but not quite, intoxicated Irena. I could see Gerta hanging on Květomil the Adonis with her beautiful Jewish eyes – and suddenly I realized what the mistake had been. Of course. Gerta hadn't paid much attention to his talk about the shot-put. She was in fifth heaven when they sat down on the moss, in sixth when she breathed in its aroma, and when he started babbling on about how she was the most mature and the most interesting of all the girls in the school, she arrived in seventh heaven. Then she was overwhelmed by that feeling they write about in novels, and she flew to him, as they say, on the wings of love, and cleaved to him in a long, passionate kiss until his lip swelled up, and he never managed to blurt out his more important message to her.

Thou art the jewel of hiiiiighest heaven...

"Well, and then I said it," I heard Květomil say. "That we'd decided to invite her into our resistance group –"

And again, for the tenth time, he fell silent.

"And what did she say?" Harýk blurted out.

For a moment, Květomil looked as though he'd just tumbled out of the sky. "She slapped my face," he said. "And then she ran away."

A silence fell over the warehouse. The only sound was the singing of the old women in the church on the square.

"You can't figure women out," said Květomil. "At least I sure can't."

Bill Meissner

DRAWING SWASTIKAS ON THE FOGGED WINDOWS OF ST. JOSEPH'S GRADE SCHOOL, 1959

After school we cleaned bruised boards,
clapped white explosions from erasers.
The nun sat in her silence;
in ours, we drew bombers in notebooks.

Sisters, we meant nothing by it.
We were only apprentices at war –
gray blood something that grinned at us from the screen.
Buds on the girls and triggers excited us.
We dreamed of Nazis: how they could scrape off
the horizon with their fingernails.

We didn't understand the world
was once a mountain, ready to avalanche.
For us history was that pine forest
behind the playground, filling with snow.

Noon hours in the basement,
we rationed cigarettes, laughed
at bomb shelter signs, fingered dirty pictures
smuggled in bag lunches
until the boilers hissed.

After an hour she dismissed us.
We saw fish in the aquarium by the cloakroom
swimming in squadrons.
At home we drew on our arms with red Magic Marker.

Sisters, no enemy planes ever tore the air
above your school. It was just a target
for the wrecking ball, a decade later.
When the first bricks collapsed,
ghosts of the kids we once were
  cowered in the basement,
    the lights blacked out,
      the windows steamed.

FAINTING

WE DIDN'T KNOW much then – what we did know were the insides of cigarette packages and the inside of the boys' room where, during recess, we sneaked in to try some fainting. There we were, Bill Keyhoe, Tom Pollard, and I, three cocky eighth-graders crouched on our haunches in the middle of the bathroom. We'd gulp in ten or twelve deep breaths, then stand up quickly, pinch our mouths shut with our fingers, and blow hard into our taut cheeks until the blood rushed back into our heads and we'd faint.

It was a good way to spend time during recess that spring, we all agreed – a good way to forget Catechism lessons drilled into our heads by black and white nuns. The bathroom was an oasis of clean beige and aqua tiled walls, gray metal stalls, and high, opaque windows so no one could see in or out. The urinals were always too white. We kept it quiet so Sister Agatha, with her hooked fingers, didn't discover us down there – she'd march us to see Father Henry for sure. We kept our talk to whispers that echoed off the polished walls of the room.

Somewhere that year, Tom started stealing Kools from his old man. We'd slip between the moist, dark walls of the A & P and Cashman's Garage and we'd each smoke one. Near grade school graduation we got braver and smoked them at dusk on the edge of the school playground. The orange tips glowed like fireflies. We took smoke as deep into our lungs as we could and held it there, savoring the taste. Sometimes Bill would smirk, then let loose that repressed chuckle, his laugh coming out in little bursts of smoke. Between puffs, and after we finished a cigarette, we'd eat the strawberry taffy we bought at the theater candy counter. We thought it disguised the smell on our breaths. We all agreed the strawberry taffy and the smoke tasted great together.

* * *

That first time we tried fainting, we took turns. Tom was first. Nothing happened. He just ended up red-faced, then he strolled to the mirror to comb his slicked-back hair. It was my turn. I got dizzy, and my sight turned fuzzy for a second, but it didn't work for me, either. Then Bill crouched down on the floor in his short-sleeved checkered shirt. He stood up and blew hard against his cheeks until his gaunt face brightened. Then he began to slowly topple backwards. At first Tom and I thought he was faking. But he kept falling stiffly toward the floor like a huge tree that was just cut down. I dashed over, caught him behind his bony shoulders just inches before he would have hit his head on the hard tile floor. I held him there, and he was out cold a few seconds; his arms slid limply across his chest and the air exhaled from his lungs. When he woke, he didn't remember what had happened. Later we talked about how he almost cracked his damned skull wide open.

After that, we always made certain we had one fainter and the other two standing close by. Or we'd faint in Tom's bedroom after school, where Tom cranked up Freddy Cannon on the record player and we could fall on the saggy bed if we really passed out. We all got to like the feeling of fainting – that odd numbing buzz followed by the blackness that took us far from this world for a few seconds. Sometimes we had weird dreams, and time slowed down – the few seconds we were out always seemed like half an hour.

A kid in class told us he heard about a boy somewhere who made himself faint and never woke up again. Tom said he could always see our eyes roll back into our foreheads just before we blacked out. We laughed about it.

We laughed. We couldn't have known that five years later, the summer after high school graduation, Bill would be killed when a car hoist crushed him.

I often imagined the car hoist in Cashman's Auto Body lowering on Bill, the whole weight of a Chevrolet on top of it. I tried to block it from my head: that vision of the wisps of smoke being pressed from his lungs. I never wanted to look into Cashman's garage door again, as we often did on the way to grade school those mornings. We'd rub circles on the dusty panes and peer in, and it would be cool and dark and exciting in there: the gray skeletons of unpainted cars, the stacks of oil-stained parts boxes, the girlie calendars with the smudged thumb prints on them.

Toward the end of that school year, we learned that trying to make ourselves faint was a sin, and so Bill and Tom and I rode our bikes to the church together and confessed it, one by one, behind the sweaty black curtain of the confessional. Kneeling in the pews, we'd offer up our ten Our Fathers to the plaster statues on the altar. Forgive me, Father, for I have fainted. The statues never seemed to have any eyes – only opaque marbles, as if they, too, were staring at the back walls of their skulls.

One time Bill and I were altar boys at a funeral, and we watched a woman in the front row faint dead in the aisle. The pallbearers had to lift her stocky body and lug her all the way up the aisle of the church with her gray dress riding up her thigh and her slip showing. Later, pulling our cassocks over our heads in the sacristy, we talked about it and snickered.

Tom's a policeman in town now, and I don't get together with him anymore. I only see him at church once in a while with his cigarette pack showing through his white shirt pocket; he nods without smiling.

Once he mentioned that his job keeps him busy – he said I wouldn't believe the stunts he catches kids doing these days. We never mention Bill anymore, but I know from looking behind Tom's eyes that he remembers.

* * *

Sometimes, when I'm driving around with nothing to do and I pass the old grade school, or when I'm filling up with gas or having an oil change, I still see Bill.

I see him teetering in his short-sleeved checkered shirt, see him falling backwards ever so slowly, his eyes rolling. And I always catch him just an inch from the hard tile floor.

POEM FOR THE INSECTS IN FALL

I

I have seen them:
crickets hiding beneath porches,
the black glass of their songs
broken into splinters.
Moths shivering
among pale grass blades
while this season approaches,
the blades of a lawn mower.

II

Some nights I crouch in the cold deep grass
of my sleep, hiding from
dawn. Somewhere a cricket
dreams the sound of a clock ticking,
and I dream the dream of moths:
a dance around the warm lightbulb
of the moon.

III

By mid-morning, insects lift stiff wings
above pavement, dot
the windshields,
surprised pinheads of death.

IV

Warm afternoons I would save them all,
gather them into my shirt pocket,
or I would drive
back and forth on the highway,
accelerating into them
until I can no longer see,
their tiny opaque brushstrokes coating the windshield
like first frost.

REMEMBERING THAT CITY BUS RIDE
IN QUITO, EQUADOR

I saw it first: a black dog
ambling into the cobblestone street.
Inside the battered bus
in my metal seat, I kept silent.
I didn't speak their language.
I squeezed the handrail
that was worn to a shine.

The dog moved slowly, like a shadow
hiding from the sun's path.
The driver accelerated, shifted;
passengers' heads snapped back.

A cry from an old man mingled with
the gnash of gears.
The dog didn't even glance at
the bumper inches away.

For an instant,
a silence
filled with dull claws.

Then the thud,
a gutteral yelp. The repeating
hollow thumps like an irregular
metallic heartbeat
as the dog rolled
under the bus.
The cries stopped, but the bumping
traveled down the whole length:
I watched it move along the worn floorboards,
coming closer and closer to me
until I wished I was deaf,
until it vibrated beneath
the soles of my shoes.

Years later, we show slides of the trip.
Which city did I like best?
In America, we're better drivers,
our busses are clean.

There are still nights when I see that dream approaching –
    it wraps around my bony elbows and knees
    until I let go, and roll and roll,
    my body relaxing in its grip
    so choking and comforting
    like a blanket of exhaust.

THE CONTORTIONIST

For him, any position is fine:
his heel resting casually on his shoulder,
bread dough arms twisting together.
He could even compress himself
into a 2 by 2 foot cardboard box,
still have room
to eat shredded wheat from a bowl, people
pointing and laughing above him
as he chews.

He has almost begun to enjoy arching his body
into an exact O, to feel
the breeze, the universe as it blows
through the open porthole of himself.
He knows this is his fate: to be loved,
to be remembered most
for becoming something he is not –
a chair, the entire alphabet, the ripples
on top of water.
Over the years, he has learned to erase
the wince, learned to relax
with his legs wrapped around his neck,
a thick noose.

For a final stunt, bending
backwards, a spatula between his teeth,
he flips pancakes,
listens to the floppy applause.

Alone in the dressing room
he sits naked on the floor.
Somehow he is nearly comfortable
as he wraps his whole body carefully
into a large, pink bow.
Yes, he thinks, this is his gift to himself.

Father Benedict Auer

MY GUEST

*"A strange old man
stops me,
looking out of my deep mirror."*
— Hitomaro

A stranger
lives in my room,
I don't recall
when he moved in,
I don't remember
asking for a roommate,
but I have one.
I run into him
throughout the day,
but mostly at dawn,
or at dusk,
the vulnerable hours
when I'm least
able to handle him.
I see him
mirrored in a window,
or as I shave –
a shadow without shade,
a circle not quite
centered on another –
always my glance
lowers
so as not to disturb
his tranquility.

Tom Hazuka

ALTIPLANO

THE SUN HAD set behind them. It was almost dark, and getting colder. The Chilean *carabinero* at the checkpoint, over 14,000 feet above the sea they had left only five hours before, sneered when he checked their passports. "It's crazy to be up here at this time of day," he said in Spanish, then returned the passports without looking at the gringos and offered no assistance. He waved them away. They watched another *carabinero* stoke the coal stove and warm his hands, then zipped their jackets and stepped back out into the icy wind.

"Finding two frozen bodies will give them something to do tomorrow," Hatfield said.

"It's February," Maggie said. "It's the bloody middle of summer. How could I know it would be like this?"

"You've only lived in Arica for nine months. Did it ever occur to you to ask someone?"

Maggie stopped and glared at him. "Damn it, it'll be OK."

"I've been reading that for a year now."

"Well, isn't it?"

"I miss you," he said.

"God, don't start that again."

"Slow down, Maggie." She ignored him and strode hard across the packed earth to the Volkswagen. She was already behind the wheel when he opened the passenger door, panting.

"Jesus," he said, "This altitude."

"I warned you to take it easy on the wine."

"Glad you reminded me." Hatfield pulled the cork on the liter bottle of Concha y Toro and took a swig. He held it up to the remnant of daylight; it was better than half gone.

"Brilliant," Maggie said. "The cops'll love that." She popped the clutch and spun gravel, sliding sideways for a second onto the washboard dirt road.

"That too," Hatfield said, and nestled the bottle in his crotch as they bounced north toward Bolivia.

They had a tent but no stove, having planned to cook over a campfire. But they discovered that the altiplano lay far above the timber line, and they found no wood, nothing at all to burn outside of some worthless scrub grass that somehow kept the llamas and alpacas alive. The road had no shoulder, nowhere to pull off to safety even if they saw a reasonable place to camp, which they didn't – nothing but tremendous plains stretching in all directions, cut by primitive hills, blue streams flowing like transparent ice, a pair of snow-crowned volcanoes in the distance. They shivered in their shorts. It was over 90 degrees when they left Arica.

Hatfield hugged the bottle between his thighs. "Maybe we should just turn back," he said.

"But we have to see the pink flamingos on Lake Chungará! Besides, I'm not sure we have enough gas."

"Great."

"You know, Kenny, you're not helping matters any."

"Not like Ernesto would, I know. Sorry I'm not a macho Latin."

"Check the map," she said, eyes on the road. There was no moon. The VW's headlights were thin beams in the blackness. They had seen no other vehicle for hours, since they passed a rickety Bolivian transport truck loaded with bulging sacks and unsmiling people piled on top of them. "That turn's got to be around here someplace."

"Take a left at the next woodpile," Hatfield said.

"This was supposed to be fun, Kenny."

"Tell me about it! Travel 9,000 miles to visit your girlfriend and find out she's with another guy. I'm having a blast, Maggie, time of my life. Fun is too mild a word for the pleasure I'm experiencing."

"I told you I *see* Ernesto. I'm not *with* him."

"No, you're *with* me – sorry to have bothered you. Watch out!"

Something thudded and squealed under the front bumper. It was a definitive impact, the kind when you know immediately things will not be the same. Maggie braked and killed the engine. She trembled and took deep, sucking breaths as if suffering from the altitude. "Flashlight?" she asked.

"It's back at your place. In the same bag with the toothbrushes, oranges, Swiss army knife and your diaphragm."

"Can't you let anything drop? I said I was sorry – isn't that enough for you? I feel like I'm on trial."

"Here's matches."

She turned off the lights and they entered darkness as complete as a cave's. The wind was gone and its lonely moan with it, the night as silent as space until their feet scuffed the road. Hatfield cleared his throat. Maggie struck a match and it flared in her cupped hand. On the ground lay a crumpled creature the size of a fat woodchuck, half rodent and half rabbit, its sides heaving and one bloody leg pawing at the air.

"Vizcacha," Maggie said. They had seen a dozen of them during the drive.

"It's history," Hatfield said. "Poor bastard."

"I hate to see him suffer."

"Want me to crush his head with a rock?"

"No!"

"Then it's going to suffer."

"I don't care."

"I didn't think so."

"You know what I mean."

"Get in the car," he said.

"What're you going to do?"

"Get in the car."

To his surprise, Maggie did. Hatfield lit a match, found a rock as big as a football, lit another one, and lined up his target. He raised the stone with both hands over his head, looking up for a moment to the sky, and was still thinking how amazing it was, how he had never seen a sky so full of bright, uncountable stars, as he drove the rock down hard like an ax and heard a squishing crunch in the darkness. He almost vomited, but comforted himself that it was her fault. He'd tried his best to make it better. Maggie started the car and in the red glow of the taillights Hatfield saw what he had done. He gagged as he kicked the stone off the road, then went back to the car without looking up.

"Drive," he said, and closed the door so tenderly it rattled as she pulled away. He yanked it tight.

"Did you do it?" Maggie was hunched over the steering wheel.

Hatfield hesitated, watching the little cones of light in the black everything. He sat on his hands. His stomach felt like old meat. "It feels no pain," he said finally.

"I'm sorry, Kenny."

"Yeah," he said.

A dirt road, more primitive still, branched left and they took it. It had to be the way to Parinacota, the only village in the area, though in the darkness they saw no sign. The crude map showed no distances. Twice the road narrowed to hardly more than the width of the Volkswagen; after six kilometers Maggie stopped at a flooded depression. There was no way to skirt it – a bank on the right and two-foot drop to the left prevented that – and no room to turn around. Hatfield got out to check. Ice was already crusting at the edges of the puddle. He couldn't see the bottom, but what could he expect in those dim headlights.

Maggie rolled down her window. "Well?"

"I think it's okay."

"Get in, then."

Hatfield went over, trying to rub some warmth into his hands. "Want me to drive?"

"Why, don't you trust me?"

"I used to," he said.

"Get in," she said. "Before I change my mind."

She gunned the engine and splashed through. The water was only a few inches deep.

"In Maggie I trust," Hatfield said, hand over his heart. "I pledge allegiance. My Maggie right or wrong."

"Grow up, Kenny." They rode in silence, slowly over the pitted road, rarely getting the car out of second gear. Hatfield mumbled something.

Maggie crawled around a blind curve. "What?"

"I said this is the loneliest place in the world."

"For someone by himself maybe."

"That's my point."

Maggie's chin almost rested on the wheel. "Please, Kenny. We've come such a long way."

He leaned over and peered at the odometer. "About nine kilometers," he said, and the silence returned.

Creatures appeared on the road. Maggie braked slowly, easing against traffic into a small herd of llamas, branded with multi-colored ribbons on their ears. Their herder tapped their flanks with a stick and made clucking noises, and the llamas gave ground.

"Signs of life," Maggie said. "Like a seagull on the ocean. The town's got to be close."

"This guy's wearing sandals with no socks," Hatfield said. "These people are maniacs."

"Maybe they're just *men*," she said playfully, but got only frozen quiet for an answer. She rolled down her window.

"Excuse me, señor. Is this the road to Parinacota?"

"Si."

"Is it far?"

"No."

"How far?"

His broad, Indian face was barely visible in the night. He kept several strides between him and the car. "Not far," he said.

"Two kilometers?" Hatfield said. "*Dos kilometros?*"

"*Dos kilometros.*" His voice was like a shrug. He followed his animals. Maggie thanked his back. They drove two slow kilometers, then three, four. The first building was a surprise in the high beams. Not a single light shone in the tiny village. BIENVENIDOS A PARINACOTA, said white letters on a cinder block wall. Maggie turned a corner and they found themselves in a dirt plaza the size of a basketball court, in front of a crude stone-and-mortar church with a thatched roof.

"It's like a Spanish mission," Maggie said.

Hatfield finished the bottle, corked it for nothing and tossed it into the back seat. "They could be cannibals," he said. "They could do anything to us they wanted to."

"Who?" she said, and she was right. No noise disturbed the deserted plaza. A dog barked a few times but stopped, as if it didn't have the energy. "Well?" she said, and opened the door. They got out.

Hatfield stood with head hung back, gulping the thin, cold air. Never had he seen so many stars, a glittering dome from horizon to horizon, so close and bright that they seemed real, a presence, not something far away and unimaginable like city stars. He walked around the car and hugged Maggie from behind. Heads together, looking up, they stood in silence, but it was a different kind of silence from the ride. He hugged her tighter.

"I wouldn't trade this for anything," he said.

"Me neither," she said. Her hands gripped his wrists. "Kenny, I'm so sorry for everything."

"Forget it. Yesterday's history. It's what happens next that matters."

They were still watching the sky, breathing together, when the first door opened, then another. Sandals scuffed the bare earth. A dog howled; Maggie and Hatfield heard a curse and a kick, then a whimpering that died like an unplugged fan. A dozen people slowly surrounded them. A brave boy edged up to the Volkswagen and touched the bumper; a woman spoke sharply and he jumped back. "Say something," Hatfield whispered. "Your Spanish is a lot better than mine."

"*Buenas noches*," she said. "Is there a hotel here?"

A man snorted. "No one comes to Parinacota, and if they do they don't stay."

"We came from Arica, and can't make it back tonight."

"Is it beautiful down there, in Arica?" the woman who'd scolded the boy asked.

"Sí," said Maggie and Hatfield together, holding hands now against the realization that this person's whole life had happened here.

"Someday I will go," she said.

"You should," Hatfield said, and felt ridiculous.

"*Qué pasa?*" said a voice with a thick foreign inflection. A burly man holding a kerosene lamp stood stiffly at the corner. When no one replied he walked toward them, limping slightly and leaning on a cane. No one spoke as he approached. There was no sound but the scrape of his boots, and the tap of his cane on the packed dirt. He stopped in front of Maggie and Hatfield, a cane's-length away, his broad face as lined and creased as his cracked leather jacket. He stared at the Volkswagen, then at them, then back at the car.

"*Sind sie Deutschen?*" he asked.

"No," Maggie said. "*Norteamericanos.*"

"Ah, good," he said in German-accented English. "Come with me. It has been years since I have had the opportunity to speak your language." He turned to the townspeople. "Go back to bed. These Americans will be my guests tonight."

"*Muy bien*, Doctor Schaffner," said a voice. The rest of the people dispersed without a word, slipping back into the darkness. Doors closed around them. Hatfield and Maggie gathered their stuff in the car. "Should we lock it?" Hatfield said softly in the front seat.

Before Maggie could answer they heard, "Do not worry. I guarantee your safety." The German stood at least fifteen feet away. Hatfield pulled Maggie to him and whispered directly in her ear.

"Could he possibly have heard me?"

"Does it change anything if he did?" she whispered back. They locked the doors.

The German was waiting, his face ghostly in the lantern light. He led the way with Maggie at his side, Hatfield lagging behind a step. "It's dark," he said. "Always the generator is off at night. But at least now we have electricity."

"It must have been hard before," Maggie said. "Have you lived here long?"

He paused and looked at her blankly as if calculating, or maybe translating the numbers into another language. Smiling he touched her shoulder and Hatfield tensed. "Perhaps forty years in South America," he said, walking again. "Perhaps ten years here."

"Here in Parinacota or here in Chile?" Hatfield asked from the shadows.

Schaffner gave no sign that he had heard. "Here," he said, and pushed open a door covered in peeling blue paint. His cane bumped loudly on the rough plank floor, the wood gray with age and grime. Maggie followed, then Hatfield. There was only one room. Two metal-frame twin beds, one with a tangle of bedding, one a bare mattress, extended from the opposite wall. A rickety table took up the middle of the room; a single unshaded light bulb dangled from the ceiling above a dirty plate and silverware. The only two windows were in the same wall as the door, to Hatfield's right as he entered, over a long workbench that stretched to the far corner. Hatfield held his breath. On the bench and window sills, lined up like soldiers, was jar after jar of things once alive, floating now in a pale fluid stained yellow by the lamplight.

"Please," Schaffner said, with a vague gesture at the open bed. "Make yourselves at ease."

They hesitated. Scaffner caught them staring at the jars. He smiled, slowly; Hatfield had never seen an expression take so long to happen.

"I am a biologist," he said. "Entomologist especially. I collect things to study." He smiled again, rubbing his hands together. "As you see."

"That's very interesting," Maggie said.

"We must study to learn how things work. We must experiment," Schaffner said. "I do not see any other purpose to this life."

"Where did you live in South America? Before Chile, I mean."

Schaffner glanced at Hatfield and held it an extra count. He lit a Belmount cigarette. The match reflected in his glasses like two torches. "Paraguay for many years," he said. "Then Argentina." Twin trails of smoke drifted from his nostrils. The slow smile returned. "My friends," he said, pointing with the cigarette, "make yourselves at ease."

They realized they were still hugging their gear like shields. Abashedly they dumped their stuff on the empty bed, and stood wondering what to do next. Still wearing his smile Schaffner reached for a bottle among the specimens, half full of a murky purple liquid, and poured it into three glasses. He handed them each one. Hatfield dared to inspect the drink; it looked like burgundy with milk in it.

"*Pintatani*," Schaffner said. "Wine made only one place in the world – the oasis of Codpa, hundreds of kilometers south in the Atacama Desert."

"I've heard of it," Maggie said. "Someday I'll go."

"You would be one of the few," Schaffner said. "It is very isolated."

Hatfield gripped his drink. "Like Parinacota?"

Schaffner's smile withered. "Yet somehow we are all here," he said. "Together." He held up his cup. "*Prosit.*"

They clinked glasses, and Hatfield felt a twisting sense of complicity in something illicit. He couldn't explain it, but that first sip was like a handshake closing a deal, a seal of approval to an act he should be ashamed of, though he had no idea why or even what the act was. Prepared to detest the evil-looking *pintatani*, Hatfield steeled his taste buds to the inevitable bitterness, but to his surprise it was pleasantly tart and tasty. He enjoyed it, and drank deep the second time.

Maggie was smiling at both of them. "This is good," she said.

"It's like anything else," Schaffner said. "You get used to it." He uncorked a second bottle.

Time passed quickly, or maybe slowly; Hatfield wasn't sure which when he looked at his watch and saw it was midnight. The only thing that matters up here, he thought, is that time doesn't. He watched Schaffner start to pour the third bottle. Maggie's friends in Arica had jokingly warned them that you get drunk faster the higher you climb. Now Hatfield felt giddy but clear, his head full of altiplano air. He had not exactly been a monk since she left, then reminded himself that those women didn't mean anything.

Schaffner slammed his fist on the table. "What I wouldn't give for a good German lager! We are the only ones who know how to make beer!" He left the chair and moved to his bed, walking overly straight despite his cane to demonstrate he wasn't tipsy. He sat down heavily next to Maggie, the two of them now facing Hatfield. Their thighs touched and Maggie tried to inch away invisibly. Schaffner grinned.

"The privy is outside, by the way," he said. "What do you expect from this bloody country? And Peru, Bolivia, Paraguay – all worse! What do *you* think of a country where the trains do not run on time?"

Schaffner stopped, as if expecting an answer. He topped off his guests' practically full glasses and searched their faces in turn, but they didn't speak. Maggie's legs were pressed tight together. Hatfield glanced at her and remembered their morning in Dachau two years before. It's a short train ride from Munich, a popular side-trip. "Our train to Dachau was ten minutes early," he said. "We got there before it opened."

"You think it is a joke!" Schaffner said. "You think it is a circus with clowns to be laughed at! Of course you think that unless you are a clown too!" Schaffner pointed the bottle at Hatfield. "I am no clown."

Caught in his stare, Hatfield nodded. "Yes," Maggie said, but her eyes were on the floor. Hatfield looked away to the specimen jars, standing like carnival targets for a softball throw, and thought of the child mummy they'd seen last week in the Iquique museum. It lay in a fetal scrunch with hands crossed in front of its face as if for protection, a few beads still braided in the ancient, matted hair.

"Hair," Maggie had said. "Jesus." Afterward they sat in the square and licked ice cream cones. Maggie played with his hair, stroking it and winding it around her fingers until Hatfield brought up Ernesto again and they fought all the way to the bus station.

Schaffner nodded in what appeared to be satisfaction. "That is the trouble – we do not put ourselves enough in the place of another, to try and understand." He struggled to his feet, calm now, almost eerily self-controlled. He limped to the workbench. Maggie reached to touch Hatfield's knee. "I'm sorry," she said silently.

He covered her hand with his, and felt new again. "Yes," he whispered.

"Sorry?" Schaffner said, his back to them.

"Nothing."

Schaffner turned around, beaming, a large jar in his hands. He held it out to the light and inspected it like a bottle of wine. Hatfield expected a human fetus, or worse. Schaffner brought the jar near. A tattered lump floated in the liquid. "An alpaca's heart," he said. "Very much enlarged by disease." He faced Maggie. "The crucial organ, my friend. Without it your warm, silky sweater would not be possible." He cradled the jar in one arm and touched the alpaca wool on her shoulder, slid his fingers almost to the bare skin of her throat. He grimaced and set the jar down. Slowly he flexed his fingers.

"Arthritis," he said. "I was a good flute player in my youth, but those days are gone. You give up much as you grow older, my young friends. But of course you do not believe me."

Maggie and Hatfield sat with hands folded, not meeting his eyes.

"Tired?" he asked, leaning on his cane. He tossed back the last inch in his glass. "Yes, we are all very, very tired. I will show you the WC."

He walked them around the corner. Maggie entered the shack, and they heard the bolt slide. Schaffner and Hatfield stood with hands in their pockets, silent as two strangers in an elevator. Then their eyes met, by chance it must have been, and a sad understanding like complicity passed between them. Schaffner shrugged and unzipped. Hatfield followed like an initiate, and back to back they urinated in the frozen starlight, their separate streams hissing and steaming as they spattered the frost, the only sounds in the utter stillness. Eyes to the sky, Hatfield saw the same infinity of stars that he had seen with Maggie, holding her close as the villagers tightened their circle around them.

I'm pissing on top of the world, he thought. And the stars couldn't care less. He wondered if Schaffner did, and shivered in the dead cold.

They slept in their clothes. Untying his sneakers, Hatfield saw his right toe smeared with blood. He remembered the dying vizcacha, the stone, the sounds of impact. He swallowed and slid the shoes under the bed. Schaffner killed the lamp. "Good night, my friends," he said. "Pleasant dreams." The bed springs creaked, and soon he was snoring. Hatfield hugged Maggie, hard, and she hugged back. "Good night, lover," she said, and in a minute she fell asleep. Hatfield stared at the blackness. The jars were dim memories on the windowsills, contents invisible. He fought for sleep, but every time he came close his lungs begged for oxygen in the thin air, and he gulped deep breaths that snapped him awake. He burped and tasted *pintatani*.

Tomorrow, he thought. Tomorrow we will see flamingos in the dawn.

Hatfield rolled over and gently kissed the reason he had come to this place.

Paul J. Casella

THE IDEA THAT HOLDS WATER

The atmosphere is great here
at thirty-three thousand feet:
all blue, and white, and I've left
the spectrum far behind.

Here the clouds are choppy,
like an underbubbling
before a storm.

               Beyond they rest
over deeper water,
cotton into glass,
the impossible river that weaves
itself into heavy sobs
and sky.

I do not feel thirty thousand feet
closer to the sun:
               although
today I am unusually warm
and I sense a strange gravity
tugging at my head.

Heads up! The earth! We must be falling
or descending wing by wing.

What I need is a seatbelt sign
that frees me from my head,
or some future oracle
that I can teach to blind girls

whose mismatched clothes are uniform:
white, and gray, and fuzzy at the edges,
and fuzzy in the center,
and altogether like this cloud

which drops me, drop by drop,
onto the blue face below.

Olivia Beens

WATCH THE CLOSING DOORS

TAKE THE A TRAIN

SHE HAD TO have it! She just had to!

She planned it all out. Put on her jungle dress. Punched holes into her red plaid traveling case and headed Uptown on the A train. She walked down 125th Street. Went straight to Blumberg's Department Store. Downstairs to the Pet Shop. She waited for the school children to leave. Opened the cage. Put her hand inside, around his waist. He held on to the bars with his feet and hands, SCREAMING. Now, she knew why he was called a *Howler*. She yanked him harder, freeing him from the bars. Shoved him into the traveling case. And, quickly, headed for the stairs when someone grabbed her arm. She hit him with the case, until she realized that he, the monkey that is, might get hurt. They brought her upstairs to a small room; questioned her, lectured her, and made her sign something. She promised never to return again. The store detective told her that she needed to see a psychiatrist.

"*Honey,*" *he said,* "*What you really want is a BABY.*"

DOUBLE A

IT WAS ONE of those perfect December days: bright and crisp. There was snow on the ground and the sunlight made everything shimmer. Steve and I were going to the Museum of Natural History. He wanted to see the *Venus of Willendorf*, and I wanted to buy a book about sea-monsters for my young son. It was two days before Christmas. The subway car was crowded with shoppers, but it was not oppressive as in usual rush hour traffic. I spotted a young Hispanic woman with a bottle of Budweiser at her feet. Steve and I conversed as we looked at the other passengers. Out of the corner of my eye, I saw her: *stand up, pull her pants down, squat and piss. . . .* right there on the floor. As the train swerved, the river formed tributaries. The passengers simply lifted their feet, allowing the river to flow, freely.

I saw yellow and purple sea-monsters rise from the foam as in a primordial myth.

PRAYING MANTIS

I WANT TO BECOME physically fit and spiritually enlightened. On the way to yoga, the F train pauses at Jay Street. A man dressed in black is actively involved in prayer. He surrounds himself with religious paraphernalia. The seats adjacent and opposite to him are occupied. Across the platform the A train arrives. Through different doors, two women, proud of their African heritage, enter. They are colorfully dressed and have ornately braided hair. They walk toward each other, meet, greet, and begin to chat as they look for seats. My yoga instructor walks on. I manage to radiate a blissful smile to him. He appears flustered, or offended, and vanishes. One woman asks the praying man to remove the articles so that they might sit. He pretends not to hear. Then, he blatantly refuses. They exchange words. The women contain their outrage and anger as they continue conversing. I feel the tension mounting. At West Fourth Street the subway again stops to admit and discharge passengers. The women begin to exit. The man removes the articles from the seats, permitting a male passenger to sit. Instantly, the doors are jammed open. One woman holds them. The other, in venomous display, crouches, arches her back, snarls the air, and hurls a giant spitball at him. The women retreat. The doors snap shut, and we're off. The man clad in black smiles, to himself, with satisfaction. A Chinese man without comment or grimace, wipes the spittle off his trousers. During a contorted posture at the Yoga Institute, my yoga instructor comments that he failed to recognize me earlier.

I disturb him with this tale.

Jiří Sýkora

THE MAN WITH A TRUNK

from *One Hand Clapping*
Translated by Káča Poláčková

IT WAS ALWAYS the worst in the subway. Someone would stare for a while, and then say in a stage whisper, "Look at the nose on that guy, it looks like an elephant's trunk!" And everyone would laugh till they almost derailed the train.

Following the example of the adults, children had their fun too: they would stick peanuts up his trunk, and bubble gum, and umbrellas . . . One good-sized tyke went so far as to stick his hand inside, up to the elbow, and snapped his fingers.

People would yell, "Hey, Durante!" at him, but he didn't have an auntie, and besides, his name was Novak, so he was confused.

He could remember the days when he tried to reciprocate, to return malice for malice, but they always shouted him down. Once they even went so far as to call a policeman, who asked for Mr. Novak's identification. But that only led to more trouble, because all he had was a credit card with a photo on the reverse side, a special photo to accommodate the entire trunk, which meant that a tiny piece of trunk was sticking out of the bottom of the credit card. The officer frowned and said that there was something fishy about the credit card, but by then Mr. Novak had fished out a special document from the issuing bank in which it said that the bank had on file a medical certificate confirming the fact that Mr. Novak had a trunk where other people had noses. The policeman read it, shrugged his shoulders at the bystanders, nodded to Mr. Novak, returned his credit card saying, "Now, don't let it happen again." Then he gave Mr. Novak's trunk a familiar flick of his fingertips.

The gentleman who bore this interesting phenomenon subconsciously sought out the company of people with large noses. In their company, he felt less self-conscious, because they knew what it was like to be made fun of too. They used to get together in a cafe at the edge of town. There they could behave as they wished, laugh at what suited their fancy, scratch their noses with both hands if the spirit moved them, without fear of any thoughtless remarks.

At first Mr. Novak sat in a corner and made mute comparisons. Before him was an array of noses of all sorts and varieties: pointed noses, bulbous noses, meaty and bony noses, hooked noses and beaks, even abstract noses. But only Mr. Novak had a trunk. Yet he behaved as if he had a nose, maybe a pretty big nose, but a nose nonetheless. After a while, he began to take part in their drinking sessions, to play pool and cards with them, and finally he even joined in when they laughed. Yes, it was a good feeling, nobody made him feel bad because he had a trunk. It was this realization that brought to his mind a splendid idea. He decided to force his friends to compliment him, to praise Mr. Novak for having the very longest nose of all. Even though, if the truth be told, Mr. Novak had a trunk. He kept beating around the bush, and watching to see what they would say. He would enter the conversation, for example, by saying, "I wonder whose nose is the longest!" Or else he'd say, "You know, it might be fun to take a tape measure and really find out who has the longest nose here."

At the start, no one paid much attention to him. But one rainy afternoon, somebody happened to have a tape measure along, and they really tried it. When it was Mr. Novak's turn, he approached the tape measure with considerable trepidation. His trunk turned out to be exactly one yard long. The tense silence was broken by a thunder of ovations and applause. Someone's squeal of, "That's no fair, he's got a trunk!" was drowned out by the general noise. A columnist named Drews, with a nose for the news, congratulated Mr. Novak with a somewhat sour smile. Drews had come in second in the nose-measuring contest, but of course, if the truth be told, Mr. Novak had a trunk.

Drews did not fail to mention the competition and its results in his daily syndicated column. He naturally mentioned that he, the author, had won second prize, so to speak, and that Mr. Novak is an exemplary citizen, and that you can tell a man by the company he keeps, and that Mr. Novak is Drews' good friend.

The results were apparent by the next afternoon when Mr. Novak got into the subway on his way home from work. The glances that were cast his way were admiring. Women were smiling at him and a child here and there would stuff a piece of candy in his hand instead of up his trunk. Except for one altogether insignificant little toddler who asked his mother, "Mommy, how come that man has a tru . . ."

His mother glanced around self-consciously, at the same time interrupting the little boy by clapping a hand over his mouth and beginning to sing to herself, so it sounded like "Tru-tra-la-la."

Then she smiled over at Mr. Novak, and said to the child loud enough for the passengers to hear, "You see, Johnny, that's the nice man that has the greatest trose. . .I mean the greatest nunk. . .of us all. . ." but by then she was pale with embarassment. She grabbed the little boy's hand, hurried over to the door, and disappeared as best she could in the crowd until she could flee at the next station.

But for the most part, comments that Mr. Novak overheard were kindly and admiring, and even philosophical, like "A nose by any other name would smell as sweet!" or "The nose knows."

He had Drews' article framed and he hung it over his bed. All he had to do when he got up in the morning was to look at it, and he knew that all was well with the world. He stopped hunching his back and stood straight and tall; he looked people right in the eye now instead of staring miserably along his trunk down at the floor; his step was sprightly, and, now that he could fearlessly wave his trunk from side to side, his little eyes just glowed. And soon everything began to work out just beautifully. He would approach someone and launch his attack without any provocation, "Where are you hiding your nose, lady? Here, look at me, how do you keep your glasses on if you don't have a nose?"

Pretty soon his self-confidence got him onto the ladder to success, and in time he swaggered his way all the way up to the post of director of the company where he worked. Whereupon he carried out a massive reorganization. Small noses were put to work on the assembly line, larger noses became foremen and supervisors, the people in the administrative jobs really had to have something exceptional to show for a nose, while the job of the director's first assistant went to Willie Trump, formerly a stockboy. Willie had remained a stockboy for thirty-two years as a result of his inclinations towards alcohol, and his massive scarlet nose showed it. But best of all, when he showed up for work after a binge, still in a stupor, he had always been euphemistically called Willie Trunk.

Mr. Novak stopped visiting the cafe where he used to go to congregate with his large-nosed friends. He had his picture put up in every office in the company. He repeatedly found himself being nominated to committees concerned with matters of substance, and generally stuck his nose into everything. Except, if the truth be told, Mr. Novak didn't have a nose at all, he had a trunk.

He found himself a wife. True, his bride didn't have very much of a nose, but that was all right, because by now the bridegroom had learned to look any woman in the eye. When their son was born, he threw a big party, and trumpeted the night away in sheer exhilaration. The little boy grew, but somehow his nose didn't. Daddy was desperate, but the inordinate amount of attention he received served only to swell the boy's head and not his nose. As the years passed, the boy went to college, and when he graduated, he was asked to join the company. Finally he ended up being appointed to his father's position. The old man retired, so the stockholders couldn't accuse them of keeping it all in the family.

The son, with the enthusiasm of youth, reorganized. Thoroughly. Little noses rose to the top, while long noses snuffled down to the assembly line.

The old man watched all this with some degree of bitterness, but there was nothing he could do except just to adjust. What really set him back on his heels, though, was when his son took him aside one day and said to him, "Look, Dad, you're going to have to stop coming here to see me. Try and understand,' people make fun of you and that undermines my authority. You know what it is, it's that impossible nose of yours."

But old Novak didn't have a nose, he had a trunk.

That was the end. From then on old Novak didn't ask a thing of life. He took the ridicule and sipped his beer in silence. Occasionally he would trumpet gently to himself. People didn't care for that, and so they called the law again. But Novak no longer had a credit card, and he answered all their questions with a resigned trumpeting. And so the policeman up and took him to the zoo. The keeper thanked the policeman, and shook his fist in Novak's face, saying, "Shame on you, Bimbo, trying to hide from us among all those nice people."

Then the keeper led him into a cage. Bimbo Novak adjusted. He was adjusted to adjusting. And besides, it wasn't half bad. Once in a while he would get lonesome for his beer, but aside from that, he felt pretty much at home. He was particularly happy one day when a group of children was standing out in front of his cage, with their parents. One brave little tyke stuck a finger through the bars and stroked Mr. Novak's trunk and said, "But Daddy, this one has a nose!"

But if the truth be told, Mr. Novak. . . Wait! Just then, everything was suddenly all right.

George Erml

Moravian Party, Prague

Moravian Party, Prague

Moravian Party, Prague

Moravian Party, Prague

Straznice Folk Festival

Snezka Mountain

Snezka Mountain

Local Officials at the Opening of a New Department Store, Liberec, Bohemia

Officials, Straznice

May Day Parade, Roudnice Nad Labem

Outstanding Workers in Agriculture, Cěské Budějovicé

Soviet Officer at May Day Parade, Litvinov

Freya Manfred

TOES

A woman lost both big toes
in an accident;
to her it was as if
the two trees shading her house
were cut down.
Her tongue lay in mourning
in the vault of her mouth.
Her shins fought without compromise.
She could no longer bring herself
to eat with spoons,
and her forks matched her feet.
Sex with her husband
was like being called out at third
when she expected to slide home safe.
When he left her to marry
a twelve-toed cheerleader,
she retired to a hot tub
to suck her thumbs and die.
Her gardener buried her
beneath the Brussels sprouts
seventy-two toes under.

ASSES

Whether or not I inherited my flat one
from my father or mother
was the source of intense argument – insane! –
because you couldn't rest even one beer can
on Mom's or Dad's.
The word "buttock" didn't apply to us.

Now I believe:
the bigger the better:
something to steady you, hold down the fort,
a cubby for babies, a slide for schoolkids,
a football lineman's center of gravity;
I'm speaking of those big ones
like dollops of bread dough,
like a horse's hindquarters,
like the ones some waitresses in Nebraska
turn in your direction
after they serve the burgers;
those giant gumdrops,
those chestnuts, slick and fat;
they give me such a sense of security,
combined with a lust for hugs and kisses.
Such an ass could keep you warm
through the worst snowstorm;
it could save you from drowning,
and float you home like a barrel over Niagara;
it could fix the VCR
and figure out the income taxes;
or if all else failed and there was
nothing left but to face death in the eye,
such an ass could install itself
in a chair as wide and warm as Christmas
and sing, "Rock of ages, cleft for me,
let me hide, myself in thee . . ."
That's what God must have meant
when he whispered that song

into the ear of a Lutheran organ player:
how much we all need one of those powerful,
never-say-die, adult asses
to depend upon
in this Vale of Tears.

HAIR

I'll never forget
the first time my Gramma Shorba
unwound her dead mother's hairpiece
till it fell off her head
into my hand.
"It's called a rat, honey.
Would you like to comb the tangles out?"
I was seven.
I held it by two fingers
as if it were half-alive.
"Gramma, aren't you scared
your mother will rise
from her grave at midnight
to snatch back her hair?"
"My stars, girl, if she does,
I hope she'll take me with her!"
"But Gramma . . ."
"Because I'm lonely,
too lonely for this world."

My best friend, Diane Pond,
whose hair was the same shiny brown as Gramma's rat,
said my red hair was proof I was a liar
who would live a lonely, tempestuous life
no man could share.
One night I trimmed the sails of a fallen elm
and blew down the Mississippi to the sea
where I found a handsome prince
who would love me forever.
I don't treat him the way Gramma or Diane
told me to treat a man;
but in the first gray of every dawn
I'm thankful his face emerges
from the dark bed beside me,
as the sun rises over the horizon,
its hair aflame, aflame.

Jaroslava Blažková

CIRCE

THAT AFTERNOON, he walked out of the Institute, his mind bleary after a six-hour conference concerning the current perspectives of research over the next fifty years. They had taken six hours to consider the next quarter, and the case of the young girl who had been a laboratory technician and whom they had fired for stealing atropine and selling it to her slim-hipped girl-friends. (Whereupon they went floating through town with their pupils miraculously dilated, enchanting their naïve older lady-friends who had no idea of modern cosmetics.) The girl had appealed to a labor court, the case being heard for the tenth time already. The conference was to continue the next morning. Now, out on the street, it was five o'clock and autumn. Heavy clusters of passengers hung from the doors of trolleybusses, gossamer strands of cobwebs stretched from trolley to trolley on the wires, causing stoppages and traffic jams.

He made his way through the colorful crowd, the stink of gasoline, he made his way through the world of a tense civilization. The din of the town reached the path by the vineyard like the roar of a distant ocean. The purple of grapes ran up the hillsides, thrushes hopped on the elderberry bushes, pecking at the dark little berries, ravens flew over the woods.

He proceeded with the weary tread of the chronic conferee. The ravens circled over the wood. He walked, his mind still fuzzy from the nicotine and verbal pearl-casting. The ravens glided on air currents and let themselves be borne by the breeze, they chased each other, tacked in the wind, their black wings against the translucent yellow sky painted the airy dreams of the prisoners of Chillon.

"Ah, to be one of them . . ." he said.

A stroke of lightning, a peal of thunder. The old woman walking behind him fell in the ditch, and his lips touched the ground. No, not his lips. They weren't lips anymore. His body had suddenly lost weight, and where an intelligent nose should have been was a point of bluish horn. He hopped. He made a movement of what was left of his hands, and it lifted him. A little stronger movement, and it carried him away over the elderberries, his head started to spin, he fell and tore out a little black feather. The leaves in front of him moved, a bug was creeping along the stem of a leaf; shocked, he suppressed the urge to gulp it down. He watched the bug's feet wiggle, kept swallowing saliva, he was repulsive to himself. He tried a new take-off. Three meters up, he fell victim to vertigo and panic. He thought of how hard the ground was and began to fall head first toward it. At the last moment, with a spasmodic corkscrew motion, he saved himself. Something giggled by the fence.

Two black heads were bobbing on the fencepost.

"You don't know how to fall. That's the harrrdest," commented the one on the right.

"Good afternoon," he said. One of his newly-born instincts informed him that they were ladies. The one on the right flew down to him and asked, with urgency, "Listen, can you tell me, how did Ulysses make out?"

"Ulysses? You mean the Greek?"

"Yes, that's rrright. . . I never had a chance to finish rrreading it, and we don't get to rrread any books, the way we arrre."

"Well, as I recall, he did finally get home. But it took him twenty years."

"That's a rrrelief. I can't stand books that don't have happy endings."

"And what about the international situation?" asked the one on the left. He voiced his surprise to find such a vital interest in culture and current events among the feathered species. They explained that they were also ravens-come-lately, the first was a high-school student, the one on the left a graduate of nursing school. They told him how one comes to be a member of the fraternity of birds: for every one that dies, a live one can join the flock, specifically, the first one to look at the flock after his predecessor dies, and wish to be one of them.

"And how does one get to be human again?"

"One doesn't."

"What do you mean, one doesn't?"

"One doesn't, because one doesn't want to. As a rrraven, you have no worries. You have everrrything you everrr wanted, frrreedom, brrrotherrrhood, everrrything but comforrrt, because nothing is perrrfect," said the high school student, rolling her "r's".

"But I've got work to do!"

"Somebody else will do it."

"It's researrrch work. . .!"

"Someone else will rrresearrrch it," she assured him, and he yelled at her:

"You can't just flit through life! Life has some meaning, some significance, doesn't it?"

"Flying is the significance of life."

"What about responsibilities?"

"Rrresponsi-what? I can't rrrememberrr a lot of worrrds."

He sat in a furrow, the blue-black heads bobbed high above him, and higher still flew the clear yellow clouds. The autumn leaves were fragrant, smoke of burning grape vines mixed with the fragrance of yearning rose from the vineyards. He felt like flying.

"Come play with us," said the one on the right, and took off. He followed her wings with his eyes.

"Catch me!" she teased. "Don't worrry, nothing to fearrr, it's all a matter of not being afrrraid."

She soared high into the clouds, she turned into a mere black dot, and he started out hesitantly after the voice that kept calling, "Nothing to fearrr! Come catch me! I am Cirrrce."

* * *

I came home with the baby, to a waiting basket of ironing, dirty dishes, and general disorder.

"Why ithn't Daddy home?" whined the baby.

"He probably had a conference."

"Why?"

"That's life."

"Why?"

"How about singing me a song."

"Why that'th life?"

"If you're a good boy, you can sprinkle the laundry for me."

"With my water pithtol?"

I hesitated. "All right. But you have to keep quiet."

He filled his water pistol in silence, and carefully sprayed water on the shirts, the sheets and the towels from my mother's trousseau, linen towels with absurd mottos like GOOD MORNING and THE EARLY BIRD CATCHES THE WORM.

The older boy drummed on the door. He glanced at the coat hanger and instead of saying hello, he gave a disappointed groan. "Dad isn't home yet?"

"No, he's not."

"Where is he?"

"How should I know?"

"Didn't he phone?"

"No, he didn't phone. Now take off your shoes and wash your hands."

"Why didn't he phone?"

"I know just as much as you do about it. Now, go wash!"

He strolled over to the sink, turned on the faucet and gingerly stuck a finger in the stream of the water.

"Mom," he said, his index finger outstretched, "is it true that souls migrate?"

"What?"

"Well, that after a person dies, his soul enters some other thing, or maybe animal, and lives a new life there?"

Before me was a mountain of unironed laundry, dinner to be cooked. My boss was reproaching me for being inattentive, my husband was wandering heaven knows where, and this one here was annoying me with the migration of souls.

"After they die, souls are glad to have some peace and quiet. Migrate, indeed."

"But in India, people believe in it, and there are more Indians than there are of us, so maybe it's the truth!"

"For heaven's sake, if more people believe in nonsense does the nonsense suddenly make sense? Wash your hands properly, hear?"

He stuck another finger into the stream. "If you had your choice, where would your soul migrate to, Mom?"

"My God, whoever put this whole thing into your head, now?"

"Alexander."

Alexander, the rabbi's son, is introducing irrationality into our family, enthusiasm for the wild game called soccer, and a dubious inclination towards martyrdom.

"If only you and Alexander paid more attention to your math, and less to filling your heads with all sorts of silliness. And wash those hands, already, properly, will you, water doesn't bite!"

At that moment, the little one, who had been following our discussion attentively, aimed wrong and sprayed water over half the kitchen, specifically the half that I was standing in.

"But if you really and truly had your choice, what would you rather be, a lion or Mickey Mouse?"

"A rock! A rock out on the desert, where you never see a human being, or a water pistol, or laundry, or children. Where there is peace and quiet, peace and quiet, damn it!"

I wiped myself off as best I could and went into the bedroom. All the way in the bottom drawer of the chest of drawers, I have a bottle of Zubrowka, from which my soul occasionally draws flashes of clarity. I took a drink. I was kneeling on the carpet, observing my irritated expression in the big mirror and feeling sorry for myself.

At eight o'clock, I put the boys to bed. The phone rang. I rushed over to it, a female voice asked me if Sophie is home. I explained to the voice that there is no one named Sophie living here, and then I pulled *Taras Bulba* from the bookshelf. Whenever I feel rotten, I read about how they put kindling at Taras Bulba's feet, how they lit the fire, how Taras slowly roasts and as he dies, he yells courageous exhortations at the scoundrels. Someone was coming up the stairs. He paused at the door to our apartment, fumbled for the light switch. Then he went on. A bunch of merrymakers was singing out in the street. In my mind's eye, I could see my husband making merry with those rascals from the Institute. In the tavern. On the edge of the pavement in a puddle of blood. In the hospital with an oxygen mask. In the morgue. Myself at the cemetery, dressed in black (heaven only knows what kind of a pension they'd give me), the children orphans. I got up to get myself a hankie. I saw him with that cheap blonde. With relish, I plunged a knife (the big carving knife) into her scrawny neck and into his treacherous throat; the morgue and the cemetery, and me in mourning, the children orphans – I got up to get myself another hankie. At ten I went and phoned the Davises. Carl's sleepy voice informed me that he knew nothing about my husband. But not to worry, he'll be home. I began softly singing hymns to myself. I opened out the couch and lay down, even though it was perfectly clear to me that I wasn't going to fall asleep until he came home. I composed a sum total of five speeches, each a half hour long. A speech on selfishness. A speech on the depths of anxiety. A sarcastic speech, with one last warning. A suffering speech. A reproachful speech, with tears and shouting (the most spontaneous one, that).

At eleven, I heard a dull rapping on the window. We live on the fourth floor. I turned off the light. I tiptoed to the window. On the windowsill sat a big black bird. My heart was in my throat and I began to tremble violently. When grandpa died, the chandelier fell down and something banged three times on the front gate.

The bird was rolling his eyes. He rapped again. I opened the window. He flew inside. From out on the street I could hear the streetcar clanging, quite clearly, and a car horn (the twentieth century!). The raven sat on a chair and began nibbling saltines. He ought to have croaked something symbolic (never more), instead he said, "Good evening, lovie, don't be scared, it's me, really it is."

I am not one of those women who faint. I threw a blanket around my shoulders, knocking a salt shaker onto the floor. It rolled across the floorboards leaving a wavy white line in its wake.

I could see it all perfectly clearly. There really and truly was a raven sitting there. He was polishing off the last of the saltines, he stuck his beak in the milk that the baby had left.

I said to myself, "This, after two swigs of Zubrowka? Impossible."

The raven croaked, "Say, could you give me a light?"

He sat down in the armchair and tried to cross his claws. His eyes were melancholically half-shut. I pinched myself. There was no doubt about it, it was my husband.

"How dare you come home in this – condition. You've been drinking!"

"Now logically, lovie, if I had been drinking, could you be seeing me like this?"

I stared dully. Not one of the speeches I had composed seemed to suit the occasion.

"That's life, lovie," he croaked. "Nothing to be done."

Then he told me all about it.

"That's typical," I commented. "You up and turn into a raven without batting an eye, without ever thinking about what will become of me and the children. I could fly away too, a bird on the wing, but I wouldn't think of it! Because I have some idea of where my duty lies. I know that once I agree to an obligation, I am obligated to fulfill it, and even if I wanted a thousand times over to fly off somewhere, I couldn't and I wouldn't. Ever."

"But lovie . . ."

"Don't you lovie me. Now I'm your lovie, but did you think of that before? Did you? You're going to flit around and I'm supposed to sit here like some slave, am I? That was not the agreement. You always used to say . . ."

"Come on, come on," croaked that beast, my husband, "if you think there is anything I can do about it, tell me!"

"I won't have it!"

"Won't have what?"

"Won't have you being like this. Won't have a raven for a husband."

"We have to wait. Anyway, we won't figure anything out right now. I'll try something come morning, maybe something will occur to us." He yawned. "I'm beat." He glanced at the opened-out couch. At that point, I exploded.

"First you hang around the dustiest holes and then you want to fall in my nice clean sheets. Well, if that doesn't beat all."

"Where am I supposed to sleep?"

"Sleep wherever you please. If you had the conscience to turn into a raven, go sleep with the ravens."

"You forget that there are girl ravens too. And some pretty damned attractive ones at that."

"You monster!"

"See? Be reasonable. We'll calm down by morning and then we'll see." He crept under the blanket and immediately fell sound asleep. A bluish membrane covered his beady eye, his ugly beak was buried in the pillow, a snore emerged from his nostrils. That typically masculine frivolity of his drove me up the wall. Here he comes flitting in before midnight, not a man but a bird, and falls asleep like a cherub, without the slightest – even feigned – twinge of fear, without a qualm, calmly leaving me at the mercy of solitude and anxiety.

The raven is asleep. He is sleeping as if everything were perfectly all right. As if I, in my saintly patience and forbearance, were obliged to swallow everything, even this kind of metamorphosis. That is what a women gets for her tolerance. First you allow them to smoke in the house. Then you close an eye to work and work, and overtimes. You put up with now and then a delayed return home, and evenings with the so-called boys, and then one fine day they come home and it isn't even them, just some sort of creature with purple claws, with feathers and the yen to fly. Today he felt like being a bird, but what is there to keep him, tomorrow, from succumbing to the urge to swim the river Nile, and come creeping home in the form of a crocodile, and I, a perfectly normal young woman would have to sleep with a menagerie. Those possibilities frightened me even more. I stared at the little black skull, the fluffed-up feathers, the crop, imagined the days and the nights, the days and the nights. Terror overcame me. It was nonsense. Absurd. I got up to get myself another hankie. The third. By morning, I still hadn't fallen asleep.

* * *

No sooner had the baby opened his eyes, he was out of bed as usual and up to see his Daddy. He stopped for a moment when instead of his beloved Daddy, he saw a raven in bed, but he was immediately thrown into ecstasy.

"Ooooh, look at the pwetty chickie!" he exclaimed, poking gently at the bluish beak.

"G'd morning!" sneezed the raven.

The baby understood immediately, with no apparent astonishment, that the "chickie" was his father. The older one came, and lit into me right off. "See? What did I tell you? And you said there was no such thing as the migration of souls! So tell me, Dad, how did you do it? I'd like to be able to fly too."

The raven hopped down from the couch, the children clapped their hands.

I stood by the door and, horror-struck, observed their pink trembling fingers. And the black feathers flapping about near the ceiling: the end of a ten-years' love. "This is the way to fly . . ." croaked my husband, and the children skipped around eagerly behind him.

* * *

"Please, come!" I shouted to Carl over the telephone. "Yes, yes, something's happened, yes, it's serious. I'm waiting for you."

He rang the doorbell in ten minutes. I led him toward the living room. Through the glass door, I showed him the happy group. He froze. He grabbed his forehead and staggered into the kitchen.

He lit a cigarette. "This is terrible. But the fact is that he was always an odd bird."

"He was what . . . !?"

He waved a hand. "That flying business, you've got to be brave about it, it was always inside of him, somehow. I mean, he was always after something that normal people aren't interested in. I know how you feel, but you have to try to be objective. He had too little reality in him, far too little. Did he ever know how to make a sober evaluation of things? Remember the time with the gluing of the plywood, or that time with Brown. . . ."

I wasn't interested in plywood, or in Brown, or the most sober of evaluations. I just wanted to hear what I was supposed to do.

"You can be assured that I'll arrange everything. Everything that is in my power," he patted me on the shoulder. It was a gesture that you use when you are consoling a widow.

"Do you think he can stay working at the Institute like this?"

"Like that? In his position?"

"What position?"

"If it were anybody else but him, of all people . . ."

"He worked harder than the whole bunch of you. Lecture after lecture, he worked like a mule."

"That's just it. He hasn't got a friend. You know how he fought with everyone."

"That was just because he was always interested in doing a good job, and not in being popular. You, on the other hand . . ."

"Look, never mind me, now. The fact is that if they were to have to take a vote for a decision about him, then everyone would have a reason to vote against him." All of a sudden, I got the distinct impression that he, Carl, would vote against him too.

I said wearily, "You're his friend."

"Look, I'll see to things, I'll do something, for certain . . . but . . . you must admit that the situation is truly an odd one. How would the Institute look to the public if it employed . . . a raven! And then, a creature like that cannot be kept under control. Who's to guarantee that he would not defect . . . with his knowledge of . . . figures that are essential to state security . . ."

"How dare you talk like that. You've worked with him for years. You know what kind of a person he is."

"Of a person? You mean of a bird . . . and what he did now turns upside down everything we knew about him. And look what he has done to you. And the kids. To all of us. How does it make us all look now? Have you ever heard of a decent person turning into a raven? This was no accident. No misfortune. This is simply – a display of unreliability. If he was capable from one minute to the next of turning from a mammal to a bird, who is to guarantee that he won't turn about on something like his political reliability?"

We were silent. Laughter and carefree croaking sounded from the living room. My head was burdened by a feeling of sticky disgust. It was just my mouth, not my mind, that repeated, "You were his friend. You have to do something."

"I'll see to it you get a decent pension," he said.

* * *

After three hours of useless debating, I repeated my suggestion, "The only sensible thing to do is to go to the zoologists, or the veterinary institute, or the university. There must be some sort of research where they would examine you."

"You might just as well buy me a little coffin," croaked my husband. "I know research institutions all too well! The first week they'll feed me carrots, the next week calcium-free granules, the third week they'll test me to see how long I'll last without water, and then, when all my feathers fall out and I'm a basket case, they'll declare me incurable."

"But maybe they could think up something after all. We'll go and . . ."

"Listen, I'm telling you, if you try something like that, I won't speak a word, I'll be the commonest, most ordinary garden-variety raven you ever saw, and the one they'll start to examine will be you!"

"Now it's threats!"

He stroked my cheek with his wing, a condescending gesture if I ever saw one, and he retained it even in his current form. He declared, "I'll see to it myself." It was an absent-minded reply. His eyes kept turning to the roof across the street. I pretended that the reason I got up was to straighten the curtain. On top of the house opposite sat another raven, making provocative signs toward our building.

"Who is that?"

"That's a . . . a guy I know." He glanced at himself in the window pane and smoothed his feathers.

"It'll all turn out okay, just wait and see," he croaked light-heartedly and kept glancing at the roof opposite. The "guy he knew" was waving "his" wings and hopping about coquettishly.

"Well, so long," he croaked and flew outside with an anxious effort at grace. It occurred to me, entirely out of context, that somewhere in the closet, right by the ski poles as I recalled, must be father's old air rifle. I used to be a pretty good shot.

I looked after him as he rose gracefully and lightly, freed of all burdens. If only he would at least stumble a little. If only he would wobble just a bit, or show signs of struggling with space, and with pale shades of self-reproach. But he was flying freely, soaring just out of rifle range. His wings danced Swan Lake around the other bird.

I picked up the phone and dialed Professor Ferance, and just incidentally tried to find out how to tell a male raven from a female.

* * *

They soared.

Circe was laughing. It had never occurred to him that birds know how to laugh too. From above, the countryside looked different, its colors more bluish, its shapes softer, but what was the most enchanting of all was that he was above it all. He had the feeling that he was invulnerable. They climbed high above the clouds, they laughed, they soared.

Joy that had forgotten what it felt like to have to walk on the earth. Space. Bluish eddies, white fluffy clouds. Happiness not subjected to the law of gravity.

Ozone.

Laughter.

His reduced skull volume did not allow for a single one of the everyday emotions common to those who are obliged to walk the earth (tension, worry, fatigue, emptiness), all that remained was a lavender current, clear scintillating sparks. He was happy.

He played with Circe. Far below them spun the world.

Gods and ravens.

* * *

I reported his loss to the police. They recorded him, ironically, under Missing Persons. The children had adapted to the new situation splendidly. The baby kept singing about "Along came a black bird and pecked off her nose." The older one went around the courtyard gathering pigeon feathers, and tried to glue them together with wax to make a pair of wings. I had read about something like that somewhere before. The one who was the happiest of all was my husband. On the first day he had been willing to see some unpleasant aspects of his transformation, but as time dragged on, he became more and more adjusted to it. Adjusted? He was downright enthusiastic. He flew off morning after morning with the unconvincing consolation that soon he would determine how to do away with his birdness. I was certain that he would do no such thing. On the contrary. If he were to find some cure, he would take and drop it in the Danube River. His eyes grew glassier from one day to the next. More and more frequently, his gaze would come to rest on the roof opposite. At night, he would toss and turn in his sleep. I had the impression that I could discern a female name repeated in among his croaks. The fifth day it became absolutely clear to me that I would have to take some action.

* * *

He flew in, as usual, after dark. The children were asleep.

"We have to talk," I said.

His eyes flitted around the room as if he had just fallen from the sky. As if he were seeing me for the first time, and our home, as if we, not he, were the ones who had changed species, changed natures and everything else.

"What are you looking like that for?" I yelled. My voice didn't sound very pleasant. "You promised you'd find out what could be done. What have you found out?"

"Nothing."

"Then you know what we'll do? First thing tomorrow, we'll go have you examined, or else . . ."

"Orrr else what?"

"Or else I won't let you out anymore."

"What good would that do?"

"Not much. But I'm not willing to squat on the ground while you fly around like the Holy Spirit under the stars."

"You think you can hold me down by forrrce?"

I smiled: "Well? Will you go with me?"

He sat down in the armchair, but not the way he did before. Now he was sitting differently, sitting, perching like a raven. Everything about him irritated me now.

"I have a betterrr idea. Let's brrreak up. We have verrry little in common any morrre anyway. You arrre you, and as forrr me, I'm a rrraven."

What he was saying was bad enough, but wonder of wonders, what infuriated me most in that absurd scene was the way he rolled his "r's." "So you'd be willing just to fly away and never come back again?"

Quoth the raven, "Neverrr morrre."

We stared at each other. Everything was clear.

"In the morning, you say?"

"That's rrright. In the morrrning." (That unbearable "rrr" again!)

I made up my mind.

"Maybe you're right. Actually, I've been expecting it." My voice softened. "It wouldn't be right for us to break up as enemies. Maybe I'll calm down in time, and you can fly by every so often to see us, the children could put crumbs out on the windowsill for you. You know what? Let's have a drink together, for old time's sake."

He was on his guard. His purple bird-eyelids fluttered a little.

"Not that I was entirrrely without fault," he croaked .

"All right, all right, let's change the subject." I brought out the remainder of the Zubrowka. I poured it out, and held the glass up to his beak. He didn't trust me. I took the first sip. Only then did he submerge his bluish beak, and he drank with his neck stretched up, the way birds do. I poured another glass. Slowly, he began to glow. He said something about space, and angels with burning wings.

I poured the last drop.

He drank it, his little black head nodded, he fell asleep.

I picked up a pair of shears. I lifted up one wing, the black quills spread limply on the pillow. The feathers were warm, they shone like silk.

For a moment, I hesitated.

He moved in his sleep, and moaned: "Cirrrce, Cirrrce!" It was the voice of love.

There was no reason to hesitate.

I slipped my fingers into the handles of the large, dull tailor's shears and opened them.

I pressed them to the bird's body.

The bone in the wing gave a gristly snap.

The raven exclaimed "Cirrrce!" The linen sheet drank up the bloody stain.
I pressed the beak into the pillow.
He squirmed.
I pressed with all my might.
I was laughing aloud.
Black feathers floated to the floor.
I cut and cut and cut.

Chris Semansky

THE MAP IS NOT THE TERRITORY

Once when the roof flew off
and wind splintered what remaining
furniture I had, I was forced
to the streets, my eyes glutted with a clutch
of blue propects. Winter in the islands?
Summer on the slopes? No. I wanted to trip
barefoot through a field of shivering fruit,
hammer steel hands into the blind
foreheads of downtown buildings.
So when a poodle-faced masseuse
with Milk Dud moles picked me up
at the 7-11 and offered me her bed,
what could I say? It didn't matter
that the moonlight that night was rented
and soon we were out of dip and conversation.
There was always cable, and the microwave
for some quick snacks. The next day
I jimmied a jukebox clean, bought a ticket
to Topeka on the 10 o'clock Greyhound.
I was reading the countryside through the grease
stained windows when some fat tongued drunk
with a plastic briefcase and effeminate scowl
asked me what I was doing, just what
did I think I was doing? About then
the driver crunched to a stop and ordered
everyone off. I was the first one through
the emergency door, turned around just in time
to see the last lick of flame consume the bus.
I hid out for days in the third stall
of a men's room in a small town library
off Route 80, thinking of the faces on that bus,
covering the walls with a novel about a man

so scared of the world he pursued it
with the dizzying vengeance of an orphan
on amphetamine. In the end the man jumped
a steamboat for the islands, where he married
a savage, had a dozen children, and died,
years later, of a common cold gone wild,
his memory clean as ice.

Milan Kovacovic

MA'S DICTIONARY

for Joseph and Lisa Ohmann-Krause

I

"Dat not it! Dat not same vone again! Letters was different! You throw mine dictionnaire away, like everyt'ing dat belong to me!"

Slumped in her wheelchiar, my mother pushes the shiny new Thorndike-Barnard illustrated children's dictionary back into my hands. Her rebuke spews out from deep inside her chest in a raw, frightening tone. She no longer looks feeble. All her strength is concentrated in her accusation.

At the nursing home where she has been a resident now more than five years, I have finally joined the support group for caregivers. The facilitator has raised our consciousness: "Let's face it, folks, these sweet little old ladies have been too nice too long. When they let go, look out! There's lifelong anger and resentment pent up in those women. Some of it will be directed at you, simply because you're there. Try not to take it too personally. At times you won't recognize your own mothers." The fathers are long dead, and I'm the only son in the group, an uneasy intruder in the women's circle.

"Okay, Ma, I'll return this one too. Don't worry, eventually I'll find the exact same one we lost."

"You lose it, not me."

"Okay, Okay."

Hell, there are only so many children's illustrated dictionaries being published. I should be able to find the one she wants. I don't remember throwing away her old dictionary (was it a Random House, a Webster, an American Heritage? they all look the same . . .), but I don't have a clear conscience either. I know that periodically, I do succumb to violent impulses to throw things out, only to regret those rash actions later. I shall forever pine for my leather schoolbag from the Lycée in Paris, stored away as a needless object (what a shock that was!) soon after our arrival in America, then dragged along through every move from Chicago to San Francisco to Los Angeles and back to Minnesota, only to be discarded two and a half decades later, in a fit of housecleaning frenzy. My mother's dictionary had fallen apart over the years. She had mended the torn pages with tape, and patched up the binding with needle and thread and a strip of cloth. It could easily have passed for junk . . .

The quirks of heredity are amazing. My mother and I have at least one trait in common: a weird attachment to dictionaries. I still have my old Larousse illustrated, worn coverless (I did not inherit her skill and patience for repairs). Madame Mercier, our primary school teacher in Saint-Aquilin, had given it to me to keep me occupied during my entire last year in her one-room schoolhouse. I had read and reread The Book backward and forward from Z to A countless times, never tiring of it. Along with Madame Mercier's moral and intellectual instruction, it had formed the backbone of my education.

Pangs of guilt. My mother's reproach is probably justified. I must resolve the situation. What other publishers are left? Macmillan? Yes, I'll try that one. What a puzzle, this mother of mine! Why her sudden fixation on her lost dictionary? But wouldn't I feel the same way if my old Larousse disappeared?

II

"Of thought, in relation to Françoise, one could hardly speak. She knew nothing, in that absolute sense in which to know nothing means to understand nothing, save the rare truths to which the heart is capable of directly attaining. The vast world of ideas did not exist for her. But when one studied the clearness of her gaze, the delicate lines of the nose and the lips, all those signs lacking from so many cultivated people in whom they would have signified a supreme distinction, the noble detachment of a rare mind, one was disquieted . . . and one might have been led to wonder whether there may not be, among those other humbler brethren, the peasants, individuals who are as it were the élite of the world of the simple-minded, or rather who, condemned by an unjust fate to live among the simple-minded, deprived of enlightenment and yet more naturally, more essentially akin to the chosen spirits than most educated people, are members as it were, dispersed, strayed, robbed of their heritage of reason, of the sacred family, kinsfolk, left behind in infancy, of the loftiest minds, in whom – as is apparent from the unmistakable light in their eyes, although it is applied to nothing – there has been lacking, to endow them with talent, only the gift of *knowledge*."

I was deeply moved by the discovery of this portrait of the servant Françoise in Marcel Proust's autobiographical novel *Remembrance of Things Past*.

Proust's geography had long evoked in me vivid personal memories. The lilacs, the hawthorns, the poppies, the flowering apple trees etched so brightly in the landscape of his native Combray had reawakened in me those same radiant blossoms which had illuminated my childhood in the village of Saint-Aquilin. The water lilies dotting the surface of Proust's gently flowing Vivonne had brought back the sight, the smell of those lush aquatic plants which glistened in wet patches of green punctuated with brilliant eruptions of yellow on my own river Eure, meandering between two unbroken rows of tall poplars through the luxuriant meadows of Normandy, in a valley bordered by thickly wooded hills. In Paris too, at the Kapférers' mansion on Avenue Henri-Martin, where my mother worked as a live-in cook, I had observed many aspects of upperclass life portrayed by Proust, and during a subsequent trip to Venice, had experienced the aesthetic euphoria he describes in "place names." I knew the *places* in Proust's great work; but here suddenly, I was recognizing a *human* character, Françoise, also utterly familiar.

Whenever I teach Proust at the university, I like to linger on this passage. I ask my students whether they have ever met anyone like Françoise, who despite her inherent distinction and obvious intelligence "knew nothing, in that absolute sense in which to know nothing means to understand nothing, save the rare truths to which the heart is capable of directly attaining." They shake their heads, unable to imagine absolute ignorance. I have to provide an illustration:

"Okay, let's say, for instance, someone who has moved during her lifetime from Czechoslovakia to Paris to Chicago to California and finally to Minnesota, without any idea where those places are located on a map, nor any desire to find out . . ."

"Impossible! How can anyone supposedly so smart also be so ignorant?"

My example is not hypothetical. The world traveler I have described is my mother, a peasant woman from Slovakia whose most startling endeavor, among others, was to emigrate from France to America in 1956, at age 50, for no apparent reason, with her 14-year-old son, me, as her not very responsible guide . . .

Like Proust's Françoise, my mother's intelligence was evident. In France she had become an expert cook and pastry maker without formal training, simply through observation and instinct. She did not use measuring cups or recipes; she disdained the exhaustive cookbook which her employer, Madame Kapférer, had provided her for reference. To pay for our one-way ship passage to America, she had devised a clever strategem, of which Madame must have surely been aware, but feigned not to: In the weekly budget entrusted her for the food purchases of the Kapférer household of twelve, including a domestic staff of six, plus frequent guests, my mother listed the produce prices of nearby Rue de la Pompe's exclusive shops, while in fact she bought those items at the much cheaper, but one kilometer distant, Passy covered market. Sunday mornings, when I visited "home" from boarding school and relieved her of this daily chore, I was the one who lugged the two shopping bags filled with leeks, carrots, artichokes, melons, apricots, or whatever fruits and vegetables were in season, pausing for a brief rest at every street corner. Our aching arms and backs signaled we had legitimately earned the difference in price. My mother's ploy required strong stamina and, even more, sophisticated bookkeeping.

The graceful curve of her forehead, her straight bearing, the poise and confidence gained by osmosis from living among the wealthy whom she had served, all these signs confirmed the impression that my mother was a woman of distinction. During our voyage to America in March 1956 aboard the "Liberté," when most of the passengers and a good number of the crew had been immobilized in their cabins by an awesome North Atlantic storm, and wracked with nausea as soon as they dared rise from their bunks, my mother, normally prone to motion sickness even in busses, marched forward surefootedly for every meal along the mirrored vestibule leading to the ship's heaving dining salon, her right hand clutching the railing on the wall, her left arm folded over her purse. The pale headwaiter posted below the crystal chandelier at the entrance to the empty dining room would greet her with an admirative: *"Madame doit faire souvent la traversée!"* "Madame must often make these crossings!" Only obsequiousness and decorum prevented him from exclaiming *"Chapeau!"* "Hats off!" to this seasoned traveler. Little did he know that Milady was literally lost at sea.

My mother's clarity of mind and powers of synthesis were likewise impressive. She could reduce any problem, no matter how complex, to three or four salient elements, and conclude with an unnerving, detached, philosophical: *"Však, dělaj si jak si myslíš."* ("Well, do as you think best.") She was a woman of few words, easily irritated by gabbing or wordiness (*"C'est une pipelette"* – "S/he's a chatterbox" was her most frequent judg ment of people). In my present academic milieu, where specialized knowledge is commonplace but thought more rare, I have seldom encountered PhD's endowed with my mother's intelligence. Unfortunately, as with Proust's Françoise, her "lofty mind was applied to nothing."

I could not anticipate how my mother's ignorance might manifest itself. For instance, our son Paul having written a musical composition at age seven, a friend had one day commented in her presence that her grandson might become another Beethoven. After the friend had departed, she asked me to clarify a point: Was this person named Beethoven an acquaintance of ours, and if so would he be coming over for dinner sometime? (She lived in an independent addition to our house, and liked to continue using her skills and feel needed, especially for festive meal preparations.)

Other times, her reactions were more predictable. Each Friday, when I took her to the supermarket (early in the afternoon so she wouldn't have to fight the crowds), I'd engage her in the same uninspired conversation, just to break silence, as we drove past the university:

"That's where I work" (I'd nod towards the campus).

"*Tam robíš?*" (with astonishment each time, pointing in the same direction). You work there? In dis buildings. (The Slovak verb *robit* denotes manual labor).

"*Ano.* Yes."

"*A jak to* že nerobíš ted̄? And why aren't you working now? (again with renewed surprise each time).

There was no point using too abstract a verb like "teach" to describe my activities, or trying to explain that as a university professor my hours were somewhat flexible and I didn't have to punch in and out of those buildings, even if they did look like a factory. Similarly, she could not understand why I might sometimes go off to complete something at the office at 9 P.M. We lived together in different worlds. Once, as I was rejoicing over the news that I had had a scholarly article accepted for publication, her deadpan reaction appeared as startling, to me, as my answer no doubt was to her:

"And how mach maney dey pay you for it?"

"Nothing."

My mother's entire existence revolved around practical activities which kept her busy: cooking, baking, sewing, gardening (for some reason, she disliked knitting). She did not know the meaning of boredom. She needed no entertainment, wasn't interested in listening to the radio, turned her TV on only for the afternoon soaps. She was not illiterate, she could read, with facility in Slovak, slowly in English, her index finger following the letters, her lips silently mispronouncing the words, but I can't remember her ever opening a book, a newspaper, or a magazine, except in three instances.

First, the dictionary. Soon after her arrival in the U.S. in 1956, her employer suggested she enroll in a night class in English for immigrants and refugees. A child's illustrated dictionary with large typeface and simple sentences was recommended to her by her instructor. She spent most of her spare time as a live-in domestic in the Chicago suburb of Elmhurst religiously pouring over the dictionary, and continued reading it occasionally throughout the years.

Then, nine years later, in 1965, when she turned sixty, there was the naturalization booklet which she studied to apply for American citizenship, so she could obtain a passport and visit my two sisters in France and Czechoslovakia. She had entered the U.S. with a "stateless refugee" travel document and now needed to get her disjointed papers in order. As with bureaucracies everywhere, this would present some difficulties: at the San Francisco Immigration and Naturalization office, an intimidating examiner ("He vas ordinaire, he look mean, he shout at me") made her so flustered she confused Lincoln with Washington, forgot that Eisenhower, not Roosevelt, had preceded Kennedy, couldn't remember the first amendment, or the length of a senator's term of office, or the number of representatives in Congress, or the minimum age for a presidential candidate (fifty, she thought).

"You failed the citizenship test, Ma'am," concluded her torturer.

"Vat can I do now?"

"Learn the material better, Ma'am, and take the test again. Minimum time before retake is two months. Next!"

"Mister, my son he go in Army, maybe Vietnam. He not be able help me. Vat can I do?"

"I said, Next! You'll have to move on, Ma'am."

That's one of the rare times I have seen my mother cry.

Two months later, having foregone her afternoon soaps and indelibly seared into her memory the facts of U.S. history, the articles of the Constitution, and the rules of government, she was fortunate to be tested by a different examiner. She passed with a perfect score.

That was the extent of her intellectual activity until the summer of 1977, when at the age of seventy-two, she suddenly plunged into a Czech translation of Stendhal's novel, *The Charterhouse of Parma*, and reemerged only after she had devoured the entire work, in three days of total absorption. I was horrified, as one is in the face of an unexplainable, monstrous event.

I never felt contemptuous of my mother, but I was often irritated by her abysmal ignorance, which caused her to suffer also, by her own admission (*"Já som tak hlúpá!"* "I'm so stupid!"). Besides, it imposed drastic limits on the range of our communication, tenuous already because of our various language barriers. She depended on me, imposed on me, and in exchange accepted my outbursts of impatience. However, just as insane people sometimes exploit their alleged mental illness as an excuse for their unrestrained behavior, or just as people with an otherwise remarkable memory seem incapable of recalling names or faces, only because in truth they are indifferent and make no effort to remember, so did I begin to suspect that my mother's submission to ignorance was for her a convenient refuge of some kind.

I knew from personal experience that the mind is capable of working in peculiar ways. For instance, when I moved to France in 1972-73 with my wife and toddler son for a year of graduate studies, our family then on the skimpiest of budgets (thank you, staff of the Nice university restaurant, for doting on *"le bébé américain"* and feeding him free on the sly!), I purchased for our transportation needs an old Peugot 403, one of those indestructible vehicles which were favored at the time by Arab guest workers, the successors in France to my parents' Slavic generation. I soon discovered that the 403's transmission did not engage into fourth gear. Faced with already plentiful difficulties, I convinced myself that the car had only three gears. I completely shut out the problem from my mind for that entire year. In fact, I was genuinely surprised (and reawakened from my self-induced hypnosis) when a mechanic who was considering buying the car from us before our departure back to the States exclaimed upon returning from his test drive with the old Peugeot: "Hey, Monsieur, you realize this car is missing a fourth gear!" Embarassed, I let him keep it for free . . . and subsequent resale to the next set of Arab owners.

Another experience which convinced me that the mind can behave in strange ways was my mother's stroke in 1975, when she turned seventy. At the time, she expressed herself most easily in her native Slovak language, which remained surprisingly unadulterated despite almost half a century abroad. Her English was still minimal after twenty years in America, and she seemed to remember only a few French words from her twenty-six years in Paris and Normandy. The stroke had caused her entire left side to be paralyzed. Nearly as frightening as the paralysis, however, and much more mysterious, were the linguistic upheavals triggered by the stroke. Slovak and English both vanished completely from my mother's registry. Gone! Instead her pidgin French of two decades earlier resurfaced, preserved intact, frozen in its mispronunciations and scrambled syntax. The hospital staff could not communicate with her and needed me to interpret. Hearing my mother's fractured French, it was as if her voice was now transmitting live an earlier recording of itself, or as if a mummy suddenly began to talk in an extinct language. Then, over the next several weeks, as the paralysis slowly regressed, my mother's language returned to "normal." French again disappeared, and Slovak and English reemerged in their former configuration.

The conjunction of these bewildering experiences, along with her one-time Stendhal reading binge, her infantile attachment to her dictionary, and my fascination with the Proust excerpt about Françoise, prodded me to delve into the mystery of my mother's bizarre intellectual development.

III

"Ma, why is it you never want to read? Why is it you don't know anything beside cooking, baking, sewing, and gardening? Not that these things are unimportant, but what about *knowledge*? Why? Did something happen to you when you were young?"

Accustomed to the unrelenting candor of the caregiver support group, I am steeled in my resolve to unearth an explanation.

"*Protože já som bola Popelka!*" ("Because I was Cinderella!"), my mother blurts out. "Já! som! bola! Popelka!"

The floodgates are open. She straightens up in her wheelchair, relieved of her heavy secret. Why didn't I ask before? She recalls for me that fateful day in her childhood Slovakia, when the schoolteacher of her native village of Bzince pod Javorinou paid her father a visit:

"Please, Mr. Stano, I beg of you again, let Eva continue with her schooling. She learns so well. She always ranks first in the class. She could still help you at home in the evening and work the fields during the summer!"

"Look, Mister Teacher, enough of this. I'm her father, and I already told you NO once before, so don't insist. See the door? Leave my house this moment and never come back! You hear!"

And so my mother's schooling ended on her fourteenth birthday, June 30, 1919. Like Cinderella, she became her family's servant, envious of the independence and the small income that her four older brothers and sisters earned from working the fields of the village's three landowners. Her father had survived the carnage of war, turned in his rifle, put away his spiked helmet. Borders in Central Europe were reshuffled, the new nation of Czechoslovakia created. But in the timeless village, life remained unchanged as ever. My mother deplored her fate; still, she would not have consented to continue her studies at the expense of her siblings. She had strong egalitarian instincts. At age twenty-five, unable to withstand her condition any longer, she ran away to France.

Five years before the War, in 1909, my grandfather Stano had returned to the village empty-handed and embittered after a three-year stint working in a gold mine in Alaska. That had been his last attempt at earning a living. Following his return to Slovakia, he spent his days sitting by the window, smoking cigarettes and bantering with passersby, and otherwise directing the household. Meanwhile his wife crisscrossed the heart of Europe like a gypsy from Budapest to Prague to Vienna, hawking lace embroidered by the women of the village. Grandfather despised the earth, the muddy peasant earth. He hated work. Until they were old enough to fend for themselves, his five children were raised by relatives, my mother until the age of twelve by an aunt in the nearby hamlet of Lubina. There was little money, but no one ever lacked food or a roof overhead. Vegetable gardens, chicken and rabbit coops, the yearly killing of a pig and the harvest of plums for slivovitz brandy provided the basic necessities.

Popelka! From her days at school, my mother had acquired a passion for reading stories and novels. At every opportunity during her housekeeping tasks, she'd try to sneak in a few pages, only to be rebuked by her father, who did not hesitate to tear books from her grasp, and fling them to the ground. "You're supposed to work, not loaf around!" Finally, defeated, she stopped reading.

For some people, like grandfather Stano, reading is synonymous with boredom or idleness. I experienced this myself during basic training in the Army at Ford Ord. One day, I had taken advantage of a break during kitchen duty ("Smoke 'em if you got 'em") to open a paperback novel which I carried in my fatigue pocket for precisely such occasions, when there'd be "time to kill." Several of my KP colleagues sat around an adjoining table in the mess hall, and whiled away the rest period solemnly puffing on their cigarettes and blowing smoke rings to the ceiling. No sooner had I started reading, a sergeant barked: "Hey, you, the guy who's readin' and not doin' nothin', go clean the grease drain."

IV

"Well, what do you think? Is that it?"

I hand my mother the Macmillan dictionary. She puts on her glasses, leafs through the pages, hones in on a detail. Her eyes light up with a gleam I haven't seen for years.

"Yes, dat is it! Dat is it! Oh, I am so happy. Tank you very mach."

V

A few weeks later, the nursing home social worker phones me at the office:

"When you visit your mother, have you noticed a change?"

"Yes, she seems depressed. She says she's losing her memory."

"She says the same thing to the staff. She no longer complains about her dictionary, but now it's her memory."

"Well, isn't loss of memory normal with old age?"

"Yes and no. So far we haven't really seen any evidence of Alzheimer's in your mother. She still complains about phantom pains in her amputated leg, but that's to be expected, even after several years."

VI

"Ma, how do you know your memory is going bad? You seem to remember all the details of your childhood."

"It's mine dictionnaire."

"How so?"

"I not remember words."

"What do you mean?"

She puts on her glasses, grabs the dictionary from the sidepocket on her wheelchair, opens it up at the letter "F," where she has inserted a piece of cloth as a marker.

"See, I not can remember more than here."

Suddenly, it dawns on me. I recoil in shock and disbelief. "No, Ma, No, No!"

She has been attempting to *memorize* the dictionary.

Susan Firer

1956, THE YEAR MY SISTER, USING HER ILL HEALTH ONCE AGAIN, BLACKMAILED MY PARENTS INTO AN ACCORDION

My mother even hated
the name of the store where she had to pick it up:
Lo Duca Bros.

She waited until dark
to smuggle it from her Olds Holiday trunk
into our house.

Everytime my sister unsnapped
and opened it my mother ducked as if fruit bats
were flying from its pleats.

To my mother the accordion was an immigrant,
one of my father's relatives,
one that didn't speak ENGLISH,
one that was pierogi fat,
one that wore a babushka and anklets
to church, one she thought she had
talked him out of writing to.

My sister would go out on my parents' suburban front
lawn between the maple & china berry tree
on the even, green, Bay Ridge, well watered lawn
and practice LADY OF SPAIN.

My mother imagined the clouds above
her house taking Lawrence Welk cut out shapes
that rained kolackys. Frankie Yankovic
was at her door. THE NEIGHBORS KNEW!

My mother hoped my sister would abandon the accordion
as quickly as she did her charm school, her twirling,
her water ballet and Mamie Eisenhower scrapbook.

My mother dreamt the Six Fat Dutchmen heard
all about her sick daughter and came
and taught her the "Too Fat Polka";
all my father's unrecognized relatives came
from Czechoslovakia to see the Six Fat Dutchmen
and do the Slovenian twirl at twilight
under plastic, electric, Chinese lanterns
strung around my parents'
newly landscaped suburban lot.

My mother bribed my sister away from her accordion
with a trip to New York to visit Uncle Jack, a professor
who taught Labor Relations at Cornell, (ACCEPTABLE).
Uncle Jack, my mother's brother. It was what my sister
wanted all along. The accordion was her wardrobe door
to Narnia, New York. My mother would
return satisfied and exhausted, reporting
"Professors' houses are filthy; ideas
seem more important to them than cleanliness."

While they were gone the accordion sat alone
as the night convent of Saint Mary of Czestochowa
across the river. The accordion had rows of nubs of wonderful black buttons. I wasn't big enough to carry it.
It was beauty. I imagined
it vast and pearl as a confessional,
gay as a Polkafest. I sat next to it;
I heard my sister's silent accordion stop playing the past.
It began playing music I didn't know yet. Years later
I'd call it zydeco and dance to it on sweet, full summer
nights, on side city streets of the future
with holy card beautiful men
who loved nothing more than a woman
with an ear for a good accordion
and all the musics one can make.

RELICS

Not fountains, grottoes, or statuary, but pieces
of cloth, bone, wood, and hair touched
to other people or places was what
we found when we undressed you. After
you died, we found a conniption of medals
shinier than the gem collection room in Chicago's
Field Museum. Relics like soldiers' decorations
pinned and blazing on your hospital gown, tulip
green scapulas clamped to the buzzer that called
your nurse. Stuffed in your purse: pieces of uncooked
spaghetti colored palm touched to the Holy Cross,
a chip of St. Catherine's bone sealed
& filigreed in metal; a piece of bicycle
blue cloth blessed by the pope & sealed in plastic;
a silver Saint Christopher medal touched
by Padre Pio; a Saint Jude medal.
That late afternoon relics rained deep
as the voice of Bishop Sheen
whose recordings of the rosary you'd played
us to sleep with when we were your baby girls.

Zdena Salivarová

IF THOU SHOULDST MARK INIQUITIES

Translated by Káča Poláčková-Henley

Si iniquitates observaveris, Domine:
Domine, quis sustinebit?
Psalm 130

"HONZA, GET UP!"

The voice that pierced my half-sleep that morning was hoarse more from overuse than from any morning indisposition. I squirmed to show that I'm not deaf, and proceeded behind closed eyelids to clarify reality. Every time that awful moment approaches when I have to get up, I have trouble grasping reality right off, I just have a sense of the real, a sense of tossing aside the quilt, breaking out in goosebumps, slipping on my slippers, stretching, going and washing, and sitting down in the streetcar, on my way. Except that I'm generally not on my way, that's the trouble.

Today, thanks to that dreadful voice and the even more dreadful intonation ordering me to get up, my thoughts clarified themselves relatively quickly.

"Did you hear what I said? Get your fanny out of the sack, they'll be starting to arrive in a little while!"

Vlasta's voice sliced into my brain like a broad-axe, and prevented me from counting to three, the way I always did. One, two, three, ready-set-go! Generally it worked on the sixth try or more. This time it worked without counting. It seemed better to pull oneself together and get up than to give her another chance to assert the rights of the elder.

Vlasta is ten years older than me, my married, smartest, sweetest, loveliest sister of all sisters. If I had the power, I'd name her commander in chief of the Czechoslovak armed forces, or the warden of the reformatory at Bonebreaks. And if I were her child, I would have filed an application for a writ of divorcement from my maternal womb in the earliest stages of my development as an embryo. I'd rather develop in a test tube with a governmental nutritive solution.

"Hurry up!" She ripped the quilt from around me. "You're going shopping!"

I picked myself up and only then did I open my eyes. She was standing beside the bed, black as a raven, her eyebrows, her hair, her eyes, her legs, everything except the white-powdered face. She was convinced that God must have created her for the color black, so the best opportunity for showing off her charms was a funeral, which was exactly what was happening today at eleven hundred hours on top of Thundercloud Hill, the site of the local cemetery. The whole family would be arriving, because today we were burying grandpa.

I dashed into the kitchen. It was like jumping into a warm bath, lathered with vanilla and lemon peel. It reminded me of Christmas. Except that it wasn't Christmas, it was the second of February, and it was grandpa's funeral. At Christmas he'd still given Vlasta a pair of felt slippers that grandma had left, along with some thick woolen socks, knit two, purl two, remarking that a woman had ought to keep her feet warm, to keep her from getting a chill in her snatch. Our mannequin was thoroughly insulted by grandpa's barracks humor. She never did forgive him for it, either, not till the day he died.

Behind the glass door of the china cabinet, the black and white death announcement was on display, with four dense columns of the bereaved. We were a large family. Making her selection from the ten officially sanctioned samples of announcements, Mom picked the one with the quotation from Wolker's poem about difficult dying, because grandpa's dying had indeed been difficult, with cancer of the lungs. He avoided the sawbones till the very last minute, so that he made his dying truly the most difficult of all.

Mother was slicing the braided coffee cake, and the tears trickled down the steamy window. I read the quotation behind the glass, and lines from Wolker's poems started spinning in my head: Death is not evil – the mailbox on the corner is blue – today is orange – I sliced you open, love of mine – will it not be born? – Antonín, you power plant stoker –. Mother rattled the coal scuttle, and poured some water from the pot on the stove into a wash basin for me.

"Do a good job on your ears," she said discreetly, and turned back to her coffee cakes.

Just then my sister walked into the kitchen and rested her gaze on the steam rising from basin.

"A deadbeat like this ought to be washing outdoors! With snow! You just wait till the army gets a hold of you!"

"Right you are, sis, the army won't coddle me," I decided to be agreeable.
"Don't you be sassy, brat!" She gave me a shove till I almost drowned.
"Come on, now," said mother. She handed me a towel and dumped the water out of the wash basin. "There's a clean shirt for you in the bedroom, dear."

I put on the black suit I wore to dancing class. I didn't look half bad and I noted with satisfaction that I'd sprouted some new whiskers since the last dancing class.

"Hadn't I better shave?" I asked mother when I came back into the kitchen.

"Let's see," mother pulled me over to the winodw and stroked my cheek. Her hand smelled good, like coffee cake. "You still can't tell unless you touch."

"So I don't have to shave?" I asked in a manly voice, and looked at my sister.

"What's there to shave, dummy?" she snapped. "Grab a shopping bag and get cracking!"

She wouldn't accept the fact that I was growing up. She couldn't push me around any more the way she was used to, and when she wanted to haul off and slap my face, she had to wait for me to bend down to tie my shoelace. It really cheesed her off that she was such a shrimp. Particularly now, when the fashion is long, leggy, skinny girls. When I wanted to piss her off a lot, I used to say to her not to let it bother her. "Small people usually have great souls. Like look at Napoleon He was a runt too, and look at the confusion he caused in the world." She hated me so much for that that if she'd been just a little bigger, she'd have strangled me on the spot. I was beyond her reach already. This time, I ignored her.

"What do you want me to buy, Mom?" I asked resonantly. Mother straightened my shirt collar, put a shopping bag and some money in my hand and I went.

From the shed came the hysterical barking of grandpa's Polly. I untied her, so she wouldn't go nuts or something. She was jumping around like crazy and she stamped her pawprints on my coat.

It was freezing. The snow in the fields looked like sand dunes in the Sahara. The white sun was just rising from behind Thundercloud Hill.

I took the long way, past the Ráž place. It would be rather nice to run into Hanka today, looking as spiffy as I did. Polly was honest to God going nuts. She zipped around like a whip, behind me for a while, then ahead of me, until I finally figured out that she wanted to play. I made a snowball and tossed it way out in the field. She threw herself after it and screwed her muzzle into the snowbank, except somewhere else entirely from where the snowball had fallen. When she got tired of that, she came running back to me. She had frost on her whiskers like the Old Man of the Mountain.

"You're a screwball, Polly! Do you have any idea of what's happened?"

She yipped and wanted me to throw her another snowball.

"No more playing. A really faithful dog lays down and dies when she loses her master, and doesn't fool around like you are."

She tilted her head to hear better. Her long, dangling cocker spaniel ears stuck out and it looked as if she was making fun of me. She didn't have the slightest idea. I tossed her another snowball. She ran after it, and for a while disappeared in the clouds of blowing powder. I quit paying attention to her, because the door at the Ráž place opened and Hanka walked outside. I speeded up. When I ran up to their fence, Hanka was just closing the ashcan. She had a kerchief on her head, and colored curlers showed from under it like chunks of hard candy.

"Hi, Hanka," I said. You could tell she was uncomfortable on account of the curlers, but all the same, she came over to the fence and reached out an ashy hand. She couldn't even shake it right.

"I wish you my sincerest condolences," she said gravely. I didn't feel like talking about condolence. She didn't know what it is, anyways. She'd never had anybody die yet. Except for Kiki, the angora cat, but that was a few years back. I cried too, then, and felt condolence when I helped Hanka look for Kiki, and when we found her by the railway tracks, with her head cut off. Hanka wanted to put the head back on the body, but it didn't work. We buried the cat in the ditch and we cried. Since then, Hanka has turned into kind of a pretty girl. I didn't know what to talk about.

"Are you coming to the funeral?" I asked stupidly, as if I didn't know that her grandpa and my grandpa were old buddies from the war.

"Sure we are," she whispered, drawing a circle in the snow with the toe of her slipper. "Well, so long then," she said after a while, and skipped away. There was a dusting of ashes in her wake, a bit like a veil. I stood beside the fence until Hanka was inside the house.

"Woof!" said Polly behind me, and when I turned around, she lit out as if we were going to play tag. Her ears were waving like banners. I started running too, and we chased each other all the way to the village.

There was the usual crowd in the self-service grocery. When I walked in, everyone fell silent. Someone gave me a basket, so I wouldn't have to wait. As if I were an invalid. I tossed the shopping bag into it and stood in line at the cash register. Again, they let me in ahead.

"Thirty and twenty is fifty," the cashier said to me sympathetically, "and fifty is a hundred. It's all over for him now, eh? Poor fellow, he could've had few more good years here." She clinked her words like coins. "It's a pity, my best to your mom."

Everybody was watching me and they forgot their shopping. I got a cramp in my face from trying so hard not to smile, even a little. I put my groceries in the shopping bag and walked out of the store with dignity. Polly jumped up on me again right off and wanted to run again. She would stop in front of me, tilt her head, wag her tail and then, all of a sudden, jump straight up in the air and take off a few steps down the road. When she realized that I wasn't running, she came back and repeated the whole act. But I couldn't possibly run across the square, today of all days, with a dog. I gave her a bit of salami, to quiet her down.

I stopped off at the greengrocer's, the baker's and the butcher's. Mrs. Feigl, the baker, apologized about not being able to go to the funeral because they were getting a shipment of goods, so did the butcher, and the woman at the greengrocer's said that she'd be there if she sells the four cabbages that she's got left of her stock.

"Now it'll be up to you to take your grandpa's place. Now you're going to be the head of the family."

In fact, she was right. We hadn't had a Dad for a long time. At least I couldn't remember him. I was born a few days after he was hit by a truck here on the square. It was my grandpa who raised me, with the callused hands of a farmer. He didn't spoil me, so that actually I ought to be glad that he isn't going to be raising me any more. But somehow I wasn't glad. Come to think of him now, it all seemed unreal. There won't be any more fun at home now. Grandpa's humor was corny, it belonged to the old empire, but sometimes his jokes were really excellent. And as far as me and Vlasta were concerned, he was always on my side. He and Vlasta had been at loggerheads since time immemorial, and I think it started out with the game of Meat. That was a game that grandpa used to like to play with us. One of us would have to bend over, cover his eyes, and the other two would whip his behind. If he guessed who had just hit him, he would take the place of the one he had guessed. Grandpa always used to give Vlasta easy ones so she'd think it was me, and I could really slice her, till she burst into tears, and grandpa would tease her that her behind was like a bloody steak. That insulted her worse than the blows. She would always throw herself on the settee and cry herself to sleep. Then grandpa would wake her up with the words, "Get up, it's time to go to bed," and when she didn't get up, he'd put a five-heller coin on the stove to get it good and hot, then he spit on her rump and put the red-hot coin on the spit. She was on her feet in a moment and burst into wails all over again, that now she has a blister on her bum and that it's going to leave a scar. That was grandpa's kind of joke.

I pictured him alone and immobile upstairs in the morgue, never again to make fun and tell the same war stories over and over again, and suddenly a sadness came over me.

The clock in the tower struck nine. The sun peered glassily through the fog, white like a big snowball, and it didn't bother me to look right into it. Then when I shut my eyes and covered them with my hand to make it completely dark in there, the white circle turned gold, and pink, red, and it took a while before it melted into the black darkness behind my eyelids. And even then you could still see a dark red dot in there.

"Don't cry, Honza," I heard behind me.

I took my hand away from my eyes and looked.

"I'm not crying, Mr. Ráž."

"You needn't be ashamed, a fellow has got to get it out."

Then why was he telling me not to cry? I left it at that. He shook my hand and scratched Polly behind the ears.

"We'll see each other later. After all, I have to go see my old buddy off, good lord, but I never expected him to go before me."

I took a different route home, across the hill called the Bump, so as to get home as late as possible. Besides, my righteous sister would find something else to send me out for, anyway. I couldn't stand her, and I was really relieved three years ago when she got married and moved away. She had to get married and it darned well served her right. But even so, she was at our place more than she was at home, and she always acted as if she were my legal guardian at the very least.

The view from the Bump across to Thundercloud Hill was a good one, and down at its foot stood our place like a gingerbread cottage. Before Christmas, grandpa had painted all the shutters red, and I remembered how he had cursed the paint for taking so long to dry. As a matter of fact, it's still a bit tacky today. The smoke was rising from the chimney, and the snow was shining all around.

A pale blue Trabant was rolling up the road to our place, behind it the Volga that belonged to our economical uncle from Týniště, and the ugly green Moskvich of my sister's legal spouse, hence also her Moskvich. He was bringing my prematurely born niece, blood of the blood of that selfsame sister of mine, Vlasta.

I slid down the hillside path to the foot of the Bump, and with Polly in tow, I dawdled my way over to our place.

My brother-in-law's big feet in their rubber boots were sticking out from under the Moskvich.

"Hi, Vláďa," I bent under the car, "what are you working on?"

He wheezed and reached for one of the tools he had spread out on the snow.

"I want to change the oil while it's still warm."

He wheezed again, and a stream of dense black oil squirted into the pristine snow. It drilled a deep hole in it.

"It'll really soak in proper here, besides, I never know what to do with the old stuff."

It was soaking in and the snow was turning into a greenish mash.

"Can I help any?"

"Here, take this can and bring it inside to the stove to warm up. Otherwise it'll never pour in this cold."

I picked up the can and climbed the steps to the house.

The front hall looked like a store selling thick black overcoats, there were boots all over the floor, melting snow ran off them and turned the floor into a wading pool. My aunt came out of the kitchen with a bucket. "Hello, lad," she smiled with her mouth closed and gave me a kiss.

"Hi, auntie, how are you doing?"

"I can't smile, look, they pulled out all of my teeth, and it'll be at least six months before I get my plates."

She put down the bucket and grinned her bare red gums at me.

"That's all right, you're not going to do much smiling today anyway."

"You're right." Her eyes rushed full of tears and she snuffled. "Poor Dad." Then she bent down for the bucket. "Run on inside. I've got to wipe it up out here. It's awful, really awful."

I didn't know if she meant all the muck or the death in the family. Probably the muck, because my aunt always thought in a single plane.

I set the can beside the stove and sat down on the woodbox to take off my boots.

"What are you loafing around here for," my sister addressed me. "Get out of here and see to it you keep busy."

I sat there as if I hadn't heard her. The best thing is always to act as if my hearing had momentarily failed. I rubbed my chin with the palm of my hand. In the silence of the kitchen, you could hear my whiskers scraping my hand. That infuriated her even more.

"Did you hear me! See to it you get out of here and get busy, hear?" she said intelligently.

"What is it that I am to do, madame?" I asked, displaying my excellent good manners.

She couldn't think of anything. She made a very annoyed face, sat down at the table, and on her hand rested her head with its fancy hairdo. As she sat there, she was twisting her foot in her slipper, lifting and dropping her instep. Mom handed me a tray, cups and a teapot, and asked me to take it into the other room.

The shivering aunts sat around the red-hot stove, beating their gums. When

I walked in, they fell silent and turned to the tea tray. The uncles looked for all the world as if they'd like nothing more than a good old game of cards and something decent to drink. They sat around the table in the corner, criticizing the president. It was stuffy in the room, I felt faint. I opened the door to the next room. The light was on in there. My sister's premarital lapse was sitting before the mirror, smearing her little face with Vlasta's hard-bought cosmetics.

"What're you doing?" I jumped at her as if I were the bogeyman. It never occurred to her to be frightened. She finished putting green on her eyelid, and then she pulled Vlasta's mourning veil on her head, crown and all. She never so much as looked at me, and began to dance in front of the mirror. For a while she couldn't take her eyes off herself, and then she pirouetted off into the other room among the relatives. It didn't surprise me in the least. A year ago, at cousin Lenka's wedding, she did the same thing in white. That time, Lenka fainted when she saw the child had destroyed the myrtle symbol of her long-since non-existent virginity, and Vlasta dislocated her shoulder administering corporal punishment to her daughter. They had to put it in a cast, which caused her to lose considerably in dignity. I was really beginning to look forward to the outcome today.

The child danced to a tune of her own devising: "I'm a sad princess, the good old king is dead," and she would have continued in her creativity if it hadn't been for the dislocated arm of justice reaching out at the right moment. The hat was ripped off the child's head and she was dragged out into the hall. Immediately a zoological yowl sounded from there. The toothless auntie from Týniště tried to cover up the scandal a little. She took advantage of a pause from the hall and laughed aloud with her lips tightly closed.

"Poor little thing, she hasn't got the remotest idea. But she was cute, wasn't she? So little and look how cute she can be."

The other aunts and great aunts nodded sourly. The silence that followed was uneasy. Mother's soothing voice came through from the kitchen, as did Helenka's sobbing. Out in the hall, Vlád'a and Vlasta argued in low voices over methods of childrearing. He was totally defeated.

Cringing, he returned among us and plopped down at the table with the uncles. I didn't feel sorry for him at all. When he married into our family, he was a pretty good-looking guy, full of energy and self-confidence. Dear little Vlasta waited on him hand and foot, dear old Vlád'a was always right, but just until the wedding. She was smart enough for that. She had to be, Helenka was becoming all too obvious beneath her rapidly rising waistline. She tapped her beak sweetly and softly, fluttering around him, and even I was fooled. I'd read in some pamphlet on marital harmony that some women are completely transformed by pregnancy. Was I ever wrong! Before they even left city hall, after they'd signed the papers, Vlasta climbed in the driver's seat. From that moment on, she had him well in hand and Vláďa began to waste away. He had long since quit being a handsome curly-haired boy, and was rapidly turning into a milk-toast with a belly and the constant inclination to hide his sorrow under the green Moskvich.

The aunt from Týniště felt sorry for him. She handed him a cup of tea and pushed a plate of coffee-cake over to him too.

"Eat up, Vláďa my boy, eat up, what else is there in this old world?"

Vláďa pushed himself away from the table and leapt on his briefcase by the window. As if by magic, he came up with a bottle of rum, rammed the cork into the neck of the bottle with his little finger, and poured some into every man's cup of tea.

"Just a little something to warm up with," he remarked apologetically, and poured the healthy shot that remained into his own cup. The uncles livened up, hurried to raise their cups, and came close to singing "Glorious!"

"I happen to have brought a little something," confessed the economical uncle from Týniště, placing a bottle on the table.

"That's for the ladies," auntie smiled with her bare gums. "It's made out of our own elderberries, just wait and see how you're going to love it."

A few more bottles emerged and it looked like it would turn into quite a promising party. Vláďa was putting it away, regardless of his driver's license, but the furrow on his red face stayed deep. I didn't understand him. I was used to my sister's occasionally showing signs of mental illness, and on occasion I would use physical force on her. It was, after all, the only thing her femininity could inspire a man to. I would have liked to have asked Vláďa if he occasionally doesn't feel like stuffing a gag in her mouth. He probably did, but it stopped at the feeling. He was beyond help. That was confirmed when Vlasta burst into the room and unerringly sniffed the air. Vláďa swiftly slid his cup in front of me and made an innocent face. He really did himself in, as far as I was concerned.

Her presence put the brakes on the fun that had started to develop. She suggested that maybe we'd better get going, because we have to walk, you can't drive up the road to the graveyard, grandpa's being taken to the graveyard on a horse-drawn sleigh and it'd be embarrassing to be late. Those were her very words. Then, in private, she whispered to Vláďa that he couldn't have driven anyway after drinking all that rum, so he'd better get cracking. Everyone rose obediently and there was confusion in the front hall. I went to the kitchen.

The child was kneeling in the corner on a grater, smearing the lipstick that she rubbed off her face onto the wall. Vlasta ordered me to wash and dress her. Me! Then she slammed the door and went to settle accounts with her husband.

I addressed little Helenka in a voice which should have told her I was on her side.

"Vlasta told me I should wash you."

"Don't want to," she replied because it told her nothing. She ran her reddened finger up her nose and turned back to the wall.

"That's too bad. Mother Vlasta-pasta ordered us to."

I didn't dare to remind her that nice little girls don't pick their noses. That's all she ever heard about, anyway. I hoped that she'd respond better to a lighter note. The finger stopped inside the nose and the child smiled. Right away, I took off one slipper. The smile vanished and the small girl moved to the opposite corner of the kitchen. The finger went deeper in the nose and stubbornly drilled inside there. For tactical reasons, I stuck with the first person plural: "Vlasta-pasta's gonna slap us."

That was when she pulled her finger out of her nose and gave a gleeful squeal.

"More!"

"When you get dressed!"

She came over to me and allowed me to undress her.

"Say some more. Like, who's gonna slap us?"

"Vlasta-pasta."

She gurgled and insisted that I continue. "More, say some more!"

"Vlasta-pasta gobbles faster," I whispered, as if it were the biggest secret in the world, and then I pulled her over to the wash basin. She was washed in a flash and she even let me comb her hair. The charming poetry acted like a soothing balm on the welts she had so unjustly received.

"Vlasta-pasta gobbles faster," she whispered back to me, "right?" She put her arms around my neck and I could tell she loved me.

"That's right," I said, and I didn't hesitate to proceed with one of the many verses that could follow, which I used so often to compensate for my debased position in the family: "Goose-grease and sugar to make her grow bigger." Then, just to be certain, I sang the whole thing to her one more time, to the tune of an old evergreen nursery rhyme about the kitty amd the barley. Helenka's enthusiasm grew, and she screamed the song at the top of her lungs. Then she wanted some more. I saw no reason to continue, since I'd achieved the desired effect. Helenka was washed and dressed, and as a bonus, even had her hair combed. That was all the instructions I'd received.

"There isn't any more."

She looked at me suspiciously. "Is too," she said after a moment's thought.
"Personally, I don't know any more."
"Personally, I do, and even better!"
"Well?"
"Not supposed to say it."
"You're just saying that because you don't know any more, because there isn't any more."
"Is too, so there."
"So sing it to me."
"Can't."
"See? There isn't any more."
"Is too. But it's something you can't say."
"So whisper it to me."
She whispered in my ear an original rhyme that even followed logically from the first part.
"When she's done with all of it, then she has to have a – " she fell silent and waited for me to say the last word for her. I pretended not to understand.
"A what?"
"I can't say it. Don't you know what you can't say?"
"Well," I pretended, "stupid, dummy, – "
"No. That's not it. Listen: when she's done with all of it, then she has to have a – sh – sh – come on, you know what you're not supposed to say?"
"Oh, that," I made as if I got it already. "Well, let me tell you, you really thought up a good one. I'd never have thought of it."
"Really," she declared self-confidently.
"But that's not the way it is, anyway."
"Is too."
"Is not."
"Is too, so there."
"Then tell me where you learned it."
"No place. That's just the way I sing it."
"You mean you knew it already?"
"No. But that's the way I sing it."
"Okay, but who taught it to you?"
"You did."
"Now, I never taught you that."
"Did too. That's the way you sang it."
"Liar! Just wait till your mom hears you. She'll make hamburger out of us."
The child laughed with glee, but the devil we were speaking of stuck her

head in the door in a rumpled veil and snapped, "We're going! See to it you catch up with us! And see it doesn't take you all day!"

The door slammed, and swift, slightly weighty footsteps sounded from the hall. The house fell silent as death.

I stuck a fur cap on my niece's head, put on my own coat, and we left the house hand in hand.

Polly was barking again in the shed, somebody had shut her up in there so she wouldn't scare the company. I was sorry I couldn't take her along. But then, why not? After all, she was grandpa's dog, wasn't she? Sure she was. I untied her. She came bursting out of the shed, obviously looking forward to some more fun. Helenka suggested that we go sliding down the Bump.

"We've got to go to the funeral."

"Why?"

"To pay our respects to grandpa."

"Why?"

"Before they bury him."

"Who?"

"The priest."

"Will he sing for him?"

"Yes."

"So will I."

"What? Vlasta-pasta?"

"Sure."

"He'd like that."

"No, I'll sing him about the blooming roses, that's prettier."

"You think so?"

"Yes. He'll like that."

I wondered how to expand her knowledge by the one item, according to most the saddest one of all, the knowledge of death. But how? I had trouble understanding it myself.

"He won't like it."

"Why not?"

"He won't like anything or dislike anything ever again, because he's dead."

"Then we'll sing him Vlasta-pasta."

"I told you he's dead, which means he can't see anything or hear anything, he can't move and never will, even if the sky were to fall in."

"Why won't he move?"

"Because he died, because I'm going to die too, and so will you, and everybody, even the ones who aren't even born yet, everybody is going to die and be dead."

"And when are you going to die, Honza?"

"I don't know. Maybe tomorrow, maybe in fifty years, it's hard to tell."

"Why?"

"Because."

"I'm not going to die."

"All right, and let's forget it."

"I'm not going to die and neither are you, if you're a good boy."

"Grandpa was good, and he died."

"He wasn't good."

"Was too."

"Wasn't. He called me a brat."

"Big deal!"

"And he said he'd put a five-heller piece on my bum."

"There, see?"

"See? That's why he died, because he was naughty. But I won't die, so there."

I left her at that. She's not going to be an intellectual anyway. And anything little is cute. But I don't want to know her when she's twenty. When she turns into the same dimwit, according to the laws of heredity and environment and how they influence the development of character.

We walked through the garden out onto the field. The procession was way ahead of us already. They were climbing the white hillside and treading a narrow path in the snow. It looked like a zigzag scar on a girl's complexion. Suddenly I felt awfully sad at the thought that grandpa was dead.

I started running up the hill.

Helenka stumbled behind me, squealing that it's slippery. Polly leaped in and out between us. She was apparently convinced that the real fun was about to begin now. We caught up with the procession on the hilltop by the cemetery.

A little cluster of friends from the village were standing there, and a few people had come all the way from Prague. They took mom by the hand and shook it and in a rather stereotyped way expressed emotions that they didn't feel. I looked around to see if Hanka wasn't around someplace. She was standing to one side with her grandfather, with a black kerchief with tassles on her head, covering all the curls from those baby-blue curlers. She was holding a bouquet in her hand and she looked beautiful.

"Hi, Hanka," I said. She dropped her eyes and I noticed that she has eyelashes that reach all the way to her cheeks. She was silent. "I'm going to have a look inside," I said. I tied Polly up by the gate and turned Helenka over to mom.

There wasn't a soul inside the cemetery except our Vlasta. She was strolling alone among the graves, feeling like Sarah Bernhardt. The wind was fluffing up her veil so that she looked like something out of a Soviet movie, but the fact is that hidden by all that veiling she was a whole lot prettier.

I went back out the gate to where mother was, took her arm and slowly walked with her to the cemetery chapel. Along the way we were stopped by a cemetery employee in a muddy uniform, he pulled off his cap and wrung it in his hands that the graveyard dirt had eaten into like a tattoo.

"Missus, d'you want to show him?"

"I don't know," mother said helplessly. "Maybe not, or – "

"They always does," the fellow waved his cap. "So you will, eh?"

The death knell sounded from the steeple.

We entered the chapel. Right in the middle was the coffin with the lid raised, like an open box in the display window of a jewelry store, and inside lay grandpa. I had never seen a dead person before. His lips receded between his gums and maybe that's why his nose seemed to stick out so far. I couldn't understand why they had removed his dentures. After all, he'd paid for them. His arms were crossed on his chest, unwillingly, it seemed, and between the yellowed fingers of his right hand, he was holding a holy picture like a cigar. Everyone who came in first went over to the coffin, reaching over and touching grandpa, making the sign of the cross on him. I made one too, but just above his forehead so as not to touch him. I felt queer. Helenka grabbed hold of the coffin with both hands and tried to raise herself up to get her chin over the edge.

"I can't see, I need a boost!"

Vláďa picked her up and lifted her for a moment.

"Gee, he's not moving. Daddy, he's not moving!" her howl sliced through the entire chapel, and then, fortissimo, she bellowed, "Why isn't he moving? . . . Daddy, he's not asleep . . . he's deaded . . ."

Tears rose to everyone's eyes. Vláďa jerked her into a side pew. The child fell silent. She was intrigued by the kneeling cushion. She tried standing up on it. Her foot slipped, she hit her knee and started to scream all over again. Vlasta tossed her a dignified swat across the back of the head, picked her up and rammed her down on the seat, the thump echoing through the chapel.

All the seats were taken and a lot of people were standing. I stood too, in the aisle. Somebody yanked at my coat.

"Here, young man, have a seat, you'll have a good view from here."

I squeezed in beside old lady Konečný. The view was in fact very good. The performance could begin.

The organist was preparing to get the pedals moving. At first he succeeded in getting the snuffly organ to give off a long wheeze in the bass, and only after that came several dissonant chords. First a few major ones, and right afterwards, some minor preluding, to soften the listeners up. Two female figures emerged from behind the organ, put down their shopping bags at their feet and started up a dreadful duet of "Shine, Oh Thou Golden Sun." From outside, Polly joined in. She gave such a mournful howl that everyone jumped.

"Poor little thing, she's crying for her master," the old woman beside me whispered.

Vlasta-pasta was gently patting her eyes with a miniature hankie, acting as if she were shaking with sobs. Of course, like any amateur, she overacted. Her shoulders twitched as if she were having an epileptic fit. She was in fact moved, but more over her own self, because this was just about the only kind of moment when she could bring herself to an awareness of her own mortality. But mainly on account of how they would talk it up all over the village, how she had wept until she could hardly walk.

". . . dry the floow of tears awaay . . ." sang the two bleaters, each in a different key, presenting the ideal backdrop for her dramatic performance. God knows who invited them here. They apparently had a contract with the Funeral Service, Municipal Enterprise of the City of Prague, or maybe with the Prague Cultural Center. They were probably retired choir singers, released from the group for their appearance, and for asthma. Each of them inhaled at different places, mostly in the middle of words, their voices quavered with a heavy vibrato, it was hard to tell a tierce from a sixth. I kept expecting grandpa to sit up in his coffin and yell for them to quit their caterwauling. But in spite of the fact that he was very musical, grandpa didn't budge. When they finished singing, the priest appeared, and his clear baritone sounding through the chapel came as a relief. Except the two women responded, so the relief didn't last, and to save us undue suffering, the priest rushed through the mass. Relieved again, I breathed a sigh, even though today I'd be willing to recite the Lord's Prayer for grandpa from morning till night. We still had to suffer through the finale, "God Be With You, I Depart," which was supposed to inspire purification through tears, but with the glissando and the articulation of the singers, we could be purified at best by means of a cramp in our bellies. Their exaggerated pronunciation of silent letters made the entire thing sound like a parody. But it was no parody. The organ wheezed on a long time after the organist had risen and left.

The cemetery employee pulled out the sticks that held the lid up and, with a bang, closed grandpa up for good. He blew out the candle, removed the wreath and ribbons, snapped his fingers and his two buddies leaped up from behind the door.

We started out in a procession through the cemetery. They took us all the way around, although our family plot was waiting for us, open, right opposite the chapel door. That's where my daddy is, the one I've never even seen. The brass band launched a heartfelt rendition of a funeral march, the tempo very slow so it would last us all the way around the cemetery. The procession dragged its slow steps like a slow-motion film. I got my left and my right feet straight and joined the others. Old man Ráž was blowing on a horn, puffing up his cheeks, and tears flowed down the wrinkles in his face like mountain streams.

A broad circle formed around the grave, the priest stood in the middle to sprinkle the coffin with holy water and to say goodbye to the dear departed. He sang beautiful words about human iniquity, and for a while even reconciled me with the fact that Vlasta is a dimwit, and I was suddenly rather fond of her. When he finished, old grandpa Ráž got up and said goodbye to grandpa for all his friends and mainly for himself, because he was the last one who had been to war with him at Zboro in 1917. He couldn't handle it and burst into entirely unofficial tears, how come he's still here in this world, he could've gone instead of old Loyza here, "because compared to him, I'm an old Methusalem." Hanka stood behind him and there was a tear sitting on the end of her nose like a little pearl. Suddenly I felt as if my heart were growing, I looked at her and I felt like weeping too. Grandpa Ráž got hold of himself, to the coffin he said, "For you, old buddy," and blew taps on his horn. The low, sad tones, carried down to the village and bounced off the Bump on the other side. Beyond the gate Polly gave a mournful wail.

The cemetery employees yanked the straps and began to let the coffin down into the grave. Grandpa Ráž kept playing until it disappeared. By now, Vlasta's crying was entirely unaffected, and Mom was standing with her face in her hands. The last note of taps faded away, as long a note as old man Ráž had breath. There was a second of beautiful, conciliatory silence. Everyone stood with head bowed, as if they had turned to stone.

Except the singers hadn't finished their stint yet. They broke the sad silence, only here, out in the open, they were completely impossible. Their shopping bags were at their feet, one had rice spilling out of it. The priest held up two fingers to indicate that they were to stop after the second verse, he waved his hand with increasing impatience. They misunderstood, thinking that he was waving his hand to get them to speed up the tempo. They gave an honest rendition of all six verses, picked up their shopping bags and hurried toward the gate. Everything seemed to be too long already. My ears were freezing, and my fingernails hurt from the cold. I wasn't the only one. Everyone was shuffling and stamping, clouds rising from their lips. Vlasta leaned on me as if she were about to faint, and weakly thanked people for their condolences. I was afraid she might make like she really fainted. Fortunately, she didn't fall all the way, she just wavered. People shook our hands and were careful about the expression on their faces. Hanka and her grandfather came too. She shook my hand, hers was warm, she smiled but it was such a beautifully sad smile, she was lovely. I would have liked to take her hand and run down the hill with her, someplace where there isn't anyone except maybe Polly. I watched her as she walked with her grandfather along the paths among the graves, and everything fogged up in front of my eyes.

My aunt from Týniště stood beside me, and she was crying very hard. But you could tell she was still thinking about her teeth all the time. Vlasta stayed in character to the very end. Her veil was up and the paint on her eyes was still in perfect condition. Last to come were the cemetery employees, they reached out a palm and they each got beer money from mom. They backed away, bowing so fervently that they almost fell in after grandpa.

We were the last to leave the cemetery. I untied Polly from the gate. She jumped up on me and gave me a silly lick on my face. Snow was tumbling out of the sky, little black clumps of people were plowing down the hillside, disappearing in the thickening snowfall. Cousin Lenka took a transistor radio out of her purse and pressed it to her ear.

"What are you listening to, Lenka?" asked mother.

"A mystery serial. I was afraid I might miss today's episode. Ever a lot of corpses, auntie!"

I got a shiver up my back. Mom, on the other hand, had a completely angelic expression. Our tragedienne rushed over to Lenka. "Oh, do turn it up, I can't wait to find out if somebody's going to do in the one with the high voice."

"He's been dead since last time already."

Lenka turned it up, Vlasta took her arm and they marched down the hillside together.

J. L. Kubicek

FROM THE RETRIEVED NOTEBOOK

Miroslav Holub

You lasso your words deftly
    as the American cowboy
pulling them to an abrupt halt
    flopping them, side exposed
stamp your brand
    on the corralled; they rise
stand quivering
    free with a brand?

Tom Domek

WILL COGAN'S MAP

As the Northern Plains began to mend from the searing heat of the Great Depression, my great-uncle Will Cogan began his well-drilling operation for farming and ranching families in the bluffs of central North Dakota.

Mine are the drills
that have probed
this earth for water

through seams of lignite
beneath this ground. Within
these breaks of hills

off the Big Muddy Mo, stones
and pottery unfurl through
the clay I've brought up

to the first lick of sky.
I've found by chance
the graves of river tribes

that rise on the wedge
of my auger. I've drawn a
map, accurate to the bluffs

my boots have crossed.
Archaeologists have come
around, pleading

for the lay
of my mind.
Nothing they say

can persuade me.
I'll take this map
to my grave, its lines,

its markers turning
to ash, settling
like dust in my skull.

GEO. KUPPER'S FATHER

As Mandan, North Dakota, grew in size prior to the First World War, my grandfather George Kupper, then a boy, watched as sewer lines were dug near the banks of the Heart River, exposing the graves of the Mandan Indians who had thrived in the area not more than a hundred years earlier.

My father drives spikes
into elms and ash,
making caskets for Slavs
and Germans in our town.

He works by the wick
of kerosene lamps,
the shadow of his hammer
on the wall reminding

us that death is
an end. Once, by the banks
of the winding Heart,
I watched as fathers

sank sewer lines
for the immigrants
they hoped would take
homes under bluffs.

I watched the horse-drawn
carts dump earth into mounds
near the moats. Skulls
stirred with the loam,

rose like newly formed
moons. The town fathers
knew. I ran for home,
my feet kicking joy

for the work I thought my
father would have.
Here were bones
ready for tombs

in our Catholic
cemetery. The priest
would sprinkle
his words, holding

his book to the sky.
But oh how my father
scoffed! When I

returned to the Heart,
the bones still rose
to the air. Finally,
shovels and blades

scraped them back
into moats where pipes
had been so carefully
laid. Within these

sewer lines, they left
a tribe of skulls to watch
the wooden homes cover
their graves, the town

grown white and more white
with its churches and bars.

AN EXTRACT FROM THE EDWIN MEESE COMMISSION ON PORNOGRAPHY IN AMERICA: PAGE 1246. NIGHTCRAWLERS.

They're out there now, slick
as fornication, balled up together,
mixing their genes. They've
shoved up from their dark, dirty

holes, pink as centerfolds, naked
clear through to their black, lusting
hearts. They'd like to rub skin
with your young daughter's flesh,

put slime and disgrace on her
unblotted soul. Never trust
them. Lock your flashlights
in safes, tie your children

to beds. They have links
to the worldwide underground.
Most become perverts
and pornography stars.

When the moon comes out,
their orgies turn wild. Be wise.
Keep your shades pulled down,
and shut your eyes.

Joyce deVries Kehoe

THE TEXAS BABY

I IMAGINE I WAS as amazed as my mama was to find out that Mrs. Lipps, the most beautiful woman I had ever seen, was barren.

She and her husband, who was a dean at the college, lived next door to us. She was a good deal younger than Dean Lipps; he had met her six or seven years before when he was chaperoning the Miss Cotton Pageant. Mrs. Lipps was Miss Tishomingo County, Mississippi, and she came in second. But I thought she was far more beautiful than the winner, with her shiny black hair and eyebrows as thin as they could be without being trashy. As thin as leeches.

When I found out she was barren, I was ten, and of course I wasn't supposed to be hearing the conversation.

She was sitting at our new maple kitchen table, and my mama was patting the shoulder of her sheer white blouse, through which I could see the most exquisite, dainty slip. Mrs. Lipps was dabbing frantically at her dark eyes with a rose-embroidered handkerchief. "It just can't be, Virgie," she said.

My mama pulled out one of the new maple chairs and sat down beside her. She said, "Are you sure, Betty Jo?"

Mrs. Lipps shook her head up and down. "It's my ovaries," she said, and I moved a teeny bit closer to the doorway, my habitual lurking-to-listen spot from which I often overheard very interesting conversations between my mama and Mrs. Lipps. I knew already, for example, that Mrs. Lipps and Dean Lipps had been trying to get a baby for a long time and that Dean Lipps was too tired some nights to give Mrs. Lipps a baby, and my mama would tell Mrs. Lipps some ways to make him not be so tired (most of the ways of which didn't seem to me like they would make someone not be tired – maybe be tireder.) I didn't know if my mama was always right about things like that. My daddy was a scientist so he had to be right – he got his degree from Emory University and studied bugs. But my mama only went to college for just one year and studied home economics. That means about taking care of houses and children and she did okay with my little sister Terry and me, but about *getting* babies, I wasn't sure if she knew.

Obviously, she hadn't been able to help Mrs. Lipps.

"Yes, Dr. Campeau is positive," Mrs. Lipps was saying. "He says there's something in my fallopians and no eggs can get through."

Now, I had *no* idea what fallopians were, and I didn't know why eggs would have anything to do with babies, but I *did* know that Dr. Campeau was the doctor in the hospital when me and Terry were born, so he probably knew.

"Oh Virgie!" Mrs. Lipps was moaning again, and I peeked into the kitchen in time to see exquisite fat tears making little furrows in her powder.

From behind me I heard, "You're peeping," and hot pricklies went up my neck. It was my little sister Terry.

"I'm tellin'," she said, and started into the kitchen, but I grabbed her by one skinny arm.

"Owwww!" she howled, and I wrestled her into the bathroom.

"Mrs. Lipps is sick," I said. "You leave them alone."

"You were peeping," Terry repeated, staring at me through her thick glasses. Terry had came out of our mother's stomach too soon and they put her in a box with oxygen and it made her need glasses, but it wasn't fair that she got blue ones with jewels when I didn't even get to wear glasses at all.

"Oh Terry," I said, thinking of the days after she was born but before they brought her home and my mama cried a lot. "Mrs. Lipps can't have babies!" I hugged her, and she fought me off with her scratchy legs.

* * *

The next day I was spying from my room when Dean Lipps and Mrs. Lipps stood in the back of their house. A bamboo hedge separated their yard from ours, but it had a few thin spots and I loved to peep out through my yellow flowered curtains to watch Mrs. Lipps as she worked in the yard, pruning azaleas and potting violets. Never, never in public could a dean's wife be seen without hose, I knew, but in the back yard she wore shorts sometimes, and her hair in big pink curlers. I would stare at her until she went back inside, and then I would run to the gold-flecked mirror over my new white vanity to look at my own face – it was never a pleasant comparison. My hair wasn't blonde and it wasn't dark – no color, really. And my lips were always chapped. Winter, summer, any time – ugly yellowy flecks hung off my mouth. My mother would follow me around with the black metal Chapstick tube – "Libby, you've got to stop licking that mouth. Stop *right now!*" I never noticed myself licking, even if that's what my mama said. And I knew they'd never get better until I could wear lipstick like Mrs. Lipps that looked like thick, shiny blood, which she put on with a tiny little brush made of the same stuff as fur coats.

This time, Dean Lipps was standing with her. He wasn't quite as tall as she was; he stood there in his suit, with his arm sort of around her. She was just staring into the bamboo, and all of a sudden she pushed his arm away and ran to the back of the yard, throwing herself into the back hedge. She seemed to be growing from the bougainvillaea, and the dean dropped his briefcase as he ran to pull her out. She shook her head. Her sleek black hair – she always wore it like Jackie Kennedy – wasn't even combed, and her mouth was pale. The dean patted her and patted her.

* * *

"I don't know, Virgina," my daddy was saying.

"It's their only hope, Raymond," my mama said. They were sitting at the new table, which wasn't quite as new-looking now, since Terry had scraped one edge of it with the pink bike she got for her seventh birthday.

"Why don't they go through a reputable agency, then?" my daddy said.

I was washing the dishes; it was night and I could see the reflection of their faces in the window, which Ida, our maid, had just washed that morning.

"Well, this place *is* legal, Raymond," my mama said. She was lacing her fingers together, looking at him across the table, which was covered with bugs in their little white paper trays. It was part of my daddy's job to grade bug collections.

"There's agencies in Louisiana," my daddy said, peering carefully under the wing of a beetle, which he held by a tiny plastic-headed push pin stuck through its abdomen.

"They don't like to give babies to people Dean Lipps' age," my mama said.

"Awww," my daddy scoffed. "Lipps knows all kinds of people. If he can't find a suitable baby, I don't know who can,"

"This place in Texas gets them right away. Nobody has to wait,"

My daddy looked up at my mama. He rubbed the bald spot on the back of his head. "They waited six years. Why can't they wait a little longer?"

"She's just going crazy, Raymond," my mama said. She backed up a little as he held a tiny glass vial up to the light. If the bugs were too tiny to be impaled on the colored pins, the students could float them inside those bottles. Terry loved to get ahold of the bottles and fill them with an individual item each: a pine needle, tiny colored rocks, a wadded up pull string from a roll of cherry lifesavers. Sometimes they ended up in her toy box, and sometimes they'd break and she'd cut her fingers.

* * *

"Did you fill the thermos, Betty Jo?" my mama said.

Mrs. Lipps held it up gaily. Looking both ways, she scampered out to the car. It must have been 103 degrees, and we were on our way to Texas.

A week ago my daddy had looked up from a tray of spiders and had said plaintively, "What about Libby and Terry?"

"Ida can watch them during the day, Raymond," my mama had said. She was doing her hair in pin curls with her hairpins that always seemed to still have their rubber tips.

"That's finals week," my daddy said sternly.

"Maybe she can stay the night, then," she said, winding her a strand of yellow hair into a careful whorl and capturing it with the dark pin.

"I thought you said you didn't want a Negro staying overnight in your house," he said.

"Well, this is an exception, and by now we can trust Ida." She looked up. "Libby, you go put on your pajamas."

I walked slowly, reluctantly into the hall, while he said, "Ida has her own family, she can't be staying here all night."

"I haven't been to Texas in years," my mama sniffed.

"Not during finals week," he said.

"Then I'll take them along," she said, loud enough that I could hear her from the bathroom.

Now they were loading the brand new blue Ford station wagon with blankets and food and suitcases, including one little one, and a blue quilted bed, and a box that said "Six infant feeding bottles," with a picture of a smiling baby on it. Mrs. Lipps smiled back at Terry and me, who had already made a little nest in the back-facing rear seat. "Y'all be sure not to put your feet on that suitcase. It's got Jimmy's little clothes in it," she said.

"Who's Jimmy?" Terry whispered to me, unsticking one thigh from the plastic seat. Sweat fogged up her glasses.

"I don't know," I whispered back. "But I heard Mrs. Lipps say he was just born yesterday."

"I couldn't even sleep," Mrs. Lipps said as my mama hopped behind the wheel. "I kept thinking about him! I know he must be crying without me."

* * *

I had never been to Texas at all. I couldn't wait – I wanted to see tall cowboys roping dogies, and to sneak into a saloon for a sarsaparilla. This would be the most exciting trip of my life, I was sure.

We were almost out of the Freeland city limits when Terry and I had our first fight. Terry had this problem with cars: when she got in one, she would fall asleep really fast – first, the bottom part of her mouth would drop open, then her head started to go forward, then it jerked up a few times and she would close her mouth; finally she'd just keel over, and if she was leaning the wrong way, she'd take up more than her share of the seat.

I carefully inserted the sharpest part of my elbow into her sweaty thigh. She woke up tattling. "Mama! Libby's hurting me!"

"She's laying on my side of the seat," I said, but my heart wasn't in it: I was going to Texas.

We drove past the paper mill on the edge of town; I could smell the worst smell in the world. All this was still familiar territory – the Chicken House restaurant, the fairgrounds, Moe Bentley State Park. Then the houses got farther and farther apart. We were going to Texas!

"Can't you drive any faster?" Mrs. Lipps said to mama. At first I thought she was talking mean, but then I saw her red mouth smiling, and my mama looked back at her through her sunglasses with jewels, smiling too. Then they looked back forward.

Now we were going through the poor part of West Freeland. I craned my neck over Terry to catch a glimpse of Cheese's, an old gray shack with a shiny tin roof that people called a "juke joint"; once when my daddy was driving my friend Nedra Walls and me to go horseback riding, we drove by Cheese's and Nedra said, "My daddy says that the niggers stab each other with big knifes there." My daddy said, "We don't use that word, Nedra."

"Oh, look at that cute little guy," Mrs. Lipps said. A big tall woman was sweeping the porch of Cheese's; a fat little baby sat there looking at the cars go by. My mama and Mrs. Lipps smiled at each other again.

The things I was seeing didn't get to be too different right away. As a matter of fact, even after my mama and Mrs. Lipps took turns driving all day, it didn't change much at all. We made one stop at a Big Barrel root beer stand for lunch, and three stops at filling stations – one for gas and two for Terry to go to the bathroom (the first one was too dirty so we went on to the next town), and then for supper we stopped at a town called Brownell. That was right after we passed a sign with a cowboy on a bucking horse that said "Welcome to Texas." There were pictures of cowboys in the restaurant, too, but I didn't think the town looked much different than Freeland, or maybe West Freeland. We had chicken fried steak and heavy yellowish mashed potatoes and mushy green beans that I didn't think was the kind of beans cowboys ate, but Terry and I both ate some anyway, so Mrs. Lipps bought us each a big clear plastic cane filled with colored sprinkles. I have to say, it never got any more Texasy the whole rest of the day.

"Y'all lay down, now," Mama said, opening the tailgate of the station wagon; a shower of red dust fell down on her and she brushed it off and said, "Texas dirt!" She folded the turquoise and white seat down, rearranged the suitcases, pushed the baby bed forward, and over the still-scratchy new carpet she spread an old quilt. Terry and I climbed under it, giggling, prying open the red cone-shaped lids from the sprinkles, licking our fingers and sticking them inside the cones. "I'm getting tired of this old baby bed," Terry sniffed, pushing it as far up against the front seat as she could. Then we settled in like baby animals. Mrs. Lipps started the station wagon, and we went further into Texas.

I woke up later; the car was stopped and a filling station light was shining into my eyes. I sat up a little bit. "Filler up, May-am?" the attendant was saying.

Mama nodded and craned her neck back. "Do you need to go tee-tee, Libby?" she said. I shook my head no and snuggled back into the quilt; soon, the station wagon started up again and I sunk happily back into the hard black rug. I couldn't have stayed awake for anything, seduced back into sleep by the hum of the Texas highway only a couple of feet beneath me.

"Terry, Libby, y'all wake up," Mama was saying. The car was stopped. Terry was feeling around for her glasses; she had yellow gunk in her eyes, just like at home. "Are we in Texas yet?" she said.

"Stupid," I said. "We were there before dinner yesterday."

"Where's Roy Rogers?" she said.

I looked out the window. We were stopped in front of a big white house. I didn't know where Roy Rogers was; I didn't see any oil wells, either. Just this big white house with a big porch and a big weeping willow. "We're here, girls," my mama said. Her voice sounded funny. She got out of the car and so did Mrs. Lipps. "Wait here, girls," Mama said. We scrunched down to watch her and Mrs. Lipps walk slowly up the steps, across the wide porch, and up to the dark-painted front door. They knocked.

"Where are we?" Terry said.

"I don't know," I said. "Just some place in Texas." I craned my neck. In the back of the white house I could see another building, long and flat with a row of small windows, in front of which stood two girls, hands on their hips like Marilyn Monroe. They were both blonde and pretty and would have looked like Marilyn Monore too, except that they had big fat stomachs. Then a girl with a black pony tail came out, and her stomach was the biggest of all.

Mama came out of the house and walked back to the car, glancing briefly at the big-stomached girls, then at us. She was wearing a sleeveless pink and white dress that was pretty wrinkled; one of her arms was sunburned.

She took the suitcase out of the second seat, moving the baby bed to one side. "Come on, girls," she said. "Let's go in. Y'all need to be real good at Mrs. Gangle's, now."

"I can't walk," Terry complained all the way up the sidewalk. "My legs forgot how to."

"Hush," Mama said.

An old glider swing with a green and orange awning took up half the porch. Terry looked interested, but Mama hurried us past it and into the warm musty air of the house.

It was one of those houses with way too much furniture – sideboards and little tables and china figurines and paperweights and pictures of Jesus and mountain scenes in fancy frames. Mama stood with us and finally a skinny little old lady with her hair in curls like Vienna sausages came into the room, closing the French doors behind her. "Girls, this is Mrs. Gangle," said my mama.

Mrs. Gangle looked as us through her glasses with tiny blue eyes. "You need to be very quiet," she said. "Miz Lipps' baby is sleeping."

Terry and I looked at each other. "Mrs. Lipps doesn't have a baby," Terry whispered, and looked at Mrs. Gangle like she was kind of scary, like Mrs. Groney in church who sang too loud, even sometimes when the song was already over. Terry never could whisper very quiet, though, and Mama gave her a look and Mrs. Gangle put her long spidery hands on her hips and said, "Well, she does now, little girl."

Then I heard it: from behind the French doors, a little noise, like an animal saying "What?" and then another little "What?" then a choking little noise and then, yes: it was a baby crying.

I pushed up against my mama's silky skirt.

She looked down at me, and her eyes were red.

"Mama, I thought Mrs. Lipps couldn't have babies," I said.

"Hush," she said, but she didn't look mad. I moved towards the French doors, but Mrs. Gangle barred them, pursing her wrinkly lips at Terry and me, and said, "The children will have to stay out of the nursery. They can stay upstairs, in the green room."

"Come on, girls," Mama said, taking each of us by the hand and leading us up the curved stairway. On the landing was a huge, beautiful painting. This one was of Jesus, too; he was holding a little lamb.

The room we stayed in that night was about as green as it could be. There was a green bedspread and a green lamp shade and light green curtains with ugly dark-green flowers; the walls were green and an old threadbare olive green rug, cut open for the heat register at one end, was laid lopsided on top of the green linoleum. Mama gave us a bath in the big bathroom that had a bathtub with scary lion paw legs like the tub did in our house when we first moved in. Like I always did in a strange bathtub, I started to miss my house and our own melon-colored tub with the gold-flecked shower doors.

"How long are we staying here?" I asked my mama, who was reaching in the tub to remove Terry's hand from under her bottom.

"A couple of days," Mama said, pushing her hair away from her face. "Until the papers go through."

"What papers?" I said.

Mama looked at Terry, who was now playing with the old corroded chain of the plug. "For the adoption," she said.

"What's that?" I said; I thought I knew, but I wasn't quite sure.

"Mrs. Lipps will be bringing a little baby boy home, honey," Mama said. She looked sort of happy, and sort of sad at the same time, and she leaned into the bathtub to scrub our faces.

We didn't see Mrs. Lipps that whole day. Mama took us around town; we went to some cowboy stores after all, and I got a shiny red plastic cowgirl hat. Terry's was green. We went to a farm right in town where you could pet some baby animals; the pig was stinky and there was just one old horse with pieces missing out of his coat, but I planned carefully the braggartly speech I would make in show and tell. Texas, however, still didn't seem too different from Louisiana. Laying on the fold-up cot in the green room that night, I listened to the same cicadas outside that we had at home; later on I woke up and heard baby cries, and singing from downstairs.

The next morning we sat at a big table in the crowded kitchen. One of the big-stomached girls made bacon and scrambled eggs that weren't either one of them cooked enough. As Terry and I ate, the door opened, and Mrs. Lipps stepped shyly into the room, holding the little blue blanket she had brought. Something was in it, and I knew what it was. She didn't say anything; she just was smiling and she sat down by my mother. Then she looked across the table to me. "Want to see him, Libby?" she said. She was tired-looking, and didn't have any powder or lipstick on, but she had a real pretty smile on her face. I had never noticed before that she had three cinnamon-colored freckles on her nose.

I gave Terry a superior look because Mrs. Lipps asked me and not Terry to look at the baby, but Terry didn't seem to notice; she was on her third English muffin. I stood up and walked past Mrs. Gangle, who said, "Careful now," to Mrs. Lipps, and I leaned over, and here, in the blue wool, was a tiny little red-haired face, all screwed up and not looking like the baby on the box of bottles in the car, but for sure a baby. "He's pretty," I said, not because he was, but because I knew it was what I ought to say, and Mrs. Lipps said, "He's beautiful." She rocked back and forth.

"Some breakfast, Mrs. Lipps?" asked Mrs. Gangle. Mrs. Lipps looked at the wet scrambled eggs and still-translucent bacon and shook her head. "Maybe later." She looked back at me. "Thank you, Libby. He *is* beautiful." She looked back at the baby. "He's going to grow up to be the most handsome man in the world, aren't you?" she said to the baby, who didn't answer.

So, we had to stay in Texas until those papers were ready. Mrs. Lipps and the baby spent most of the time shut up in the room behind the French doors. Mama would go in there with her a lot. The baby seemed like he was crying more every day; from the cluttered living room where we had to sit motionless on the yellow brocade couch, I heard my mama telling Mrs. Lipps, "That's just how Libby was. While I was in the hospital for the week, she was an absolute dream. But after that, she cried half the day. Then she got to be an angel again." Terry smirked at me. I pulled up my upper lip at her and said, "At least I didn't have to be in a *box* when I was born." Terry swatted at me, and I had to grab her by the hair to pull her down on the clam-colored carpet.

"This is not allowed."

It was Mrs. Gangle. I looked directly up her long green skirt; her thick brown hose were held up by a white girdle.

We stopped immediately.

Mrs. Gangle didn't lean over. She crossed her bony arms. "Children are *not* usually allowed in my establishment," she said. "When I *do* make an exception – which I had no choice about since Mrs. Lipps neglected to tell me you two were coming – I only allow well-behaved children."

I stood back up, untwisting my red cotton shorts.

"You young ladies go outside now," Mrs. Gangle said. I noticed she almost had a moustache.

"Okay, we will," I said.

"Is there anything to do?" Terry whined.

"Shhhh," I said.

"Y'all play on the sidewalk," Mrs. Gangle said. "Your mother is helping Mrs. Lipps with the new blessed arrival. When she is done, I will send her out to fetch you."

Terry and I edged towards the heavy door with the yellowed lace curtain over the window. I turned the brass knob with difficulty, pulling open the door to admit a wave of hot air.

From behind us Mrs. Gangle said, "And don't go back there by the sleeping quarters." She shook her finger back and forth, back and forth, and I dragged Terry out the door.

Texas was if anything hotter than Louisiana. I had never thought about it being hot when I was watching cowboy pictures; the cowboys never complained, never seemed to mop at their faces with their bandannas. "I wanta see a cowboy," I told Terry.

She sunk onto the painted gray board of the front porch. "I wanta go home," she said. Her thick glasses were fogging up and her bangs stuck to her forehead.

"Me too," I admitted. "You'd think a place where you get babies would have some toys."

"I want my Barbie bunk beds," she sniffed. "And I wanta go in and see Mama."

"Maybe she'll be out pretty soon," I said. "When she's done helping Mrs. Lipps with the baby." I looked across the yellow grass of the yard to the big weeping willow. "Let's go under there," I said.

It was cooler in the dome-shaped space beneath the sagging branches, and it made a pretty good fort. We squatted down to watch some fire ants work on a nest; I stirred them up with a stick and we stood back, watching them run around in panic before settling back in to patiently repair their quarters. After awhile we could see some of the big-stomach girls come out of the long building out back. They looked up at the porch, smiled at each other, and tiptoed past the front of the house, ducking around in front of our tree; we lay still so they wouldn't hear us. "Shoot," said one girl, one of the blonde ones I saw before. "If Old Lady Gangle catches us past the front steps, we're gonna catch it."

The other one, the black-haired one, laughed – it was a laugh like she didn't think anything was funny. I heard a scratching sound and smelled smoke; the black-haired girl put a cigarette into her red mouth, sucking hungrily on it. She said, "Finally!" and then, "Who cares if she catches us. What's she gonna do?"

"Send us back home, that's what," said the blonde-haired girl.

"I don't care," said the black-haired one.

They sat on the curb. There weren't any sidewalks like we had in Louisiana; cars drove by and dust flew up. I peeked through the willow leaves. The black-haired girl was kind of pretty, and the blonde-haired one was one of the ones that looked like Marilyn Monroe. "You hear from Bobby?" the black-haired one said.

The blonde girl shook her head.

"He still in the Army?"

The blonde girl nodded. She was looking down the street. From inside the house, the baby started to cry.

"That June Fay's baby?" the black-haired girl said.

The blonde girl nodded again. "Miz Gangle gave him to some Louisiana people. A real pretty lady."

The black-haired one nodded. "I saw her. She's got nice clothes. That other lady with her's got a pink and white dress like in the window at Reber's."

"We'd look good in that pink dress, wouldn't we," the blonde-haired one said, pulling at the front of her white flowered blouse, which was stretched tight across her stomach, the lacy sleeves cutting into the flesh of her upper arm. She took a cigarette from the crumpled pack and said, "I hope they don't send my baby to no Louisiana."

"I told Reverend Gangle that I wanted some rich people to have mine," the black-haired girl said. "I told him I wouldn't stay with his mama until the baby was borned unless the people would have a big house and a nice car."

They both smoked cigarettes, not saying anything else. The black-haired girl would take a big mouthful of smoke and then open her mouth up and breathe it through her nose. I thought that was the most grown-up looking thing I had ever seen; I resolved to develop that skill as soon as possible. They leaned back on their elbows, shifting position uncomfortably every so often. I looked at Terry; she had fallen asleep, her mouth slack, her glasses fallen off and lying beside her. Suddenly, the girls sat up and looked at each other; another girl was running across the street. She peeked around the tree towards the porch, and pushed herself between the other two with her bottom. "Brenda, Vickie!" she said. "Did Old Lady Gangle see me?"

"I don't think so," said Vickie, the black-haired one, looking through the trees, almost right at me but not seeing me. I froze.

"Gimme a cigarette," the new girl said. She wasn't pretty like the other two. She was wearing a big baggy blouse like the other two, but her stomach wasn't as big. The rest of her was, though; she was fat. She sat only inches from me on the other side of the drooping leaves; I could see that she had big teeth, spaced far apart, the front ones like big kernels of corn. Her rat-colored hair was frizzy, and she had a pig nose.

"You better not let her catch you here, June Fay," said Brenda, the blonde one.

"I don't care," June Fay said. "What's she going to do to me now?"

"I don't know, and I don't want to know," shuddered Brenda. She handed June Fay the last cigarette in the pack, and June Fay lit it with one of the straight wooden matches. Mrs. Lipps's baby's thin reedy cry came through the open screen, and June Fay sat up straight; Brenda and Vickie looked at each other behind her back. Finally Vickie said, "Was it pretty bad?"

June Fay nodded her head up and down, up and down. "Hurt," she said.

"Didn't they give you no shot?" Vickie said suspiciously.

June Fay shrugged; she lifted her big head, sensing the air for sound. "Well?" Vickie said, wrapping her arms around her belly.

"I don't know," June Fay said. "When I went in there, they shaved me . . . down there, and they put this water up my butt . . ."

"No!" Brenda said.

"They did!" said June Fay. She started to chew at the skin on the side of her thumbnail. "Then they made me lay down on this hard bed all by myself for a long time and it hurt. And then these nurses would come in and put their hands up me."

Brenda shook her head again. "Not really," she said.

June Fay looked meanly at her. "You wait," she said. "You'll see."

"But didn't they give you a shot?" Vickie said again, moving closer to June Fay. "Miz Gangle and the doctor told me you could get a shot and you wouldn't feel anything."

"They finally give me one," said June Fay. "They had this needle that looked like it was about a yard long. They stuck it in my back. Then I woke up later and threw up about ten times."

"Did you feel the baby come out?" Vickie said.

June Fay shook her head. "They don't let you do that," she said. "If it was anything like what I *did* feel, then I'm glad." She put her hands in her lap. "I'm never ever going to let Wayne do nothing to me again. Nor anybody else." I could see she had some pimples on her face, which looked mean and mad, but her eyes were red. Brenda and Vickie didn't say anything. They just sat there. I heard the baby again – it sounded like "Laaah, laaaah."

"Did you see him?" June Fay demanded.

"No," said Brenda.

"I did," said Vickie. "I was scrubbing the downstairs bathroom and the lady came in with him. He was real cute."

"When are they going to take him to Louisiana? Those people?" June Fay said. She was looking hard at the station wagon, which my mama had pulled up half on the yellow grass strip.

"Tomorrow, I think," Vickie said.

"Did *you* see the lady?" June Fay said to Brenda.

"Yeah. She's pretty."

"Do you think she's rich?"

"I'm sure she is," Brenda said. She laid her pale puffy hand on June Fay's fat back, and June Fay leaned her head between the legs of her green shorts, wrapping her arms around her chest. "I don't know why," she said. "When I hear that crying, I get this real strange feeling, right here. Like I'm full of a bunch of old bees."

"So, did you tell Wayne yet?" Vickie said.

"I just came out of the hospital an hour ago," June Fay said. "I took my suitcase by my mama's, but she was at the fact'ry."

"I still don't know why you stayed at a place in your own town," Vickie said. "I don't want no one in Wichita Falls to know."

Brenda nudged her.

June Fay shrugged. "I don't care."

"You just thought Wayne would change his mind and marry you," Vickie said.

"He still might, sometime," June Fay said. "At least he ain't already married, like that guy you went with."

Vickie glared at her. Then they sat there, the three of them huddled together in the thin shade of the tree, until "Girls?" a voice called from across the yard, and Brenda and Vickie stood up quickly. "Girls!" It was Mrs. Gangle. "Come get these clothes washed, right now! Girls?" Brenda and Vickie moved across the yard, swaying back and forth like circus elephants. June Fay huddled closer into the tree; I could hear her sniffling. She said, "Ohhh!" and said it again, and hugged her fat chest more tightly.

There were turnip greens *again* for dinner that night; yet another of the big-stomached girls served us and then took our plates. "When are we going home?" I said, looking at the watery gray-green glob on my plate.

"In the morning, sweetie," Mama said. "The papers are all done, and the baby's ready for the trip now."

"Good," I said, pushing a strange flat brown thing that might have been a meatball around the plate with my bent fork. Mrs. Gangle gave me a look that made me stop. "Now you mind the heat tomorrow," she said to my mama.

"Of course," my mama said.

"And stop frequently."

"We will," my mama said.

"More greens?" Mrs. Gangle said. "You all paid for it."

"No thank you," said my mama, and that night while Mrs. Lipps was feeding the baby his bottle, she said to Mrs. Gangle, "I think I'll take these children out for some air," and we snuck out to the Dairy Delight around the corner and got giant dipped cones. My mama took a big vanilla malted back in a crisp white bag; she looked both ways before disappearing with it into the room behind the French doors. That night it seemed like I could finally sleep in the big scratchy beds; I hardly heard the cicadas at all.

＊ ＊ ＊

"Y'all got ever'thing?" Mrs. Gangle said, peering into the station wagon as if checking for stolen bent forks. "You got ever'thing you need for the baby?"

"Yes, thank you, Mrs. Gangle," said Mrs. Lipps. She was sitting next to my mama, wearing my favorite sheer yellow blouse, holding the baby in the blue blanket she'd brought. She looked very beautiful.

"Well," Mrs. Gangle said. She stood up, placing her hands on her bony hips.

"Thank you again," Mama said politely, and she backed the station wagon away from the dusty yard. As soon as she did a U-turn and rounded the corner, she and Mrs. Lipps started laughing. "Drive like heck!" Mrs. Lipps said. "She might decide to come with us!"

"I'll do ninety," Mama said. "Could you believe that slop she fed us!"

"I guess you shouldn't expect any better, she has those poor girls do the cooking, in that kitchen – did you go in there, the oven couldn't have been any hotter than the room!"

My mama laughed. "You'll always have to tell Jimmy what you took him away from. From Texas!"

Mrs. Lipps smiled, and looked down at the baby. I craned my neck from the back of the station wagon. Mrs. Lipps looked like pictures in my Bible of Mary with Baby Jesus. "I wonder what she was like," Mrs. Lipps said. "Jimmy's mother."

"Probably just wonderful," my mama said. "Probably just a nice girl who just got carried away one time," and then she looked in the rear view mirror at us and said, "We better stop for gas before we get out there in the middle of nowhere."

"Let me pay, now, Virgie," Mrs. Lipps said, but my mama said, "My turn this time."

"You've just been wonderful, Virgie," said Mrs. Lipps, and they smiled at each other.

"Here's a Standard Oil," my mama said, and she pulled into the filling station. "You girls need to go?" she called back to us.

"Yes!" I said, having not obeyed orders to go before we left; I had wanted to spend the least time possible in Mrs. Gangle's smelly, murky bathroom.

"Come on then," Mama said, and walked around to free me from the rear, just as the gas station attendant appeared. "Fill it up, Ma'am?" he said. He was a mean-looking red-haired boy with big red pimples on his farmer-looking sunburnt face. He wasn't even wearing a white hat like filling station workers in Louisiana wore. I couldn't wait to get home.

"Fill it with regular," my mama said to him.

The boy nodded and walked over to the pump. I lingered there for a second to get a delicious whiff of gasoline. "Come on, Libby," my mother said, looking around like we might get hit by a car, though none were anywhere in sight.

The bathroom was dirty, too. I decided that all the bathrooms in Texas were. My mama lined the seat with toilet paper, then went out to pay for the gas. Sitting on the wobbly toilet, I heard voices through the thin wall, someone talking in the garage. "That *is* them," a girl's voice was saying.

"What am I supposed to do about it?" a boy's voice said.

"Don't you even want to see your own baby, Wayne?" the girl's voice said. There was no answer. I pulled down the rusty wet metal flusher quickly, pulled up my elastic shorts, and edged quietly out of the bathroom, making my way around some oily barrels in back of the filling station rather than over the concrete. Edging around a rusty propane tank, I moved up to the small plate-glass window. It was June Fay; she was holding onto the filling station boy's sleeve, trying to get him to look at her face, but he was putting money in the cash register; he peeled her arm off his like it was bindweed on an oak tree. Out front, my mama was waiting for me. I could see Mrs. Lipps in the passenger seat, still smiling. June Fay went into the repair garage and was peeking around the corner. She looked back at Wayne, her mouth open a little bit, her big corn teeth with their big spaces showing, like a run-over dog I once saw while I was riding my bike to buy comic books at Pic 'n' Pac.

Wayne took a couple of quarters and some pennies out of the cash register drawer and took them to my mama; I walked back around the building.

"Wayne!" I heard June Fay say. He didn't look back at her.

"Did you check the oil?" my mama was saying.

"No'm," he said. "But I was about to."

My mama nodded her head, looking at him with that face she makes when she will say after the person is out of earshot, "He wasn't very nice, was he?"

Wayne opened the hood and stuck the dipstick deep into wherever it went.

"She's fine," he said, wiping it off on his pants, which were probably pinstriped but you couldn't really tell.

"Thank you," my mama said. When she thought someone was rude, she would always be twice as polite.

He shut the hood and came back around. As he did, he looked down real quick at Mrs. Lipps. The baby was fussing a little bit. "You're okay, sweetie," Mrs. Lipps was saying, holding him a little closer.

"That there's a good looking baby," Wayne said.

Mrs. Lipps looked up and gave him one of her Miss Cotton Pageant smiles. "Thank you," she said.

"There you are, Libby," my mama said. "Come on, let's get going."

I hopped in the back. Terry was playing with her new Barbie that mama had produced for the return trip. This was the new model Barbie, with a bubble cut, not a pony tail. And I was in awe; Mama had also given her the ultimate Barbie outfit: the Barbie bride dress.

Mama got in the driver's seat and, slamming the door, she said jovially, "Let's go." She started up the station wagon and pulled away from the pump. I looked back. June Fay was watching us. Wayne was fiddling with the air hose. I saw June Fay go over to him, but he didn't stop doing what he was doing. Watching our car, she moved to the very edge of the filling station pavement. I lifted my hand and waved to her through the rear window.

Aedan Alexander Hanley

LOUANNE AND THE BIKER

She met him at a flea market
while looking for beaded earrings.
He said, "You're a rose, baby."
So she took it as a compliment
and said she'd tatoo her thigh
if he'd be her boyfriend. He was
twenty and not what normal girls
went for. He had thick lips,
long, greasy brown hair, and his name
was Franky. He rode a Harley
in an all leather suit. When lifting
his leg over his bike, he creaked;
all his zippers unzipped.
"It's creepy and sexy all at the same time,"
Louanne said. She liked his leather,
and petted it like an animal
in front of people. Once he got
an erection while taking a picture.
I know because Mrs. Berg said
she looked at the picture and saw
a funny bump down there. I looked
for it, but couldn't see what she saw.
I figured you had to be old
to see things clearly. Anyway,
Louanne got rid of him for cheating
with a fourteen year old farm girl.
I guess he gave this girl rides
on the sly, and told her how pretty
she was, like roses. "He'd say, 'A rose
is a rose is a rose,' like it was something
Shakespeare would say," Louanne said.
But some of us knew Franky wasn't any
poet. After all, it's only in public
school books that you read that stuff.

LOUANNE AND THE MUSIC LESSON

"You ride them saddle-less, you see,
so you can feel them sweat
through your jeans." Louanne hoisted
herself onto a horse, holding
his hair with a fist. He snorted,
choked and coughed, shaking loose
the flies on his thighs. He studied
the ground then shook his head
"yes" with a jerky toss. With a kick
in the gut, Louanne was flying.
The horse jumped John Bergs' two-foot fence,
then headed for the cows. Louanne
screamed, and her large legs
kicked up both sides. Soon, she became
a yellow spot on the horizon.
I remembered those songs with the dancing
dots, always yellow or red,
hitting each word as you sang it.

Eva Konrad

PEELING OFF

THE ONE-ARMED forester and the flowering cactus made of glass beads were the only objects colored by a hesitant slant of light. The rest were in grayness. Mirek twisted his neck close to the leaded glass panels, straining to hear any movement inside. He had cleaned up after work and run all the way; it had to be done quickly while he felt the courage. Now it seemed the old woman wasn't in and he would be reprieved; he couldn't very well make a ruckus by banging on the gate. She wasn't at home either. Suppose she's upstairs, thought Mirek, she might be staring at the case with military head-gear; there was nothing more desolate than that pile of caps which had been blown off young heads by cannon balls. Like Petr's helmet left lying in the ditch. . . . Mirek had it hidden in his room. I must clean it and give it to the old woman when I finally talk to her, when I find her, when I figure out what to say.

He wandered off toward the square. The angles of the street, the cob-blestone designs, the geraniums in plastic pots were becoming strange again, unnecessary. He forgot about Petr's grandma. His own body was barely holding together; his head threatening to fly off like a firecracker, and that would be a good thing because if it exploded it would make an angry sound, and then there would be nothing.

"Wait, Mirek!" Old Vanek was blocking the street. Trapped, Mirek stood looking down on a piece of dog shit until the fat man waddled close.

"So you didn't tell them, you let the son-of-a-bitch get away with it!"

Vanek's piggy eyes were darting around; he spoke low. He doesn't want anyone to hear him say this, thought Mirek with contempt, he just wants to fart through his teeth, torment me.

"I told them," he said to Vanek. "They wouldn't believe me. . . . Somebody else, a grown-up, would have had to . . . somebody who saw him take drink before it happened; plenty did but they didn't speak up. You were in the pub too, you could have. . . ." His voice rose: "Leave me alone!"

Vanek was about to cuff him one for being cheeky when Mirek found his legs were still in working order; he dashed toward the little park in the middle of the square and made for the bandstand.

The bandstand had been their favorite joke; when they first discovered its uses they were still short enough to walk in without ducking. Now Mirek had to bend over, grasp the bizarre columns and twist himself down so he could sit on the cement floor with his legs squeezed against his stomach. Oh the wit that Petr had expended on the pink-and-yellow metal enclosure! They had conjured a midget band conductor in a yellow and pink uniform waving a tiny baton at giant tubas and bassoons honking in the rain. They were the authors of many graffiti now clumsily painted over. One of them was still legible on the little structure's misshapen roof: 'To every town the bandstand it deserves!' Then there were periods when they had felt sorry for the toy stand and brought it little presents. They had enjoyed placing bones inside it, thus encouraging the local dogs in their already considerable patronage of it.

It began to rain. Uncomfortable among the smelly refuse on the tiny cement floor, Mirek started shaking: yeah, it had really happened, and it seemed worse here than any other place. The jokes had been kids' stuff, but who else but Petr could have made something of this disaster; who else could help him, Mirek, to see things in funny ways, so he could feel different from the people around them, different and free, ready to go. . . .

"We're not glued to this town – when we're ready we'll just peel off from it, like those airplanes at the airshow, remember how they got away, one by one?"

Yeah, that's what he used to say, but now I'm alone – he got away, but how can I . . . on my own? He squeezed out of the bandstand and started running toward the ramparts.

* * *

A few years before, an artist had come to the town of Duby and started sketching the church and the town hall, the views from the ramparts. Children trailed after him, and in the pub he was pestered to put his work on view. Petr had run errands for him and told him all the scandals about the Duby élite. The bandstand was also recorded in garish colors. What was it for? The town had some old parts but who'd be interested in the little old museum or the pock-marked Pietá at the crossroads?

"You'll see boys, you'll see!" The artist left in a fine mood; the publican's wife had been good to him, it was said.

Some six months later Petr got a package in the mail from the artist. There were several sheets of heavy paper and a list of instructions. They turned the sheets every which way; there was a familiar roof, and weren't those the tiles from the churchyard wall? Perforated lines ran up and down the sheets . . . it was a pop-up town of Duby! And there it said on the bottom: Colorful towns of Bohemia, a series of easily assembled places of interest. . . . Petr and Mirek laughed their heads off but hurried to assemble the quaint cardboard town just the same. The red roof of the church (renovated by the artist's imagination) was the highest; the ramparts circled the naïvely rendered renaissance backs of the old houses; the square was a three-dimensional picture of civic pride and tasteful restoration; the bandstand had been unfortunately omitted for reasons of boring good taste; whimsical cats dozed on window-sills. And there at the end of Church Street was the museum, squatting in its tarted-up garden!

There developed a shortage of the idealized paper town but eventually everyone in Duby managed to get one of their own. The one assembled by Mirek and Petr ended up in the museum because it had an inscription from the artist on the wall of its cardboard counterpart.

❊ ❊ ❊

Mirek had run all the way from the square to the outskirts; in Duby everything was only a short distance away, but he was out of breath when he reached the refuse dump above the railway. The rain was sucking out the smells from the discarded rags and rusty bedsteads sprawling under the "Dumping prohibited" sign. A glass shard cut Mirek's ankle, and he looked down with satisfaction at the drops of blood beginning to stain his sneaker. He wanted to run on or rather run round and round Duby, faster and faster — even faster than Petr had driven on his motorcycle, but suddenly he was surprised by a shout; his lungs were straining to let out more air and sound. The fireman's mutt who had been vaguely following him took up the howls and scared Mirek into silence. He started to kick around an old chamber pot. If I hadn't been his friend, if he hadn't given me all those notions, I could be kicking a real football with the others . . . or screwing fat Anča behind the garage . . . or doing something like everybody else. He's made me crazy, the son-of-a-bitch, what did I need all this for? For the first time in those five days he felt hungry. I'll go home and stuff myself like everybody else and then I'll talk to the old bag and that'll be it; that'll end it .

❊ ❊ ❊

The two women stopped talking when he walked into the low-ceilinged kitchen that opened right onto the street. They were gathering fresh venom. Mirek went to the stove; the sight of congealing potato dumplings from yesterday discouraged him. He sat down on the stool by the range.

"The gentleman expects to be served – maybe we should give him one of those huge menus, like they do in class A restaurants." Mirek's mother was repairing a reddish hair piece which she sometimes wore on top of her head when she had a date. His grandmother laughed at her daughter's wit. They seemed closest when they had a chance of picking at him.

"I'll eat in a minute – is there something else, some cheese or eggs?"

"The dumplings were good enough for us; they must be eaten."

His grandmother was looking at him with that avidity she had exhibited ever since Petr's death.

"Did you finally go see her? It's a scandal really – you his best friend and you can't find a moment to do the right thing by his grandmother."

"If you had gone to the funeral like every decent person. . . ."

Mirek's resolution not to talk to them about it deserted him. He had eaten one bite of the dumplings and his hunger was gone.

"You know why I didn't go, JesusMaria, how could you go listen to that crap and watch that fucking bastard make long faces. He killed him; you know he killed him. . . . "

The lumpy starchy mess was gluing his throat and made him cough. The grandmother got up from her rocker and stretched across the table; at first Mirek stared at her stupidly and then realized that she wanted to hit him. He held onto her arm.

"So that's what you've been saying around town, you want to make trouble, yeah, you want to get us in real trouble, you stupid lout, after we've been so careful and for whose sake I ask you? Yeah, you just let your mouth run on, you'll see, Manka will lose her job; I won't get my pension sup- plemental . . . !" She was spitting through her ill-fitting dentures.

"Old Vanek thinks so too . . . he told me just now, they all know Ran- dal was drunk and took that corner too sharp, I'm telling you. . . ."

Mirek always underestimated what the two women could do to him.

His mother said in a bored way: "Old Vanek is crazy; nobody pays any attention to him; he would say anything against Randal, the two families were always at each other. It was bad luck, that's all – your friend tearing around on that bike, asking for it. . . ."

"Not one word out of you about this – you know the Chairman saves the good cuts for your mother and . . . and where would we be if he turned against us?"

Yeah, he saves meat, meat, meat . . . but that's already been paid for, hasn't it, mother already paid for it, in the back of his truck! Mirek felt dizzy and had to put his head down. Just like this town to have a butcher for the local Party Chairman and a Chairman who's also a butcher, butchering people on the road with his bloody truck . . . he'd hit an old woman before, and things were always hushed up.

His mother thumped him on the back: "Sit up straight, Mirek – you're acting like a kid. And you're going to see old Veselá today, today you hear – or she'll tell people we didn't teach you any manners."

"What's it to you, you never have a good word for her; suppose she doesn't want to be bothered; I'll do it when I'm ready."

The smell of cheap sweet rum filled the air. Grandmother was fixing herself tea. "Good words!" she mumbled. "Good words for those who deserve them. Old Veselá . . . I never saw such a woman for giving herself airs; if there's one thing I hate it's people who puff themselves up. And right here in Duby where everybody knows what rubbish heap she comes from. Remember Manka, what a laugh everybody had when she was made that curator, she who could barely read . . . and sure enough, people say she's mixing everything up. . . ."

She was slurping her tea. Pretty soon she'll get herself a rum refill, thought Mirek. It seemed to him he would never be able to get up from the table. Their voices pinned him down – his mother's lazy contemptuous comments, his grandmother's indignant invective – he could feel how much relief they were getting, energy even. And he had none. . . . How much easier it was throwing dirt like this, how much easier than . . . loving. The word scared him. It was absurd to think that he had loved Petr, they were two guys; if he had loved him, he wouldn't be so mad at him now. Petr, after all, had been a bit of a shit, for all he was dead and buried now. He too had thought his grandmother was ridiculous with her curating, yeah, Petr had been ashamed of her all right, though he didn't say so. And the way he was showing off on his bike, and how he bragged about having been the first to screw girls, and the books he was forever pushing on him though he probably never read them himself. . . . And how about when that artist was here, didn't he just lick his ass, thinking the man'd help him get into the Arts and Crafts School in Prague? That he'd get away by being an artist himself?

He jumped up so hard that he knocked down his chair. He ran out of the house not hearing what the women were shouting after him.

* * *

There was an open window in the museum annex. Mirek knocked on the painted door of the cottage. He heard her shuffling inside; it would be easy now; he didn't feel a thing; he'd mumble a few words and then be off; it didn't matter where.

"Ah, it's you Mirek." She was looking at him dry-eyed, without expression;

her black and yellow polyester dress was hanging on her as if she had lost a lot of weight. Mirek averted his eyes from her beard; a few long black hairs sticking out on the shrunken chin.

"I came to say that I'm sorry I didn't make it to the funeral; we're real busy at the garage, you know and . . . oh, I meant to bring his helmet, I forgot, it's in one piece, I thought maybe you could sell it . . ."

Of all the idiotic things he could have said! He looked to her for help but she only shook her head.

"I don't want it."

Could I leave now? wondered Mirek. He looked beyond her into the room. On the large peasant kitchen table were some ledgers; it looked like she was doing accounts.

"Are you all right? Could I help with something?"

"You're good at numbers, aren't you? Petr used to do it, though he wasn't much better than me."

The moment for escape had passed. He stepped into the room.

The columns under the ledgers showed only small sums under the headings of the past months. Mirek wasn't surprised; the groups of children who came during the school year didn't pay, and the occasional sightseers were rare.

"Would you add it all up, I mean for all those years – I want to give them a sort of final count." She still sounded as if her words were strung on a sagging rope.

So she's quitting, registered Mirek while he turned the stiff paper of the ledger. He started quickly adding the years' totals of the various columns. The artificially antique room was quiet; this is where the guided tours would start, in the more or less authentic weaver's workshop. Several kinds of looms took up most of the space but there were also decorated wardrobes and chests; antique cooking utensils hung from the sides of the large fireplace.

Mirek was done. A few more words. . . . Petr had been the one good with words, what would he have said to get away without feeling absolutely shitty?

"I hope this doesn't mean you're not going to be a guide any more, Paní Veselá – there's no one who knows the museum as well as you."

"Peter hated it, my going on repeating it . . . and the jokes, he couldn't stand it when he overheard my jokes."

There was no denying what she said. Mirek tried just the same:

"That's no reason . . . excuse me, but well . . . just because Petr – and anyway he was proud of you, really. . . ."

She looked at him hard as if she didn't mind showing her dislike.

"That's not why I'm quitting; Petr didn't like a lot of things . . . all of

Duby for that matter. I'm quitting because it all went out of my head, that's why."

She made an impatient gesture as Mirek started to speak. "I can't think of a single word and that's that. It's written down somewhere, not what I used to say, but what all those things are; I won't begin learning it again though, like I did when I was younger. And the committee – they'll be glad to get rid of me – they can all crawl in my ass!"

Mirek looked at her in surprise. Petr's grandma had never used words like that; she had been almost ladylike compared to the other women in Duby – after all she had been the curator!

"Petr and I used to hide – here behind the oven and in the museum . . . all over the place. He knew it all by heart – well, I don't mean to say that it was always the same, but we knew most of it."

She made no comment. Mirek had another idea: "Paní Veselá, what about the house – it goes with being curator doesn't it?"

"Yes, he didn't think of that . . . where am I going to go, just tell me that; he gets himself killed, my brain goes, and what now?"

She spoke without emphasis or self-pity, she was really asking him a question.

"I know you can't help being smart," she went on, "but it won't do here in Duby; Petr got all roused up about those ideas of yours; they all boiled inside him, he knew he couldn't do anything about anything; so he rode that bike fast and faster . . . well I'm not saying it's your fault . . . he was like a pike in a muddy pond, a bit like his father. . . ."

Mirek was so amazed by her words he found none to defend himself. The idea that he, Mirek, had been the leader! He, an apprentice in the local garage! The woman must really be losing her stuffing; and didn't she know that it was the butcher and not any fast driving that killed Petr?

He got up, almost ready to shake her. She looked up at him: "Yes, I know what you're going to say, but don't you see, it doesn't matter how it happened. Have you finished with the numbers? I must write a letter to the Committee, so you better go, it'll take me a mortal long time."

Mirek took two steps toward her. Her beard didn't bother him anymore. "So, you'll give up the house, the garden? You may just as well get a bike like Petr, yeah, you'll last just as long as he did if you move into some hole in the wall – that's all you'll get, you know, somewhere with strangers, real nice, like my folks maybe."

She backed off from him but he kept on. "Come on, that's all nonsense about your forgetting, come on, how does it go? . . . 'Here we stand in the cottage of a weaver's family just like it was over a hundred years ago. My own family were weavers, I remember my grandmother bending over this very loom . . . come on . . . this chest was painted for the dowery of a rich bride, well richer than I was – I had only my pretty face, though you wouldn't believe it now to look at me. . . ."

"I never did . . . never did put in all that about myself – that's not the right way!"

"Say it right then, try. . . ." All he could think of were swear words; she was so stubborn, an impossible bearded hag! She'd had nothing but grief all her life until she landed this cushy bit, and now she was ready to turn it over to those fat cats from the district. . . .

She had retreated into the shadow of the fireplace. Mirek finally got it: she was scared, shrunken scared, like a maimed bird trying to be overlooked by cats.

"I'm sorry Paní Veselá . . . I shouldn't have talked to you like that; but you see Petr told me about you, how you were in the Party way back when they really cared for working people, how you fed the strikers and went to Prague to protest, lost your job, went to jail . . . all that. You deserve to keep the house, it's supposed to be yours for life and you did . . . you're doing a good job here in the museum . . . don't give them the satisfaction . . . give it time. And I'll . . . well, I'll come to see you if you need something, like repairs, you know – I'd like to, really. . . ."

He was shouting and wheedling as if all this were terribly important to him; he could barely credit that he was committing himself, but there was no way he could let go of her now. She was sitting on the bench, mumbling:

"Yes, Duby was a better place then, we were all in it, against the fabricants. We had to do without . . . Petr and you can't even imagine how we lived but we cared, we cared. . . ."

He let her rest for a bit. She got up of her own accord.

"Well, if you want to stay, help me sort of remember, I'll try, but I want to start in the garden."

Mirek couldn't believe he heard right, but she was already out the door. I did it, I got through to her, nobody except Petr ever listened to me; he rushed after her before she could change her mind.

The garden was only a corridor between the weaver's cottage and the little renaissance museum building. She slipped into her own house at the end of the garden to get keys. Mirek waited looking at the frescoes that Petr had started painting on the museum wall. They were supposed to supply a kind of an optical illusion by adding a green background to the narrow strip of vegetation, but as he had worked, the plants became less and less realistic; now, in the fading light, Mirek could barely discern the menacing branches, the aggressive flowers that looked as if they were going to spit at you. Instead of blending with the living greenery, the painted flora seemed to work hard at being ugly.

"Awful, isn't it?" Grandma was standing next to him. "But I won't let them take it down, I'll tell them it's art, they know nothing about it."

She started naming the plants as she would for visitors: "Marjoram, that's all poor people often had to make soup; St. Peter's keys – if you tend them you'll have a short-cut to heaven; our Lady's slippers, and the border, those are Waiting Maids; they are supposed to be just weeds, but have you ever looked at them? Where else can you see such blue color – only in the eyes of poor girls waiting for something. . . ."

"That's good Grandma, you're doing just fine." Mirek was grinning at her in the dark, impossibly pleased. "Now for the museum."

"Ach, the garden's easy, I planted all of it, but that junk in there. . . ."

Junk – Petr's favorite word. She opened the gate and put the lights on. Mirek noticed that when she had fetched the keys she had taken the trouble to pull some of the worst black hairs from her beard.

"Here downstairs, we have all kinds of mementos people donated; upstairs is the historical part from the 1866 war; professors come here to look at it – it was here around Duby that they had the worst fighting."

She seemed to falter. "Now I tell them something about all these . . . mostly they don't listen much any more after they've been through the cottage. They like it upstairs when I talk about the gory details from the war, but I usually make it real brief down here." She took the one-armed forester from his shelf. "I would have missed him, and this chipped vase; that's a real pretty flower painted on it."

"Okay, it's okay, we don't have to do the whole thing tonight; you can change it maybe, just as long as you know . . . you're sure you can do it."

She wasn't listening; a wound up voice insided her started intoning: "and now ladies and gentlemen you'll get a real treat – I always leave it to the last. This is a genuine old hurdy-gurdy, some of you may never have heard one; beggars used to play them on street corners, but this is a special one, an old craftsman made it right here in Duby, we used to dance to it when I was a girl."

She was cranking it up. Mirek had forgotten about the hurdy-gurdy, the most embarassing item in the collection. How could she? He himself had had enough. But it was too late; the sloppy, grinding sounds filled the room, filled his guts, tightened his throat. She kept turning the lever with merciless energy; what was she trying to do to him?

She was crying, her whole thin body shaking, tears and snot falling on the varnished top of the hurdy-gurdy. Still, she never faltered, the sounds were coming out evenly, the cheating bitch of that music, breezy one moment and choking the next. Mirek had never heard it like that before, two strands coming out of that dumb box, one of them almost killing you with sorrow, the other strident – music for angry idiots. He cupped his hands and made a shield of them in front of his face and ears but the music kept getting through until he gave in and joined the old woman in the crying.

MaryAnn Franta

BEGINNING GRIEF

Solitaire,
the flutter-slap
shuffle, then black-red-black.
Phone the one friend who won't mind
how long you cry. Bike ride,
run, shortcut through mud,
then laugh, actually laugh
at your brown-crusted shoes.

Claim your right to be sick,
then sleep. Peppermint tea,
chicken soup, a little chocolate.
In your red shirt and socks
sweep the patio.
Feed the chickadees.
Talk longer to a neighbor
you don't know. Open
the photo album and
let it rain. Bake a batch
for the gang at work.
Letters of thanks.

Now become a stumbling kitten
or prairie dog, scan
your horizon. Meditate
on the animals
too small to be brave.

SUGAR CUBE

As you reach for keys in your purse,
there it is, reminder from this morning;
wrapped in white stiff paper, blue printed:
Domino Sugar, lifted from the restaurant table
at breakfast. And you! The dentist's daughter!
Must have been bitter coffee
to even consider it. But you have it now,
as you open the car door in the winter night.

In your mouth, a tiny brick of beach sand
quickly liquefied, the definition
of each grain gone, but momentarily
stinging like snow blown
off the crest of a drift
to your cheek, which is red with the wind.

Sweet as the virgin white of a bride
on her Daddy's arm down the aisle,
and just as edgy. And when it's gone
there's a flavor lingering, like a love
that didn't work out. Crumpled wrapper
in your pocket.

But already you can't say for sure
how it felt on your tongue; nor recall
your father's glance, exactly,
when the wedding march began.
To think of a beach, of going
barefoot, seems absurd,
even dangerous on such a night.
More important that you have your keys,
the necessary equipment, as you
wait for the car to warm.

Little internal combustions; crumbling
the white, tumbling off glacier's edge
into the sea, the sea. Old love,
summer, sugar cube. You want another.
You want another.

ECZEMA

That miserable itch of the skin
    on your wrist. At least this time
    it doesn't show on your face.
    The doctor says, *You know*
    there is no cure. You don't believe him
    for a second. You are sensitive
    to something.
Can you blame caffeine
    your hormones in a swing
    the summer moon?
    Formaldehyde, cats,
    latex, love? Is it
    the trembling earth when a train roars by,
    radioactive clouds in the sky?
Did you break a mirror, salt
    a robin's tail? Kiss a toad lately?
    Stare too long at a dusky portrait,
    those stunning gunmetal eyes, or
    watch the tornado till your
    skin turned to stone?
    Something in the water,
    Something in your dreams?
    Ripe mangoes, Grandma on your nerves,
    those two dogs you could never train?
Lizard skin. Scratch it in your sleep.
    Allergic to old vows, new friends,
    your own tears? Is it injected
    by insects? The neighbor woman dead
    yet alive, dust on your desk,
    your last poem or the next?

Into any noxious weeds?
    Storms at the synapses, racing the aurora,
    mis-spoken criticism, unpriestly exorcism,
    amethyst, copper, mercury, lust,
    some kind of soap, chocolate ice cream,
    tanned leather, the color orange leaking
    volatile gases?
    Too much casual sex
    in the undersea world of public TV?
    All that over-conditioned air? Did you
    cut off your long hair?
Whatever it is, you keep looking.
    you fight
    that screaming urge to scratch
    to rub, to get at it.
    There is something deep
    under your skin
    that needs to be touched.

Ludek Snepp

DAYS ON THE EDGE OF RAZORBLADES

HOLDING THE LETTER, I felt like Archimedes witnessing the destruction of his circles by the soldier.

For the third time I read: "My Old Pal, for over twenty years I've been waiting for your invitation to visit Canada. Since you have done nothing about it, I'm inviting myself. Simply put, I'm already in the middle of preparations for my trip over the 'big puddle.' Be so kind as to reply with the necessary invitation."

I sat stiffly, my head spinning like a merry-go-round. So Eman (my best friend until he got married) wants to come. . . .

His letter had started like a poem: "In May, the month of love, you will hear my rich voice instead of the dove's song."

Flashes from my youth were popping into my head. All the mischievous things we rogues had done.

I could see him in front of me now as clearly as that last time. I could even hear him: "You shouldn't be going, it won't be so bad. Nothing is forever, even Communism will fuck itself."

"You are probably right, but we don't live forever. Besides I've always wanted to see the world," I had told him.

"Well, are you really leaving me here at the mercy of the comrades?"

"You can come with me."

"As if I could. I have a woman and two bastards around my neck."

"Sure and the cottage, car and a good position as well," I added sarcastically.

He was offended: "It cost me part of my life. Lots of hard work. And besides, I'm at home here. I can't run away now."

"So I'm a coward. Have a good time, hero."

We parted without a handshake.

"Don't be an idiot," he shouted after me, "I didn't mean anything. . . . "

I didn't turn back. Surprisingly, I wasn't angry with him. It was clear that he envied me. How many times we dreamt about distant places behind the barbed wire borders. But he was also right. I did see my departure as a cowardly act, maybe because of my fear of prison. Fear is the father of cowardice.

Now I am sitting here, imagining Eman's face. How could it be, that I didn't feel happy at the chance to see him after all these years?

With a moan I folded the letter. I have gotten used to a quiet life. (Actually I live like a pig in a field of rye.) My life without complications could end with my friend's visit.

I spent days filling out invitation letters, legal bureaucratic machinery with air tickets, reservation and medical insurance (most important of all, Eman is as old as I am). Anything could happen. . . . The possibility that without insurance he could end up in a hospital brought a cold sweat to my spine. All my savings would disappear into the doctor's pocket.

I tried to reason with my lack of enthusiasm. It came down to money. How big an expense could I run into? No, I don't think that is the case . . . to hell with money.

Before I managed to visit a notary, Eman's second letter arrived.

"My dear wife will not let me come alone, she doesn't trust me. Since I'm looking forward to seeing you, please invite both of us."

Oh, Lord, what a disaster are you sending my way? Is Eman planning to land here with all his relatives? So Anna, Ani, Annita will honor me with her visit. She used to be a good looking girl, but the two of us were never fond of each other. After their wedding she did not hide her animosity. Maybe she anticipated my bad influence on her hubby. Myself, I did not like her, because she took my old friend away from me. Anyway, I never felt right in her presence. Now I would be forced to spend eight weeks with her.

I felt gloomy when I was mailing the thick manila envelope with the official invitation. I was not sure if I was lying: ". . . looking forward to seeing you."

The sudden urge to throw the envelope into the wastebasket was followed by shame for my selfish ego. Overwhelmed by conflicting feelings I felt anger at myself, at Eman and his wife; but at the same time I was planning what to show them of this free world.

. . . In four months May came, time filled with nervousness and impatience.

Then the last step, two hundred miles to the airport. (Airports have the magic power of attraction. Those beautiful monstrous birds with wings spread over the ground symbolize people's dreams fulfilled. We can fly anywhere, anytime. . . .)

I was standing in the arrival terminal observing the rush around me. A wave of activity followed each flight announcement.

Passengers with heavy suitcases and worried faces suddenly appeared in a strange world far away from home. Their eyes wandered in seach of the one person waving to them. And when found, all their suitcases lost their load, they walked with sudden vigor, I watched their tears of relief, hugs, and laughter. At this moment I almost believed that love still lives.

The young couple beside me spoke fluent Czech. The man in a brown leather jacket said angrily: "Fuck, how I hate waiting."

The girl was calming him: "Come on, it's only a twenty minute delay, no big deal." Her pleasant voice changed suddenly to a sharp shriek: "There they are, there they are," and jumped as though trying to fly above our heads, her arms waving in the air.

"Oh yes, that's mum and dad," said her companion. When he lit his cigarette, his hand was shaking.

I started to search among the passengers, guessing and trying to recognize my guests. The crowd got thinner, Eman and Anna nowhere. The young girl was hugging her mother, her companion hugging the old man. Four bulky suitcases beside them were the center of the young man's attention.

I had given up hope of seeing my guests. Maybe Eman got ill, or maybe he was caught trying to bring in prohibited items. God knows what could have happened. I was so disappointed at not seeing my friend. All my preparations, rough plans for travel, shopping, financial calculations . . . all for nothing. . . .

My eyes were burning from staring at the arrival gate, here and there the late arrivals appeared, almost as if spat out of a giant's jaws. Suddenly they appeared, two silhouettes pulling three oversized suitcases. Their faces showed the same worry as those before them: is anybody waiting for us?

They recognized me sooner than I could them. The woman started waving in fear that I might leave. Sure, that is Anna! I waved back. Finally they stood before me, smiling. For a moment we scrutinized each other, curious to see whose face showed the heaviest traces of time, the most harm of the past twenty years.

Eman and Anna were both dressed in brand new clothing. They looked like they were leaving the fashion house. A small hat crowned my friend's wrinkled face. Only his blue eyes were as I knew them.

"So here we are," started Eman and hugged me the way Eastern officials do. His round body hit my bony chest: "So glad to see you." Eman's voice trembled.

"Me too, old buddy," I assured him. I smiled at him. He reminded me of the late Khrushchev. Really, he looked just like him.

"You haven't changed much in these long years," Eman continued: "I expected to see a shrunken old man."

"You haven't changed either, you just look more grown up." I patted his fat stomach.

Anna had been momentarily forgotten. She was standing politely by her suitcase, observing us with understanding. Two old friends met again.

"Do you recognize my dear wife," Eman laughed.

"Hi, Anicka," I reached out with my right arm, maybe to avoid a hug, but she had no intention of hugging me, she pressed my hand slightly. She reacted with a quick smile to my compliment: "Still a nice girl."

"And you're still a nice boy."

I did lie, because the slim young girl I remembered had changed to an all round woman. Only her face retained the same shape, and her sea-blue eyes – which I used to call 'goose-eyes' – were staring at me with the same old irony.

"I was afraid you were not going to show up," I said.

"You know Eman, Mister Forgetful, could not find his wallet," Anna explained, "and there was also a mix-up with our luggage."

"Go ahead, blame everything on me, I can bear it, darling," he teased.

"How was your flight?" I changed the subject.

"Great, no problems, smooth as if we do it all the time. Good food, drinks, nice flight attendants."

"You see, he hasn't changed a bit: food, drinks, girls." Anna made a wry face.

"Let's move, people, we should get home before dark. I don't like night driving. We will have plenty of time to talk."

I grabbed one of three suitcases, expecting a heavy load, but judging by its lightness, it must have been half empty.

We marched to the shuttle bus, which took us to my car in the parking lot.

"Nice car," Eman expertly touched the hood.

"A bit old, but a dependable Pontiac." I opened the trunk and put the luggage in.

Eman sat beside me, his wife occupied the back seat.

He talked nonstop, remembering our youth. My replies were short. I do not like to talk while driving. Maybe he got the message, or he got tired. I welcomed the sudden silence. When I looked at his quiet body, he was sleeping, comfortably spread out, mouth open. The body of my pal was like a barrel of fat. . . . He is heading for suicide. . . . I have to talk to him. . . . In the rear mirror I saw Anna, her eyes wide in an effort not to miss anything of the passing landscape.

"Are you not tired?" I asked.

"Not really. New impressions always bring me to life."

"Do you already have some?"

"When you hear Canada at home, you imagine mountains of snow and people dressed in furs, but it is totally different here: so clean, big. Just look at that farm," she pointed at the red building far away.

"You are right, this is an enormous land. It's so big that even the dirt gets lost." I laughed, and concentrated on my driving. After a moment's silence I added, "The trip overpowered Eman completely."

"He would oversleep even on his day of execution," said Anna. "When he cannot eat, drink, or babble, he sleeps."

"His nerves must be in great shape."

"Not really. Sometimes he gets enraged like a mad dog."

Judging from the bitterness in her voice, the love must have evaporated from their relationship.

She felt ashamed for her admission and added, "You have to understand, it's not easy back home, every stupid household item has to be hunted for."

"Eman always had a gift to get even the impossible." I evaluated my snoring passenger. What irony: Eman with his business talent and real enterprising spirit, was left in the old country, where the political regime cut down all roots of natural healthy enterprise. But who got out? Me, the one with his head in the books, a person with no business inclination, got into a world where business and money are the leading power. Eman actually was a born capitalist, raped by communism. But me, a dreamer with dreams dying slowly, romantic without romances, a writer with the sap of creation drying out . . .

"It is a fact, Eman is a good businessman," Anna continued. "He should have gone with you, he would have been succesful here."

"Are you two gossiping about me?" grumbled Eman.

"We are praising you for a change," I said to him.

"Don't tell me, I missed a lot." Finally he opened his eyes and turned his head to Anna: "And you too were praising me? That must be some Canadian miracle."

It was getting dark when we reached my house – nothing imposing. Eman's cottage at home was better looking.

With one suitcase in hand I led the way: "So this is my castle, not a millionaire's place, but I'm quite happy here." I couldn't read much from Eman's expression. Anna was observing the flower beds in the front. I opened the door inviting my guests to enter the living room. Besides the couch and chair, tall bookcases filled the room. I build more bookcases when finances allowed me to buy more books.

"That's you. I was for wine and women, you were for women and books." Eman's voice warmed my heart. Maybe I had not changed that much in twenty years.

Anna's watery blue eyes fluttered around the room. She evaluated my efforts at housekeeping: "You have it so clean, as if a woman has done it for you." She added: "I expected to be welcomed by your new wife." She gave me a thorough lookover.

"You would be wasting your time in waiting. I live like a lonely monk."

"Stop kidding," said Eman. "You would not give up female companionship. Or are your juices dry?"

"That is not the case; I simply have had no luck with women here."

Eman came alive: "What are you talking about? Beautiful girls are everywhere."

"Of course they are, but I guesss I am a nationalist even in love. I always search for those imported from home."

"You couldn't find any during these years?" Eman shook his head in disbelief.

"Those who search, will find. The first was a young widow, she lost her husband to a heart attack. I was afraid I would follow his path."

"Was she so demanding?"

"Enough, and she wanted to get married right away. I came here for freedom, I did not want to lose it so quickly. So we parted in peace." My thoughts ran through three months of life with Marie.

"What happened after that?"

"In two years I found a fresh immigrant from Plzeň, but my hopes fell through."

"Was she more demanding in bed?" Eman's excitement grew.

"On the contrary, she was as cold as a dog's snout. I would forgive her that, but she would have run me to the ground on another field. She wanted to get rich fast. She had two jobs herself, and she pushed me to look for more work too. She could not concentrate on anything but dollars."

"And what was wrong with that? She only wanted the egg nest for your future," Anna objected.

"It was much more than an egg nest, more like a mania slavery. Life with her meant to sell my soul to money. I refused to waste the rest of my days in such a greedy way, so we parted. I could never live with a woman who has a calculator heart."

"What else did you try?" Eman would not let go of me.

"I tried one more time." I went to the kitchen; I did not want to touch the most painful experience of my love life.

"Wait, pal, you would not let me die of thirst, would you? Can't you see my curiosity?" Eman stopped me.

"What else is there to say, just bad luck with women."

"But what about the third time, who was she?"

"A beautiful girl from Prague, cuddly like a lost kitten."

"And what did she do? Was she homesick for Wenceslas Square?"

"She secretly drank and smoked. I only found out when money was missing and when she sold my things to get money for drinking."

"So you threw her out?"

"First I tried to help her, begged her. She promised, swore that she would not touch that stuff again, but in a couple of days we were back where we started. Lord, she would have even drunk away this house."

Tactfulness was never Eman's strong side. "And how was she in bed?"

Anna's hand punched Eman's ribs.

Eman got angry. "Why are you hitting me? I can ask how my best friend lived."

"What else do you want to know? That I was an imbecile? I was crazy about her, so I kept forgiving her over and over again. I believed she could change, because I wanted to prove that our feelings can cure her. Useless, totally useless. I had to end it. She was a lost cause. Why she left her home, I will never understand. Is that satisfactory?" It dawned on him, how difficult it was for me to talk about that disastrous affair. But he could not resist his advice: "You should have given up nationalism and searched for native girls."

"Maybe you're right, I was an asshole. But let's go, I will show you your sleeping quarters, where you can go on sinning."

"Wait a moment," Anna opened one suitcase and Eman followed her example. They started to pull gifts from their half-empty luggage.

"Understand, we did not bring much for you, there are strict rules about that," Anna handed me a heavy box. I unwrapped a beautiful crystal ashtray.

"And here is one bottle of rum and one slivovice," Eman held two bottles above his head. "And one fur hat to save your brain from freezing," With the move of a real magician he exhibited a handsome kozack hat.

Twenty years without any gifts, these first ones melted my heart. Standing with the bottles and the hat on my head, I felt emotional. My voice softened: "Folks, you should not have done it."

"Don't be silly. We had to bring something for you. Money will be here even after we are gone," said Eman generously. He was never stingy.

"Thank you very much. I hope I can pay you back." And I went to put my gifts away. Then I gave them a big tour through the house. Eman was excited with my fully equipped workshop downstairs. I disclosed all my secrets of the kitchen cupboards and my food supply: "This is going to be your kingdom now," and I handed the wooden spoon to Anna as a king's sceptre.

We spent the evening remembering old times, bringing to life even the dead ones. I was surprised at how many friends had gone to eternity. Eman was amazing, through the whole evening he managed to eat and drink. Our first evening was crowned by Eman's falling asleep on the chesterfield.

"He is the same at home." Anna gave a sigh.

I felt sorry for her, but at the same time I was sorry for my friend. This must be the end for most marriages: in boredom, in search for some escape. Eman found his in drinking, but what about Anna?

Days went by, my financial account grew thinner, my old Pontiac's engine never got cold, and my guests felt happy here. They visited Niagara Falls, Toronto, Ottawa, points of interest close by, and since they came with a visa to the USA, their last wish was to see a part of America. So they saw the White House, paraded through Manhattan, Broadway, got rained on in the Smoky Mountains, got their skin burned on a beach in Florida. But most of all they loved the giant shopping malls. There they felt like they were in heaven.

After the two months long visit I was surprised at myself. I did not feel pity at how upset my life had become, I did not mind buying gifts to fill up their suitcases. Anna went through the house with an all-over cleaning. She did the cooking, baking, she was so kind to me that even Eman commented on it. Whenever Anna happened to be alone with me, Eman suddenly appeared. It could have been coincidence.

Two days before their departure we were going through a big mall, and Anna tried on a coat she really liked. It was on sale. So I played the role of a cavalier: "Take this coat, I will pay for it."

"Are you serious?" Her eyes grew bigger.

"Deadly serious," I assured her, and she touched my hand.

I knew Eman would not be happy to see this, but when I looked around, I could not find him. We had lost him a couple of times before. This time he came back with a lady.

Eman's face was flushed, close to a stroke. His eyes looked down to the carpet, his companion's expression was strict, official. Could she be a countrywoman?

"Do you know this man?" she asked.

I nodded.

"He says he does not speak English."

"That is true," I looked straight into her beautiful green eyes set in her well-shaped face.

"I have to call the police."

"Police?"

"This gentleman tried to steal these items." She extended her right hand with a bottle of aftershave and a packet of razorblades.

I could not believe Eman's stupidity to steal from the store. I shook my head: "It must be a misunderstanding."

"These items were in his pocket. I know my business, sir."

Now my face got red. I turned to Eman: "You stupid fool, is it possible, that you are such an idiot?" Eman did not answer, his head got heavier.

I went back to the lady-guard. I liked her. "Unpleasant situation," I began.

"That is always the story," she answered dryly.

"Are you serious about the police?" I stared straight into her eyes.

"It's my duty."

"I know, but could you make one exception and arrange for me to pay the bill and for you to forget about his?"

"No, you can't ask me to do that." We were staring into each other's eyes. Slowly I inched towards her: "Look, these two are my visitors from the old country, where all the stores are empty most of the time. It's not at all like here," I swung my arms. "They are amazed, shocked by the variety, abundance, and all this choice. This idiot," I pointed behind me, where the sinner stood listening to his wife's strong words, "This man obviously went momentarily berserk. He took what he cannot buy at home. I know him, believe me," I lied with ease, "he would never touch what is not his."

"Anybody could afford to buy these little things," she answered.

"That is the problem. He can't," I said and watched with pleasure how she got interested in my explanations: "Everyone who gets the permission to visit the West, receives only twenty dollars, nothing more. That is barely enough for postcards. The rest of the expenses is on the host, me in this case."

The woman nodded: "I understand, but that does not change anything. My duty is to call the police."

"Okay, so we give him to the police. And what happens next? He will go to court and to jail. But imagine, these people were saving money for years to fulfill their dream, they feel they are in heaven here, and such a tragic end for a couple of meager dollars." My words were speeding like a recordplayer out of control. "Above all of this I could be in lots of trouble with more expenses, and their return flight might expire."

"You can thank your friend for that."

"I would love to thank him with my fist right now," I assured her.

For the first time a smile lit her face. It suited her. I had a strange feeling that we were being drawn together. So far she did not move her eyes. I used this chance and continued: "I don't believe that you don't have a heart."

"In my business there is no place for heart."

"Not even place for conscience? You do not want to destroy three poor souls, do you?"

"God, what will I do with you?" she sighed.

"That's simple." A plan struck me. "First you will join me for dinner."

"Dinner?" Surprise lit her face.

"Yes, I am inviting you. And look, I am buying this coat," I pointed to the coat over Anna's arm, "I will pay for those blades. I am an old customer here, so you could make an exception. I will be grateful until my death and maybe even after." I took my visiting card out of my breast pocket: "I hope I am not impudent. Please call me, if you accept my dinner invitation. I would be grateful to hear from you."

"So grateful to death, you said, eh?" She was amused.

"My gratitude has no limits."

Finally she took my card and I received the stolen items in exchange. "Thanks a lot," I said. "You really saved three souls."

"I hope the dinner will be worth my services." She smiled. "Wine included?"

"Whatever you wish, even heavenly ambrosia. Could I wait for you after work?"

"No, I have other plans. But tomorrow I am free at eight."

"Excellent. See you tomorrow." I shook her hand. Her handshake was surprisingly strong. "Thanks again." She turned away and I watched her slim figure with delight. They say: everything bad contains five percent good and five percent fun. It sure seemed that way this time. My five percent of goodness disappeared between shelves of merchandise.

I turned back to my guests. Anna was angry, she must hate her husband now. Eman was not redfaced anymore. His eyes fluttered around.

"Here are your stolen goods, you robber." I handed him both items. He looked at me with surprise, mouth open, but without much spirit.

"No police?" Finally he managed to form a question. "How did you arrange this?"

"You know about my charm," I boasted. "It will cost me a dinner tomorrow."

"You got a date? Really?" He came back to life fast: "She is one great looking lady. So you will cash in on my stupidity."

"I will lose at least a hundred bucks. And you should be grateful for her soft spot. How could you steal in the store? Here it is punished almost as severely as murder, because it is the matter of omnipotent dollars. You would rot in jail. I had no idea how stupid you can be."

"I really cannot explain what came over me," Eman stammered.

"Let's thank God for this end," I said and started to walk to the cashier services.

Late that afternoon when Anna was busy with supper preparation, Eman went for a walk – to air his head after that depressing day. I did not waste any time. I entered their bedroom. Eman's big suitcase was in the corner; I opened it. There I found more of Eman's loot: many blades, a box of screws and a cheap digital watch with a price tag of three dollars.

So our little thief was busy. It was surprising that he was not caught earlier. But why did he have to steal that? I would have bought these things for him. Maybe he was ashamed to ask for more. I already had bought him a radio, clothing and some tools for his workshop.

There is a motto back home: When you do not steal from the state, you steal from your family. People followed that motto, they believed it. Prices were high, and there was never enough merchandise available, so the black market flourished. There was another rule people followed: I scratch your back, you scratch mine.

A person who started cottage construction as Eman did was in a desperate need of building materials, concrete, brick, lumber. Market supply was poor, so the merry-go-round started: Mr. X had concrete, but was in need of new tires for his car. Our cottage builder has a relative in the car supply business, he got the tires after a certain fee was given to the relative and then he got the needed concrete. Of course the owner of the concrete had stolen it originally, or purchased it on the black market himself.

Eman was a real master in that 'exchange economy.' He could get anything he needed. But poor individuals unable to steal and without connections had nothing, bare minimum. I was one of those.

I closed the suitcase and decided not to mention my knowledge. After supper we sat in the living room as usual, but our conversation was awkward. Anna was angry with Eman and I was preoccupied with tomorrow's date.

After a few shots of whiskey Eman for the first time that evening opened the conversation: "You are cross with me, aren't you? I really am an old idiot. You should slap me, I earned it."

"I know you earned it, but it all ended well, so forget about it." I raised my glass and drank with him.

"Thanks, you are a good friend," and Eman poured himself another whiskey. In less than an hour he was drunk, but it did not stop him from babbling: "Oh, boy, what an idiot . . . ain't that the truth . . . but I have accomplished more than anybody else back home . . . I have more . . . I did not do it just for myself, but for her and for the kids. . . ." He pointed at his frowning wife. "No gratitude . . . everybody just takes and takes from you . . . just do more, Eman . . . you old fool . . . Not one thanks you ever . . . not a shit, pal. . . . " He wiped his eyes and went on: "I should have gone with you that time . . . we could have lived like kings by now. . . ." He whispered: "All my efforts were for nothing . . ." and then his head dropped and he was asleep.

With Anna's help I got him to bed.

"Drunkard," she murmured, "stupid drunkard. I sure have a life with him."

"Hold your horses, he just had one too many." I tried to calm her down. I felt sorry for Eman.

Lying in my bed, I went though the day's events, ending with my date. Thanks to the drinks my fantasy worked overtime, brought scenes of life with the new lady. . . . Almost asleep I heard my bedroom door squeak. I could see a silhouette in the door frame. It was Anna. She came nearer and stooped above me: "Are you awake?" She threw off her housecoat. She was still bending over me. All I could see were her breasts, two balloons. Then her soft body was all over me.

"I feel so alone," she whispered.

I was squeezed down like a big ant and as soon as I could shake off the surprise, I muffled my shout: "Are you crazy? Eman is next door."

"Not even a shotgun can wake him up. When he is drunk, he sleeps like a corpse. I hate him. . . . You were so different." She hugged me with great power. Her lips found mine.

I didn't even know how she managed to get me on top of her, but Anna was an experienced lover. Thanks to mother nature, the whiskey, and my long celibacy, I could not refuse this body any longer. In spite of the darkness I saw her shining eyes and the whiteness of her skin. She had the softness of a mossy carpet. The waves of her were moving faster in a plan to absorb me totally, and suddenly that white carpet became an earthquake, and my body went along with tremors of harmony. We were two rivals: she tried to swallow me and I tried to fulfill her. My cool common sense flew away like a *colibri* out of my skull. I was left with the eternal instinct of a man and a woman as two parts of a circle, united for a brief moment. Suddenly the storm was over then, all was quiet, my brain returned to the cage of my skull, and the circle disconnected.

Anna was still hugging me, her bosom moving in the rhythm of a runner. My lean chest had sunken into her enormous breast. She whispered how beautiful it was, that she would love to be with me forever. Maybe she believed it herself, maybe that was her way of thanking me for our eight weeks together.

I did not feel any gratitude. I was empty as a barrel. I had betrayed my friend.

"You know, it was totally different with you," Anna said. I did not believe her. The basic and most important feeling of love was missing. It must be easier for Anna, I reasoned. She wanted it, it was a way of revenge towards her husband. Could it be the result of long years of marriage and boredom? Or was Eman too good to her, that he appeared weak in her eyes?

I could not find the answer, but I was glad to be single. . . . My body raised and I broke her embrace.

"You should go, Eman could wake up any time."

"Can we stay together for a while?" She tried to get me back into her arms.

"Be reasonable, Anna. You are forgetting, I am not twenty any more." She released me with a deep sigh. I helped her to get up, her body shining with perspiration. I had never had such a strong woman . . . when she bent down to pick up her housecoat, everything on her moved. She gave me a short kiss and said: "I would like to come again."

I did not answer her. When she disappeared, I went back to bed. I fell asleep and did not suffer any bad dreams.

The freshness of the morning woke me. Breakfast was waiting in the kitchen. Eman was feeding himself diligently. He greeted me with a full mouth: "Did you dream about that fine lady who caught me stealing yesterday?"

I looked steadily into his eyes. No, he was not suspicious. To my surprise I did not feel guilty about the evening with Anna.

Anna gave me a radiant smile. "Sit down, breakfast is getting cold." She looked well, as if she had gotten younger overnight. She was kind even to her husband.

When Eman left the kitchen, Anna did not say a word about last night, only her eyes gave away our secret. I was glad that it all went so well.

My day was centered around preparations for the evening. From the darkest corner of my closet I took out my best suit, gave it a good brushing and went downstairs to iron it.

Anna stopped me and said with a tone of sarcasm: "This looks like wedding preparations."

"Maybe a funeral," I answered.

"Let me do the ironing, bring the shirt too."

The coming evening found me as nervous as a teenager before his first date.

I drove to the mall and waited at the entrance with flowers behind my back. The lady I was expecting came out of the building wearing a modern coat and a matching hat. She did not look like a strict watch dog. She recognized me and we said our greetings like old friends. I gave her the bouquet.

"How nice of you." She thanked me with her warm green eyes.

After dinner in a good restaurant we drank wine and enjoyed a long conversation. It seemed as if we had known each other for a long time. I disclosed a lot about myself and she let me peek into her life story. Suzanne was a widow. Her husband died five years ago of lung cancer. She had a sufficient pension, but to get out of boredom and to make some extra money, she got the job in the store. She had one grown-up son, married, living in Vancouver. She sold her house and lived in an apartment because it was convenient and economical; she could also travel.

Two hours together flew like half an hour. I paid the bill and took Suzanne home, I stopped the car in front of her high rise and while I searched for words to invite her to a second date, she surprised me: "Would you like to have a cup of coffee?"

There was no need to persuade me. I would not dream of such an invitation on the first date, but she was from the younger generation, eighteen years younger.

I parked my car, and we took the elevator to the top floor. I played my role of a gentleman and helped Suzanne out of her coat.

"Thanks. So this is where I live." Her arms circled the space decorated with modern furniture and a couple of pictures on the walls. The huge bookcases attracted my attention.

"You like reading, too?" she asked.

"That's my passion," I admitted. "Your home is really nice, quite different from mine."

"Of course, every person is different." She took a vase out of the cupboard and put the flowers in it. "Please, make yourself at home, I'll bring some refreshments."

I sank into one of the living room chairs. She returned unexpectedly soon, as if she had everything prepared ahead of time. A bottle of wine instead of coffee was crowning the middle of the tray.

The time was flying, the wine disappearing and I could not remember the last time I was in such an excellent mood. I guess it proves again that it takes two to make a person feel complete.

Suzanne's youth was disclosed with the help of photograph-filled albums. She talked about her tragic marriage and about her son. In turn she learned about my fate. This two-way confession helped us take the load from each other. We felt closer.

At midnight I said, "Where did the evening go? You should throw me out, otherwise I will sit here until morning."

"Don't worry, if I thought you were boring, I would have sent you home a long time ago." She squeezed my hand, and it sent shivers through my body. But I did not know what to do next. I left the decision up to my hostess.

"Actually I can't let you leave after drinking all that wine. I don't want you on my conscience."

I was about to suggest calling a taxi, but I did not say a word.

"You will stay overnight, simple as that," and with her eyes gazing into mine, she continued: "I don't think we have to cover up our feelings. Correct me, if I'm wrong."

I shook my head. She was not wrong at all.

"I will take a shower first." She stood up. Still holding my hand, she made me get up too.

Motionless, I felt stupid, not knowing what to do. She had an amused expression on her face, like a puppeteer controlling the leading strings. She pulled me towards her and we kissed for the first time.

Sitting in the armchair, I listened to the rush of water, I felt overwhelmed by the speed of what was happening. I did not expect our relationship to go this fast.

Suzanne came out of the bathroom wrapped in a see-through nightgown and handed me a bathrobe. "From my husband's wardrobe, but it was never worn."

Obediently, I took the robe and went to take a shower. Clean and refreshed I went straight to the bedroom, which was poorly lit by one lamp, but I could recognize every item around, including the queen size bed, with Suzanne as the real queen dressed in Eve's clothing, slim, well shaped. I thought that Anna's body would take double the space here.

"You are so beautiful." I greeted her with outstreched arms, they accepted me as a long awaited friend.

Suzanne had waited a long time for a man; I did not dare ask how long.

She reminded me of all my three previous loves, my three countrywomen. She combined the features of all three: a hungry passion, joyful cuddliness, and a certain calculated self-interest. She was also incredibly understanding; I felt happy in her presence.

How entirely different from the night with Anna. Here we had the big chance to fall into the nice slavery called love. With Suzanne, I felt like the writer just starting the introduction to a successful novel. It must have been early morning when we fell asleep, our bodies joined like Siamese twins.

I woke up weak, disoriented. My hand searched next to me for proof that it was not a dream, but Suzanne was not there. I opened my eyes. The strong morning light hurt. I closed them again. A laugh from above me made me sit up.

Suzanne stood by the bed fully dressed. I could smell her perfume.

"Did you have nice dreams?"

"So far I can't tell what's real and what was a dream." I touched her lips: "But you are real, not a phantom, so I couldn't have dreamt it." I suppressed the urge to yawn.

"Breakfast is served. I have to run."

"Wait, I will drive you," and I left the comfort of the bed.

"I have my car," she assured me. "When will we see each other again? Tonight at eight?"

"I can't, I have to drive to Toronto airport, my visitors are leaving. I will be back late."

"Fine, tomorrow, then." She kissed me and looked at her wristwatch: "I really have to go. Enjoy your breakfast," and she departed. I watched her with envy. How is it, that women are so fresh after a night of loving?

I dressed fast, had a hot breakfast, cheese-ham rolls and coffee, and I left her apartment. What can my guests be thinking? Gone all night. . . .

I could hear noise from the kitchen. It was Anna's racket with the dishes. Her greeting said it all: "You were with her all night?"

"Of course." How dare she judge me. "Do you mind?"

She shook her head, and I saw the moisture raising in her eyes; it softened my tone: "Look, Anna, you have Eman."

"I . . . I don't think I love him. Sometimes I can't stand him." She wiped her eyes.

"That happens to all of us. Sometimes I can't stand myself, I hate my guts, but that passes and I forgive myself, and all is right again." I touched her arm: "That's the law of common life, one has to learn to forget and forgive. Without that we would die from anger and hatred. You would not like to get wrinkled before your time, would you?" I patted her on the cheek. "Eman is a good man despite his faults. Just remember how much he has done for you. It will be all right again between you two."

She gazed at me, her eyes moist again. She nodded like a doll with a weak battery.

"Where is Eman?"

"I am coming," his voice shouted from the bedroom. He burst into the kitchen: "Lord, our Romeo has returned. Did you have a great time?" Eman shouted with joy as if it was he who spent the night with a nice girl. "I just finished packing. You will be free again. What a relief."

"Don't be silly, pal. I was glad to have you."

"I should be packing too." Anna left.

"So tell me everything," Eman poked my ribs as an anxious accomplice.

"What is there to tell? I spent the night with a woman."

"With a gorgeous woman," Eman stressed. "Will there be more nights like this one?"

"I hope so."

"Isn't life interesting?" he continued. "Two days ago I almost pulled my hair out in despair because of my stupidity, that I got caught stealing, and today I could dance with joy, because I'm leaving you the most promising legacy in the form of a beautiful lady. So keep it alive and think of me everytime you are with her."

"Not only will I remember you, but I will do it once for me, and once for you. Satisfied?"

"Heavenly!" His laugh went out of control.

He was right. I would not have met Suzanne without his shoplifting . . .

At five o'clock in the afternoon, we were at the airport. We looked into each other's misty eyes; that look contained all our years together, our youth, memories, all compacted, similar to the amount of information jammed into a computer disk.

"You have to come for a visit soon," Eman begged. "Ice is melting, spring is in the air, and communism is dying of consumption. You don't have to fear jail any more."

"I am sure we will see each other soon, maybe next spring." I was serious with this sudden plan. "You have to promise me to stop killing yourself with overeating," I poked my finger into his belly. "You might get a stroke and be gone before your time."

"I get your message, I will go on a diet."

The flight to Prague was called. We shared our last hugs.

"Have a good life, my old buddy," Eman's powerful arms squeezed me and took the air out of me.

"You, too, and stop crying. I will come as soon as possible."

Eman wiped his eyes and blew his nose.

I turned to Anna and shook her hand. "Anna, it was nice to have you. And take care of your hubby, so we can see each other in good health."

"I will try. So long." She kissed me.

I watched them leave, their heavy luggage reminding me of Egyptian slaves carrying stones to the pyramids. Last turn and waves. I watched them through a thick fog. I lifted my hand and wiped the fog away.

After two months I was alone again, the stirred waters of my life once again calm. Well, not quite. Eman's legacy, Suzanne would, I hoped, keep things stirring.

I returned to my car and watched the huge birds roaring in the horizon. They brought back memories of war, air-raids, bombing . . .

It occurred to me, that there are also air-raids now, air-raids of our excessive civilization, which could destroy us in the future . . . The knowledge that neither of us would be here to witness it, calmed me down.

Lorraine Duggin

THE LEGEND OF LIBUŠE

for Zdena Libuše Bodlak Jansky, my mother

When Dad blacked out
from a stroke they thought
a heart attack
on the restaurant floor
on their forty-fourth,
she rode the ambulance
home, scrubbed by hand
his soiled underclothes.

As a girl I used to
dread that mixture, stink
of fat and lye, admired
her deftness though
of hand on sharpened
butcher knife slicing
bricks of laundry
soap she'd made.

How the old Maytag
used to waddle round
the basement's concrete floor
on washdays. She'd poke
with bamboo pole and stick;
in my small hands, I'd catch
squeegeed layers of clothing,
towels, sheets dropped
into sudsy galvanized tubs
through wringer's rolls.

Oh, Libuše, the name
some cruel irony or joke.
Founding queen of the Czech nation,
once-honored, beautiful
maiden, like a step-sister
whose foot the slipper
didn't fit, bumped from
rightful throne to scullery
by a race of men
more certain of her place.

FOR MY MOTHER, WHO LIVES

We come from a long line
of ancestors who didn't survive,
thought suicide more satisfying
than miserable lives
that threatened their destinies.
Dedicek waited till eighty-five,
put the knife to his throat.
When angina didn't improve,
Uncle Tony took the noose.

Cather's Mr. Shimerda, another
pioneer Bohemian deprived
of violins in the concert hall,
saw one other avenue, like
many refined, cultured folk
defying life on the surface
the only way they knew. Too
used to beauty, legacy of books,
music, fine architectural lines,
the golden, ancient city
of Mozart, home of the oldest
universities, Don Giovanni's
debut, despite long reigns
of oppressive rule,

how could they live now,
crude peasants, where soil
blew away like a house
of sand with the first gust
of wind, where ships filled
with immigrants spilled
onto prairie seas of wild
Nebraska grass without rock
for anchor, without roots?

Even today my daughter
studies accounts in the news,
numerous teen-age suicides.
Hopeless kids, sick with addiction,
no sense of family, nation,
pride, says she can sympathize.
In school they read "Paul's Case,"
see him a hero, identify,
believe his dying justified.

I wonder at the sins of the fathers,
heritage, history we pass on,
remember Mother's veiled asides,
defeated sighs, Dad's revolver
in her bedside dresser drawer
atop a pile of crocheted
handkerchiefs she'd made,
my brother's illness at one
of its heights of violent pain.

I remember coming into the bedroom
late at night, terrified, my
brother's cries momentarily
subsiding. I'd lie silently
on the rose-edged pillowcase,
my body a living blockade
separating them from the drawer,
the gun inside, trying to remind
my mother of one thing I knew
with a child's quiet certainty,
making sure, too, she wouldn't
reach a despairing hand across me,
not that night, anyway.

Ronald J. Rindo

CYCLONE EDDIE KING

I WAS SITTING at the office last week trying to decide whether to bet the Lakers and take the points or whether to give the points and bet Detroit, and my editor comes in and says he wants a feature on Eddie King for next week's paper. Says call the coaches, the doctors, his girlfriends if you have to, but get that story. I'll give you a week, he says. And don't spill any beer on it.

Better if he'd asked for a short piece on the Resurrection. To begin with, I'm not much of a sportswriter. It's a dead end job in a little high school town wilting in the shadow of Chicago, where all the blue chippers live. It's just a weekly paper called the *South Suburban Star*, with more grocery store ads than articles if you want to know the truth. But I go to the high school ballgames, the track meets, the catered awards banquets, and I type up boring little blurbs about how so-and-so placed fourth in the mile, and so-and-so scored 15 points in the game, and so-and-so was voted most improved by his teammates. Get all the kids' names in, my editor says. And spell them right for Chrissake. Don't need any angry mothers throwing curlers at me in the grocery store because you spelled Schichowski with a y.

But it could be worse. People know me. I walk up in the bleachers, kids look at me. The men shake my hand. Women point and whisper. And every once in a while, I get to watch something special – a conference championship, a state record. No goddamn Superbowl, I'll grant you. But it gives you a good feeling, makes you happy to be alive in a way. Then there's kids you see once in a lifetime – like Eddie King – with a beauty you can't completely describe, the kind of kid who takes the body to a new standard and drags the rest of us with him, like Mozart in music, or a young Bobby Fischer in chess. It's something mysterious and magical. And when that magic fails, everyone wants an explanation. But believe me, no one can tell *this* story.

You see, Cyclone Eddie King is like quicksilver on a wet rock. He's like stocking feet on a polished wooden floor. I mean he's smooth as a cheerleader's thighs – got a little wink and piano key smile that could charm the black dress right off of a widow. Everybody who knows him knows it too, which is what makes this story such trouble.

Used to be, Eddie was an extraordinary athlete. I'm talking Division I, professional caliber. Had muscles that would make a racehorse cry – could run like the goddamn wind, this kid. I saw him in junior high coming up, a nice looking kid, a big kid, a little cocky maybe. Already had hamstrings so thick and shiny they looked like black earth turned over by a plow. Put a football under his arm and it was like nothing you'd ever seen. In high school, the kid gained 300 yards a game. Could run 100 yards in something like 9.2 seconds, and, get this: could dunk a fricking basketball with his little brother hanging on his back.

I saw that one myself. Drove by the playground one Sunday afternoon and they're all out there shooting in the rain, no net, the rim all rusted, paint peeling off the blackboard. Eddie, he was a junior then, he starts dunking – reversers, 360s, triple pumps, putting on a goddamn show, and pretty soon he's got his little brother – must be seven or eight – up on his back, arms wrapped around his throat, ankles locked across his belly. Eddie, he starts out where the free throw line should be, bounces the ball twice on the concrete and takes off (little brother holding on for dear life, eyes bulging like ripe fruit). Up, up, up he goes, basketball double-handed, cocked behind his head, his forearms shining like a couple of eggplants, and slam! he tomahawks the ball through the rim. Had no respect for gravity, this kid. And I thought then: Legs like that in his mama's womb, the poor woman must still have bruises.

Eddie's high school career was glorious. I don't think I missed a game. Even the *Tribune* sent a guy out regularly to see the Cyclone. And Eddie, before it was through, he was the most famous kid in town – folks had my news clips and photos taped to the glass doors of grocery stores, on the wall of the barber shop, even on the bulletin board of the dentist's office. Eddie's legs and my words, we were a good combination. But the best part of it was, this was just a kid playing for fun and doing things the rest of us could only dream about. I mean, one time I'm on the sidelines with a press pass looped around my neck, and Eddie goes flying by, loose turf spraying up behind his cleats, opposing tacklers trying to break his neck, and he winks at me and gives me a thumbs up. Effortless. The best picture I ever took, won some little award if you want to know the truth, shows Eddie leaping over a pile of tacklers at the five yard line, his knee pads clear over everyone's goddamn helmets, his thick arms covering the ball, and a wide smile stretched across his face.

His senior year, as you can well imagine, the kid's got college recruiters sleeping on his porch and climbing down his goddamn chimney. I mean, they're flying in like locusts from all over the country. Eddie says he wants to go south someplace where it's warm, keep his hamstrings soft and flexible. Chooses Alabama – wants to be a tidal wave in the Crimson Tide. Turns out, though, that his grades aren't too hot. One recruiter from California says to me, if Eddie's gradepoint average was an earthquake, it wouldn't even show up on the Richter Scale.

From there things only get worse. In the fall Eddie goes to some junior college in Missouri so he can pull his grades up high enough for big time ball. By then, already, he's fighting for his life. People are beginning to talk about how here was just another black kid who let it all slip away, who had the world by the ass but couldn't hold on.

The big news come in about Christmas time: The Cyclone has dropped out of school. Rumors flying. One guys says Eddie opened a book and couldn't read a line. Another says he knocked up two coeds, rich white girls from out East someplace, and was facing double paternity. Somebody else says cocaine.

But it was all nonsense, every bit of it. Eddie comes home Christmas Eve, plane lands at O'Hare in the snow, and when Eddie comes out of the tunnel he's wearing his blue high school letterjacket, and he's sitting like Buddha in a silver wheelchair. Paralyzed. I says to myself, Oh Lord, now what the hell you done?

* * *

As for me, I never had an ounce of ability athletic-wise. Bowl a few frames here and there, play some softball and a little poker, but that's about where it stops. Got a bit of a pot hanging over my belt buckle, smoke and drink too much, got an ex-wife who thinks her sole purpose in life is to keep my blood pressure in the danger zone. Spend half my time sitting in the dark. There's a group of regulars who hang out at Barney's Tap on Orchard Street, across from the high school, call ourselves the weight lifters. We must have lifted a hundred semi-trucks of Budweiser in our life, twelve ounces at a time. That's our claim to goddamn fame.

There's four of us most of the time. Barney – he owns the place and lives upstairs – calls us the four quarters, because he says sometimes it takes all four of us together to come up with a buck. After me there's Marvin Harris, who chews cigars and bets the Bears like a madman, and Johnny Drake, at thirty-seven the youngest of us, a garbage man. Kid pulls in a good buck, but he smells like rotten vegetables all the time and hasn't saved a penny in his life. Next is Hal Wisniewski, who became a born-again Christian after he found out he had diabetes and his legs were going cold. He's a drunk like the rest of us, but a holy drunk. He doesn't get along too good sometimes with Marvin, who will blaspheme the Mother of God if it will help the Bears beat the point spread.

Anyways, Christmas Day it's the four of us and Barney, about three o'clock, watching a college ballgame. Someone, Johnny I believe, comes in with a gallon of eggnog, and Hal's wearing a cross about as big as a goddamn dinner plate. But we're enjoying ourselves, getting by, feeling good. Then the door pops open, the sunshine cutting through, burning our eyes, ice-cold wind whistling, and in rolls Cyclone Eddie King. He's got a two-piece pool cue tucked under his arm, biceps bulging out of his coat like footballs, one of those skinny cigars between his teeth. The glare off the chrome spokes of his wheels spins across the ceiling like a mirror ball at a wedding dance.

When the door slams closed, I can see just the shadow of him roll slowly to the billiards table, the tip of his cigar glowing orange like a sunset. Barney reaches behind the bar and flicks on the house lights above the table, and the green felt glows – just like a ballfield, I'm thinking. Eddie racks up the balls, screws his stick together, and lines himself up behind the cue ball. He draws the stick back even and slow, blows out two lungs full of smoke, and crack! he lets it go. On the break it sounds like the cue ball's been split by lightning, and there's balls scattered all over the table, a few in the pockets, a couple more bouncing across the cold tile floor.

Jesus Christ, says Marvin, it's like he hit them with a sledgehammer.

I toss some change on the bar and bring Eddie a cold one, setting it on a small table beside him. He winks and smiles, then turns back to his game. Plays all afternoon and into the evening, me just sitting there, watching, drinking one beer after another. I couldn't believe it. Here's a comet fallen from the sky, I says to myself, and he rolls into Barney's to drink with us river rocks. Christmas goddamn Day.

Around closing time, it gets too much for me. I says, Eddie, what was it, a linebacker cheap-shot you? Spear you in the back after the whistle?

He looks at me but doesn't answer. The irises of his eyes are black and as large as dimes.

I says, Then you were up in the fricking clouds with a basketball cocked behind your head, and when you come down from the stratosphere, a little white guard from Indiana undercut you?

He looks down and takes his cue stick apart, rolling it in his hands so that the small muscles in his wrists twitch under his shiny skin.

Then Eddie, I says, what could it be? I mean, Jesus kid, you got a raw deal. You could goddamn *fly*.

He doesn't say anything, doesn't even nod or shake his head. And I don't notice it right away, but now he's got the cue ball in his right hand, and he's squeezing that ball so hard the veins on the back of his hand are bulging, thick as nightcrawlers. And it may be my imagination, but when he rolls the ball back across the table, it doesn't roll true but wobbles a bit, like an egg would. Then he looks down one leg, tracing the crease in his pants with his eyes all the way down to his ankle. He's wearing leather high tops, unlaced, and when he takes a breath, drawing the wind in through his nose, the muscles in his thighs seem to swell like they're filling with air. He exhales and winks at me, then rolls toward the door.

I have a feeling then that I need to know something I don't want to find out.

※ ※ ※

Driving into the black neighborhoods was never something that bothered me much. Lots of kids know me there, see me parked at the curb by the playgrounds in the summer, watching the pickup games, drinking beer. Eddie lives with his mama in a small bungalow near the railroad tracks. It's a house with an open porch in front, clapboard siding, gray paint peeling everywhere. The porch steps are weathered and rotted, snow drifted across them, one small set of footprints punched down the middle.

Eddie's mama smiles when she sees it's me at the door. The house is bright but sparsely furnished, with colorful afghans thrown over the chairs and couch. A wooden crucifix hangs on one white wall, surrounded by framed pictures of Eddie and his brother. A small television sits on a wheeled stand under one window, Eddie's little brother in a chair watching it, watching *Oprah*. The tile floor is a checkerboard design, gray and white. Eddie's wheelchair sits empty by the door.

Eddie's little brother sees me and says, You comin' to write about Cyclone?

Hush child, his mama says. But I nod.

It's Jesus, the boy says. Jesus don't want him to run no more. Preacher says. Don't want him walkin' neither. Wants—

I hear a muffled slapping behind me, through an open doorway into the kitchen. It's a quiet noise, getting louder. Eddie's shadow comes first, then the head, those hands and shoulders, the wide, wide back, and those legs, wrapped in a blue blanket to the waist, sliding across the floor.

—Wants him crawling, the boys says, in a whisper.

Eddie sees me, pushes himself up on his hands and drags his legs behind him into the room. It takes him almost a minute to move twelve feet. Then he rolls to his back and pushes himself up against the couch, keeping his elbows sunk into the cushion behind him. The blanket pinned around his legs is covered with dust and dirt.

I clean these floors, his mama says. It don't seem to do no good. She looks at me imploringly.

You have a beautiful home, I tell her, but I'm looking at Eddie's legs. She says, Lookit what Jesus done to my boy.

Eddie stares up at me and smiles, and right then I'm feeling everything go wrong. I can feel the spiral binding of my notebook in my shirt pocket pressing the pen against my chest, but it's as if my own arms are paralyzed. I can look a kid in the eye and ask, How's it feel to be a conference champ? or, Is 51.2 your personal best in the 400 meters? But I can't do this. What do I want to know? I'm thinking. What am I going to say? I thought I saw your legs move? Are you really paralyzed? Who am I to do that? If I find out, I've got to carry it around, have to write it all down, and I can't do that. Editor would run the story on a page backed by grocery coupons printed in red and green like sheets of money, and people like me, who get winded climbing the goddamn stairs, would cut it up into dollar-sized pieces to save a few bucks on their grocery bill. What's that worth?

So I stand there, just staring at those legs wrapped in a blue cotton blanket.

Don't feel so bad, Eddie's mama says. You ain't alone. Everybody come by, want to know what happen. Natural thing. My heart's already broken, bleedin' into my chest, and they come by sayin' here Mrs. King, bleed some more. Tell us how you're feelin', havin' your Eddie crawl on the floor like a baby.

I'm sorry, I tell her.

Oh, I understand it, she says. If it happen on the field, people would leave us alone. They could watch it on the TV in slow motion. Doctors could explain it, then. Seem to me it's a miracle we walkin' at all, any of us. It's the bad news that make us start wonderin'.

So it wasn't an accident? This is what I'm thinking, but the woman reads my mind.

Nobody knows what it was, she says. Eddie just call me up one day cryin', sayin', Mama, I can't walk no more. I told him, Baby, come on home.

Driving home, I stop for a six pack and drive by Eddie's playground, which is empty and covered with snow. The dirty shred of a tattered net is hanging from one of the rusty hoops, and I can see Eddie's face in it, framed in a frightened, mute, conspiratorial smile.

In the *Star* we run just a little blurb on the Cyclone, a celebration of his high school accomplishments mostly, with a picture, and then a somber note on his paralysis without much explanation. We finish with the announcement that an anonymous donor in town has established a fund for Eddie's family at Lincoln Savings and Loan, and we run the address so people can contribute. We passed a mug at Barney's to get it started. Got seventeen dollars, ten of it from Barney's till.

* * *

In two or three weeks, Eddie becomes Houdini with a pool cue, starts to hustle a buck here and there from guys wanting to come in and see the Cyclone. Marvin thinks Eddie found some trouble with the wrong kind of people, drugs maybe, crack or something, and caught a bullet. Johnny says it could have been a freak accident, something he's embarassed about, fell off his bed and landed on a beer bottle, something like that. You read about those things, you know. He says you have a spinal cord that runs like a piano wire from your brain down to the tip of your tailbone, and if you snip it, your legs just go dead. You push the key but there isn't any sound. Hal believes it's God's will.

Marvin says to me, What do you think, superfan?

I don't know, I says. I just don't know. All I know is when a racehorse loses his legs, they put him out of his misery.

The whole thing though, Marvin says, is that Eddie don't seem so miserable a lot of the time. The college insurance has picked up the slack. He's got a shiny new van with hand controls. He can park right at the front door at restaurants and shopping centers. Hell, even Barney lets him use the driveway when he comes here.

Then Johnny says, That's right. And you know he's wearing pretty fancy clothes, a leather jacket, gold chains. You don't see us wearing that kind of money.

What, I says. I'm angry now and they can feel it. What you think? You think he's goddamn faking it? Is that it? A black kid on food stamps buying steaks when you're frying hamburger?

Easy, easy, says Marvin. No one said nothing about that. It's just that he ain't so bad off, you know, all things considered.

All things considered, I says, you should be in the goddamn wheelchair. All your legs are good for is hanging like ballast off a bar stool.

Christ, would you cool off, Johnny says. None of us are happy about this.

We all wanted to see him in the pros, Hal says.

Yeah, yeah, yeah, I says. I know. I know.

* * *

Soon springtime comes and the snow starts melting, and the kids start coming out. Across from my place there's a small park, and it's like the kids sprout from the asphalt when the snow's gone. Inside a tall fence there's a basketball court, cracked blacktop. Poles on each end with steel backboards, red rims, and no nets. Kids'll bring their own nets, sit on tall shoulders to put them on, and take them down when they're through. They make a net last half the year that way. Soon as February sometimes they're out there in high-tops they got for Christmas, dribbling through the puddles, blowing on their hands, laughing, going three-on-three, five-on-five.

In March, I'm thinking maybe Eddie can get into one of those wheelchair leagues, you know, with Vietnam Vets and others like that. I tried it once, some benefit the newspaper got in on, for publicity. It isn't easy, I'll tell you that. I spun around in one place mostly, like a man with his boot nailed to the floor. These other guys, huge arms, hairy chests heaving under their jerseys, their legs shriveled and strapped together, they roll up and down the court so fast it's like the real thing. It would only take Eddie a few hours and he'd be great at it. All he does is drink and shoot pool. No one asks for autographs any more. Newspaper clippings up on the wall behind the pool table, including the headline where I gave him his nickname – "Cyclone Twists For Record 423 Yards " – are yellowed from all the smoke, and to tell the truth by now I don't like going in there too much. But I got nothing better to do.

Then one afternoon, a Sunday it was, week or two after Easter, we're all of us sitting along the rail, drinking beer, watching the NBA playoffs on television. Eddie, as usual, is at the billiards table in his wheelchair, practicing trick shots, shooting with his cue behind his neck, making three balls at once, things like that. There's a few guys watching him, sucking on celery that they're dipping into their Bloody Marys.

This strange guy comes in out of the sunshine, lets the door slam behind him and sits down at the the end of the bar. Barney gives him a beer, and the fellow sips it a little bit, nervously, like it's his first one or something. But he's about forty I'd say, with a mustache, nice hair. He's wearing a blue suit that's a bit too big for him, but he's a nice looking guy really, just different.

So, says Marvin, where you from?

When Eddie was a franchise player, strangers were constantly stopping in at Barney's to pump the locals for information, something that might give them a recruiting edge. They'd ask us questions – What does Eddie's mother do? Does she date anybody? Does Eddie have a girlfriend? Do they have family in such-and-such a state? We never told them much but always made sure to meet them, find out what university they were from.

This guy, he stands up, walks over to Marvin and extends his hand. When he speaks, he's got a little bit of a drawl. I come, he says, from the house of the Lord.

Hal, he perks up a little, thinks he can finally share his testimony with someone who'll listen. Marvin rolls his eyes at us and says, Came all that way, did you?

It's not an earthly place, my friend. It's the home of the spirit, a sanctuary for the soul.

Jesus Christ, says Marvin, a holy lunatic.

Are you born again? Hal asks.

Through Jesus we are all born again, he says, and then he rattles off some long quotation from the Bible. I didn't have my pad with me, so I didn't get it down. But I could have. After a game, in the locker room, high school coaches go on and on, and I scribble it all down pretty much as they say it and get it in the paper. Sometimes they'll call me later to change something, or they'll ask me to make up something positive, a great learning experience for our ball club, we showed a lot of poise out there, something like that.

I didn't notice it right away, but this guy has a briefcase with him, and he lifts it onto the bar and fumbles with the latches. I've seen his kind before at O'Hare, selling religious books. Once I had one of those Hare Krishnas, bald as a beer mug, trying to sell me some crazy holy book with a paisley cover. Those Krishnas, they shake your hand and stare right through you. You're running to catch a plane, and they stop you and it's hypnotic in a way. I gave him five bucks and told him to keep the goddamn book and stop making his mother ashamed of him.

This guy can't get his briefcase open, but Hal shuffles over with his cane – his diabetes is bad by now – and helps him. He's got his pocketknife out, digging at one of the latches.

I've come to show you something that is literally one of its kind, the stranger says. It's all I have. It feeds me and clothes me and renews my soul.

There you go! Hal says, snapping the briefcase open.

The man raises the top and shuffles around inside with his hand. There are papers inside, and some loose dollar bills, but he pulls out this little glass case, about as big as a deck of cards, and he cups it in his hands gently, like he's holding water.

This, he says, is an artifact of the miracle of the ages.

He's got us curious, and I know that's the way these guys work. We're all of us leaning towards him, moving in that direction.

Marvin, who's sitting closest, says, It's a piece of Kirk Gibson's bat from the World Series. The one he homered with. Cost me fifty bucks.

But Hal, who's basically a shy guy, drops to his knees. I mean, here's a guy who has made his life a study in being inconspicuous, and he makes this dramatic gesture, falling right to the floor. It's like he's praying, and his chin is level with the seat of a bar stool.

The Holy Cross, he says. It's a piece of the Cross.

And it's like he feels this power, this divine weight pressing him to his knees. And the man doesn't even have to say anything and Hal is reaching for his wallet. It's brown and cracked along the creases, and he opens it with his thumb and just pulls out several bills – could have been tens or twenties because he didn't even look, but they're all singles as far as I can tell. He puts them on the bar. Marvin slides one across to Barney with his glass and says, Barney, give me a refill.

What is it? Johnny asks. What is it really?

Jesus, Marvin says, annoyed, it's a hunk of wood, a pencil shaving or something.

It is the Cross, the man says. A branch of the tree where they hung our Lord.

This kind of talk makes Marvin uneasy, so he heads for the bathroom. Then Johnny looks closer, and I'm next to him. It's a little piece of wood, kind of gray and weathered, but you can't see the grain. It's only about an inch long and maybe a half-inch wide. All you can hear now is the television – the announcer's voice, sneakers squeaking on the floor, and crowd noise.

Then I feel this nudge at the back of my leg, and it's Eddie in his wheelchair, rolling in between me and Johnny to get a closer look. Moses parting the Red Sea. He's got his pool cue between his knees pointing straight up at the sky.

The man holds the case lower down so Eddie can get a look. Eddie looks at it and shrugs, and then looks around at the rest of us, as if he's waiting for us before he makes up his mind.

Where'd you get it? Johnny asks.

Jerusalem, the man says.

How? I ask. You dig it up someplace, like in *Raiders of the Lost Ark* or something? This is how these things go. Just by your questions, he's got you.

How's not important, he says. On earth, seeing is believing. But believing is truly seeing.

Is he still here, says Marvin, from out of the bathroom, yanking on his zipper and walking bowlegged. He turns to go back in but mumbles, The hell with it, and comes and sits back down. He brushes against the guy kind of rudely as he goes by, but this fellow doesn't know enough to be offended. He's just holding that little glass box like it's the most fragile thing in the world, and we're watching him waiting for what comes next.

Then Marvin gets this idea. He says, Ever have that thing out of the box?

It's sealed, Hal says, from the floor. Airtight, to prevent decay, like in a museum.

No, my faithful friend, the guy says, it isn't air sealed. I would not prevent the needy and the faithful from having direct and sacred contact with this holy relic.

I'll give you a five spot to open it up, Marvin says. The man nudges his briefcase open a little wider with his elbow, and Marvin pulls a wadded five dollar bill from his pocket and tosses it inside.

Then ever so slowly, the man opens the case. And I swear, as it opens, I have to think about breathing. He holds it up to Marvin, and Marvin reaches in with his thick fingers, dirt under his nails, picks up this little sliver of wood, and holds it over his beer.

Does it float? Marvin asks.

Hal is beside himself, silent in his building rage, his head shaking wildly, but the stranger just smiles like someone who has seen hecklers before. When Marvin drops the wood into his beer, we all gasp in surprise, but then Hal starts yelling like a madman and tugging on Marvin's leg when Marvin lifts the glass to his lips and chugs it all down before slamming the empty mug on the bar.

You're all a bunch of lunatics, Marvin says, and when he smiles, he's got the wood between his front teeth. With one puff of his cheeks, he spits it out at Hal. And then – and then, uncoiled by reflexes you have to be born with, the sinewy, black hand of the Cyclone fires out and snatches that little sliver of wood right out of the air. Then he opens his palm, the pale, wrinkled skin unfolding like the petals of a rose, and he looks at this little piece of wood, stares at it closely, then hands it back up to the man, who returns it to the case and snaps it closed.

You see, the guy says, looking around at all of us, the Lord can protect his own. He slides his hand over the money Hal put on the bar and puts it in his briefcse. Then he looks at me, at Johnny, at Barney, and when he sees that no more money is on the way, he closes the case and snaps the latches. Hal, with the aid of his cane and a little help from Johnny, gets back to his feet.

Marvin laughs and shakes his head. That's quite a show, he says.

May the Lord bless you all, the man says, and then he kind of bows his head at all of us and heads for the door.

The rest of that day and into the night, it's all anyone can talk about. Crazy Marvin, pretending to swallow a piece of a fake cross – and paying five bucks for the privilege, Johnny adds. After Marvin buys him a beer, even Hal loosens up a bit and chuckles.

And then around closing time, this thing happens. It's one of those moments when everything that you know becomes less certain, when you read that the plane you missed because you overslept has crashed, killing all on board, or when you wake up at midnight and smell cigar smoke –

the brand your father, long dead, used to smoke. Marvin turns to put on his coat, and he mutters, What in the living hell. . . . The rest of us look to see what he's cursing now, and he's looking over by the pool table, and when I see it, I can't stop swallowing, because I'm thinking that somehow I'm part of this. What we see is Eddie King's wheelchair, empty. The Cyclone is gone.

* * *

It's been over a week since that night, and that's pretty much where things stand. Hal has taken over Eddie's chair. Doctors are about to take one of his legs below the knee, but he's getting around better now than he has for years. Quit wearing his king-sized crucifix, too, all of a sudden. Marvin, he's starting to go the other way. Still bets and curses like a madman, but says he intends to drink ginger ale now on Sundays, says it couldn't hurt to show a little reverence once a week. Watching the ball games on TV, we'll see something spectacular, and someone will say, the Cyclone could have done that. All of us, every time the door opens, we think it might be Eddie coming back. We can't get it off our minds.

Of course, everyone's thinking there's a plausible explanation for this: a coincidence, a medical fluke, a scam, anything but what we're thinking it might be, you see. My editor says, You were there, just write what you saw. He says, call around, ask some questions, you're a reporter for Chrissake. But what did I see? Who can tell me that?

The thing is, Eddie hasn't shown up anyplace. He hasn't been at Barney's, not anywhere in town, not back at college in Missouri. Nobody has seen him. And I've tried to find out the truth, but it doesn't seem to be out there, available. Doctors in Missouri won't talk about it, citing confidentiality, like they do. Eddie doesn't have a girlfriend. And his coaches in Missouri say they don't know what it was – that one day he was running with a football like he was born with it in his hands, and the next day he wasn't even walking. But his legs were shriveling in that chair, and that's a fact. I did see that. Thighs looked like softball bats in the end.

Eddie's mama is sitting on the porch when I drive up to her place, smiling like a woman delivered. No, she says, she hasn't see Eddie. But she expects to, someday. She says, When Eddie's running so fast his legs look like spinning fan blades, no one come and ask me, how's he do it? When he jump up on the roof of the porch from the ground to fetch his brother's baseball, no one say, it's a miracle! So now he just get up from a chair, and my phone be ringing and ringing all day. Natural thing. But if you got to ask – She shrugs. She says, The answer will pass right through your head without stickin'. Write that down.

* * *

So you see my problem. Editor wants a story, but I know what I have to tell him. It's either a story that's been told too often or a story that can't be told.

I'm just not sure which one it is.

Charlotte Nekola

DON'T READ THOSE STORIES

My mother said don't read those stories.

I want to watch the streets of a city
turn their hands up at night.

My grandmother said *In California
I moved my breadboard next to the window.*

They cut the feet off a girl in red shoes.

This is my father's story
of a woman he never forgot:
*She stood on a ferryboat
wearing a mauve dress.*

I want to sleep with rivers.

My aunt said *I made Edna a skirt
with 104 pleats, once.*

A mermaid sold her tongue for legs.

My grandmother said *I went to school until the eighth year
then my knee was lame and I had to go home.*

I ran at night from streets and rivers.

But now I am making a promise:
I will write a story
where women can walk.

GOOD TO EAT

I

We travel north to the edge of a continent,
for salt, for water, we say.
Each of us tries to part from the other.
We pace the aisles as the train cuts
fields of fireweed and flax.
Small-town children wave the train on.
Dusk lights the water of the St. Lawrence Seaway,
and codfish hang in backyard nets.
We dream of sleeping side by side.

II

Further north, the stars look larger.
At the end of the train line,
a man cradles a bucket of spit clams.
We walk on opposite sides
of the road to the boardinghouse
and watch the town form a hilltop.
A woman rushes home from noon mass,
and fishermen pull in eels.
A mill saws wood
and schoolchildren sing "Claire de Lune."
At night, we lose each other's shoulders.

III

We walk down to the water.
A man in a salt-eaten truck offers us mackerals.
He says he's Pierre LeBeau, ice hockey star of 1918.
His wife Yvette sits in the cab of the truck
and tries a new lipstick in the rear-view mirror.
Pierre says he takes her here each morning,
to smell the sea.
He says that everything from the sea,
lobster, snails, worms, is good to eat.
He turns up the collar of her coat
and fluffs the pink wool at her neck.
Later, we make a bed like deer in brush
and find the field of our arms.

DESIRE

The man steps off a lighted bus
and carries home a bag of sardines and snails.
On the subway, the woman tries not to watch
another man and another woman, leaning
against the door of the train, how
her hair and his shoulders, together,
look like a tree. The streets steam
with coffee, coriander.
Then the man and woman meet, first at a diner
on a road that leaves the city.
Later, they walk past warehouses
full of circus tents, electrical parts, hats.
Their dreams, they find, are still lucky.
One says "Had I known"
as they stop to look at a row of cabbages
planted in the windowbox of a trailer.
By the river they sift air
and survey the procession of a green barge.
"Finally" one says and the streets
seem full of hope and not regret.
At home, the woman licks a shell,
hides it in her bureau drawer,
and rerolls her winter stockings.
The man sits in the bay window
of a hotel in a foreign city.
Behind him, a truck turns north,
cicadas mourn, and he does not know why
he listens, now.

Hana Demetz

A BEAUTIFUL FRIENDSHIP

IT STARTED WITH that watch, four years ago it was. In he came, tapping his blind man's cane, and Rudy, the guard, almost fell over himself trying to hold the door for him. I guess Rudy knows quality when he sees it. Working at Worthington's does that to you, even if you are only a guard. I, being a saleslady, stood behind my counter, black skirt and blouse and pearls and all, and watched him tap-tapping his way across. He was what you would call a handsome man, tall and slim, with gray hair, a narrow face, very up and straight. His suit must have been at least four hundred dollars, if it wasn't custom-made. I have an eye for such things, working at Worthington's does that to you. Well, so he tap-tapped his way directly at me, leaned his cane on the counter, and said "Hello." Now, people who shop at Worthington's don't usually do that, they usually come right out with what they came for, they don't look at you and say "Hello" first. So, I said "Hello" too, and smiled at him. I know I have a nice smile. Then I thought right away, what am I smiling for, he can't see me. But he must have seen some of it because he smiled right back. And I tell you, that smile of his is something. His whole face lights up when he smiles, the sad blind man's face all lights up. I thought right there and then, that man is beautiful. And I know a beautiful man when I see one, I do.

So, we said hello, and then he said that he would like to buy a watch, it had to have a white face because otherwise he couldn't see the time on it. I started pulling out the trays with the men's watches and looking for the ones with a white face. There were just two of them, I never thought of it, but most watches have black faces nowadays. One was a Seiko and one was an Omega. He fingered them both with beautiful long fingers, and said that he would take the Omega. Then I tried it on him, and the wristband was too loose. It was a metal wristband, and I said that it would take the jeweler about one hour to shorten it, and could we send the watch to him when it was done. He said no, he would come back for it at the end of the afternoon, he had dealings in the courthouse, he was getting divorced that day, and he would need something to cheer him up after. He paid with a gold American Express. I like men with gold American Express, Chuck used to have one, before he came upon hard times. Chuck is my dear husband, we've been married thirty-seven years, and we have a good marriage. He used to be in carpeting, wool carpeting, and we were what you call well off. Then nylon came in, and by and by wool went out, and that's when Chuck started having a hard time. And what does a wife do, when she is going on fifty and her husband starts having a hard time? She sticks by him, that's what she does. That's what I did, and that's why I started working at Worthington's, though I never worked a day in my life before that. But one of Chuck's partners, the one who jumped into nylon carpeting right off, he knew the assistant manager, and that's how I came to work at Worthington's. I don't mind it much, it's a beautiful store, I'm very artistic myself, and I have always liked beautiful things. My children used to tell me, "Mother, you would give your life away for your beautiful things," and that's how I am.

So, where was I? The blind man came back for his watch at four that afternoon, and he said that since this was a sad day for him, would I come and have a drink? I said sure, I'm always ready for some fun. So we went for a drink at Harvey's, and he told me about his divorce. I tell you, some women really are bitches, they really are. This one ran away with her psychiatrist, left the poor blind man with two college-age daughters, just like that, no qualms about anything. And he ends up paying her alimony, would you believe it? Not that Clarence – his name is Clarence, by the way – not that he was poor or anything. You could see from the way he carried himself, from the way he bought that watch, that he was loaded. Good's Candies, that's his family's business, if you know what I mean. Well, anyway, so we had two drinks each, and then we said goodbye. I went home to my Chuck and he went back to the Park Plaza, because that's where he was staying after his separation. I thought that would be that.

One week later he came in again, Rudy almost killed himself opening the door for him, and I heard him asking for me. He greeted me like an old friend, Hello, Elaine, he said. Then he told me that he would like to buy a bracelet for his younger daughter's birthday, and I showed him what I thought would be right for a college girl. He bought a nice gold number, didn't even ask after the price, and when I was gift-wrapping it for him, he invited me to lunch. By then all the other girls were gaping, there goes Elaine's admirer, they said, and I said, why not, I'm not so bad-looking at fifty-eight, I have better legs than many of the young kids. And besides, I'm on commission, and whoever buys something from me is my friend.

We had a nice time, I told him right off the bat that I was married, I'm not like some women who go fooling around behind their husbands' backs, I like to be honest about things. He said that he would like to meet my

Chuck one day, and I said, sure, my Chuck would like to meet you too one day. The next week he called me at the store and said could we have lunch again, and I said sure. We had lunch, and then I invited him to come for drinks the following Saturday. Chuck goes swimming from five to six, we have a swimming pool in our apartment house. It's a real nice place with a view of the Museum, we moved there after we had to sell the house. The apartment is small and my things are sort of crowded there, but who cares, the children are grown and it's just the two of us. So I invited him to come at five-thirty, that way we would have a while before Chuck comes barging in. I sat him down in my kitchen and fed him some blueberries, one for you and one for me, and we were laughing and giggling like two fools. Then Chuck came in in his terry robe, and I could see right away that the two of them would hit it off like a stroke of lightning. It really was interesting to see. Then he invited us both to come out for dinner, we went to La Niçoise, and we ate and drank and had a ball together. That's how we started being friends, the three of us.

Sometimes Clarence would take me out for lunch, sometimes he would take Chuck, and most of the time it was dinner for the three of us. Sure, he always picked up the bill. Chuck would usually make gestures and pull out his wallet, but Clarence wouldn't hear of it. And, to tell you the truth, we couldn't afford to eat in those places anyway, so it was just as well. And it certainly helped with my food bill, sometimes I would take home a doggie bag and we would have two more dinners from those left-over steaks.

So it went for a while, then Clarence said one day that he had rented himself an apartment out on the East River, and that a decorator from Bloomingdale's was just doing it for him, and could I come and see that the decorator was doing it right. So I went there. I'm sure you are thinking that he used this as an excuse to get me into with bed him, but I can tell you that he didn't, the bed wasn't even there yet.

Then he came into the store and asked me to help him pick some china and glasses and silver, as his wife had taken it all. I thought he would buy one or two settings, but no, he went at it big and did eight of everything, and the best Lenox, too. So I picked what I would have picked for myself, the lovely Gorham Tradition, and the Waterford crystal wine goblets. The girls were snickering and giggling all over the place as I picked out the gravy boats and the punch bowl and the covered vegetable dish that you would also use as a centerpiece. But it was envy, pure envy, because of course my commission went up sky-high. That year even the vice-president wrote me a letter of congratulations.

Of course I was in the apartment supervising the unpacking. He could have done that by himself perfectly well, because he was quite amazing about all the things he could do, in spite of his handicap. But I felt very involved with all of it, seeing that they were all things I would have picked for myself, and seeing that I am an interior decorator myself, almost. I do have quite good taste. When the apartment was finished, I sold him one of my watercolors to hang up, I paint in watercolors, you know. And he had it framed in an expensive metal frame and had an electrician come and put a spotlight on it, so that he could see it better.

Then Chuck had a heart attack, he was in intensive care for three days, and in the hospital for two weeks. I worried about him, of course, we'd been married thirty-six years then. He always ate too much and drank too much too. When he was real bad the first day I had a moment's thought, I thought if Chuck should die, then I'll take Clarence, with all the Lenox and the Waterford and the Gorham which I picked anyway. I really liked the man, you see, in spite of his being blind and all. It was just a thought, of course, I would never say a thing like that out loud. Chuck didn't die. He had to promise to eat less and drink less, and that was a pain when Clarence took us out, because the restaurants were always the best. And you can't very well ask for a doggie bag for the third martini.

Well, it was a beautiful friendship. We would eat and drink and fool around, the three of us. I can eat and drink as much as I want and never put on weight, and Clarence would say, "Elaine, you are some beautiful woman." He bought two more of my watercolors, he could see some and he really liked my artwork, and had spotlights put on them in his bedroom. But we were always very proper, even when we were out alone. He would come to the store and look around, and then he would buy something from me, graduation presents for his daughters, and candlesticks, or a bonbon dish, or a figurine. I always gave him expert advice, and also told him where to place the stuff once he got it home, to show it to its advantage. He bought a tall breakfront, I found it for him at an auction, with glass doors, and the things I picked looked just lovely in it. Sometimes Chuck would call him up and say, "I'll be in your neighborhood tomorrow," Chuck is in real estate now, so he gets around, and they would go out together. It was a beautiful friendship.

But then we didn't hear from him for some time. When Chuck called him the next weekend, the housekeeper told him that Clarence had gone away for four days, he would be back on Tuesday. So we called on Tuesday night. He sounded glad to talk to us, I was on the other extension, but he was also sort of distant at the same time. And he said that he couldn't get together the next weekend either, he was sort of very busy. Well, we didn't see him for a whole month, he was either going away for the weekend or too busy, and my Chuck said, "I bet you there's a woman behind it," and he sounded sort of pleased, you know how men are. I really got mad at my Chuck that instant, because I surely wasn't pleased about it, I wasn't. "What's the matter with you, you jealous or something?" said Chuck, and I got even madder and I said, "If that's the case," I said, "then we will soon lose our good life with him." Chuck looked at me dumb, but I knew right there and then what I was talking about. A woman has her instincts.

Then, after another month when we didn't see him, Clarence called one day and said that he would like us to meet a woman friend who would be visiting that weekend, and could we all have dinner together. "What did I tell you," Chuck said to me, and I said, "You just watch, she's after his money."

I was sort of nervous all week, and on Friday I picked up my mink from storage, although it was only September and I hadn't planned to pay the storage fee until after October payday. Well, we met the "woman friend" on that Saturday night, her name is Anne and she is about my age, a bit younger maybe but definitely not as good-looking, a bit overweight too, and all tweedy, and she didn't even notice my genuine Emba. It was clear right away that she was more than a "friend." Clarence could not take his thoughts off her, oh sure, he joked and bantered with Chuck as usual, but his whole heart wasn't in it. All he really wanted was to talk to this Anne, or at least talk about her to us. She had done some recordings for the blind, he told us, up where she teaches at Northampton, and he had heard them and fallen in love with her voice on them. And so he wrote to her, and she wrote back, and they started a long correspondence. Then he went up there to meet her, and now, he said, he hoped she loved him as much as he loved her. And she actually blushed, plain as she was, she did, and patted his hand, and he grabbed her hand and kissed it. The whole spectacle made me sick, I had trouble swallowing my quail, and I looked at her schoolteacher face and all I could think was, I know what you're after, Miss Plain.

Chuck was behaving like a fool, "You son of a gun," he told Clarence, "and you never let on," and "when is the wedding?" To that she blushed again, and Clarence looked at her and said, "I don't know yet if Anne will have me." The whole evening was like that, Miss Plain was the center of everything. When Chuck and I got home we had a fight about it, and I had indigestion all night long.

Then one month later Clarence came to the store and told me that Anne had consented to marry him. He would be moving to Northampton to live there with her, she had her teaching job there and many friends, he was sure that we would be happy for him. And, would I help him pick an engagement ring, Anne just wanted a small one. I did my best not to show how I was feeling about it, a small diamond, I beg you, at our age. I certainly would not let on in front of the girls. So I picked out a small number for him and we joked while I gift-wrapped it and wrote "Thank You" on the receipt.

We didn't hear again for weeks, it was sort of hard getting used to not going out every weekend. After four years you sort of get used to going out. Clarence called us and said the wedding would be up in Northampton and could we come, and Chuck said sure, but I butted in and said that our first grandchild was due in Arizona just about that time, and that we might have to go there. That was really true, but I was glad to have it as an excuse. So we didn't go to the wedding, didn't even know when Clarence moved away. He would call from time to time, asking how we were, and talking about how happy he was up there in Northampton, that we had a standing invitation to come and visit, and how he liked Anne's friends, and how his daughters were fond of her.

Then Worthington's fired me because they were cutting down on staff and I hadn't had any spectacular sales for a long time. Chuck was ready to retire, so we decided to pay a visit to our son up in New Hampshire, and on the way back we would stop at Clarence's in Northampton. They had bought a little house there, all old and with sagging floors, and I really mean little. Clarence's study had to double as a guest room.

Everything of hers was New England simple, Shaker furniture and pottery, and she had put cotton fabric inside my breakfront's glass doors, so as not to show off the Lenox and the Waterford crystal. "It looked much too ostentatious," she said to me. Clarence did not wear his nice expensive suits any more, he was all tweedy, too, with baggy pants and suede elbows. And there were books, books everywhere you looked. I have nothing against books as decoration, but they should be used moderately, every good decorator will tell you that.

She did cook a nice dinner, I have to grant her that, but it really broke my heart to eat off some Italian pottery plates and to know that the Lenox I had picked for us was there hidden behind a cotton curtain. We drank from some simple stemware, and two of the Waterford goblets held daisies instead of wine. The cute little imitation Louis Fifteenth chifonnier was hidden away in the hallway closet. And would you believe that I didn't find my watercolors at all?

On the way back I said to my Chuck, "If that woman didn't marry Clarence for his money, what did she marry him for?" And Chuck, happy to be driving his Cadillac, he buys old Cadillacs all the time, said, "Maybe he married her for hers?" Then we broke up laughing, because everybody knows what college teachers' salaries are like.

Well, it was a beautiful friendship while it lasted, and nothing in life lasts forever. Now that I'm not at Worthington's any more, I go swimming with my Chuck every day from five to six. We have a good marriage.

Oldřich Mikulášek

DEVASTATED BY LOVE

Translated by Bronislava Volková and James Felak

Confused by love, I feel
from you a gust of coolness.

Tortured by love, I see
two flowers huddle up
in the rain-drenched grass of November.

Disappointed by love, I feel
that our hunger has no appetite,
just as you can't get drunk on an autumn rain –
and in vain I am putting my arms around your neck.

Devastated by love, I feel
in my heart – there somewhere in the back –
the leafless time.
And I see you in the empty orchard,
as if you yourself were leafless –

devastated by love.

MUTENESSES

Translated by Bronislava Volková

It is not necessary and some things one shouldn't
even say.
There are words mute,
known by the confessor –
and the hangman,
the wind that suddenly died
in the leaves,
the wailing, the drawn out howling,
the verse, whose groaning doesn't reach
and thus will repent,
a little seed buried in the sand,
scars and slashes and seams,
a breath intangible, born in the squeeze,
an execution wall and a screen,
the nameless war fields
and the names on the tablets of honor –
and one sad
woman condemned to love
for life.

Janet Bohač

IN THE LANGUAGE OF MARRIAGE

On Saturday nights, before the elder members of the American-Czechoslovak Club retired to their stucco homes on Miami Beach and condominiums near the IntraCoastal, the younger members confined themselves to the small bar of the clubhouse and to the Pilsner Urquell. Someone, usually Miloš, the bus driver, would seat himself at the end of the bar, open his concertina, set his legs wide at the knees, his feet flat on the cement floor, and begin to play for the others who sometimes closed their eyes while they danced, knocking into wooden chairs with their hips and lifted feet, and imagined for a fraction of a painful second that they were home. For some, the pain came to them because they had left. For others, because they had had to live there at all.

When the elders left, the younger members pushed open the wooden doors of the barroom and arranged themselves into groups at the long tables, stripped of the white paper tablecloths that had been present during dinner. They danced on the hardwood floor, and if one of the men was willing, or already drunk enough, they might have drums to go with the concertina. Whiskey, usually scotch, or vodka appeared out of pockets and disappeared into styrofoam cups. The circles of the dancers grew larger; the volume of voices rose. The women, most of them in their forties, curved their backs, leaned an elbow on the bare table, and squinted through the smoke of their cigarettes while they spoke in Czech. During the lulls in conversation, they straightened their backs, feeling an ache between their shoulder blades, and stamped out their cigarettes in a cup that had held someone's scotch earlier. Having completed all those movements, if the conversation did not readily renew itself, they watched the couples dance. It was on one such night that Jan met Colleen and the women for once had something to look at.

They didn't know where she had come from; they didn't ask. That she had suddenly appeared seemed somehow inevitable. To ask Why? to ask From where? would not make her retreat any more than it had the Russians.

To be sure, she "belonged" there. She had the wide face, the brown eyes and hair, the high cheekbones that could be a dead giveaway. She knew how to dance with Jan and wore a dress with the right kind of hem that made her circles around the floor all the more dramatic. But of course, none of them were in the least bit surprised to hear her answer "I'm sorry. I don't speak Czech" when Rose asked "*Mluviš česky?*" Their curiosity stopped there. But it was, as they all knew, exactly where Jan's began.

With them he flirted, he teased, he even made promises that later he could back out of, saying, "Magda, come on. You take me too seriously. Besides, you're friends with Lena. How could that work?" And ultimately, because they all were friends with Lena, he could tell them the same thing; he could stopper their desire at the same point and leave it full as if Lena, or themselves, were to blame for their frustrations. As they sat, tapping their ashes into the communal ashtray, they knew the second inevitable thing about Colleen: she would become Jan's mistress.

Revenge swelled and died within their breasts. At least once, each separately saw herself getting up from her seat, crushing out her cigarette, and using the phone in the now-empty bar to call Lena. And just as quickly each saw the other women's reproachful eyebrows rise, even if they did not bother to turn their heads. What was the use in calling Lena? Even if she did care – which most of them knew she did not – alerting her to her husband's flirtations would not solve the problem, because the problem was that each wanted to be the one whose hem twirled as Jan led her around the floor.

"You have never been here before. I would have seen you," Jan said as they danced.

Colleen laughed. "You mean you are always here?"

Jan smiled. "I mean I am here too much. I'm here so much I'm becoming infamous, like Al Capone. You know he used to hide out here."

"I know. I read the article in the newspaper. That's how I found the place," she said. "Is that what you're doing here? Hiding out?"

"Me? No. There's only one thing dangerous enough to hide from and they keep finding me anyway."

Colleen kept her face turned toward his. She waited.

"Women," he answered at last, twirling her around.

* * *

Later, as they lay in the bed at the Holiday Inn, he discovered that she called out his name with a voice that could have been Lena's. It was eerie the first time she said it, but then he decided he liked the fact that his wife and this young woman said his name in the same nasal, pleading way.

The Holiday Inn was next to I-95, and with the lights off and the curtains parted a bit, he could see the white headlights and red taillights of Mercedes and Porsches and BMWs flash by. He worked in the hotel as a waiter for room service. He had gotten the key from Javier at the front desk and placed a Do Not Disturb sign on the door and knew that they would be all right for a few hours.

"Teach me to say something in Czech," Colleen said in the dark.

"No."

"Why?"

"You're not a parakeet. You're not going to visit Czechoslovakia, are you? There's no reason to learn."

"How do you know? Maybe I will visit someday."

"Then you will get a book and study before you go."

"You won't teach me one word?"

"No. One word will not make a difference."

"What kind of difference would more words make?"

"They wouldn't make a difference either. Life is too short to learn a dying language."

He turned to watch the lights on the highway flash and disappear. He did not want to hear her fumbles, tentative and sloppy, with his language. When he wanted to hear it, he would go to Lena. That finally was what she was for him and he for her: vowels trapped between the tongue and palate, certain consonants hissing around the teeth. She could disregard the flirtations she knew about, because they were confined to the language she shared with him, and in that lanugage he could not betray her.

"You know one word already," he said. "My name."

"Jan," she said, as he knew she would.

"You say it the same way as my wife."

"Oh," she said after a moment. "Is she Czech or American?"

"Czech."

"Were you married here or there?"

"Does it matter?"

"No. I'm just curious."

"We met over here. In New York City. She works for a cruise line and one week a year we get a free cruise."

"That's nice."

"Yes. It's nice," he repeated, and they fell silent.

"Do you miss it?" Colleen asked at last.

"What?"

"Your country."

"This is my country."

"Then, do you miss Czechoslovakia?"

If he said yes, she might take him again into her arms and make love to him with tenderness and pity. If he said no, they might lie there for hours until it was time to go, but it would be a more honest answer.

"Yes," he answered, feeling her arms twine about him. "Now. Say '*dobré lhář*,'" he said, hoping that she would sound just like his wife.

Barbara Goldberg

HOW THE PAST INHABITS

When she was twelve, my mother
contracted scarlet fever, before
antibiotics, before the war
would make living in Bohemia
obsolete. Now she is twelve,
she wants to sing in the opera,
paint her lips red, wear gowns
that expose her shoulders.

Soon she will walk in the orchard
with her brother, the one she lifted
aloft with a fireplace poker while
he slept, an infant swaddled in linen
in his bassinet. Now it is spring
and the tiny hard green apples
fit neatly in her palm. They smell
tart and spicy, as yet unripened

by a blowzy summer sun. She is about
to take a bite, though the apples
are unripe and she is only recently
completely well. Her lips hover
over the unblemished skin. Suddenly
her father, following secretly behind,
strikes them from her hand.
This is how much he loves her

though the line between protection
and possession is unclear. Is this
the story I want to tell? Or how
later she begs him to flee to America
and he refuses, saying, What would I do,
an old man of sixty, sell sausages
in a foreign land? He and his wife
will die prematurely and his son,

the boy who walks in the orchard,
will survive because he knows how
to weld. And my mother will take
sleeping pills night after night
to prevent her father from surfacing
even in dream. Her granddaughters
sing beautifully, but my mother
frets daily over what she should eat.

HEARING HIM TALK

Eric Heymann, 1903-1957

My own father died of swine flu, spent
his days reading Talmud in the back
room while my mother ran the store,
work-horse daughter of horse thieves.
That was my stock: one foot in heaven,
the other in mud. Never forgot that.

War already brewing when I first danced
with your mother in Carlsbad, she making
eyes at that dark Hungarian who looked
like Robert Taylor, American film star.
I know she didn't think much of me, though
for a stout man I dance a mean tango.

Followed her back to Prague with clear
intentions, ended up yelling at that
chicken-brained idiot who was her best
friend's brother, he believing Hitler
wouldn't invade: too well-off to be smart.
Hand-delivered twelve long-stemmed roses.

Had to drag your mother out. The others
perished. No matter how bad things are
they can always get worse. Stay liquid.
Avoid real estate, handsome men. Choose
one like a rock. Never cheat on taxes.
This country deserves every dime.

Sometimes I have no patience with lumps
in the horseradish sauce, you girls
for refusing to practice your scales.
I go up and down with the market.
You shouldn't take it so hard.
A lot of noise. The way I am.

Joseph Bruchac, III

PLUMS

Grandma Bruchac lies with closed eyes,
her hair blue as the skin of a plum,
that color because she washed it before
beginning dinner – the pots were bubbling
on the iron stove when she had the stroke.

In the neatly-made hospital bed
she has slept three days, a traveler
gaining strength before climbing one final hill.
The blue of European plums surrounds
her face like flower petals
or fingers stained from picking fruit.

Her face, a pale cloud, drifts further away.
She dreams of Turnava, where the boy
she'll marry years later in this land is waiting.
He has brought her something from his uncle's orchard.
Her hand moves from yours to accept that gift.

Zdena Hyblova Heller

RESISTANCE

Six of us, shadows among shadows, peel away from the walls of the school building and silently, purposefully, go our ways. Four have bundles of underground papers to distribute around the town, you and I work together on the public bulletin cases.

Sometimes I lead, other times I follow you.

Tonight I make the first move and head out for the Workers' Union Hall. We walk shoulder to shoulder through the silent empty streets passing buildings with dark windows. On these missions I am always very tense and alert, but what happens, what I do, is automatic, detached. A wound-up clock ticks and directs me, possesses me, until I am safe back in bed.

We understand each other without words and usually work in silence. Quickly, like a thief, you unlock the bulletin case and hold the front page up for me to pin; next to it we pin the reverse side. You lock the case while I pick up the papers.

Now to the post office. The Party has a freestanding two-sided case in the middle of the square there, completely exposed from every side. Our risk is greater here. Electrified by the sense of danger I finish my side within seconds while you do the other. As I close the glass door of the case I see it's all steamed up by my hot breath and so I open it again to wipe the pane with my sleeve. If the vapor froze on it nobody could see what we posted. Too few people get a chance to read our pamphlets anyway before some Party official or the police arrive and tear them down.

By silent agreement we save the Party Secretariat Building for last. This is pure bravado and we know it. Only communists come to read here, everybody else gives the place a wide berth. But you and I have planned this, the ultimate act of defiance, a joke on the regime.

I walk into the dark recess of the entrance, try the door. It's locked. In front of the building I beckon into the dark, knowing that you are watching me from some shadow, holding the incriminating paraphernalia in case I get stopped on my reconnaissance. But I do have the skeleton key on me, and so, without waiting for you, I open the case. My nerves twang like high voltage wires but my movements are precise, my senses sharp; I can see like a cat in the dark. What cannot be seen I feel with exceptional accuracy: the lock, the edge of the glassed door.

Here you are, the sheet spread already. I have to wait for you to pin it, and while I wait, listening, I hear footsteps in the empty street. I touch your arm, squeeze – you understand instantly. I push the door closed, and we slip into a small depression behind a downspout at the side of the building. Shortly two men are upon us, passing within a foot. I close my eyes so the whites don't attract their attention and hold my breath, I can smell the warmth of their bodies rising from the clothes for a moment.

They stop at the Secretariat entrance and talk. One is going inside to do some urgent work. Parting words, shaking of hands, they take a few steps, have more to say and stop again. At last they part.

We breathe, then look out from the shadow. The sidewalk is now illuminated by the entrance light inside the building. The door of the bulletin box has swung open. You put your mouth to my ear and pour in hot whisper: I'll see you at the meeting place. This is a job for one.

I shake my head violently before you even finish. You nod and squeeze my arm until it hurts. I shake and squeeze just as hard. We stand face to face in the small space. Shivers run through me. It's freezing and we haven't moved in some time.

No, it's not cold and it's not fear. In spite of the utter darkness I see your face so close it almost touches mine. And on it, I read love. It makes me shiver. But that detached wound-up clock inside my head is ticking on; our work is sacred, it comes first and above everything. So I nod in agreement and step out into the street. I move quickly, knowing that you are waiting for me to be out of sight.

* * *

I am watching over you as you pin up the second sheet. Of course, I fooled you. I am hiding among the trucks in the lot across the street. In my frozen hand I am clutching a piece of icy iron pipe – should anyone threaten you I will pounce on them and I will destroy them.

You lock the case and start up the street.

* * *

Two of the boys are back already when I get to the school building. They have unlocked the back door and are waiting inside, out of the cold. When we break into the school at night to work on the paper, or just to gather after a job, like now, I am very aware of the building's smell which I never even notice during the day. Now I inhale it happily. Its familiarity is soothing.

You arrive next, then the other two, one at a time. We are all safe.

Good night, we say, but it's almost four o'clock.

Going between my house and the school I usually take a shortcut which doesn't keep me in the street too long. So on the way home I climb a solid board fence and drop into the darkness on the other side. This is the courtyard of an old deserted house; when I cross it I'll walk through the wicket at the other end and I'll be across the street from the back of our house.

The first time I tried this I had trouble letting go; jumping down six feet without seeing the ground is unnerving. But I found that my body remembers what to do without any clues; after all, I go this way every day – and quite a few nights – to and from school.

As I straighten up after landing on the ground, I sense someone near me and, instantly, before I can get frightened, I know it's you.

"Why did you hang around across the street! There was no need for both of us to get caught."

Like you, I resist giving up this pretense between us so I say nothing. My heart is pounding, but as we stand there, in silence for a while, I realize my feet have been numb with cold for some time and the toes are hurting.

"Cold?" you ask.

"What do you think!"

I don't give in easy! I am tough! I am the only girl in the group, and I am tougher than all of them. But, suddenly, I change my mind.

"Yes," I say softly.

You step behind me, put your arms around me, and with your face pressed between my shoulder blades blow a hot breath on my back. It works! Heat spreads through my body and for an instant I don't feel the pain of the cold, but then I start shaking.

You pull me close to you by the coat collar and I feel warmth on my lips. Caught by surprise I see the astonishing starry sky; my heart has stopped, time has stopped, there is nothing but the blazing stars and the imprint of fleeting warm softness on my lips. By the time I am sure it was a kiss, you have run away.

STEP INSIDE A DARK ROOM

Excerpt

EVA MET THE Doctor on the hill one night. The old man was poking at the weeds with his cane and every now and then he bent down to pluck up a plant.

"What are you looking for?" she asked him very politely.

"Something for my rabbit," he said but didn't look up.

This offended her. Fists on her hips, she demanded sharply of the stranger: "Is he your pet or are you going to eat him?" These days many people in Prague kept rabbit hutches in the service yards or even on their balconies.

Surprised by her tone, the old man now straightened up and looked her over. "You really must know?" His face was serious but she knew he was laughing at her. That only made her more stubborn; she nodded emphatically.

"So, you have to know! Hmmm . . ."

Hoping not to let him know how she felt she glared at him through narrowed eyes, but the tears were on the way.

He was taking his time. "Hm-hm-No! I decided not to eat him!" he said at last, still making fun of her. Now the tears poured down her cheeks, but she made no sound, just glared at him.

"Listen," he yielded, "he is my pet, always been my pet, I could never eat him. Would you like me to show you what he loves?" She nodded again and bent down over the weeds, glad to hide her face.

"I call him Ushak, all ears."

"That's what my grandfather calls me!"

At seven thirty, Eva was sitting on the polished granite ledge in front of her apartment building, waiting for the Doctor. She dangled her bare legs in the air, impatiently lifted herself up on her hands and let herself down again, she pressed the back of her calves against the cool surface. Finally, he was coming – slowly – limping and leaning on his cane. She lifted herself up and swung forward from the ledge.

"Good evening."

Without a word or a look he extended his hand; she took it and tried to fall into his limping rhythm. When they reached the corner, he stopped, rummaged in his trouser pocket, then pulled out an apricot and held it up high.

"Do you know what this is?"

"An apricot, I think. My grandfather planted an apricot tree when I was born but I never got to eat from it because he lives in Sudeten and that's Germany now, you know. I am the only one in the family who is allowed to visit him because I am only a child; the grownups are not allowed into Germany. I can only go once a year but there are no apricots then."

"Well, here's an apricot for you."

"I go on the *Schnellzug*, it takes four hours. Everybody on the train is German; there are never any children. Sometimes the people ask me where I am going but then they talk to each other as if I weren't there. They talk about the English attacking the trains – "

"Eat your apricot and don't talk nonsense," he interrupted.

While she ate her apricot, very slowly, Eva was thinking how much she liked talking to the Doctor. They talked about everything: how dinosaurs turned into oil, how coal formed underground millions of years ago, they guessed where the universe ended. They talked about everything, everything but politics. Father had told Eva she couldn't talk politics with anybody but the people who could be trusted, people in the family, mostly, not even all of them. She trusted the Doctor.

"Well, what do you want to talk about tonight?"

"Could we talk about God?"

"Maybe, what's your question?"

"People go to prison when they are really bad, right?"

"Sometimes."

"Does God decide?"

"Not always."

"How come?"

"What do you want to know, little girl?" He stopped again and impatiently hit the sidewalk with his cane. They studied each other in silence. At last, he shook his head and offered her a hand again. They walked on without saying anything, he led her straight up the steep part of the hill, something he had never done before.

"I want to know why children go to prison."

The high evening sky turned orange above them. He said nothing.

"My grandmother says that if a child dies it goes to heaven and becomes an angel. That's because children are innocent. My mother says that nobody would shoot little children but a man once told me they would."

The Doctor turned and held up her chin. "Are you afraid of being killed?"

"Nah! I'm not afraid at all. But my friend Sylvie, she is really scared. If you knew Sylvie – she is never bad, she never fights, she doesn't even argue, she doesn't even fight back when somebody fights with her, and they sent her to prison." She didn't say concentration camp because he might stop her from talking.

"First they sent her parents and she could stay behind because she had to have an operation but when she got better she had to go. She told me she wanted to go, she wanted to be with her parents. And my mother told her that her parents were waiting for her, but she told me that Sylvie would never see them again and I was scared."

"What were you scared of, Evichka?"

"I wasn't scared! She was, Sylvie, because she was never going to see her parents and because they do hurt little children and because my mother – and she was never bad."

They had reached the crest of the hill. The sun had just set and Prague was dark chocolate brown against a lemon sky.

"I am scared. Quite often, as a matter of fact," the old man said so quietly she could hardly hear him, "and of some of the same things you are."

For a long time they watched; lemon turned to aquamarine over the city. At last he bestirred himself.

"Well, let's see. A person needs to know how to fight one's fears, right? In order to do that properly, one has to know exactly what one is afraid of. Do you know what you are afraid of?"

She thought. "Snakes, I'm afraid of snakes. And the dark, and the skeleton. During the day I'm afraid of snakes but only in the country and only when it's hot. I'm not really afraid during the day. But at night I dream about the skeleton coming to get me and I can't sleep; and I get these headaches and my father is worried, so worried that he comes back home from work and he asks me questions, but I can't remember how to say the words to answer him; and the doctors looked at me and they said they have never seen such a headache in such a little child, that's what my mother said to one of her friends; and one doctor told my mother to let me sleep in her bed and he told me to hold onto her when I go to sleep and then the skeleton won't be able to get me, but when I go to sleep I dream she turns into a skeleton herself and then I wake up screaming and everybody's awake and they are angry.

"You know the skeletons? They are the angels of death, Grandmother told me. The Gestapo come and they seal over the door-locks of the Jewish apartments in our building. Almost all of my friends in the building have now gone. The seals have skulls and cross-bones on them. Nobody knows what that means, some think that it's a warning for anybody who'd try to get into the apartment, my mother thinks it's a warning that the gas they use to fumigate the apartments is poison. You know, they fumigate the apartments and the smell of disinfectant is all through the house. And then German officers come with their families and move right into all the apartments, Sylvie's apartment, and everything is there just the way it used to be, except for the plants and the bird, they died from the smell. The German children have Sylvie's toys and one of them wears Sylvie's red sweater; and Sylvie is all alone with the SS men, they have skulls and cross-bones on their uniforms, and she doesn't know where she is going, and she can't find her parents and they can't find her and everything is – ."

Oh, she said too much! She looked at him, worried, but the old man was still watching the darkening city.

"Come here," he said, finally, "I need to lean on your shoulder as we go down the hill."

He leaned on her heavily; she felt strong and was glad. In the meanwhile the sky turned cobalt, translucent and very high. Above them everywhere bright stars were bursting into the blue. They descended in silence. By the time they reached the street the sky over the blacked-out city was tremulous with stars. He kept his hand on her shoulder, lightly now, as they stood on the corner.

"I know what to do with your fear of the dark. Think of a place you're afraid of in the dark as it is in the daytime. Same place, nothing to be afraid of, right? That's because the fear is in your mind." He paused, reconsidered, tapped himself on the chest with the cane knob. "In your heart.

"Fear, because it's inside you, is wherever you are, you can't get away from it. What you need to do is make up your mind to fight it; step inside a dark room and fight it.

"You won't have to fight the darkness, you'll see! Just yourself in the dark. You can do this, I know. And once you've walked into a dark room and fought the fear until it's gone, you'll never be afraid of the dark again. I know that, too. You might still be afraid of the skeleton, though, but we'll think of something."

He looked sad to her as he patted her cheek good night but it was getting dark and she couldn't be sure.

"One more thing: Don't talk to anyone about God and the children and those things. Let's keep that for our own talks. Remind yourself that you're my little philosopher, and that's our own secret."

Jan Lukas

Portrait of a girl, 1942
Vendulka Vogelová a few hours before the transportation to a concentration camp.
She survived and lives now in Columbus, Ohio.

Prague, July 6, 1948
Anti-government manifestation four months after the communist coup.

September 14, 1948
The funeral of ex-president Edward Benes – communist militia in foreground.

Discussion on Wall Street, 1972

West Berlin View: From West to East, 1980

The Great Wall – Entrance to a Night Club

Carolyn Forché

PHOTOGRAPH OF MY ROOM

after Walker Evans

Thirty years from now, you might
hold this room in your hands.
So that you will not wonder:
the china cups are from Serbia
where a man filled them with plum
wine and one night talked
of his life with the partisans
and in prison, his life
as a poet, Slavko, his life
as if it could not have been otherwise.
The quilt was Anna's.
There are swatches taken
from her own clothes, curtains
that hung in a kitchen in Prague,
aprons she never took off
in all her years in America.
Since her death, the stitches,
one scrap to another
have come loose.

The bundle of army letters
was sent from Southeast Asia
during '67, kept near a bottle
of vodka drained by a woman
in that same year who wanted
only to sleep; the fatigues
were his, it is she
whom I now least resemble.

In the trunk, the white eyelet
and cheap lace of underthings,
a coat that may have belonged
to a woman who approached me
on a street in April
saying, as it was spring,
would I spare her a smoke?

Under the bed, a pouch of money:
pesetas, dinar, francs, the coins
of no value in any other place.
In the notebooks you will find
those places: the damp inner thighs,
the delicate rash left by kisses,
fingers on the tongue, a swallow
of brandy, a fire.
It is all there, the lies
told to myself because of Paris,
the stories I believed in Salvador
and Granada, and every so often
simply the words calling back
a basket of lemons and eggs,
a bowl of olives.

Wrapped in a tissue you will find
a bullet, as if from the rifle
on the wall, spooned from the flesh
of a friend who must have thought
it was worth something.
Latched to its shell, a lattice
of muscle. *One regime
is like another* said the face
of a doctor who slid
the bullet from the flat
of his blade to my hands saying
this one won't live to the morning.

In the black cheese crock
are the ashes, flecked
with white slivers of bone,
that should have been scattered
years ago, but the thing
did not seem possible.
The rest of the room remains
a mystery, as it was
in the shutter of memory
that was 1936, when it belonged
to someone already dead, someone
who has no belongings.

ON RETURNING TO DETROIT

Over the plum snow, the train's blonde smoke,
dawn coming into Detroit but like Bratislava

the icy undersides of the train, the passengers
asleep on one another and those who cannot

pace the aisles touching seats to steady themselves
and between the cars their hair is silvered

by the fine ice that covers everything; a man
slamming his hand into a morning paper

a woman who has so rubbed her bright gray eyes
during grief that all she has seen can be seen in them

the century, of which twenty years are left,
several wars, a fire of black potatoes

and maybe a moment when across a table
she was loved and as a much younger woman

wet her fingertip and played the bells of empty
glasses of wine, impossible not to imagine her

doing that, drawing the shade and then in its ochre
light, the first button of his shirt, the rest

the plants boarded up along the wide black river,
the spools of unraveling light that are the rails

the domed Greek church, the glass hopes of the city
beside one another; the man whose clothes

he carries in a pillowcase, the woman whose old love
walks into her eyes each morning and with a pole

lowers the awnings over the shop stalls of fruit.

ENDURANCE

In Belgrade, the windows of the tourist
hotel opened over seven storeys of lilacs,
rain clearing sidewalk tables of linens
and liquor, the silk flags of the non-
aligned nations like colorful underthings
pinned to the wind. Tito was living.
I bought English, was mistaken for Czech,
walked to the fountains, the market
of garlic and tents, where I saw
my dead Anna again and again,
hard yellow beans in her lap,
her babushka of white summer cotton,
her eyes the hard pits of her past.
She was gossiping among her friends,
saying the rosary or trying to sell
me something. Anna. Peeling her hands
with a paring knife, saying *in your country
you have nothing.* Each word was the husk
of a vegetable tossed to the street
or a mountain rounded by trains
with cargoes of sheep-dung and grief.
I searched in Belgrade for some holy
face painted *without hands* as when
an ikon painter goes to sleep and awakens
with an image come from the dead.
On each corner Anna dropped
her work in her lap and looked up.
I am a childless poet, I said.
I have not painted an egg, made prayers
or finished my Easter duty in years.
I left Belgrade for Frankfurt last
summer, Frankfurt for New York,
New York for the Roanoke valley
where mountains hold the breath
of the dead between them and lift
from each morning a fresh bandage of mist.
New York, Roanoke, the valley –
to this Cape where in the dunes

the wind takes a body of its own
and a fir tree comes to the window
at night, tapping on the glass like
a woman who has lived too much.
Piskata, hold your tongue, she says.
I am trying to tell you something.

Peter Kulka

A FLY IN THE OINTMENT

IN THE FINAL YEAR of her long life, 'Oma' Grosz, Lem's step-grandmother (as nasty an old woman as one's likely to meet), offered as a special birthday treat to take the boy to the circus. Her offer was special because Lem, the offspring of her son's wife by a previous marriage, was no blood relation of hers, thus no better than a stranger as far as she was concerned, and because she, a peasant born and raised in Central Europe, did not believe in pampering children. Children were a burden. Even on a farm it took forever until they were strong enough to pull their own weight. Given her druthers, she'd have drowned the lot at birth and settled for a pair of oxen or a horse. She could appreciate plowhorses.

Lem's stepfather, the sole survivor of seven, no longer heeded his humpbacked mother's misanthropic outbursts. He chucked Lem under the chin and urged him to act his age (a double-edged invitation since eleven-year-olds are notoriously obnoxious – unruly wiseacres and scaredy-cats by turn).

"Don't let the old witch frighten you, sonny-boy," he said. "Oma talks mean but she's tame as a pussy cat. Anyway, you're a head taller than her and twice as heavy, you big sissy, you!"

Lem wondered if Lucy, his half sister and two years younger than he, wouldn't like to go to the circus in his place. "Kid stuff," he sneered. He'd already been to the Garden on a school outing the year before.

But that excuse didn't work. Oma Grosz had no intention of taking him or anyone else to that Disneyfied 'Greatest Show on Earth' with its three rings, royal menagerie and death-defying aerial acts, one-hundred-piece orchestra and more costume changes than in a fashion parade and musical comedy combined. That commercialized travesty had no right to call itself a circus. She was taking him to the *real* thing – she yanked on Lem's earlobe to help him appreciate the difference – straight from the Old World where it had all begun! A Czech company, on a once in a lifetime tour of the West, was in town. What an opportunity! As rare as the return of Halley's comet.

Not rare enough for Lem, who mistrusted his step-grandmother's unprecedented and unexplained interest in him. And why wouldn't she take his half sister along as well? He didn't believe her excuse that Lucy wasn't mature enough. No, Lem suspected that Oma Grosz had some sinister surprise up her sleeve, some object lesson just for him. Yet, short of running away, there was nothing Lem could do to get out of going.

The circus tent had been erected under an abandoned section of the elevated highway, close by the river. (The following week, Xmas-tree hawkers would set up their stands there.) The single ring was no larger than a volleyball court. No more than a couple of hundred spectators could crowd into the tent, but that was no problem since only a handful had shown up. (The troupe from behind the Iron Curtain had been boycotted by the New York culture critics for ideological reasons.)

The ringmaster raised his whip and and motioned the customers to move closer to the action.

"Don't be reticent," he urged. "No extra charge for ringside seats. All patrons are equal in our socialist circus. Princes may sit next to paupers, though women and children are traditionally favored. . . . They're fed to the lions first." He winked. "A joke, dear people. Don't be afraid. Our wild animals have no claws to scratch out your eyes, no teeth with which to bite your ass."

Which proved to be the second joke, for the "wildest" of the circus' animals was a skinny black garden snake that the ringmaster wore around his neck instead of a bow tie. The other creatures in the menagerie must have been donated by the Slovakian SPCA: a broken-back goat, a one-eyed goose, a tired rooster pursued by six scolding hens, a triad of mangy dogs that looked more like underfed pigs than the wolves they were billed as (blame the translator if you feel cheated), half a dozen alley cats, and something in a bird cage (a ferret, Oma Grosz whispered, useful for flushing baby hares out of their holes).

The third joke was the performance of the Kapek family itself.

Instead of such fabled acts as the High Tea Ceremony in which (so Oma Grosz remembered from her childhood) a nonet of aerialists sipped Russian tea from bone china cups and nibbled on petit beurre biscuits, saucers balanced on their knees, feet tucked under, while swinging high above the heads of the spectators, swinging not on a trapeze but – get this – By The Hair Of Their Heads! (as the poster promised), females by their thick black braids, males by the handlebars of their mustaches, children by their forelocks (Lord, it gives you a headache merely to think about it) – instead of performing such magnificent feats on a tightrope a hundred feet off the ground, the "Flying Kapeks" from Moravia teetered on a washline barely an arm's span above the ringmaster's top hat: a bare-chested, not-so-young man, hair dyed butter yellow, juggled three grass-stained tennis balls; a buxom redhead with muscular, hairy legs struck a provocative pose (copied from a 1940s girlie calendar), then executed a half split; finally, an androgynous teenager grudgingly prodded a hoop across the rope.

As for the magician's bag of tricks, it came from some mail-order catalog: a see-through blindfold, tinfoil gold doubloons, a stuffed rabbit that leaked sawdust, trick handcuffs that snapped open before Brno's own Houdini (the ringmaster, who else?) could say "Open Sesame!"

The circus was a family affair, each member of the Kapek clan playing several parts. Just as the ringmaster doubled as prestidigitator, his wife held center stage as acrobat, snake charmer, and bare-back rider (the goat her steed). Their pouting offspring did multiple duty as trapeze artist, prima ballerina, and fire-eater. The proud-chested blond juggler, the ringmaster's brother (though apparently on closer than brotherly terms with his sister-in-law) could bend "iron" bars, swallow swords, and play "Yankee Doodle" on the musical saw. Granny and Grandpa Kapek, grounded because of arthritis, contributed their share as black-faced clowns when they weren't hawking peanuts and crackerjack or pushing mimeographed programs:

"One U.S. dollar per autographed copy. Sure to be a collector's item! The only way to tell the actor from the act, the gooser from the goosed."

The humor, both by gesture and words, was barnyard variety smut: "Why did the Volga (pronounced Vulgar) boatman cross the river to unbutton his fly?" . . . "Why did the shepherd apologize to his neighbor's ewe?" or ethnic jokes with Hungarians the main target: "How many Magyars does it take to light a candle?" . . . "What's the difference between a Buda jackass and a Pest mule?" etc.

Madame Kapek's generously rounded rear end (outlined like a Rouault painting by her dayglow tights) was the direct object of everybody's desire, yet the trick she was coaxed to perform was more gymnastic than erotic. Inserting a walnut into the cleft, she applied the muscle power of her mighty buttocks to crack its shell. The men groveled for the scattered nut meat. Grandma Kapek, holding her nose, provided the appropriate sound effects while, overhead, the youngest of the tribe mooned the spectators on each orbit of the flying trapeze (a kiddy swing). Next, the family staged a series of sporting contests: a burping duel, a hiccup face off, a farting match, *und so weiter.*

"Gross, isn't it?" the ringmaster begged the audience's pardon. "But what else did you expect from a backward region like ours?" He held up both hands as if to shield himself from a barrage of rotten eggs. "So, what do you say, children, to letting our wild animals do their stuff?"

Invited to respond, the children, expecting less than nothing from the flea-bitten and underfed menagerie, hooted and hollered. But, as it turned out, the animals performed like professionals.

On command, the dogs in wolf costumes jumped through a flaming hoop – singly, in pairs, all three together. (If they singed their tails, it wasn't their fault, rather that of the hoop holder, the redheaded temptress who was more interested in flirting with a natty type in the first row than in upholding her part of the act.) The zebra-striped cats followed, leaping onto each other's shoulders to form a picture-perfect pyramid. The nanny goat, playing toro to Kapek Junior's effeminate toreador, put her heart into the charge, goring her tormentor and drawing what looked like real ketchup. Even the ferret did its level best, crawling through a spiraling glass tube, not much thicker than a straw, in pursuit of a mouse.

Lem wasn't the only one who would have liked to have the four-legged creatures give an encore, but the ringmaster (who must have known he was outclasssed) couldn't wait to crack his whip and clear the stage of his rivals. His excuse was intermission time.

Sausages and sauerkraut, beer as well as sodapop could be purchased right now at the refreshment stand. He urged the audience to dig in and be sure to take in the spectacular side shows also, where, for a reasonable fee, they could gawk at freaks of nature and wonders of science never before displayed in the New World:

"Listen with your own ears to the inimitable barking fish! Bottle-feed a two-headed wooly lamb! Have your palm read by the topless Gypsy beauty queen! Visit the India rubber man who, if encouraged, will kiss his own royal Bohemian *tuckus*! (Pardon my French.) Catch the theatrical extravaganza of the trained fleas, formerly of Vienna, before they hop away! Examine, at your leisure, the pickled fetuses of Siamese quintuplets, smuggled out of mainland China by your impressario at the risk of his life!"

Lem was all for taking a peek at the pickled Siamese, but Oma Grosz had other ideas. Her heart was set on the flea circus. She had last seen one eons ago in the old country when she was about Lem's age. Could this be the same group? Why not. No one knows the life span of a flea. They can survive for scores of years, like ticks, without feeding, until the day when . . .

She pushed Lem into the booth ahead of her.

* * *

When Lem's eyes had adjusted to the dark, he found himself looking down at a small stage, not much bigger than his desk at school. The set, executed with three-dimensional super-realism, represented the courtyard of a fortress, encircled by high towers and crenellated walls. Stage left: amid a copse of bonsai olive trees, the wreckage of a primitive engine of war. Stage right: a statue of a horse on wheels.

"Good grief! The topless towers of Ilium!" Lem's step-grandmother exclaimed.

"Topless what?" Lem responded.

"Ilium. The wooden horse." The old lady's voice rose with excitement. "Blind Homer's best story, by far. Don't they teach you anything at school? Oh, never mind! You're in for a treat. Wait till you see the blond whore that caused all the trouble. Ach, what fools men are to be taken in by the skin-deep appearance of things – "

"Hush!" commanded a bodyless voice from the pitch black behind the stage. (Lem recognized it as the clown-faced crackerjack hawker, the patriarch of the Kapek family circus.) The admonition was followed by three thunderous thumps (a convention of European theater), then – could it be? – a trumpet blast, a tiny trumpet blast, no louder than the squeak of a mouse. There! Lem heard it once more.

And look: as the stage lights brightened, the bronze-studded, teak gates to the inner palace (stage center) swung open. A phalanx of greaved warriors, brandishing gleaming shields and battle-bloodied swords, squeezed through the opening, six abreast. A dozen chariots followed the infantry, prancing black steeds glistening with sweat, visored charioteers in parade costumes, white fustanellas and crimson vests, their golden shakos topped with blue plumes.

"Keep your distance, if you please," the ghostly voice of the director cautioned. "Ladies and gents, you are privileged to witness an historic pageant." (He paused to clear his throat.) "The siege is over. The towers of Troy have been toppled, not by might of sword or starve-them-out blockade, but by the artifice of the Wooden Horse. That's it, on your left, my right, constructed to exact scale, its hollow belly capacious enough to hold a platoon of shock troops." (He paused again to spit into his handkerchief.) "See the conquering Greek heroes in parade – cheer them if you like – ruthless Agamemnon, tricky Odysseus, Ajax the strongman. Pity the vanquished Trojans. King Priam bereft of crown, Queen Hecuba in tears, princes of the realm put to the sword, once haughty princesses now lowly slaves. Weep for mad Cassandra, the fortune teller whom none believe. Be dazzled by fair Helen whose terrible beauty bewitched Paris, sank a thousand ships, and destroyed a mighty empire."

As the stage lights brightened from blood-streaked gold to electric blue, the leading characters of the drama exited from the sober depth of the palace: victorious warriors in stained battle dress, heads high, chests inflated; a marching band, tooting fifes and rattling drums; and then, drawn by a magnificent white horse, larger by half than its fellows, reins held by two captive princesses, a see-through glass chariot, and standing in it, affecting the pose of a fashion model, none other than the woman herself, hourglass figure encased in a gold lamé gown of daring design, hair more golden than the lamé, topped by a diamond tiara . . . but her face – that face – masked by a black veil, alas.

"That's her, the bitch!" Oma Grosz's fingers bit into Lem's arm.

He leaned forward to get a closer look, but the glass chariot had passed. A cloud of dust raised by the mob that followed (rowdy soldiers, archers and infantry mixed, street musicians, camp followers, beggars, cripples, pickpockets, gutter urchins) obscured the stage. The light, following the pattern of the sun's course, began to dim.

Lem couldn't control himself a second longer. "The fleas! Where are the fleas?"

"They're all fleas, you lummox!" said Oma Grosz. "Don't you understand anything? Use your eyes. Yes, the horses as well as the warriors, and the pretty ladies too. Fleas every last one."

"They don't look like fleas."

"They're fleas all the same," said the old woman. "If you don't believe me, just roll up your sleeves and offer them a bite. They'd like a taste of fresh blood for a change. Old man Kapek has been drained dry."

"But their size. Look at the size of them!"

"You'd be suprised what make-up and costumes can do. Naturally they're not your common house flea. They've been specially selected and bred. And they've spent a lifetime training. Professor Kapek is a genius, the Stanislavsky of flea circuses."

Lem regarded his step-grandmother with new respect. How come she knew so much about fleas? "How do you train them?" he asked.

"Any animal can be educated by punishment and rewards, just like children, only better. The trainer is both mother and father to them. And God. One wrong step and he squashes them between thumb and forefinger." She gave Lem time to think that over.

"Maybe Professor Kapek will let you watch them being fed," she continued. "After a performance they're famished, down to a fraction of their weight. They'll want their pay. Look at the scars on his forearms. The lead players get to suck at his wrist. That's the most tender part. The richest blood is closest to the pulse, sweeter than mother's milk. The young ones are greedy, don't know when they've had enough. One gulp too much and they explode. Poof! Serves them right. And no great loss. Plenty more where they came from. The breeders don't appear on stage. Kapek keeps the nits warm in the hair of his armpits."

The idea made Lem shudder. He wished Oma Grosz would shut up, but there was no stopping her once she warmed to a subject.

"The training takes years," she informed him. "Losing one of the veterans would be a catastrophe. The flea that plays Helen of Troy is worth a king's ransom. More. This may be the last flea circus in the western world. It's a dying art, though I hear there's an avant-garde Romanian playwright who's training a troupe of a thousand flies, bluebottles, no less, to star in his new tragedy. Only the health officer closed down the theater. A threat to public safety, he called it. It's no different over here, maybe worse. People have no imagination nowadays, what with TV and 3-D movies. Who appreciates the classics anymore, I'd like to know?"

Lem was no longer listening to his step-grandmother's commentary. His attention was on the feeding fleas.

The trainer, having rolled up his shirt sleeves, exposed wrinkled white arms, the skin pockmarked with a thousand red spots. Now, Lem could see with his own eyes the insect-shaped bodies of the performers beneath their costumes, the tiny bald heads under their luxuriant wigs. The prancing horses had six legs instead of four (a detail that had escaped him during the show), and Helen's snow white steed was nothing but an ingeniously fashioned shell strapped to the backs of three sweat-drenched fleas whose muscular legs had been spray-painted white. Unmasked, the beauteous faces of the captured noblewomen revealed pointed snouts and protruding teeth. The golden helmets of the soldiers covered grotesque pin heads.

The legendary Odysseus, hero of heroes, the first to receive his pay in blood, leaped from the stage to his host's wrist with a spring so powerful Lem swore he had grown a pair of wings. He hadn't, of course, yet his agility served to remind the youth of the potential menace of these insects. If ever the trainer were to lose control . . . or were to choose to set them loose. . . .

Lem retreated a step, then a second and a third.

But something else was happening. Although Lem had put distance between himself and the feeding fleas, their size did not diminish. Just the opposite, they grew larger, upsetting the proportions of the stage set. Was it an optical illusion that the six-legged black horses stood two hands taller than the toy castle's turrets? Did Lem imagine it or had fair Helen's breasts swelled to the point of spilling out of their gold lamé halters?

The sole exit was blocked by a phalanx of stout warriors, their razor-sharp swords unsheathed, their battle-axes raised to strike – that was no illusion!

And where was Oma Grosz? Why had she run out on him after having pushed him into this nest of vermin?

Deliverance came from an unexpected source. Professor Kapek snapped his fingers and the spell was broken. "Show's over," he said. "Hoopla!" he called, and the fleas, shrunken to normal size, leaped back into the plush-lined casket that served as their nest.

"All accounted for?" Lem asked.

"Certainly," said the trainer without hesitation. "Every last one of them."

Lem wanted to believe him, but couldn't. Not then, not ever.

When, not a week later, his step-grandmother lay on her death bed, Lem approached to ask her for an explanation. What was behind her having dragged him to the circus? And what, so to say, was the moral of the story the fleas had acted out? She seemed to expect his questions and motioned for him to draw closer. He knelt at her side and bent his head over her mouth. Perhaps she meant to reassure him, but it was too late for words. All she could finally manage was to spit in his ear.

Terrance J. Lappin

PITTSBURGH

surly drunk
below the whisper

steel mills
keep the silence.

TO A CHILD RUNNING

I am a warn-
ing in myself
a fear that tremors
put birds to flight
When close
me, myself!
With the rib fixed
arch of an aviary.

Jan Skácel

WORDS

Translated by Bronislava Volková

Those begged out at the last minute
remaining before the little
they must now be enough

Tell me
how many of them a verse needs
so it wouldn't be too much

And how many little stones fit into a child's palm
and how many into the hurting mouth

The whole day you threw out words
so in the evening you would have some left for a poem

Somebody comes after us and collects

Jarda Cervenka

LOSS OF AN ENEMY

"Life is made of stories, not atoms."
— *Muriel Rukeyser, poet*

LIFE WAS VERY GOOD, there were smiles and happiness on the faces of everyone in the classroom. The air-raid siren sounded like sweet music to them because it was "preparation" and because it was afternoon. And "preparation," the long uninterrupted howl of the siren after the noon hour, meant that they all would go home and need not return that day for classes. No more torturing math, no more tortured history or Czech grammar, so incomprehensible to natives and occupants alike.

Maybe the "acute" will follow, a series of short undulating wails of the siren, announcing that the American planes are actually high above the city, silvery beautiful birds from the far away, unimaginable world, on the way to Germany for a bombing raid. Creeping home from school the students will be showered with Christmas decorations, falling like snow over the alleys and grim streets, roofs of ancient buildings, glistening on grass and linden trees of nearby parks. And free for the taking. Those thin strips of aluminum foil were supposed to confuse radar, but also, Peter was quite sure, were intended to be saved for Christmas. To adorn the spruce, to be scattered over its branches decorated with real candles, candies and magic glass balls. Even the wire star at the top could be improved by American aluminum.

Today the explosions of anti-aircraft artillery boomed from the distance and that was good news, too.

The artillery had never harmed the aircraft anyway. Peter could see clearly the puffs of explosions well below the planes. But exploding shrapnel was made of handsome material – shining bronze fragments were falling back on the city, still hot. Sometimes, with luck, nice pieces could be found with letters or numbers on the shiny surface. Such a find was of real value. With careful bargaining, it could be exchanged for marbles, even for the yellow ones (but almost never for the glass ones with colored stripes inside).

Peter was not lucky today. On the way from school there were no shrapnel fragments and only one small bunch of aluminum strips, which he stuck in the pocket of his short pants. He found it near his apartment house in Marinenstrasse.

It used to be a peaceful street of unchanging moods and changing and not peaceful names. Before the occupation it was known as Verdun street, after the battle of the French Verdun. During the occupation, it was named after Marinen – the German Navy. After the war it would be renamed Thälman Street after the German communist revolutionary. For Peter it never changed, he knew every single pavement stone there – those few missing ones were in his room because they contained precious fossils, such as orthoceras, graptolites and one, extracted from the sidewalk across from his apartment, a real trilobite. He knew every acacia tree there, climbing almost all of them for blossoms, which tasted like honey, and were "good for the lungs," as Grandma taught him. He often wondered how different the trees were from pictures he remembered of the acacias under Kilimanjaro, shading the olive-colored baboons from the scorching sun of East Africa. Sun was a rare visitor to Marinenstrasse. Crowns of acacia there were ragged with leaves more gray than green.

He entered the apartment house, closed the main door and looked around to be sure nobody could see him doing the task he thought to be pretty humiliating. He had to change his clothes fast before being seen by his mother.

His hated, brown, thigh-high stockings were rolled under the knees and held there with a red rubber band, which was intended to be used under the lid of a glass container for canning marmalade and compotes. Now the rubber band went into the pocket and stockings were rolled back up under the short pants where they were attached to the equally humiliating garter. The indescribable rubber devices for the stocking attachment were broken, so a one heller coin, the smallest, had to be used to join the stocking to the garter.

Then he removed his cotton sweater and pulled it over his head again, only backwards, on purpose. Breathing heavily after this secret operation, Peter decided to have one more look at the street before going up the stairs to the apartment.

And there he was – Hans. Just in front of the house next door.

Peter's reaction was instant and swift. In a second, the stone was airborne in the direction of the unsuspecting German. He missed by quite a bit, almost two feet. Since many stone projectiles had left Peter's practiced hand in the past and since stone throwing was considered one of the very basic, almost primitive skills in the Bubenec section of Prague, the miss by two feet must have been intentional.

"Czechische Schweinhunde!" screamed Hans, surprised, as his eye caught the parabola of flying stone. "Czechische Schweinhunde!" Czech pig-dog. Swine-dog. What a nonsensical animal, Peter thought. To be called swine only would be pretty offensive, so much that revenge, or better a swift attack, would be required to maintain some degree of honor. Especially if a third person were around. But swine-dog? Czech swine-dog? What to do about the "Czech" part? The "Czech" part made it so much less personal. It included in the offense so many people – in fact, all the people Peter knew. Some might deserve the name – Peter thought of the history teacher who liked to hit him over the knuckles with a wooden ruler in front of the class: "All stand up and watch what Peter Cermak deserves!" Some others, in Peter's mind, were so far above any name calling that the "Czech" part of "Czechische Schweinhunde" made this offensive call just a sort of political, all encompassing statement – and therefore of lesser impact on a pragmatic twelve-year-old's mind.

Hans began his approach. It was a strange attack. The start was indecisive and a careful observer would notice hesitancy in Hans's steps. And Peter was a careful observer. He recognized that Hans's attack was a ritualistic response and thus he also responded in a ritualistic withdrawal to the door. The exaggerated and faked expression of fear on his face changed in seconds to an aggressive sneer as pronounced and perfected as only a Kabuki actor could perform. With the sneer, just in front of the door, Peter turned to face the approaching Hans.

"So come on Hans, come on, you miserable coward."

Hans stopped on the spot. He expected to be stopped anyway, his face vainly trying to contort into hate.

There they stood, a few feet apart, under a gray sky deserted by drifting bombers, in the echo of the air raid siren. Somehow their aggression abated. The scene did not resemble a Diane Arbus photograph. One might think more of a Norman Rockwell painting. A slightly grim painting, though. Hair of no color, just sort of brown, unwashed for a week – only on Saturday when the water was heated by coal under the water tank in the bathroom. Faces without a trace of tan – spring had not yet descended into the depths of Marinenstrasse. Their stomachs longing for a better future – better than dry bread dipped in chicori coffee for a smoother trip through the esophagus, better future than daily dinners of mashed potatoes, with chopped onions fried in lard and poured over them for some taste. Two hearts, beating fast now, ready for acceleration. Two brains, seats of two gentle souls, laboring hard on the decision for action. Since action must follow this standoff. And soon.

Many times before Peter and Hans had performed their routine. By now the rules were well-established and followed with only small deviations.

They both knew by now how "real" enemies should behave. Peter, with the threatening mask still on his face, imitated a mock counterattack, Hans performed a short retreat. And that was enough for today.

By evening, supposedly doing the homework assignment for school, Peter allowed himself a few pleasant daydreams. He liked the one about the handgun the most. It had actually happened a few weeks ago. Peter found a real revolver in the bushes of Stromovka park. Wrapped in oiled cloth, in perfect condition, its white opaque mother-of-pearl handle and blue steel barrel gave him a feeling of great power and excitement. On the way home, that luckiest of days, Peter met Hans again in Marinenstrasse.

Hans must have sensed things were different that day. He retreated right away to his apartment house entrance, with surprise on his face, watching carefully every move of his adversary. Peter's steps were springy. He felt a thrilling feebleness in his knees, though, and could barely suppress the urge to sing of happiness. He also forgot, for the first time, about the rituals, about all the apprehensions and pleasant fears of Hans. Just when he passed Hans, at a safe distance, as was the custom, he made a decision. As he walked away from him, he pulled the gun from his pocket, looked at it with admiration, turned around and slowly, as slowly as his control would allow, pointed the gun at Hans. Right at the face of Hans which changed in an instant. Perhaps a great painter could recreate the boy's face which was expressing not only fear, but also admiration for the winner, the conqueror, Peter the Great.

Life is so nice, Peter thought, and decided to replay this movie in his mind again each night, before falling asleep, with new variations.

* * *

In the following weeks Peter and Hans, the enemies, continued their rites without ever touching each other, repeated their offenses without ever feeling offended. They never talked but they became an important part of each other's daily life. Peter had to assure himself, often with an effort, that he hated the miserable Kraut. Sometimes he even felt he had succeeded in hating Hans but wished to be more sure about it.

Then came the end of the war, and with it a revolution in the country. Russian tanks roared over the border crushing the feeble resistance of the Germans. They reached Prague on a sunny pleasant day in May.

People rose up with an excitement unparalleled before. Barricades dammed the streets, weapons hidden for five years appeared in the hands of clerks, bakers, grandfathers. Smoke filled the air, gunshots and explosions reverberated from Gothic arches of a hundred cathedrals, rattling the ancient stained glass windows, killing Germans and Czechs, puzzling the children, thrilling the teenagers, saddening the mothers. Remnants of SS-troops cut breasts off of women in the Vrsovice quarter, executed husbands in front of their wives and children in Pankrac, burned the ancient city hall in Stare Mesto. The Czech Revolutionary Guard shot to death whole families of Germans forced to swim over Smetana's Moldau, near the suburb of Podbaba.

Peter listened to the news with fear and astonishment. He guarded Marinenstrasse from the window of the apartment all those days. One afternoon an unknown youngster was crossing the street. Peter saw two soldiers kneel down, and when the echo of gunshots subsided the boy was dead, strangely curled, with one arm reaching in the direction of Peter. That evening Peter saw his father being led home by German soldiers, with guns in his back, his arms high above his head. Peter's father was a proud man, strong willed. He would never bow to Germans, he would never raise his arms above his head. And yet there he was, surrendering.

In those four days of the uprising Peter did not remember Hans. And if the image of him flashed through Peter's mind, it was suppressed instantly. There was no place for Hans in Peter's thoughts now. He vanished, was vanished.

The fifth day of the uprising the Russians reached Prague. That time in history they were cheered and welcomed with flowers and joy. They rode in on giant tanks, primitive machines with a wooden mallet to shift the gears; broad suntanned faces, wide with victory smiles, were admired by Peter and all his friends. The soldiers ate butter, real butter, from one hand and tore pieces of white bread from the other. They drank any alcohol they could get, and when drunk enough, drank gasoline and died. They stole watches and many wore several on their forearms. In Marinenstrasse, a soldier stole a bicycle from an old woman and was shot to death by his officer. Another Russian visited Peter's home, to everybody's great excitement. He had the expression and tired, kind manner of Peter's favorite teacher. He showed Peter the worn tinted photograph of his twin daughters – in pigtails – he hoped to find at home still. Peter liked him because he was a plain soldier and not one of the officers who set up a simple court in the yard of Peter's old primary school. The court was just a long row of classroom benches. There the officers sat facing German soldiers brought in front of them. After the sentence was pronounced the German was walked to the back of the yard and shot. The gunfire from barricades was not heard in the streets and squares anymore, only from the elementary school. They were single shots, at regular intervals.

Peter got a piece of real chocolate from his dad's friend. It was dark brown with an exotic sweetness and the aroma of a tropical paradise.

Father and mother were happy most of the time now and Peter liked to watch them smile, enjoyed listening to the radio which played cheerful music all day. Acacias in Marinenstrasse bloomed more profusely than ever and the war was over.

"All Germans must be relocated. All must be sent back to Germany," announced the radio and the newspapers. War is no more, peace will come in the future, the people thought. And they moved the Germans through the streets of an ancient city in long processions. Grim women, children and old men with eyes turned down, sad suitcases, uncertain steps. Their presence alone disturbed the celebrations. Infuriated passersby yelled hateful things at them. Peter knew it was all true about the many unspeakable things done by the husbands of those women and the fathers of those children. So they had to be marched out of the city. Yes, they had to go and never return, to go where they belong. And he was determined to be clear about this, despite their sad faces and worn suitcases. No, he must not feel confused – or even sad, God forbid.

On May 14 it drizzled all day. It was not windy but the humid cold made one pull up his collar and warm his hands in his pockets. The blossoms of acacias hung sadly wet. People were rushing home with thoughts of a warm stove and hot soup. At five o'clock Peter was coming home from Ural park wondering where all his friends were. School was out and there was nobody in the park, just a few little kids. Near home, in Marinenstrasse he lingered awhile hoping that somebody might pass by to be coerced into a game of marbles or planning an expedition to big Stromovka park. It was still too early to go upstairs.

From around the corner a procession appeared. Peter knew who they were; he had seen German civilians marching to detention and repatriation centers before. Again today they were accompanied by a couple of young Revolutionary Guards with rifles on their shoulders. This time it was a big group – a few hundred people. They walked slowly, dragging their suitcases and rucksacks, not looking up. They seemed to concentrate on the road just in front of their feet. Their faces stressed the unreality of this situation, this event without precedent in this middle class, orderly, and pleasantly unexciting neighborhood. Peter decided to go inside the apartment house. He was alone in the street and did not feel enough courage to watch alone.

As the grim procession approached, he changed his mind. At the far end of the formation something was happening. An older man was gesticulating and shouting. He was not one of the Germans. It was clear he had survived many beers that day, and he was stumbling around, kicking the suitcase of an elderly woman who was barely keeping pace with the others. Peter opened the door of his apartment house and stood there, wanting to go upstairs yet at the same time compelled to watch. The end of the procession approached, with the drunkard shouting and the old woman still barely holding onto her possessions.

Next to the woman walked Hans. Shabby wet jacket, too small to fit him, a shawl around his neck and a cap, a worker's cap Peter never saw on him before. His head was bent down, staring in front of his little body bent to one side to keep his suitcase off the pavement.

A small drizzle was still falling on the city. It was getting dark, people were coming home from work now. They did not seem to pay attention to anything. They walked quickly.

All Peter saw now was the small figure of Hans, framed in the misery of the street, slowly fading away as the procession disappeared. Climbing the stairs, he felt a heaviness and an unknown pain in his chest. In his room his scream was muted by the pillow, then it changed to sobs, and finally, the relief of sleep.

※ ※ ※

It is known that Peter woke up the next morning, but that one part of him did not. That part did not die, but rather remained alive in his dreams. Nothing is known about the dreams of his enemy.

Jiřina Fuchsová

FREEDOM

To Jan Palach

Yes
I am burning
And burning bright
I
Young freedom
Thousand times over
drenched in my children's blood
Yes
I am burning

Yes
I am burning
In Prague
In Warsaw
In Budapest
In
What does it matter
where
I am burning
And there is no rain upon this very earth
that could extinguish my fire

Yes
I am burning
For all of you
Whose eyes went blind
Whose ears went deaf
Whose lives have turned to dust
Yes
I am burning

Yes
I am burning
For all of you
Who have washed me off your easy minds
With beer
Or with a curse
Or with a few helpless tears
Yes I am burning

Yes
I am burning
I
Young freedom
A thousand times over resurrected from the dead
And trampled again under a giant's foot
I am burning
        And burn on I shall
        Forever
             1969-1989

V. NEZVAL

– A Czech poet, 1900-1958

Through the park
walks the wonderful wizard
plays the shawm
And leaves
    trees
    and
    grass

follow him
          At the traffic island
          a raincoated sun
          waits for a tram
Through the city
walks the wonderful wizard
plays the flute
And windows
    cars
    and bouquets of chimneys
follow him in a beeline
          Through the park
          walks the wonderful wizard
          and lightning strikes
          out of clear blue skies
Through the city
walks the wonderful wizard
and leads imagination by the string
like a dog

AN ABANDONED HOTHOUSE

Rows of roses
like lines of men
whom someone bade to stand ready
but who – before the onset of the battle –
                have been told
NOT to fight

So they stand
in full armor
taller than the weedy circle of enemies
furiously crowding around their ankles

In bitter rage
carefully sharpened thorns
pierce the warm air

The glowing enthusiasm
which first made the blooms glow red and hot
evaporates day by day

The intoxicating fragrance of overpowering sweetness
daily threatens to burst to the sky
and demolish the hothouse

But every night
stealthily and invisibly
a slight waft of a decay-like odor
little by little encircles the fragile stalks
furiously strangles their unspent beauty
and one by one
wrestles the rusting swords
from their
endlessly waiting
death tired
hands

                1971

Vladimír Holan

DAWN

Translated by Bronislava Volková and Andrew Durkin

It is the hour when the priest goes to Mass
along the devil's back.

It is the hour when dawn's heavy suitcase
takes our backbone for a zipper.

It is the hour when it freezes and the sun does not shine
but nevertheless the tombstone is warm,
because it moves.

It is the hour when the lake freezes over, inward from its shores,
but a man outward from the heart.

It is the hour when dreams are nothing
but fleabites on Marsyas's skin.

It is the hour when the trees, wounded by a doe,
wait for her to lick it away.

It is the hour when scraps of hourly words
are collected by the cunt of the tower clock.

It is the hour when only someone's love
dares to descend to the stalactite cave of those tears
that were in secret suppressed, that in secret toiled.

It is the hour when you must write a poem
where you must say it differently, quite differently . . .

IT IS NOT

Translated by Bronislava Volková and Andrew Durkin

It is not all the same where precisely we are.
Certain stars approach each other
dangerously. Here below, too,
it happens that lovers are forced to part
only to increase time's speed
by the beating of their hearts.

Only simple people do not seek happiness.

BUT

Translated by Bronislava Volková and Andrew Durkin

The god of laughter and songs long ago
shut eternity behind him.
Since then, only from time to time
the waning memory will sound in us.
But since those days only pain
never comes life-size,
it is always larger than a man,
and yet it has to fit into his heart . . .

Erazim V. Kohák

THE GIFT OF THE NIGHT

Excerpt from *The Embers and the Stars:
A Philosphical Inquiry into the Moral Sense of Nature*

THE NIGHT COMES SOFTLY, beyond the powerline and the blacktop, where the long-abandoned wagon road fades amid the new growth. It does not crowd the lingering day. There is a time of passage as the bright light of the summer day, cool green and intensely blue, slowly yields to the deep, virgin darkness. Quietly, the darkness grows in the forest, seeping into the clearing and penetrating the soul, all-healing, all-reconciling, renewing the world for a new day. Were there no darkness to restore the soul, humans would quickly burn out their finite store of dreams. Unresting, unreconciled, they would grow brittle and break easily, like an oak flag dried through the seasons. When electric glare takes away the all-reconciling night, the hours added to the day are a dubious gain. A mile beyond the powerline, the night still comes to restore the soul, deep virgin darkness between the embers of the dying fire and the star-scattered vastness of the sky.

The night comes softly, almost imperceptibly. The darkness gathers unnoted amid the undergrowth, in the shelter of the hemlocks and beneath the boulders of the old dam, slowly seeping out to cover the ground. There is still light on high. Only down on the ground the splitting wedges, bright and keen through the day, melt with the shards of bark around the splitting block. Then it is time to gather up the tools, to straighten a body bent with the day's toil, and to look up from the darkling earth to the still light sky. It is the time of radiant maples.

The sun has not yet set: though its rays no longer reach down to the ground, they go on shining above it across the treetops, letting the shadows rise up among the trees and fill the valley. Contrary to legend, evening shadows do not fall: they rise up from the thickets as the sun edges toward the rim of the treeline. Only the tallest maples reach up above the pool of shadow and, for a few moments, catch the last rays of sun. That is their moment of glory. All through the day they had merged with the profuse green of the treetops. Now they exult in the sunlight, radiant clusters above the darkened forest. It is a time to lean back and to give thanks for the miracle of the radiant maples.

Then the shadows rise up and drown the fire of the maples. The trees around the clearing gradually darken, their trunks merging into the curtain of the forest. There is still light in the air, diffused in the particles of dust and the droplets of moisture from the water tumbling over the boulders. There still is light, but a human eye cannot gather it. Neither can the tree trunks, the satin maples, the coarse oaks and the flaking cherries, nor the ageless, lichen-covered boulders. They stand subdued in the gathering dusk. Only the birches, the glorious great birches, focus that light. Their chalk-white bark comes aglow, rising out of the gathering darkness, white, glowing, glorious. Theirs, too, is a moment of immense wonder. I can understand why the good people of Shelburne, in the northern part of the state, erected no marble war monument but chose instead to plant great birches in memory of all who did not return. No monument could speak out the sorrow. Only the birches, glowing at dusk, can do that.

Then the birches, too, merge in the curtain of the forest. There is darkness all around, only high above the sky is still pale, outlining the black lace of the treetops and leading the eyes of humans, earth-bound through the day, up to the heavens. You would watch in vain for the stars to emerge from it. The stars do not emerge: they happen with the suddenness of a pinprick in the celestial dome. Many a night I have watched the sky, knowing full well where the first star would appear, yet have never seen it happen. Perhaps I rested my eyes momentarily, perhaps I let my attention wander. One moment there is only the unbroken sky, growing dark overhead. Then, without a transition, a star is there, bright and clear, then another and another until the entire wondrous dome sparkles with lights. That, too, is a moment of wonder, precious in our time. The stars do not insist: even the glare of a white gas lantern or the reflected glow of neon will drown them out. Only where humans respect the night can they see the wonder of the starry heaven as the Psalmist saw it.

The night has other lights as well. There are the fireflies of a summer night, the flies of Saint John to my ancestors, tracing their paths across the clearing in occulting flashes of cool green light. There are the mushrooms, glowing yellow in the tree stumps slowly reverting to humus. The lights of human presence are warm, a match struck among the trees, the glow of a cigarette, a flashlight. The lights of the night are as cool as the night to which they belong, Saint John's flies, mushrooms, the blue lights on the bog and the silver-white lights which appear, unexplained, deep among the trees. All through one August moon, one would appear each night after the last traces of daylight faded, always in the same spot atop the old dam, a cool glowing disk the size of my palm. Was it the moon reflected on a damp leaf? A flake of silica in a boulder? Or a tobacco can dropped by a logger? I do not know. Several times I tried to walk up to a night light among the trees, carefully keeping it in view. Each time it would disappear before me. One night I drove in aiming stakes so that I could inspect the spot by daylight, yet I found nothing and gave up the effort. There are things which it is so beside the point to explain! It is much more important to cherish and give thanks for the lights that enrich the night. Explaining, making, those are the priorities of the day which conceal the world around us. In the dusk of a forest clearing, other things matter – to respect first, then to understand, only then, perhaps, to explain.

Al Masarik

WIDOW

together so many years
they begin to look
like each other
resemble a couple of
infantry privates
trudging in heavy
blood filled shoes
thru foreign snows

finishing each other's
sentences giving you
the name rank &
serial number
of their love

when whiskey takes
him to where she
aims her rosary

the light in the hall
stays on all night

a pair of work boots
carefully placed
before her door

telling anyone who enters
a man is here with her
love is just inside
this door

here are his empty shoes.

FAMILY BIBLE

I didn't know him long
remember a short old man
with a bald head

shiny & tan & freckled
& that he somehow held
the family together

in spite of the fact
everyone seemed to hate
everyone else

& the Christmas he sat
perfectly still
allowing the blue parakeet

to land on his bronze head
sat there smiling
thru his no teeth

& the years after his death
the holiday get-togethers
that would end in feuds

the telling of the story
the Christmas the parakeet
pooped on Pop's head

passed on
like a reading
from the family bible.

RUNOFF

we live in a very small place
but for years it seems as if
we've each had a house of our own

this is not a bad thing
we have been civil &
neighborly your barking dogs
do not bother me

sometimes I steal your paper
but always fold it neatly
& return it before you're up

there is much talk of food
& weather we trade recipes
& point out snow clouds

right now it is spring
the winter has been harsh
nights & mornings are cool

I wake to the gurgling sound
of water the mountains
sending us their frothy
bouquet

I see smoke from your chimney
& picture you in the yard
rubbing sleep from your eyes

immediately I think of excuses
to be outside.

Joanne Hvizdak Meehl

THE LINDEN SNOW

THE IMAGE OF THE Czechoslovakian men in dark caps and rumpled clothing, men scattered across the fields and along the culverts, each with a flashing scythe, arcing slowly and steadily back and forth, back and forth, back and forth, turning the tense grasses into sleeping seas of green – this she could not forget.

They are joined by women and men in the fields, turning over the earth by hand with hoes, tilling between each row of potatoes or cabbages, slowly, breaking the crust, being part of the soil, row after row, on and on, even after their long day in the city.

And she still sees the bicycles, especially the plump, babooshka'd women on bicycles, their puffy and stiff black skirts swallowing the seats, black shoes and black stockings working around and around and around, white embroidered blouses under short patterned vests, hands steady on the handlebars, seemingly hairless heads under their scarves tied unlike Western scarves: tied once in one big knot that by some Slovak magic never needed adjustment during the day. And others on bicycles: an old man, concentrating with every pedal-push; young women with smooth faces, in their office clothes, their straight skirts somehow bending with their knees as they move up and down; and the achingly tired gravel pit worker with just enough strength left in his face to make it to his village.

She cannot forget the accident they pass. She is being driven from one village to the next when along the road ahead are dozens of cars, all pulled over as if for a Little League game. But there is no baseball here. A car has careened off the narrow highway, driver probably asleep, and hurtled into a field where it lies on its side, windshield smashed. The other drivers are all running to help, trying to pull open the door, trying to right the car, their faces twisting in anguish over the inability of even several hands to make the metal move. A man at the guardrail between the road and the field begins waving at them to slow down, his face pulled into a tearful, Munch-like cry, and more drivers stop to see if they could help. She remembers this, and remembers thinking, Why don't they call 911? and then realizing, There is no 911.

Everywhere on the fields, the roads, the roofs, the trees – everywhere is the linden snow, puffs of white cottony flowers that the linden trees are shedding – floating, blowing, even coating the streets and roads after the rain. It is a constant in the ever-shifting light of this place.

She still sees babies in carriages. Not the kind of strollers they have back in her own country, but real trams with big chrome wheels, simple yet elegant, perched so high off the ground, like the stork nests she sees on the chimneys. So many babies, wheeled by so many young women, barely more than girls; young women alone, the men having done their job. She remembers one young woman who parks her carriage outside an open door on a side street, leaving the sleeping baby there, covered with an embroidered blanket. She follows the girl/mother as she goes inside. It is a church, cool and dark. As her eyes adjust, she sees a nun hurriedly changing flowers, as if a service is about to begin: armfuls of deep rose peonies, huge poms of color splashing the ochre light. The young girl/mother has a western haircut and is reverential as she stands, melding with the whispering tourists who hang back at the door; she alone steals time to worship secretly. Then the girl blesses herself, turns, and leaves, wheeling her precious cargo ahead of her as she walks down to the shops that have nothing to sell.

She remembers the Russian soldiers who were leaving here now and moving east, and she and her driver become tangled with them for miles. They pass trucks and mortar machines time and again but there is always another line of them ahead, awash with brown dust, red stars dimmed by mud. One vehicle with several men is pulled over and she is struck by the taut figure of the man poised on top, his back to her: even from behind his large yet fit body proclaims a confidence that is matched by his pose – one leg higher than the other, propped on a turret. His uniform's shirtsleeves are rolled up above his wrists, and his hands are on his hips. He looks to her like a hero about to re-enter his village, allowing his triumphant troops to run ahead, modest in his victory. As her car passes him she sees he is Mongolian or some other Soviet version of Oriental, and she wants to know what he smells like and moves like and if his skin is smooth after so many months in the field. Her driver is waving to the soldiers and the other soldiers wave back but the conqueror keeps his gaze steady, on the horizon, and she thinks of the word *beautiful.*

Paul Martin

CLOSING DISTANCES

The arbor, like a complex cross,
is up, the vines are ordered
and I'm ready to try to kill the pheasant
that steps nervously out of the field into our yard.
I'm ready to close distances
the way my grandmother did when she pinned a chicken
between her knees and drew the blade across its throat:
the stiff, spasmodic beating of wings,
a rain of blood in the dust.
If I'd have been tall enough, I could've looked
across the fence into Siska's, Johannes's,
down to Matusik's and Luchman's yards,
seen chicken coops, pigeon lofts, smoke houses,
grape arbors, every vegetable garden and chopping block.
At the table on summer Sundays the sweat
of my grandfather's brow dripped into his soup,
he held up the bone showing me how
to stuck out the marrow.
After dinner he sat on the back steps, smoked his cigar,
his round face floating in blue smoke
above the pages of the *Zrkadlow* or the *Nevy Yorsky Denik*.
In the afternoon he'd take me down to the ground cellar
and lifting the thin hose to his mouth inhale
the cold sweet wine out of the barrel into his glass.

I'd like to think the town they're buried in
grows lush, abundant gardens,
that the mayor, a happy, shambling man
makes his way from one to the next, pulling scallions,
drinking beer, talking with blue-shirted men who lean on their shovels
or adjust the fine spray of the nozzle.
But all that grows is the number of stones

in the cemetary overlooking the town, the ground
bare, rutted, as hopeless as the factory now
and at 10:15 Mass where the old Slovaks
filled the church with garlic thicker than incense
and sad, passionate voices that shook the simpering marble faces
of saints, their well-dressed sons and daughters
scatter themselves through the pews
and sing such a thin, bloodless song
the church feels big as a cavern.

I've lived too long in the distance of books
but I feel distances closing now –
the garden is overtaking the lawn.
Since I've broken the rake I crawl hands and knees
breaking clods of earth in my fists,
happy with the taste of earth on my tongue.
I watch for the sweep of his tail,
the soft breast of his entrance out of the high grass
into our yard.
I'll balance that small, delicate brain in my sight, cry if I must,
throw him into a boiling bucket, pluck every feather,
save the longest one for my cap,
I'll ram my arm up his ass, pull out his heart,
invite my family and friends for bowls of pheasant
paprikash,
say more than an easy rhyme for our grace
and wash it down with the richest red wine I can buy
till I get my own vines into the ground.

WHAT I KNOW ABOUT MY GRANDMOTHER

I remember her flowered apron, her hair
pulled back in a bun.
No matter how early I woke, she was already up.
We were leaving the table before she sat.
She squeezed nickels into my palm
commanding me not to tell.
Bruises blotted the back of her hands.
The only ice cream she liked was vanilla.

Before I knew her, she had fifteen boarders.
She heated water in copper boilers
and scrubbed their heavy underwear,
back bent over the steaming tubs.
Soup, sausage, omatchka, kasha,
flat bread sprinkled with salt –
the boarders kept knocking
willing to sleep in the attic in shifts.
She knitted, crocheted,
waiting up till dawn for her grown son
and if she stepped outside
she swept dust away from the house.

We have no pictures that show her young.

Iva Pekárková

FEATHERS AND WINGS

Excerpt
Translated by Paul Wilson

MY GRANDMOTHER WAS DEVOUT. She was a Catholic. Not a very common phenomenon in Prague today, not even among old people. It was mostly the young who were rushing to join semi-legal Protestant communities, but as far as I could see it was an escape; they were only trying to squeeze out the dogma of communism, which had been drummed into our heads from nursery school on, with an opposing dogma. But Granny was a proper believer, in her black widow's dress (this was seventeen years after Granddad had died) she would go to the little church in our quarter of Prague every Sunday and – fingering her way through a rosary she'd inherited from her own great-grandmother – she spoiled my political profile.

Not that I gave a damn.

And far more than by Granny's undying effort to get me to see the light, I was converted to the right faith by Comrade Rehankova from the Street Committee. Every time Comrade Rehankova saw Granny somewhere in the street all decked out like that she would call me in for a little chat just to reassure herself that I still had the right political convictions. It might have been a lot worse if Comrade Rehankova had gone into any detail, but Comrade Rehankova was a good person, so good in fact that she was stupid. She would limit herself to one question: "Viola, you don't believe in God, do you? You believe in the ideals of communism." And I would reply: "No!" and of the two possible meanings of my answer, Comrade Rehankova (thank God for her) would choose the one I hadn't meant. As I say: the tender comradely concern of Comrade Rehankova (who had known me from childhood) did more to turn my naturally materialistic spirit to the unexplored heights of heaven than a careful study of the Bible. Whenever I would leave the office of the Agitation Committee, I would always be mumbling an Our Father or a Hail Mary.

And when I needed a personal evaluation for the university entrance procedure, Comrade Rehankova wrote: "The comrade's pro-communist consciousness is indicated, among other things, by the fact that although her grandmother believes in God, she herself does not, and she tries to convince her grandmother of the truth of Marxist ideals."

I did not try to convince my grandmother of the truth of Marxist ideals, but of this Comrade Rehankova (who was about fifty) was indulgently silent, or else she would occasionally remark that the unprogressive old folks would soon pass on and we, the young, would take our places at the head of the world. As I say, Comrade Rehankova had the brains of a chicken. Nevertheless, Granny went faithfully to church, crossed herself, knelt and prayed – and in the time that was left (the time not spent standing in line for food) she watched television.

Yes, that was probably the biggest thing wrong with Granny.

We'd been living in relative peace in that three-room apartment in Prague for a year, we had no relatives, at least none we ever saw, and every evening Granny would sit down on the bed in my little room and talk and talk, cry and then talk some more, talking and crying, on and on until I'd finally manage to get her in bed and to sleep. My evenings were unbearable.

And so I resolved to invest in a television set for Granny. It cost me the equivalent of about three months' wages.

Not out of the goodness of my heart, I hasten to add. Purely to buy myself some peace and quiet.

All good deeds, whether well-meant or otherwise, usually turn against you in the end. Whenever I came home now, coming up the stairs I could hear the sounds of jubilation echoing from the box as though they were coming out of a barrel, and there would be Granny, sunk into her threadbare old wing chair, following the action.

Granny spent eight to ten hours a day watching television. She watched the news, the song shows, the movies, the sitcoms and serials, the ten-minute political sermons, the garden show, the Russian course (she didn't know a word of Russian), the speeches of politicians, and even those moments when a cherry branch in bloom would appear on the screen along with the word INTERMISSION. She watched the bedtime cartoons and the cop shows, the westerns and the Russian war movies, the sports broadcasts and the parades of waving flags on the First of May. She watched everything indiscriminately. Once I even caught her staring at the buzzing test pattern. And in all those years of viewing, everything turned to a perfect mishmash in her head. Granny couldn't keep track of things when the same actors played in several different serials at once. The Woman Behind the Counter, The Man in City Hall, The Hospital on the Edge of Town – they all got mixed up in her aging brain with The Thirty Cases of Major Zeman or some historical nonsense, and then Granny would watch in dull astonishment as that nice surgeon climbed into a suit of armor and proceeded to run the famous detective through with a rapier. On the other hand Granny would occasionally be able to pull a plot or two out of the mists of forgetting, and during the third or fourth re-run she would rush out to tell me excitedly that she'd known all along how it would turn out.

I didn't begrudge Granny her daily dose of drivel, but I hated that box.

I hated its bluish light, I hated the sounds that came out of it and set the apartment trembling (Granny, on top of everything else, was growing deaf) and I hated the whole system of brainwashing it represented.

A television with two channels, with a political speech on one and a Russian film on the other, is to my mind the cheapest and crudest way to turn people very effectively into idiots. The vast majority of average families, evening after evening, would rush to the television like baby chicks under the mother hen's wing. Families would cut short their weekends in the country, suppers would be prepared early so they wouldn't miss IT, and people VOLUNTARILY sat in front of the radiating screen and day after day and a heigh-de-hey they would let their heads be filled up with finely ground propaganda that seeped into every single program like lead dust. The average person, although he barked his shins on reality every day, couldn't help but slowly soak up this POSITIVE THINKING. The average person no longer noticed that the pioneering spirit of socialism in the films and serials was turned completely on its head; on the contrary he began to believe it was the truth. "Historical films" on the Slovak National Uprising and the post-war years, about the February Revolution or even "film clips from the years of crisis," they would all, with premeditated cleverness, stand reality on its head. The ones upstairs seriously operated on the assumption that mankind forgets, that if there are no records, then there is no past.

How true was Goebbel's remark that a lie repeated a thousand times becomes the truth.

My television grandmother sat in front of the picture tube day after day and into the apartment, poisonous, infectious sounds escaped from the box.

Sounds that I was afraid would drive me crazy because I'd end up believing or because I'd lose my ability to keep their stupidity clearly in mind. The stupidity already made me feel pretty close to going crazy, and so did the thought that I might not notice it.

I wanted to live differently.

And in fits of rage (which thank God became less frequent) I'd have liked nothing better than to throw it out the window along with my screaming grandmother.

Our six-year-old black and white set was finally beginning to give out.

It took five minutes to warm up, the sound croaked and the picture flickered. I taught Granny how to give the box an expert wallop to make the picture settle into its frame again. I didn't feel like calling a repair man and Granny (thank God) didn't know how to use the phone.

I watched the televison die with mixed feelings. I looked forward to a time when it would be no longer. At the same time I knew that I'd have to go right out and buy another one, because Granny couldn't live without it anymore.

Yes, we each had our own drug. Our own way of surviving.

Granny, the church and the television.

I had hitchhiking.

Otto Ulč

CHINA'S SURPRISES

"ONLY THE UNPREDICTABILITY of those blokes is predictable!" insisted an old China hand in a Hong Kong bar of unexceptional repute.

Well, yes – very probably. In the name of the Cultural Revolution culture was demolished, the educational system de-activated, thus netting one hundred million young illiterates. After various great leaps forward and especially backward, the implementors of scientific socialism finally managed to attain the average level of consumption of the late 1920s. The average per capita income is about twenty times lower than in Taiwan – a backward island itself at the end of the Second World War. . . .

These blemishes notwithstanding, a large number of American academics continued to extol the allegedly monumental accomplishments and the inherently superior virtues of the communist regime. Not infrequently, the enthusiam of the fellow-traveling thinker, Shirley McLaine, was matched. That is, until the first weekend of June 1989.

* * *

"What kind of letters do you get from home?" shortly after the massacre I asked a graduate student, on loan to our campus from the Chinese Ministry of Foreign Affairs. We first met in Beijing three years ago. His family lives some five-minute walk from Tiananmen Square, a place of great historical significance.

"It was terrible, terrible, they write," he responded.

In 1989, for the first time in almost four decades, the decorations for the May Day parade did not include likenesses of Marx, Engels, Lenin and Stalin. Instead, a giant portrait of Sun Yat-sen, the pre-communist founder of the first Chinese republic, was hoisted.

Democracy movement. Euphoric students erected a thirty-foot-high Goddess of Democracy, a replica of the American Statue of Liberty. Peaceful protests, demands, hunger strikes – tele-events with global distribution. And the aftermath, thoroughly recorded by the noisy outsiders. Intrepid journalists brought into our living room the events of the fateful Sunday, the assault of thirty thousand crack troops backed by forty tanks and armored personnel carriers. A deadly peace of hellish death was restored on the Square of the Heavenly Peace, the antique rulers with their equally anti-quated concepts of rule triumphed. Two thousand and six hundred fatalities were reported by the Chinese Red Cross.

Dialectics, the mighty pillar of the Marxist-Leninist faith, commands that every reality is ever-changing and reinterpretation-prone. No surprise then over the subsequent official statements about zero losses among the students. Only the armed soldiers suffered. What the world saw on the television screen was an illusion, a chimera, a plot concocted by sworn enemies of socialism, of peace and progress.

"Nothing has happened – absolutely nothing!" insisted our student's parents in their subsequent letter, echoing the party line about the foreign-inspired wild exaggeration, slander, and hysteria.

Millions of ecstatic worshippers used to march in front of Chairman Mao, waving their little red books. "But do they believe it?" the Great Helmsman was reported expressing his worry to Chou En-lai.

On October 1, the fortieth anniversery of the People's Republic was celebrated in the presence of 100,000 very carefully screened citizens. In the place of the Goddess of Democracy a huge statue was erected – the tradi-tional worker-peasant-intellectual-soldier quartet, united in a heroic revolu-tionary pose.

No massacre ever happened.

Tiananmen Square perhaps never existed. If the party so decrees, who will be foolish enough to challenge the new truth of the day?

＊ ＊ ＊

I was born and grew up in Bohemia, the country of Franz Kafka. My ex-perience with Stalinism has infected me with a life-long interest in mat-ters absurd. China provides for bountiful satisfaction in this respect. Where else but in the People's Republic would they name their most dreaded con-centration camp "The Lake of Emergent Enthusiasm"? "Daddy, is it true you are a bloodsucking capitalist roader?" the son asks and the father whispers "You should always believe the Party and Chairman Mao," further admonishing his progeny "under no circumstances to forget class struggle." In case of fire in the foreigners' only compound in Beijing, the firefighters will be allowed on the premises only if invited in by the endangered foreigners who will vouch for their character. One should beware of the leftist as well as the rightist deviation, leftist at times being rightist and vice versa. Always obey, cognizant of the fact that "rebellion is legitimate."

The truth is quite often the postion of minority though the minority must always submit to the decisions of the majority.

Interested in the subtle intricacies of the Chinese language? *Chen* means "to stand still" but also "to gallop at full speed." *Ch'he* denotes a person, devoid of intelligence, an idiot, also a person borrowing and returning books. "To find bail for lighter sentences of females" is taken care of with the three-letter *Hoo.*

Thank you, I'd rather preserve my pristine ignorance. *Maou Tsaou* denotes "A scholar not succeeding and giving himself over to liquor."

* * *

In the early 1960s, I labored on a doctoral dissertation in political science – or pseudoscience, as the case may be – at Columbia University, a self-retired Czechoslovak judge who at the age of twenty-nine managed to flee to the west in a rather ridiculous disguise.

At a crowded New Year party in the Manhattan apartment of a Czech-born psychiatrist I became mesmerized by an exotic looking creature – what was she doing at that particular ethnic jamboree? "A Slovak dish – second generation," volunteered a kibbitzer and I, equally inebriated, nodded.

Priscilla is Swiss-Chinese, her mother Helvetian, her father from the Celestial Kingdom.

We got married. Some time after the exchange of marital vows the bride blushingly revealed a secret – her aristocratic pedigree. Her grandfather Lim Nee Kar (so states Lloyd's *Ports of China,* 1908), was a mogul, one of the richest men in the country, founder of banks, insurance houses, railroads, granted a title equal to an ambassador by the Empress Dowager, he sent all his sons to study at Cambridge University. . . . Well, that explains it: one of them went frolicking to the Alps and I married the result.

The in-laws resided in Taiwan, the family estates were not far away – in Amoy, a port city of Fukien province, across the Formosa Straits. From the Quemoy Island (a big bone of international contention, in 1958 almost triggering the outbreak of World War III) we saw Amoy through binoculars. Propaganda outposts were pouring passionate exhortations into the windy salt-air. The theater of the absurd once again.

The Museum of Psychological Warfare displayed a flock of rubber ducks carrying ideological statements in their bellies. Such a floating commando equipped with Sun Yat-sen quotations was then dispatched across the straits where it eventually met a competing commando rushing in the opposite direction with Mao Tse-tung's quotation. One spreading democracy, the best hope of mankind, the other inflated messenger carrying the torch of world revolution. How would a veteran of the Long March (a distance from Glasgow to Cape Town) react nursing his bruised aged body under the soothing sun, should he encounter such an ideologically subversive duck? To abandon his faith, to throw away the raison d'être of his entire existence?

Quemoy we visited on an even day – on odd days the other side bombarded the place and I just had enough of this experience from the days of the big war (on the ground we were the subjects of the Third Reich, at school the officials of the Race Research Institute measured our *Untermenschen* heads, comparing their shape to that of chimpanzees, whereas from the air the British and the American airforce worked on our liberation by bombarding us).

Next time we shall attempt to make the few extra miles and visit the ancestral in-law land.

* * *

Chinese organized tourism – the pampered and at the same time isolated, shamelessly, without an apology, fleeced foreigners being herded to Potemkin sites – was not what we were looking for. Instead we became the so-called FIT (Foreign Individual Tourist), unchaperoned by the authorities and far less welcome.

In 1982 – six years after the terrestial demise of Chairman Mao – in Hong Kong we obtained by somewhat irregular means the entry visa and by ship we reached Amoy overnight. The sea, during the typhoon season, was rough. However, we were even more shaken by forces of emotion: Priscilla returning to her birthplace where she had lived up to her teens. Will the place confirm the assertion of the ancient Greek, Herakleitos, the granddaddy of dialectics, that it is impossible to step twice into the same river? And what a torrent of tumultuous events had swept over China in the interim – the hundred flowers campaign, the great leap forward lunacy, the numerous rectification campaigns and one catastrophic cultural revolution on top of all that, followed by the healing process, the licking of the numerous self-inflicted wounds.

I had to cope with a different kind of apprehension. All the refugees I have ever met have been tormented by an identical dream: They dream that they are back in their native land, do not know how they got there, they are becoming gradually recognized by the people around, there is no escape, no way out – sweat and anguish terminated only by a merciful awakening.

After my treacherous vanishing act, a secret police officer made a bet with my brother that the comrades would succeed in snatching me in the

West and bringing me back for swift punishment. It did not work, my brother won the bet (and subsequently removed himself from the joys of socialism to Carmel, CA), and now I was about to crawl voluntarily into the red realm. What if they extradite me to Czechosovakia for belated punishment, the Sino-Soviet split notwithstanding?

The three of us – Priscilla, I, and Herakleitos – disembarked into the prewar days, Hollywoodish realism of shabby decaying China of the early 1930s. Did we catch a glimpse of Clark Gable leering in the direction of Carole Lombard, did we hear the whiningly innocent voice of Peter Lorre? This is supposed to be the spotlessly clean new China, didn't Mao order the extinction of all flies? They swarmed the smelly meat market, our fussy sanitation inspectors should pay a visit to get acquainted with the facts of real life. An almost silent movie it was, accompanied by the tingling bells of unhurried, methodically moving bicyclists.

The entire Lim clan had removed itself a few steps ahead of the victorious communists, behind stayed only one family of distant (which for the Chinese means close) relatives. They were our welcoming committee and guides.

The ferry delivered us to a nearby island called Kulangsu (Gulangyu in the modernized spelling), once a rather luxurious enclave, the summer home of some of the wealthiest overseas Chinese and a dozen Western con- sulates. The Mediterranean architecture, falling apart due to both the lack of upkeep and excessive attention paid by the tropical climate, nibbling away the masonry, luxuriant green growth crawling up the steps through the blind windows.

"A house whose number of rooms one can remember is not worthy of living in," was the article of faith of my eccentric father-in-law. I knew his primary residence only from the fading photos – part Grand Hotel Pupp in Karlsbad in my native country, part Taj Mahal.

Not any more. The relatives were permitted to occupy the ground floor. In the former reception rooms the walls, once draped with red velvet, had turned into an abstract design on a mildewy canvas, with blueish varicose veins meandering in weird directions. Each piece of furniture seemed to be from a different garage sale. No lacquer, porcelain, statue or painting, nothing aesthetically pleasing – this being the abode of a retired professor of art.

Easy to guess: the tornado of the cultural revolution had swept the premises.

"They came and smashed everything – piece by piece," informed uncle, the art lover, adding that this was not the worst experience. That it had been his duty to join the ideologically imbued vandals – and thus to prove his political maturity – in visiting the neighbors and demolishing their treasured possessions.

There followed an introduction to a man of significance – an *apparatchik*, an official of the Communist Party. Smiles, handshakes, a Niagara of platitudes.

Despite my best intentions to preserve an absolute ignorance of this preposterously complicated Chinese tongue, through the years of listening to it almost daily, I occasionally managed to decipher the topic of conversation.

The Party official was to be used as a part of *banfa* – a tool of shortcut arrangements without which absolutely nothing seems to be accomplished.

"Why are you trying to be so nice to us – why don't you behead us, for example?" I queried. Fairly, substantially straight-forward, no beating around the bush. Priscilla interpreted, the functionary grinned pretending not to understand.

So I obliged by elaborating on the fundamental Marxist-Leninist principle of class struggle, historically predetermined, inevitable and mercilessly to be pursued, no one to be spared. So much I remembered the hard-to-forget experience from my days in Europe.

"Oh no, no!" protested the *apparatchik* and presented a predictable pirouette of dialectics: "The honorable grandfather was no feudal oppressor, no black demon at all – to the contrary, he was a modernizer – banks, railways, and according to our leader Deng Xiaoping, his four principles of modernization . . ." and so the recital of the proper political message of the day proceeded.

The friendly functionary arranged for us lodging in a spacious, i.e. luxurious mansion – space being the most treasured luxury in China. This former property of the Lim family was reserved for visting VIPs, State and Party potentates, what an honor.

There was more to it: we entered the premises of nostalgic historical significance – this happened to be one of the last headquarters of Chiang Kaishek, before he ignominiously fled to Taiwan, a chapter in history thus closed.

There we were sleeping in the same imperial-size bed, under the antimosquito canopy that protected the generalissimo from biting insects but not from more noxious communists. There I was, perhaps sitting at the same desk at which the generalissimo had formulated his final quixotic manifesto of resistance.

The shower did not work, we, the sweaty smelly VIPs raised the point. The neither hostile nor friendly personnel agreed that indeed that particular contraption was out of order and due to shortage of manpower (in a country of one billion) it could not be fixed in the foreseeable future. We were

advised to step outside – a vigorous post-typhoon downpour would surely provide a satisfactory substitute of desired ablution.

Some parts of the island, including the mansion in which Priscilla was
born, were off-limits. The People's Army preempted much of the housing
space, often without making any discernible use of it. The public was also
barred from what was reputedly the nicest beach on the island. There it
was, I was informed, that people used to abandon their female offspring.
Either by drowning them ("to give a bath" euphemism) or, in the case of
more gentle souls, to leave them on an adjacent slope in the hope that some
good Samaritan would commiserate and rescue the unworthy creature (girls
being called "one thousand ounces of gold," baby boys, however, considered
"ten thousand ounces").

Nowadays, with the decreed one child per family policy, when a girl – a
deficit of 9,000 ounces – is born, what then? Either to divorce the guilty
spouse and try again – or to dispose of the daughter the old-fashioned way.
The local media are not entirely reticent about the matter. A sack with eight
suffocated female infants was reported found at the doorstep of a Party
secretariat. Couples should beware of conception in the month of May – it
augurs ill, it will be a girl.

One child means not only the impoverishment of the family but also
of the language – no need any more for words like "brother, sister, cousin,"
the uncles and aunties are also destined to die out. A Chinese-speaking
family of an American academic was strolling with their two children. "Is
this your mother?" asked a Chinese youngster. "And where is the mother
of the other baby?"

We were substantially taken by the demeanor of the children – how serious
they were, rarely giggling or horsing around. They rather reminded us of
somber Teutonic pensioneers on their methodical strolls in the Schwarzwald.

"Something is missing here – I just can't put my finger on it," mumbled
my expatriate spouse.

Plenty of things were in short supply – laughter, relaxation, upkeep of
houses – and yes, of course – no dogs, no howling mongrels, the standard
tormenting feature in almost every Third World country. But not here. In
1950, a few months after the installation of Mao's rule, all dogs were ordered
killed, many of them were eaten by the hungry people. This happened almost
two generations ago. Today's youngsters have never seen a live canine creature
as we have not come face-to-face with a live dinosaur.

In the countryside some dogs do survive, we were told. We did however
notice a few shy, pathetically emaciated cats, hiding in dark corners.

What about the report card according to the teacher Herakleitos?

Mores have surely changed – not for the better. Alienation may be the inevitable nemesis of a capitalist order/disorder as the Marxists never tire of reminding us. In China we did not detect much of comradely congeniality either. People rarely exchanged greetings, they pushed and shoved without apology. On a ferry, after having stepped on someone's toe, there was my automatic "sorry." Why did I do that – to a stranger? wondered my companion.

The Chinese script was simplified, Priscilla had also some difficulty with the spoken language, peppered with various coded expressions such as the word "tiger" by which the natives meant our bedfellow Chiang Kai-shek.

The wartime Japanese occupation worked as a radical social equalizer – everybody starved, regardless of pedigree. Priscilla recalled long lines, big crowds and fights over rare commodities. Somewhere here, this direction – here it must have been – a fisherman who started to disembowel a shark, and in the process from the belly of the beast retrieved a human arm that belonged to a combatant lost at sea. The fisherman swiftly removed a gold wedding ring, dropped the limb in the garbage pail and proceeded with his brisk business of parceling the man eater.

Inspection of that particular market place shattered one of my carefully honed theories, namely the proposition, verified over and over in my native Czechoslovakia as well as on the troubled island of Sri Lanka (in the days of socialist experimentation of Mrs. Bandaranaike) that socialist programs and the availability of onion and garlic are mutually exclusive: either the nirvana of a classless society or healthy, vitamin rich vegetables – but one can't have both. The moment Marxism-Leninism enters, the salutary substances vanish overnight.

Yet, at the former shark market, a cornucopia of onions dominated – no other vegetables but onions. Was there perhaps something wrong with my dogmatic equation or with the Chinese increasingly less dogmatic implementation of socialist recipes?

"Somewhere here, it can't be far away, used to be a candy store, as children we used to come for absolutely superb coconut cookies, I still remember – on the top shelf, left side. . . ."

We walked in circles until we found: yes, there it was, the same store, shelf and place, the same cookies tasting as in the days immemorial. Despite the revolutionary decades, the succession of values, canonized and condemned in turn. How about that, my dear Herakleitos?

As it is commonly known, whereas other people eat in order to keep alive, the Chinese seem to live in order to eat. Culinary goals are the alpha and, not infrequently, also the omega of their aspirations. We foreigners count heads, the Chinese count mouths. "How are you, take it easy," are the standard meaningless salutations among us, the neurotic Western barbarians. "Have you eaten?" will a Chinese greet another instead.

Our brief stay had to be crowned by a farewell feast. After a lengthy family deliberation the choice fell on the People's First Eatery, the top place in town.

Instead of Herakleitos we should have taken Dante along on this field trip. A gloomy, poorly lit place, a few morose, bone spitting patrons. A little boy with a remarkably rectangular head entered in order to urinate between the soiled tables.

First we had to approach the box office and engage in lengthy negotiations with a thoroughly disinterested state employee. An agreement finally arrived at – a multi-course dinner for five, the price the equivalent of two weeks' wages.

In front of bubbling kettles another state employee yawned semi-asleep pretending we were not there.

By then we already shared that sentiment. Self-service (shortage of labor, once again), polishing greasy chopsticks with my Central European handkerchief. Foul smelling dishes, indigestible concoctions, a revenge for the Opium War, unequal treaties, lost territories to the Russians. One spoon of soup made me believe that this was a bouillon made out of the socks of the veterans of the Long March. A cat, one of the sturdy emaciated mohicans approached us. We offered to let it sample the delights but the experienced champion of survival would not touch it.

Any souvenirs to bring home? In a special store for fleecing foreigners of their hard currency, cans of pickled mushrooms are the best bet. Priscilla selected a dozen fans, all with an identical design, no surprise in socialism.

Since my childhood, preceding the tutorial of Hitler and Stalin, I have been craving for a gong – a big gong, if possible. And suddenly we stumbled upon a store with just such merchandise. We touched, sensitively tapped, fondled and finally chose two splendidly acoustic contraptions.

The unexpected expenditure required a further exchange of then still-robust dollars into local currency. The premises of the bank might have been designed by Charles Dickens – one room with forty scribes, silently, listlessly attending to their chores. We flashed VISA, the symbol of capitalist opulence, and the machinery started to move.

During this lengthy process, one of the gongs slipped from under an arm and fell flat on the ground, shattering the tranquility of the premises. The laboring cadres froze without emitting a sound. Did we lose our face? Probably, most definitely. I started to laugh, an uninhibited kind of roar.

After a long while, the wall began cracking. First a solitary giggle, then another, an echo of Smetana's symphonic poem *Vltava*, when the trickle of a river stream is on its way to grow and turns into a roaring Wagnerian finale. The Chinese, traumatized and anesthetized for so long, have not entirely lost their capacity for what we consider elementary, normal, and substantially preferable reactions.

Fine. Not everything is lost, the situation is serious but not hopeless (and not the other way around, as Mussolini allegedly diagnosed the state of Italy of his days). On this optimistic note we left China just ahead of yet another pernicious typhoon.

* * *

We returned to China in 1986 – after four years, time long enough to graduate from college, to finish a world war, and in the case of Deng the modernizer to implement substantial domestic changes. This time we were surely not stepping into the same river.

In Hong Kong we boarded the very same Chinese ship and were put up in the same cabin. Behold, the reproduction of a standard traditional painting (steep mountain peaks, mist, wind-swept pines) was gone and instead we stared at a wall with a modernistic renditiion of a nude female with a luxuriant amount of pubic hair and one leg amputated.

The cabin boys and girls were less aloof, in the dining hall chopsticks had been replaced by plastic forks and knives. The quality of the food had improved but because of the typhoon season and the substantially choppy voyage, not all the passengers retained it and the deck was slippery.

Docking and far more efficient disembarkation this time. The waiting crowd shouted greetings and, above all, instructions on what further Western merchandise to acquire in the duty free shop. Our relatives had notified us urgently in Hong Kong to bring along a refrigerator. What about a concert piano? I grumbled. What happened to the restraint not to lean so obviously, to demand so crassly, a restraint that characterized the Chinese society for millenia and was still around a couple of years ago?

Unlike the unchanged exterior of the port, still largely run down, with little color and still plenty of bicyclists, the interior of the people had changed – altered habits with a patina of capitalist temperament, individualistic greed. A brisk black market with foreign currencies, competition among the cabbies and tricycle rickshaws (not state employees anymore), and tipping, of course.

Private shops and restaurants had sprung up, no danger of repeating the horror of the People's First Eatery. The military had surrendered the lackadaisically maintained properties, no more beaches off-limits. No more Mao jackets but men still dressed with monotonous uniformity (dark pants, light color short-sleeve shirts, plastic sandals, a watch with a metal band). The women were the trailblazers toward the antitotalitarian goal of variety and color. Some wore skirts. They handled this novelty with endearing innocence, blissfully oblivious of their providing an unimpeded view of their delicate parts. To cool themselves, they used their skirts as a fan, lifting and flapping, thus eventually raising the temperature of interested observers.

Daring pioneers appeared in what resembled semi-hot pants. T-shirts with signs such as PAPILLON or UNIVERSITY OF KENTUCKY, with statements misspelled (ENGERTIC PEOPLE) or abandoned (HOME OF STAINLESS, MADE IN), worthless Taiwan or Hong Kong rejects that make some smart operators rich.

Most importantly, the joyless, subdued people around us started opening up. Though not yet a merry wedding party, they did not resemble a funeral crowd anymore. During our first visit everybody seemed to stare at the visiting Lim princess but nobody would dare to make a step to shake her hand. This time we were swarmed. The same fellow who used to pretend blindness rushed to us announcing that his brother was about to give a piano recital at Carnegie Hall in New York.

The fruits of one child policy: gone was the ideal and reality of an exemplarily behaving offspring (treasured in a society practicing collective responsibility, i.e. parents could be punished for the misdeeds of their young). Nowadays, the one and only treasure permitted is the treasure to be protected and pampered. Permissiveness is rampant among the young parents (largely a part of the "lost generation" of the Cultural Revolution), corporal punishment unknown, the little monsters are at the worst called *taoqi* – "the somewhat naughty ones."

The media have come up with a more apt label: LITTLE EMPERORS – pampered, spoiled, lazy, and fat, so goes the offical lament.

I made a fool of myself in a fiasco of an attempt to stand up against the tide at a concert of a celebrated youth orchestra from Shanghai. Chinese traditional music, Donizetti, Rossini, Gershwin – an exemplary performance, ruined by a pernicious force. Little emperors and empresses were crawling all over the place, yelling, chasing each other. My hisses, gestures, and overall expression of ferocious displeasure merely added further decibels to the reigning anarchy. When I switched my protestations to their parents, they just indicated there was nothing they could – or possibly would be inclined to – do.

* * *

Four years ago, our son Ota stayed behind in Hong Kong, stricken with chicken pox of extravagant virulence. This time, at the age of sixteen, he was to be exposed to the ancestral terrain. Though American born, he speaks

Chinese (its Fukien dialect). In the West he is taken for a diluted Oriental of sorts, in China he passed for a Long Nose, a *Hwanna* – a hairy barbarian, a savage intruder.

"Those white people – how repulsive! Their little children, that is not that bad but once they grow up! And they all look so alike – how do they manage to see the difference and not get confused, that is beyond me," was a typical comment of local kibbitzers, happily passed on to me by my knowledgeable descendant.

He acquired a dozen local girl friends, employees of the local tourist board, a carefree crowd, enjoying a pleasant tenured existence. A guest room may or may not be cleaned. The garbage may wait or it can be tossed out of the window. When told about the efficiency of services in Hong Kong, the jolly angels were shocked over such inhuman practices.

Unauthorized contact with a foreigner used to be punished with a speedy dispatch to a reeducation camp. Not any more – Ota reported about his visit to a one room apartment: "In front of a televison sat a woman, middle age. My girl did not greet her and did not introduce me, and she ignored us all the time we were there chatting. After we left, I asked her who was that woman. It was my mother, she explained."

Filial respect is definitely a matter of the past, buried during the cultural revolution. "What do you say to your parents in the morning, when you get up?" I interrogated one of our nephews. "Nothing," he responded.

"I feel like a missionary," Ota complained about the deficient mores of his angels. They pick their noses. They spit around with the gust of a disgruntled sailor. In this, the missionary's rectification effort was partially succesful – the angels switched to spitting from the window. What if someone happens to get in their way? Oh well, it will most likely be a stranger, so what.

According to a governmental instructional booklet published in the days of Deng the modernizer, so-called music such as jazz with its abnormal rhythm resembles spasms and uncontrollable fits. Dancing continued to be viewed with disfavor as something unproductive, if not outright decadent.

But even this Spartan wall seemed to be crumbling: We spent Saturday night at an open air restaurant adjacent to the People's Botanical Gardens, once again officially known as Lim Gardens, named after the original builder and owner, my grandfather-in-law. The manager led us to the best table on which he placed Coca Cola, locally a rather expensive potion for which he refused to accept money.

A tropical setting, whispering palms, the place was filling up, the gaudily lit dance floor quadrangle empty. Families, couples, girls holding hands in tense expectations. The solemn, subdued mood was broken by a little empress of preschool age who got up, lifted her luxuriously frilled mini-undies, squatted and relieved herself on the spot. Her initiative was closely, pensively observed and then imitated by a little emperor who managed to spurt his stream to an extraordinary distance.

Some throaty messages over the public address system, an attempt made to use the microphone, or rather a macrophone. Something was about to begin – begin with what?

"The Radetzky march!" was my correct guess. What seemed to be the most popular tune in the most populous country commenced. The touch of Austro-Hungarian monarchy was followed by a couple of Verdis (*Il Trovatore, Aida*) and Bizet (*Carmen*, of course). Toreadors marching with shovels to build a dike, to divert the Yangtze river, I imagined. Still, progress – not any more ditties such as *The East Is Red*, or *The Brigade of the Collectors of Night Soil Is Descending from the Mountain.*

Surreptitious looks around, concentration on one's straw in one's coke bottle. After much hesitation the first courageous ones entered the dance floor – boy with a boy, girl with a girl. Gay preference? No such thought. No gay liberation front on this land (such predilection being swiftly cured with a bullet, we were told) but shyness, pure and simple.

After the *William Tell Overture* the functionary in charge of the record player switched to Argentinian tangos of the Thirties. And behold – a first couple emerged, with more confidence than skill, engaging in daring bends and ostentatious gestures, the gentleman firmly in control of the lady, music, and the gasping spectators. "Just like Fred Astaire and Ginger Rogers," an elderly native nodded appreciatively.

Music of Hawaii followed.

"Now, you try," I nudged Ota who objected that he did not know how to.

"What a silly excuse – neither do they," I pointed to a trio of maidens, frozen in anticipation, firmly grasping their handkerchiefs.

"Shall we dance?"

"We do not dance."

"So why are you here?"

"To see those who dance."

He then suggested that they ask him about the United States – anything. For the first time ever, they now had an opportunity to speak to a real American from MEI-KUO, "Beautiful Country," as the U.S. is called in Chinese (unlike Africa – FEI TZIU, the "Bad, Ugly Continent").

"What kind of weather is in America," they managed to utter after some hesitation.

Still, this is progress. To repeat: not long ago, swift punishment threatened for a mere whisper to a foreign devil, be that an American imperialist or any of the numerous running dogs.

Progress in the selection of music was also registered, reaching and soon exceeding my (low) level of tolerance – a local semblance of rock, the infatuation of the barbarians.

"Grandfather must be turning in his grave and Mao in his mausoleum, on hearing this," I pointed an accusatory finger in the direction of the cacophony.

Son pointed out that the grandfather was an enlightened modernizer who would not object to progress.

As expected, the grandfather did not rise from the dead to solve this generational dispute.

* * *

Asking a Chinese how far it was from place A to place B, I received the answer that it depended on how fast I would go.

"The Aristotelean logic that plus and minus are natural opposites, that one plus one equals two, that logic you cannot apply in this country," warned a knowledgeable Viennese coed studying in Shanghai. "No, you have to be equally illogical and then you will reach a perfect understanding."

I remain unconvinced – there is, for example, a system behind the infuriating sequence of standard negative responses one gets: A nod, of course, must not be taken for a sign of consensus but merely an acknowledgment that the question, request, whatever, was heard and, hopefully, understood.

This scenario develops:

1. Reaction to an unwelcome question – to pretend the question was not heard and because of the non-response the questioner will get the point and forget the whole thing.

2. In case the questioner did not get the point and will repeat the question, the Chinese party will pretend not to understand.

3. In case of further perseverance, the Chinese will resort to profuse explanation that while he wholeheartedly agrees, unfortunately, it cannot be done – it is too complicated (the most favorite rationalization), it is beyond anybody's control, is *ultra vires*.

As an advance party for our university, I was to look over some candidates for graduate studies and funding, and also to inspect the premises and to probe into some details with regard to a pending exchange program with a local institution.

I wanted to see the dormitories – any room.

"Sorry, it cannot be done, dormitories are closed. It's summer, you see."

Well, I did not see – the summer session was in full swing.

The point granted, the request not granted with the explanation that all dormitories in China were alike.

After a few hours of less than fruitful communication, as lunchtime was approaching, I suggested to have something to eat in the student cafeteria.

"Sorry, all cafeterias are closed – summer vacation. . . ."

"Summer session!"

"True. But the best cooks are on vacation."

"I don't need the best cook, an ordinary one will do."

"Very sorry, it cannot be arranged because we did not make an advance reservation."

One is likely to encounter this kind of discourse in various settings. As lamented earlier, the Chinese charge foreign devils for services (notably for accommodation) much more than what they charge the natives. The overseas Chinese are priced somewhere in between and that was the category we were aiming at, and whenever we did not succeed for the three of us, at least Priscilla should have been the beneficiary.

"You are not an overseas Chinese," objected an official in charge of such matters.

"Why not? Have a look at my passport – born in Amoy, China!"

"You are not an overseas Chinese because this is an American but not an overseas Chinese passport."

"Such passports do not exist, you foolish man!"

The less than Aristotelean verbal duel continued, the official still probing to prove his point: "You are not an overseas Chinese because you are not registered in this hotel for the overseas Chinese."

"But we want to get registered here, that is why, because. . . ." Catch 22, Joseph Heller. And Franz Kafka, my countryman, once again.

* * *

The cultural revolution was already over for ten years. The final discouraging judgment as to the qualities of the human race was already in: the majority failed, people lost their sense of decency, caused much harm and pain, did beat up, torture, denounce enemies and friends, strangers and their own family members alike.

When the nightmare was finally over, the tired, dizzy participants started to orient themselves in that multiple havoc and precious few penitents were to be found. As is usually the case, the responsibility for crimes and damages in general was shifted from specific individuals to the nebulous System, to Chairman Mao "whose thought was essentailly correct as can be clearly seen from his mistakes" (70 percent correct, 30 percent wrong, according to the current official calculus). How many thousands or millions did actually belong to the Gang of Four?

When pressing the point, I would be told about a "few thousand" ultraradicals shot, others put behind bars, yet still others escaped retribution altogether, some of them turning into opportunistic, prosperous entrepreneurs – red capitalists.

In Fukien province the cultural revolution was almost a tranquil affair, I was told. True, plenty of property destruction but not more than twenty thousand killed. "Here – everything was smashed," informed a witness in the municipal park about the revolutionaries destroying gazebos, ripping apart benches, blowing up hunchbacked bridges across bubbling brooks. At the bottom of one such stream I noticed a cupid, a chubby angelic fellow, battered, drowned, not yet rehabilitated.

Yet another distant relative was introduced to us: a shy girl, a half-orphan. Her father had been beaten to death by the advocates of a better future.

At the local university I was introduced to a jolly, optimistic professor who offered his lefthand for a hearty handshake. His right arm was paralyzed, it withered away like a dead tree branch. Revolutionary students had broken the arm and prevented medical help.

We were getting to the skeletons in local closets, step by step, as if peeling an onion: it did not produce tears but wonderment, bewilderment. An aunt of ours was paraded through the streets with a dunce cap. Her former husband, a party official and tyrant, was killed by the red guards – deservedly so, insisted some of the neighbors. The nephews, members of the lost generation, rather than victims of irrational times were among the energetic victimizers. They hounded their grandmother to death.

Everyone has his or her own truth, Luigi Pirandello. Usually, after sunset, former employees of the long gone grandfather would visit Priscilla, presenting their mutually exclusive views of who behaved decently and who swinishly. A servant's daughter who claimed to be the savior of the grandmother, becomes accused as having been one of her prime tormentors. The widow of another ex-employee, while overtly an impertinent critic of all things communist, was in fact a ferocious radical who craved to be admitted to the ranks of the red guards despite her advanced age, and so on – who denounced whom, who harmed whom.

Another visitor (a reputed former secret police informer) barged in, imploring Priscilla to file, on behalf of the Lim family, a restitution claim to the decaying, decrepit palaces.

Why should she do so, why this interest in unmaking the revolutionary accomplishment of the people – a matter of bad conscience, perhaps?

Yes, bad conscience towards the state. During the cultural revolution none of the tenants bothered to pay rent and no agency of the semi-defunct state bothered to collect. But now, as part of the non-ideological modernization drive, Deng insists on the payment – retroactively, for all the many delinquent years. Each month the collector comes to the door, each month the indignant debtor throws him out. Communism is worse than feudalism, in those days the lodging was free – so goes the claim. (Still, communism is in this respect far more compassionate than capitalism – which capitalist landlord would tolerate such procrastination?)

Therefore, the supplicant continued, if we reclaim the properties as other overseas Chinese have already done, and repair the properties, spruce them up, of course, we surely would also forgive and forget the debts, unlike the communist leeches.

I wished to find out what other properties did the family own, in addition to the decrepit mansions packed with rent-resistant tenants.

Land, some of it agricultural. A block of office buildings downtown. A brick factory, a sugar refinery. . . .

What about a brewery, a distillery of some good alcohol – have we got? Just a factory producing soy sauce.

The government already extended its apology for the destruction of grandfather's statue. A replacement was under construction. The court sculptor in charge was working with the help of faded photos and, according to Priscilla, the result thus far failed to resemble the honorable ancestor. To me it looked like Antonín Švehla, a pre-war Czechoslovak politician of rural orientation, certainly not honored in his native land.

$$* \quad * \quad *$$

Nowadays in Eastern Europe socialism is being defined as an intermediate between capitalism and capitalism.

Our junior reported that in his Chinese harem was one who claimed to be a communist. I deputized him to find out what she understood by that chiliastic creed. He returned with this definition: "She said that communism was a system in which we can make more money."

It is also a system in which values tend to perish with distressing speed and regularity. This particular loyalist youngster was perhaps among those killed at the Square of Heavenly Peace. But, of course, we must never forget – there was no killing, there perhaps has never been a Tiananmen Square. Only the unpredictability of China is predictable, so the sage in the Hong Kong bar emphasized.

Bohumil Krcil

Candymen at Work
Herat, Afghanistan

The Two Best Friends
France 1976

Passenger from the Land of Light – Nuristan
Pakistan 1978

Three in One
Sweden 1976

Trust in Vain
Manhattan

Late Years of Dr. W.

Upper East Side Conversation

Edith Piaf Imitator in Central Park

The Three Brothers from Downing Street

Waiting in Chelsea

West Side Sunset on Broadway & 60th Street

The Twins & The Wind

James Ragan

THE LAKE ISLE OF BLED

I still see the bones of Bled through mirrors
and light the rock shade stores within its sepulcher,
how from the stoneyard eyes appear
like fish nettled in spoors
of prehistoric clay. Across the rockfall
coins click down across their saintly feet
while from the gilded nave the wishbell
rings for the memory their minds will keep
long and unattended. All day I climb
with saurian soles to where the sun steam settles
and the hunched nun, blind on glacier lime,
blows the holy smoke from spears of candles.
She resents the circling swans that seine to rest.
She would rather see, and seeing, be the bones of death.

Yugoslavia, 1984

SISYPHUS BLIND

"A face that toils so close to stones
is already stone itself."
– Camus

I have imagined him always blind,
pushing stone until the hill capsizes,
and the walk back down
becomes the walk back up,
each step, a shock, a touch of air,
on course in case a passer-by
leans into his world of local forms.

He stops. I barely brush his arms
before his eyes stare down,
calculating distance as I pass.
We are not far from breathing.
We suffocate only in the lungs
and curse each other, doubled-up, tongues
dried by the dust our shoe-flaps make.

Only night deceives us. Its landscape
trails the moon, shifting sky to cut us down
where we sit. We feel the shattering underfoot
of stars, the ground rolling overhead,
the rock carving paths into our flesh.
How willingly we fall into each other's cry.
We dream, eye to eye, one suicide.

I try to think his stare awake, to rise
above the ash of moonstone, to feel his shoes,
dust lifting around them. Nothing remains,
only rock, his moon-struck face.
I am whatever stone breathes, a blind man
pounding air to escape the universe
like a meteor burning up space.

A KILLING IN THE OLD COUNTRY

In her sack she feels the rope, thinks
how quick the spokes of the neck
will snap, tighter than the braid
wheat spins in the barn's souring chaff.
She knows the air is hay,
and seeds the chickens peck are fevered.

She walks hunched down along the trough,
the rib of light lasered by the rafter's coop.
All noon long, her shifting eyes
decide the course the earth will take
to shake the sun free. And what

she thinks will the difference make
if in the killing of a hen
this morning her lone child running
a pigling through the goldenrod,
finds the feathers sickled from the gilder's hair?

She knows the old country, the earth
will never move faster than the night stars,
and hearts she keeps
locked in the bone-bowl of her bed
will never beat in her crippling hands.

Her sudden eye is caught.
She feels for the noose and swift
as the half sign of the cross,
strangle-grips the cackler's craw,
the right hand not knowing the other,
cycling the knot, has shucked the whimper off.

Cernina, Czechoslovakia, 1968

Patricia Hampl

ELEGY FOR THE BURNED

January 1969

Anthracite sours the air,
the sun's no better than a gas lamp,
and the cocaine of the fog
has confused the trees.
Later, slush chokes the gutters;
the moon will elude
the oily clouds as it rises
over the russet tiles
of the fluted roofs.
Icicles are dangling
from the eaves of the Czernin Palace
where Jan Masaryk
jumped, or was pushed,
but definitely died,
twenty-one years ago.
On Vaclavske Namesti
Jan Palach has lit his match.
He has breathed his last gold
in the golden city,
he has become many colors.
In the emergency room
of Bellevue Hospital
my brother fights to save
the melting bodies
of two other men
who tried to go up in smoke
in front of the U. N. building.
It's the fingernails, he says.
You can't get the fingernails
out of their gums.

They double over,
they crouch down and dig
into their mouths
one last time, but
the right words
aren't there anymore.

May 1977

We sit around a white
linen cloth stitched with red
geometric embroidery.
A tall bottle of *slivovice*
on the table, flecks
of caraway in the bread,
a mound of codfish roe heaped
like tiny greased ball bearings.
Outside, the engaged couples
move in and out
of the Persian lilacs.
One man, a doctor, tells us
there was never any hope,
then or now.
Later, we raise our glasses
in the high-ceilinged apartment.
Drink fast! they say. Don't think!
We throw back our heads.
Our tongues burn briefly,
then our throats.
It is gone, the colorless
abstract of blue plums,
the heat distilled
in dusty Moravian towns,
the forgotten villages,
the narrow highways
lined with fruit trees
that very soon will
rush into flower,
all those flimsy pink blossoms.

A ROMANTIC EDUCATION

Excerpts

I WAS FIVE AND WAS sitting on the floor of the vestibule hallway of my grandmother's house where the one bookcase had been pushed. The bookcase wasn't in the house itself – ours wasn't a reading family. I was holding in my lap a book of sepia photographs bound in a soft brown cover, stamped in flaking gold with the title *Zlatá Praha*. Golden Prague, views of the nineteenth century.

The album felt good, soft. First, the Hradčany Castle and its gardens, then a close-up of the astronomical clock, a view of the baroque jumble of Malá Strana. Then a whole series of photographs of the Vltava River, each showing a different bridge, photograph after pale photograph like a wild rose that opens petal by petal, exposing itself effortlessly, as if there were no such thing as regret. All the buildings in the pictures were hazy, making it seem that the air, not the stone, held the contour of the baroque villas intact.

I didn't know how to read yet, and the Czech captions under the pictures were no more incomprehensible to me than English would have been. I liked the soft, fleshlike pliancy of the book. I knew the pictures were of Europe, and that Europe was far away, unreachable. Still, it had something to do with me, with my family. I sat in the cold vestibule, turning the pages of the Prague album. I was flying; I was somewhere else. I was not in St. Paul, Minnesota, and I was happy.

My grandmother appeared at the doorway. Her hands were on her stout hips, and she wanted me to come out of the unheated hallway. She wanted me to eat coffee cake in the kitchen with everybody else, and I had been hard to find. She said, "Come eat," as if this were the family motto.

As she turned to go, she noticed the album. In a second she was down on the floor with me, taking the album carefully in her hands, turning the soft, felt pages. "Oh," she said, "Praha." She looked a long time at one picture, I don't remember which one, and then she took a white handkerchief out of her pinafore apron pocket, and dabbed at the tears under her glasses.

She took off the wire-rim glasses and made a full swipe.

Her glasses had made deep hollows on either side of her nose, two small caves. They looked as if, with a poke, the skin would give way like a ripe peach, and an entrance would be exposed into her head, into the skull, a passageway to the core of her brain. I didn't want her head to have such wounds. Yet I liked them, these unexpected dips in a familiar landscape.

"So beautiful," she was crying melodramatically over the album. "So beautiful." I had never seen an adult cry before. I was relieved, in some odd way, that there was crying in adulthood, that crying would not be taken away.

My grandmother hunched down next to me in the hallway; she held the album, reciting the gold-stamped captions as she turned the pages and dabbed at her eyes. She was having a good cry. I wanted to put my small finger into the two little caves of puckered skin, the eyeless sockets on either side of her large, drooping nose. Strange wounds, I wanted to touch them. I wanted to touch her, my father's mother. She was so *foreign*.

* * *

The sharpest memory I have of a childhood conversation – I don't mean one of those fragments of private perception from childhood that are eloquent with the oddity of life, but rather the only recollection I have of what it was like to be a child talking with other children, a *social* memory of childhood – was really a ritual. Maybe that's why I remember it: we repeated it often.

"What are you?" someone would ask as we walked, four or five of us, up Oxford Street, to St. Luke's School on Summit Avenue. Or the question might come up as we stood in a little knot, shivering on the asphalt playground that on Sundays was the church parking lot.

What are you? And each little girl answered promptly, with satisfaction, as if counting up the family silver: "I'm Norwegian," "I'm German," or the most frequent reply, "I'm Irish," "I'm Irish," "I'm Irish." Occasionally there was a rebel who said, defensively, obviously coached at home, "I'm American." But this was frowned upon and considered an affectation.

"I mean, what are you *really*?" someone would ask impatiently. We waited for the requisite foreignness to be pledged. Our contempt set in soon after our annoyance if the rebel refused to play the game as the implacable rules demanded. What are you *really*? And the girl mumbled something about being a lot of different things – German and French, a little Swiss, a little Irish and partly Finnish. "And so my Mom and Dad say we're American." This was acceptable, though I found it pretty thin gruel myself.

It is odd that we did this repeatedly and with such relish – we who spoke only English, whose parents were just buying their first television sets, ending forever, it seems now, the ancient art form, night after night filled with gossip. We had so little connection with anything "ethnic" (the word wasn't used) that our little game was all form, no content.

We were natural catechists to whom words were more rhythm and motion than meaning. The *Baltimore Catechism*, that small buff-colored lozenge of Truth, had taught us the satisfaction of recitation, the ready and absolute response:

> *Who made you?*
> God made me.

> *Why did God make you?*
> To know, love and serve Him in this world
> in order to be happy with Him forever in the next.

What exactly were we up to when we stood in a circle on the playground of St. Luke's School, huddled in the cold? (I remember all these scenes as winter ones, the crusted snowdrifts and a sharp wind bending us forward into the circle.) Why did we ask that question and what satisfaction came from our answers? It wasn't a process of drawing the self together into "wholeness," to use the current expression. Or if it was, our wholeness was a patch job with all the seams showing. Most of us weren't simply German, or Irish, or any single thing. It took us a while to dissect our reality. "I'm half Irish," I said, sweeping my hand like a cleaver exactly across my midriff, "and half Czech."

It all seems atavistic and even a little morbid. We were, in our way, out for blood. We had very little to say after we'd announced our "nationality." Those of us who had any remnant of foreignness near us (my grandmother, with her accent – I didn't hear it as one – and her inability to write English) were often ashamed of the actual presence of distinctly non-American (I mean non-Irish American) qualities. But we remained proud of, or perhaps it is more accurate to say we were enthralled by, the foreignness that was somehow ours. In a thoroughly unconscious way, we saw ourselves as the authentic products of entire nations which lay, mysteriously but definitely, over there. The Old World.

* * *

Food was the potent center of my grandmother's life. Maybe the immense amount of time it took to prepare meals during most of her life accounted for her passion. Or it may have been her years of work in various kitchens on the hill and later, in the house of Justice Butler: after all, she was professional. Much later, when she was dead and I went to Prague, I came to feel the motto I knew her by best – *Come eat* – was not, after all, a personal statement, but a racial one, the *cri de coeur* of Middle Europe.

Often, on Sundays, the entire family gathered for dinner at her house. Dinner was at 1 P.M. My grandmother would have preferred the meal to be at the old time of noon, but her children had moved their own Sunday dinner hour to the more fashionable (it was felt) 4 o'clock, so she compromised. Sunday breakfast was something my mother liked to do in a big way, so we arrived at my grandmother's hardly out of the reverie of waffles and orange rolls before we were propped like rag dolls in front of pork roast and sauerkraut, dumplings, hot buttered carrots, rye bread and rollikey, pickles and olives, apple pie and ice cream. And coffee.

Coffee was a food in that house, not a drink. I always begged for some because the magical man on the Hills Brothers can with his turban and long robe scattered with stars and his gold slippers with pointed toes, looked deeply happy as he drank from his bowl. The bowl itself reminded me of soup, Campbell's chicken noodle soup, my favorite food. The distinct adultness of coffee and the robed man with his deep-drinking pleasure made it clear why the grownups lingered so long at the table. The uncles smoked cigars then, and the aunts said, "Oh, those cigars."

My grandmother, when she served dinner, was a virtuoso hanging on the edge of her own ecstatic performance. She seemed dissatisfied, almost querulous until she had corralled everybody into their chairs around the table, which she tried to do the minute they got into the house. No cocktails, no hors d'oeuvres (pronounced, by some of the family, "horse's ovaries"), just business. She was a little power crazed: she had us and, by God, we were going to eat. She went about it like a goose breeder forcing pellets down the gullets of those dumb birds.

She flew between her chair and the kitchen, always finding more this, extra that. She'd given you the *wrong* chicken breast the first time around; now she'd found the *right* one: eat it too, eat it fast, because after the chicken comes rhubarb pie. Rhubarb pie with a thick slice of cheddar cheese that it was imperative every single person eat.

We had to eat fast because something was always out there in the kitchen panting and charging the gate, champing at the bit, some mound of rice or a Jello-O fruit salad or vegetable casserole or pie was out there, waiting to be let loose into the dining room.

She had the usual trite routines: the wheedlings, the silent pout ("What! You don't like my brussel sprouts? I thought you liked *my* brussel sprouts," versus your wife's/sister's/mother's. "I made that pie just for you," etc., etc.) But it was the way she tossed around the old cliches and the overused routines, mixing them up and dealing them out shamelessly, without irony, that made her a pro. She tended to peck at her own dinner. Her plate, piled with food, was a kind of stage prop, a mere bending to convention. She liked to eat, she was even a greedy little stuffer, but not on these occasions. She was a woman possessed by an idea, given over wholly to some phantasmagoria of food, a mirage of stuffing, a world where the endless chicken and the infinite lemon pie were united at last at the shore of the oceanic soup plate that her children and her children's children alone could drain . . . if only they would try.

She was there to bolster morale, to lead the troops, to give the sharp command should we falter on the way. The futility of saying no was supreme, and no one ever tried it. How could a son-in-law, already weakened near the point of imbecility by the once, twice, thrice charge to the barricades of pork and mashed potato, be expected to gather his feeble wit long enough to ignore the final call of his old commander when she sounded the alarm: "Pie, Fred?"

Just when it seemed as if the food-crazed world she had created was going to burst, that she had whipped and frothed us like a sack of boiled potatoes under her masher, just then she pulled it all together in one easeful stroke like the pro she was.

She stood in the kitchen doorway, her little round Napoleonic self sheathed in a cotton flowered pinafore apron, the table draped in its white lace cloth but spotted now with gravy and beet juice, the troops mumbling indistinctly as they waited at their posts for they knew not what. We looked up at her stupidly, weakly. She had said nonchalantly, "Anyone want another piece of pie?" No, no more pie, somebody said. The rest of the rabble grunted along with him. She stood there with the coffeepot and laughed and said, "Good! Because there *isn't* any more pie."

No more pie. We'd eaten it all, we'd put away everything in that kitchen. We were exhausted and she, gambler hostess that she was (but it was her house she was playing), knew she could offer what didn't exist, knew us, knew what she'd wrought. There was a sense of her having won, won something. There were no divisions among us now, no adults, no children. Power left the second and third generations and returned to the source, the grandmother who reduced us to mutters by her art.

That wasn't the end of it. At 5 P.M. there was "lunch" – sandwiches and beer; the sandwiches were made from the leftovers (mysteriously renewable resources, those roasts). And at about 8 P.M. we were at the table again for coffee cake and coffee, the little man in his turban and his coffee ecstasy and his pointed shoes set on the kitchen table as my grandmother scooped out the coffee and dumped it into a big enamel pot with a crushed eggshell.

By then everyone was alive and laughing again, the torpor gone. My grand-father had been inviting the men, one by one, into the kitchen during the afternoon where he silently (the austere version of memory – but he must have talked, must have said *something*) handed them jiggers of whiskey, and watched them put the shot down in one swallow. Then he handed them a beer, which they took out in the living room. I gathered that the *little* drink in the tiny glass shaped like a beer mug was some sort of antidote for the *big* drink of beer. He sat on the chair in the kitchen with a bottle of beer on the floor next to him and played his concertina, allowing society to form itself around him – while he lived he was the center – but not seeking it, not going into the living room. And not talking. He held to his music and the kindly, medicinal administration of whiskey.

By evening, it seemed we could eat endlessly, as if we'd had some successful inoculation at dinner and could handle anything. I stayed in the kitchen after they all reformed in the dining room at the table for coffee cake. I could hear them, but the little man in his starry yellow robe was on the table in the kitchen and I put my head down on the oil cloth very near the curled and delighted tips of his pointed shoes, and I slept. Whatever laughter there was, there was. But something sweet and starry was in the kitchen and I lay down beside it, my stomach full, warm, so safe I'll live the rest of my life off the fat of that vast family security.

SPILLVILLE

Excerpt

Pilgrimage

GOD, THE SKY IS BLUE, and the air is shot with gold. A moment ago, we passed a farmyard where a girl about twelve, wearing a blue-and-white dress, stood waving, dwarfed by a lilac bush whose blossoms were already rusted. She seemed to beckon, but of course she was just waving at the world – us – passing by. She would have been alarmed if we'd stopped. But the impression remains that she was inviting us in.

Now, down another side road, we've decided to stop for a picnic, spreading our provisions on a patch of rocky pasture overlooking the clean geometry of the fields below. Pilsner Urquell in green bottles, the heavy-gold of Bohemian hops; cheese and salami set out on butcher paper, sweating in the sun. We rip off hunks of sourdough from a big loaf, grimacing like men tearing the Manhattan telephone directory in half. For dessert, there's Belgian chocolate so bitter it makes my eyes hurt.

This trip is a variation on a theme. Even for Dvořák, the theme was already stated; even he was making a pilgrimage. He sought the familiarity of his own language in the wilderness of English, and he came to the farmland and woods Kovařík promised would remind him of Bohemia. A good place to compose, away from the city. All that, true enough.

But he sought as well, I think, the higher pitch, the experience of immigration itself. He could have found peace and quiet closer to New York. He could even have found other Czechs nearer to hand. But he could not have replicated his countrymen's experience of immigration without crossing the wider stretch of land.

Dvořák understood (it is clear from his letters) that poverty, not idealism, was the heart of immigration. "The poorest of the poor," he said, describing the background of the settlers of Spillville. He spent most of his afternoons in Spillville, after his work was done for the day, talking to the oldest townspeople. He wanted to hear their stories.

Dvořák came not to *be* an immigrant – that was of course not possible for such a celebrated man – but he could touch the experience, at least the hem of its cloak. Perhaps his coming here is best understood as an oblique homage paid to immigration, the cruel/kind song that beguiled so many of his people. The summer of 1893 he made his brief bow to what he knew was not only his countrymen's emigration, but their banishment.

The paradox: there can be no pilgrimage without a destination, but the destination is also not the real point of the endeavor. Not the destination, but the willingness to wander in pursuit characterizes pilgrimage. Willingness: to hear the tales along the way, to make the casual choices of travel, to acquiesce even to boredom. That's pilgrimage – a mind full of journey.

It's an *adagio* movement, the slow lyrical mode of travel. Everything fits. As now, lying here, eyes closed, winter face to the spring sun. Flies, attracted to the sticky smell of flat beer left in the green bottles, are making a low sizzling sound near my head. A wasp has zoned in on the salami, and I realize, touching my hand to my forehead, that my brow is furrowed.

Somebody has put Dvořák's *American* quartet on the tapedeck, and turned the volume up to the max. Our theme song, the piece he sketched his first few days in Spillville. The *scherzo*, modelled on the song of the scarlet tanager, is drilling itself over the pasture. A happy man wrote that.

Dvořák ventured this far from home; the American Midwest was the furthest reach of his travels. Such an unlikely explorer. He was so hopelessly daunted by the carriage traffic in Prague, it is said, that he would ask a student to help him cross the street. What kind of pilgrim is that?

A fearful one, the most authentic kind.

Bronislava Volková

IN THE LITTLE SATCHEL OF SILENCE

In the little satchel of silence
in the kingdom of feathers
the air
is ticking.
It bends down for kindness
from the trees.

I DIDN'T COME IN ORDER TO FORGET

Translated by the author and Lilli Parrott

I didn't come in order to forget.
I weigh my grapes,
I mark the tune with my foot.
Then senseless I fling myself into the waves
and under the surface I grow heavy
I open the shells
I listen to the seas,
I flap along the sand with my nudity.
Shyly I press the buttons of vertebrae
Like bells of strange doors.

I DO NOT SPRING FROM THE EARTH

Translated by the author and Andrew Durkin

I do not spring from the earth
                          as water
and I do not darken
                as a curtain.
I have a soul shaved
                bald.
I have days kept awake by the sun,
and on my eyes I have a scarf,
a trembling on my mouth.
At dusk
        I smuggle my prison notes
into the ears of the seafoam.

Jaroslav Seifert

LAWN TENNIS

Translated by Jarda Cervenka

Forget your dark thoughts
and heavy heart.
Remember the white lawn tennis
and light rubber balls.

Oh – old guitars and mandolins
dead history and knights in armor.
Just listen to the wailing strings of tennis racquets
sitting in the wicker easy chair.

POET

Translated by Jarda Cervenka

He sang and sang
about the grim mood
about the youth far gone
while on his chin
still drips the milky way.

LOVE

Translated by Jarda Cervenka

Dying of cholera
exhale
the scent of lilies of the valley.

Inhaling
the scent of lilies of the valley
we die of love.

SOLACE

Translated by Jarda Cervenka

My lady, my lady
you frown again
because it was raining
all your day.
What should
the mayfly say
when all her
life was rained away.

CIRCUS

Translated by Jarda Cervenka

Today it was the first itme
when fire-eater John
embraced the tiny dancer Chloe.

And tender Chloe was a virgin still.

That evening Pom the clown
in front of the saddened audience
announced, releasing the big
balloon: "Today For The Last Time."

HISTORY

Translated by Jarda Cervenka

And in the meantime on fragile parallels of Earth
an ancient vine is creeping
I am dying of thirst Miss Muguet
and you would not reveal
about the taste of wine in Cartagena.

The star was struck by lightning
it rains
the water's surface
stretched drums
the Russian revolution
conquest of Bastille
and poet Majakovskij died.

But poetry
sweet drops from honey moon
into the calices of flowers.

Eva Kanturkova

THE OLD MAN DIED

Translated by Marie Bednar

THE OLD MAN MADE me realize how the approach of death draws us closer and closer to the place where we will take our last breath. When I first moved into the village more than fifteen years ago, the old man used to take his geese to the river daily. In the late afternoon he would come to fetch them and steer them back home. He had a whole flock of geese, some of them downright mean, and with a countryfolk's malice he often watched me and my dog stand up to his belligerent gander. I gained his respect only when I, in an unladylike fashion, almost finished the gander off after it jumped at my dog from behind. The old man brought his geese to the river partly to feed, partly to be out of the way, and partly to keep them dazzling white. In the winter he and his wife would strip the goose feathers to give to their numerous relatives.

The river is quite far, and it runs deep in the valley, but twice a day the old man made it to the river over the Hradishte Hill, which was very steep. Its summit towers above the bend of the Otava River, and it may have once been a settlement of the Celts, who were the first to discover and pan for gold in the river. The Celts left behind in the Bohemian lands remnants of fortifications and tailing piles from washing gold. The Teutonic tribes also coveted the Otava River gold, and they tried to push the Celts out; in the end both were swallowed up by the Slavs. No gold is found in the river now, only fertilizer from the surrounding fields, which has killed all the crayfish. The old man never thought of the Celts, though. His historical knowledge of the local topography was limited to a hill near the town of Putim, where, rumor had it, a rich robber had once buried a treasure ever so rare which nobody has found yet.

As the time went on, the old man no longer went up and down the slope as easily. He still brought his geese to the river, but only for an hour or so, and then he steered them back home. He did that mainly from stubbornness. The goose trail went close by the townspeople's summer cottages who made a loud fuss about swimming in the river full of goose feathers and slipping on goose droppings in front of their own property. By the daily march with his flock, the old man held onto his prerogative of an old resident.

Then one spring he kept his geese in his yard; they bathed in an old wooden tub and once in a while took a reckless flight across the road into the agricultural cooperative's corn field. To save face, the old man got himself a sheep and took her grazing way up toward the top of the hill. Shmulina munched on ornamental bushes around the townspeople's cottages, while the old man hunted mushrooms in the grass. When we passed them, Shmulina stamped her forefeet at my dog, but she let me touch her wet snout. More often though, Shmulina just loitered about, while the old man was dozing off. He didn't even make it to the river to see the big spring flood.

Gradually, the old man grazed the sheep closer and closer to his house. At first, he took her beyond the meadow near the woods, then only behind the neighbor's garden, and finally just across the street by the neighbor's farmhouse. During his last year, he let Shmulina forage on our side of the road and carried a small pillow so he wouldn't get chilled sitting on the cement wall of the village well. And he mostly dozed off, although it was right in the village. Toward the end, his wife would put a chair for him in front of their gate, and Shmulina grazed close by under the steep bank, a remnant from a demolished poorhouse. A week before his death, the old man fell from the steep bank into the tall nettles, and the neighbors brought him home unconscious. "Mother," he later said to his wife, "now I know how it happened to old Kalousek." He didn't explain himself further.

His weakness made the old man stay in bed; outside, Shmulina kept bleating and trying to get in. Even lying down, he was not comfortable, so he mostly sat in the bed, since that seemed to make his breathing easier. No doctor was called in. The old man wanted no part of hospitals – he would rather give strength to his shriveled body with slivovice. When I talked to him for the last time on Monday afternoon, he was sitting on the bed in his long underwear and white shirt. Once I had planted a mountain ash, and every year we made wine from its berries. Mine was never any good but the old man's always turned out well, and his wife brought from the pantry a leftover bottle of that marvel. This year the crop of berries was meager, and on top of it there were tons of starlings. I complained to him about the starlings, but he seemed to pay scant attention to our trying to engage his interest in life. Finally he offered: "Those beastly birds, the fieldfares." From the old man's memory presents like this would often pop up: fieldfares, fieldfares; the last time I had heard that bird mentioned was back in my childhood. I went home with that word – his last gift.

When the death bell tolled the following morning, it did not dawn on me that it could be for him. As he sat on the bed the night before, wearing his sparkling white shirt, his hair neatly combed, he did not appear close to death. His wife had left him in the early evening to fetch some fodder for the sheep. He was going to listen to his favorite program on the radio – a fairy-tale reading – which usually was the highlight of his day. When she came back, he was lying next to his bed, no longer breathing. She tried breathing into his mouth, she called his name, she shook him. He did not come to.

She covered him with his eiderdown and propped up his head high with pillows. Old age had irreversibly bent him at the waist, and on cold days when he used to take his sheep grazing, wearing a peaked cap and heavy winter jacket, he was a perfect embodiment of an old man stooped over with age. The pillows piled up high tactfully concealed his stoop. To keep him company in this difficult moment, his wife lay down on the floor next to him. Later, she and his son dressed him in his black best suit, a white shirt, kept ready for that occasion, and warm gray socks. Death had straightened the old man up a little. When I saw him lying on the floor, two pillows were enough to prop up his head.

His hands were neatly folded – such skillful hands, with fingernails broken-off – they could have fixed anything and were marvelous with stone. All those retaining walls and fireplaces and chimneys he had built! Nobody could do it like that anymore. His pride and joy, though, was his son's house; he had saved up for it, designed it, and built it with his own hands. His face was a bit ashen, but he still looked as if he were only asleep. His wife was eager to hear how great he looked even in his death, and all her lady friends kept repeating just that: "He looks great, Barushka, really great." Human grief finds such amazing ways to hide itself; she did not carry on, did not reproach him for leaving her behind, and if she cried at all, it was just briefly. But she told me that later, when he lay there, waiting for the ceremony, she had heard him say to her, "Mother, give us a kiss." "Of course I will and not just one," she answered and broke into tears. And then she heard him plead with her, "Don't cry. You mustn't cry."

At the funeral she did not cry either. He was laid out in the coffin in the middle of the room; the beds had been taken out. She surrounded him with fresh flowers and pictures of saints. He still looked as if he were just sleeping. Since he never left his house without his cap, now, when his head was bare, the upper half of his forehead looked distinctly whiter. I asked her if I could lay a bouquet of pink roses on the coffin. She considered my request solemnly; the roses would look so bright against the dark wood.

Finally she said, "How did he pray for you! Every night and aloud, when they put you in jail," and she placed the roses over his legs.

Eight firemen carried the old man out of his house to the Hradishte village chapel, where they stood at attention. How many times had the old man repaired the chapel and tolled the funeral bells for all those who had preceded him! In his yard, the brass band started and followed the funeral procession to the chapel, where the priest, a very young man still, bid farewell to the old man on behalf of the village. He was late rushing over from a wedding; priests were few and far between. The funeral bus to the Putim cemetery was packed. Not only would farmers' wives not want to miss the stonemason's funeral, they also got a free ride to bring fresh flowers to their own family graves.

In his sermon in the Putim church, the young priest spoke of the blessed: the blessed just and the blessed meek who will inherit the kingdom of heaven. Then, after the funeral hymns, the choir sang an old folk tune, "That village of mine, near Shumava hills" and from the hilltop Putim cemetery, where Jan Tsimbura* was also laid to rest, the lake with its well-known swan, Honzik, could be seen. Tsimbura's family was forced to leave Putim during collectivization, they were so-called rich kulaks, but his grave was always well cared for.

At the old man's grave, the deputy of the Hradishte village council, a retired army officer, gave a speech. He had refused to attend the mass. But when he accidentally bumped into the priest at the cemetery gate and the young priest said, "It went well, didn't it?" the retired officer agreed, "It was a funeral, right and proper."

The funeral, right and proper, continued back in the village. At the pub, the firemen and the band members were drinking away their funeral pay, singing till late at night, and in the yard of the house of mourning a large table with refreshments was set for relatives and guests. Grief took refuge in ceremony, and the old man's wife maintained her poise, although there was something vaguely peculiar in what she said to me and repeated to everybody – that the old man was very worried about her.

My house and garden sit on a bank directly above the old man's yard, and when I walk over to the fence, I see right down into their kitchen. Our conversations were mainly conducted up and down like that. That evening, when all the funeral guests left, the table was put back, and she was in the house all alone with the vision of his dead body, I stood by the fence for a long time, in case she needed me. But all was dark and quiet. In the morning she said nothing except that she couldn't sleep in their marriage

*A prominent 19th century Czech farmer and a hero of a popular novel – trans.

bed, so she spent the night on the couch in the kitchen, where the old man used to take his afternoon naps with the cats.

She had been the quicker, the more imaginative of the two, and all their troubles – their refusal to vote on principle, clashes with the government and church officials, and with her own family – were her doing. He, on the other hand, was the stronger and more solid. Without him she wouldn't have been as daring, or she would've perhaps given in. But his loyalty and quiet respect gave her the strength and confidence to rise above the ordinary, even if it seemed foolhardy at times. What the villagers considered sheer lunacy, was a noble mission to him. So they complemented each other. She made the lives of their children difficult by her conflicts with the regime – they adored him; she erupted into stubbornness – he soothed the atmosphere by his good cheer.

As long as he had good wind, he played the bugle, finally only a harmonica. On Sunday mornings, they used to listen to the brass band on radio Budejovice, singing along. During birthday celebrations their little house swelled with music and songs, and for such occasions the old man had a special number about a footman whom the baroness loves, because he moves so well, ever so well, among the ladies of high class.

What will happen to her, I wondered, when she just lost one half of her being? She blurted it out to me the next morning at the well: "The body is in the grave, but not the soul. You don't believe in that, but I hear him. He is constantly around, talking to me. When I can't find something, he tells me exactly where it is. And yesterday he suddenly said, 'Stop crying. And turn on radio Budejovice.' I answered, 'I can't, people will talk,' and he said this time more firmly, 'I said, turn on Budejovice.'" The funeral guests drank all of his slivovice, but there was still some of his homemade wine left in the pantry. And she heard the old man say to her, "Mother, have some of that wine. It'll do you good." When she answered, "How could I drink wine?" she heard him almost yell at her, "Damn it, you drink some of that wine!"

Shmulina looked for the old man for a couple of days and then she obediently followed his wife to pasture. A man stopped his car by the well to get some water and when he saw the sheep, he asked, "Where is the old man who owns the sheep?" I felt a lump in my throat, but she just said, "He is here," and she made a broad gesture with her hand, "around here everywhere."

Daniel Simko

HOMAGE TO GEORG TRAKL

In the bird-light, in the dream-light, messages
of the dead drift through windows.

What house is this? What grass?

Orion inbound, tattooed against the north wind . . .
Think of it.

Think of the last grievance,
the incomprehensible need to go on and say nothing.

Perhaps now, you can recall the pale ideogram of your body,
which is the moon's,

rowing itself behind the clouds into past tense.

Or combing the hair of the dead,
as they lie, absolutely still,

as though someone was about to take their photograph.
And after all, this is why you came here.

This is why even apples fell into sin.

This bread, this wine, have silence
in their keeping.

This is how it begins.
Weaving the blood through the wrists of the damned.

This is how it continues:
The cold, the snow, the slight trembling in your hands.

One silent candle shines in the dark room.
A silver hand extinguishes it.

DEPOSITION

Yes, I know. It seems I have been talking for a long time
without making much sense.

I have mentioned fists, and departures,
the choreography of the blind.

Some invective, I suppose.
In the photograph, presented under dubious circumstances

you appear to be waving,
I mean, holding your hands up.

And that fist of ice, the knife-blade, and broken glass,
are all a rude joke.

But of course you didn't know –
the dogs, the snow coming down on our bodies

which weigh nothing.
Which are grievances.

As for the address, there is none.
What was I saying?

All right. Continue.

A FIELD OF RED POPPIES

I can see them now, I think, bowing against absence,
and trusting us.

They are, what my friend calls, a mind's glove.

Small death's heads, small bodies that are not there.

It is all right to think of them in a photograph,
or in a dream.

It is all right that they assume their sinister bend.

What else can you say about poppies?

How they remind you of your childhood,
or of someone who is not there.

That's all.

And yet, this is a field
where they threw a man once.

That's the story.

And it still matters. Because it's voiced.

AFTERWARDS

August deep,
a thin line of grief swarms around the wild cherry.

The music coming on again.

It doesn't really matter where you are.
It doesn't really matter.

What can you say to that?

Simply, that you haven't arrived anywhere.
Your destination, unknown.

Only then are you among the living.

CODA

All night you have been tearing maps in your sleep.
Your autobiography.

The crows rowing overhead are too silent to be crows.
The sky shows its overbite.

It must be raining.
There is no place to go but home.

George Erml

Before the Celebration

CONTRIBUTORS' NOTES

C. J. HRIBAL is the author of a collection of stories, *Matty's Heart* (New Rivers Press), and a novel, *American Beauty* (Simon and Schuster). He has taught in the M.F.A. writing program at Memphis State University and now teaches at Marquette University and in the M. F. A. Program for Writers at Warren Wilson College. A new novel, *Small Potatoes*, is forthcoming.

FATHER BENEDICT AUER is a fourth generation Czechoslovak-American on his father's side, and was raised in Cicero, Illinois. He is presently Director of Campus Ministry at St. Martin's College in Lacey, Washington, and teaches in the college. He has three books of published poetry, and has appeared in over 150 magazines with short stories, poems, homilies, and articles.

MARIE BEDNAR is a translator and fiction writer who lives in Bellefonte, Pennsylvania. She has published many articles, including reviews of Czech fiction in *Library Journal*. She received library training from Charles University in Prague, and has a master's degree in comparative literature from Penn State.

OLIVIA BEENS, born in Haarlem, Netherlands, is a Visual Artist/Writer who lives and works in New York City. She came to the United States in 1955 with her Czechoslovakian mother after living in Lisbon, Portugal for three years. She received a B.F.A. from Pratt Institute in 1977 and an M.F.A. from Hunter College in 1982. She has exhibited her work widely since 1980, including a performance piece titled, *Prague, CSSR 1959* at Franklin Furnace. Among other awards, Beens received a grant from the New York State Council on the Arts and a Fellowship to the MacDowell Colony in 1987 and 1990.

JAROSLAVA BLAŽKOVÁ was born in 1933, and studied philosophy at Comenius University, Bratislava. Blažková spent two years as editor in the department of literature at the Czechoslovak Radio Corporation, and four years as editor of the cultural page of the daily *Smena* in Bratislava. In 1958, she was dismissed for "revisionism." Blažková spent one year as a gardener in the communal gardens of Bratislava, and since then has been a freelance writer. She now lives in Guelph, Ontario.

JANET BOHAČ received her B.A. in Creative Writing from the University of Miami where she studied with Isaac Bashevis Singer and was a recipient of the Ila Rosenbaum Award for Scriptwriting. She has also attended the American Film Institute in Los Angeles as a Screenwriting Fellow. She holds an M.F.A. from Western Michigan University. Her fiction and poetry have recently appeared in *Zelo* and *Anima*.

JOSEPH BRUCHAC's family, on his father's side, is from Turnava, a small town near Bratislava. On his mother's side he is American Indian – Abenaki – and a good deal of his writing has been deeply influenced by the Native American side. However, like the eagle which flies with both wings, not just one, he depends on both parts of his heritage to give him balance. Aside from attending Cornell University and Syracuse and three years of teaching in West Africa, he has lived all his life in the small Adirondack foothills town of Greenfield Center. Bruhac writes both poetry and fiction, has had twenty-two books published, and has received numerous awards.

PAUL J. CASELLA grew up on Long Island, New York, and is a graduate of Dartmouth College and The Iowa Writers' Workshop. He's had poems published in *The Oklawaha Review, The New Press,* and *Bovine Interventions.* At present he is the producer and editor of *PTV: poetry television* a video magazine of poetry and other fine arts.

JAROSLAV CERVENKA was born in Prague in 1933. There he attended medical school and later obtained a degree in human genetics. After spending two years as a visiting professor at the University of Minnesota, he emigrated to the United States with his wife Alexandra and his son Vojta, in 1968. Their daughter Tereza was born the next year. Since then he has worked as a Professor of Human Genetics at the University of Minnesota in Minneapolis. He has traveled in Africa, Asia, and South America, and is currently working on a book of short stories.

HANA DEMETZ was born in 1928, in Ústíi, Czechoslovakia. Since 1952 she has lived in the United States. From 1962-1985 she was a Lector in Czech at Yale University. Among her publications are *The House on Prague Street* and *The Journey From Prague Street,* both published by St. Martin's Press, New York.

TOM DOMEK is a lecturer in the English Department at the University of North Dakota, Grand Forks. He has recently had poems published in *The Gettysburg Review* and *New Voices: College Prize Anthology* number seven, published by the Academy of American Poets.

LORRAINE DUGGIN was born in Omaha, Nebraska, the granddaughter of immigrants from Moravia and Bohemia. She taught at the University of Nebraska at Omaha's Writer's Workshop from 1974 to 1982; currently she teaches writing at Creighton University. She is a poet-in-residence through the Nebraska Arts Council and the Iowa Arts Council. Her short stories and poetry have received several prizes, including the Mari Sandoz Prairie Schooner Fiction Award and the John R. Vreeland award. Her work has been published in many magazines and anthologies, including *Prairie Schooner* and *North American Review.*

ANDREW DURKIN is Associate Professor of Slavic Languages and Literatures at Indiana University, Bloomington. His critical and translating interests extend to Russian literature and history.

JAMES FELAK, a former student of Bronislava Volková at Indiana University, is currently Assistant Professor of Slavic Languages and Literatures at the University of Washington, Seattle.

SUSAN FIRER lives, works, and writes, all within walking distance of Lake Michigan. She teaches creative writing at the University of Wisconsin-Milwaukee, and is the author of *My Life With the Tsar* (New Rivers Press). In addition, her work has been included in *The Chicago Tribune, The Christian Science Monitor* and *This Sporting Life: Contemporary American Poems About Sports and Games.*

CAROLYN FORCHÉ is the author of several books, including *Gathering the Tribes* (Yale University Press) and *The Country Between Us* (Harper and Row). Forché, whose father comes from Bratislava, currently lives in Washington, D.C.

MARYANN FRANTA is a practicing Registered Dental Hygienist, part-time senior at the University of Minnesota, majoring in English with a concentration in creative writing, and a poet when possible. Born in St. Paul, Minnesota in 1954, she has lived in that area all of her life, and currently resides in North St. Paul. Her poetry has appeared in *The Florida Review.*

JIŘINA FUCHSOVÁ was born in Plzeň, Czechoslovakia in 1943. There, during the late fifties, she began to publish her poetry. In 1963 she left Czechoslovakia and came to the United States. She is the author of eight books of poetry, all published in Czech, with the exception of *An American Baedeker.* She has also published a book of art monography with Jiri Karger and a travel book on Alaska. She lives in Los Angeles.

BARBARA GOLDBERG's mother was born in Olomouc, grew up in Teplice-sanov, and married in Prague before coming to this country in 1940. Goldberg is the author of *Berta Broadfoot and Pepin the Short: A Merovingian Romance* (The Word Works) and *Cautionary Tales* (Dryad Press), winner of the Camden Poetry Award. She has received fellowships from the National Endowment for the Arts, and is editor of *Poet Lore* magazine. Goldberg is the coeditor of *The Stones Remember,* an anthology of contemporary Israeli poetry (The Word Works) due out this spring.

PATRICIA HAMPL is perhaps best known for her memoir *A Romantic Education*, the story of her Czech family and of her travels to Prague. She has also published two collections of poems, *Woman before an Aquarium* and *Resort and Other Poems*. Her prose meditation on Antonin Dvořák's 1893 visit to Iowa, titled *Spillville*, was published in 1987 with engravings by the artist Steven Sorman. Her work has appeared in various magazines and anthologies, including *The New Yorker, Antaeus, Best American Short Stories* and *The Writer on Her Work* (Vol. 2), and she is a regular reviewer for the *New York Times Sunday Book Review*. Hampl has received numerous awards and fellowships for her work, including a Guggenheim, a National Endowment for the Arts, and a MacArthur grant. She teaches at the University of Minnesota and lives in St. Paul.

AEDAN ALEXANDER HANLEY is a poet, short story writer, and creative nonfiction writer. He is the current poetry editor for *The Cream City Review*, and a recipient of a Wisconsin Arts Board Grant for 1990, which allowed him to write the two poems included in this anthology. His poems have appeared in numerous publications, including *The Iowa Review* and *The Northern Review*.

C. G. HANZLICEK is a Professor of English at California State University, Fresno. His fifth collection of poems, *When There Are No Secrets*, was published by Carnegie-Mellon University Press in 1986. His book of translations with Dana Habova, from the Czech, *Mirroring: Selected Poems of Vladimir Holan*, appeared from Wesleyan University Press in 1985, and was the winner of the Robert Payne Award from the Columbia University Translation Center.

MARY KOLADA HARRIS has a degree in journalism and is completing her studies in English and writing at California State University, Northridge. She won the Rachel Sherwood Poetry Award at CSUN in 1987 and 1988, as well as recognition from the Academy of American Poets. Her poems, articles, fiction, and photographs have been published in magazines, newspapers, anthologies, and literary journals. In 1986, she was honored as a Woman of Achievement by the National League of American Pen Women. She lives in Simi Valley, California with her husband and son.

TOM HAZUKA served in the Peace Corps in Chile from 1978-80, got an M.A. at the University of California Davis and a Ph.D. at the University of Utah, where he co-edited *Quarterly West* from 1987-89. His stories have appeared in *Chariton Review, The Quarterly, The Florida Review* and other magazines.

VLADIMIR HOLAN (1905-1980) was known for introspection and philosophical meditation in his writing. The poems in *Pain* were written between 1949 and 1955, but could not be published until 1965 because of Stalinism. The definitive edition appeared a year later.

ZDENA HYBLOVA HELLER escaped from Czechoslovakia in 1951, and lived in London and Munich. While still in her teens and early twenties, she did a considerable amount of writing in Czech for Radio Free Europe. After the Hungarian uprising, she left Europe for the United States. She began to write and publish in English in 1976, then worked as a journalist, publicist, and communications specialist. She has been writing fiction for the last several years, and is working on a novel.

EVA KANTURKOVA's numerous novels, short stories, and essays have been published mostly during the last twenty years by Czech samizdat and emigré publishers. Her recent novel, *My Companions in the Bleak House*, has appeared in English to critical acclaim both in the United States and Great Britain. In 1988, she was awarded Prix Jan Palach for her outstanding contribution to Czech literature and to the Czechoslovak human rights movement.

JOYCE DEVRIES KEHOE, though only one quarter Czech, was greatly influenced by her Czech background. Her grandmother, Olga Plouzek, and her great-grandmother, Emilie Koza, were both very close to her. In 1983 she received her M.A. from the University of Washington, and was the recipient of the James Hall Prize for Fiction. Kehoe teaches fiction writing classes through the Creative Writing program of the University of Washington extension, and does editing. She has published essays and book reviews.

ERAZIM KOHÁK, born in Prague, left Czechoslovakia after the Communist coup of 1948 and, except for a brief return in 1969, has lived abroad ever since. He studied philosophy and theology at Yale University, and has taught philosophy at Gustavus Adolphus College and at Boston University. Kohak has published many books in both English and Czech, and has also translated widely from Czech, French, and German.

EVA KONRAD was born in Prague in 1924. After the war, she was given a scholarship to Vassar College, returned to Czechoslovakia after graduating, married an American, then found herself back in the United States, this time in California. She received an M.L.S. from Berkeley, and worked for 30 years as librarian at Mills College in Oakland. She has been writing in English for ten years, and has had her work published in several small magazines. She is now newly retired and at work on a novel about a Czech family between the wars.

MILAN KOVACOVIC teaches French language and literature at the University of Minnesota, Duluth. He writes directly in both French and English. A memoir on which he has been working for several years will be published in spring 1992 by Editions Seghers in Paris. His work has been made possible in part by two artist assistance grants provided by the Minnesota State Arts Board, through an appropriation by the Minnesota State Legislature, with additional funds coming from the National Endowment for the Arts.

J. L. KUBICEK's poems have appeared in a number of U. S. and Canadian journals, and a chapbook, "Flemish Light." He served in the infantry, ETO, WWII and has written many lines that, he relays, stumble towards the Holocaust.

PETER KULKA was born in Vienna to an Austrian-Jewish father and a Moravian mother. He spent a part of his childhood in Czechoslovakia before coming to America as a refugee at the age of ten. His fiction has been published in numerous literary magazines. His books include *The Hermetic Whore*, a collection of short stories, and *Crash-Landing*, a novel.

TERRANCE J. LAPPIN's grandfather was born in Bohemia; he emigrated to this country as a boy of seven. Formerly a student at the University of Minnesota and Carnegie-Mellon University, Lappin currently lives in Minneapolis, Minnesota, where he is a playwright and poet. His play "Hit By A Cab" appeared in the 1990 New Rivers Press anthology, *Slant/Six: New Theater From Minnesota's Playwrights Center.*

FREYA MANFRED has three published books of poetry, *A Goldenrod Will Grow, Yellow Squash Woman,* and *American Roads.* She was the Radcliffe Fellow in Poetry in 1976, and won a National Endowment for the Arts Grant in 1978. In 1988-89 she was a poetry consultant for "Good Evening" with Noah Adams (Minnesota Public Radio), and read her own work and the work of other poets on the air. She is married to screenwriter Tom Pope, and they live in Bloomington, Minnesota with their twin sons Ethan Rowan and Nicholas Bly.

PAUL MARTIN lives in Ironton, Pennsylvania with his wife, Rita, and two children. He teaches at Lehigh County Community College, and has had work published in numerous journals, including *Kansas Quarterly, Green Mountains Review* and *Passages North.* Heatherstone Press has just accepted his manuscript, *Green Tomatoes.* His father's name, when he entered this country, was Michael Marczinov.

AL MASARIK was born in Wilmington, Delaware, in 1943. He lived in San Francisco for eighteen years. Since 1984 he has traveled extensively, working in the Artists-in-Education programs of several states. His poems have appeared in many magazines and anthologies, and he is the author of several collections of poems, the most recent of which is *Van Gogh's Crows* (Black

Rabbit Press, 1989). Now living in Tennessee, he is the editor of *Swamp Root*, a poetry magazine.

JOANNE HVIZDAK MEEHL is a forty-year-old writer and businesswoman of Slovak heritage. Her father was from the Tatra region and her mother's family came from the Bratislava area. She has published business articles and social commentary, and is working on a book about Catholic women who have left the faith. She lives with her husband south of Boston, where she writes and runs a consulting business.

BILL MEISSNER is the Director of Creative Writing at St. Cloud State University in St. Cloud, Minnesota. He is the author of three books of poetry, *Learning to Breathe Underwater, The Sleepwalker's Son* (both from Ohio University Press) and *Twin Sons of Different Mirrors* (with Jack Driscoll, from Milkweed Editions). He has had numerous stories published, including three which have been syndicated by The Fiction Network in San Francisco. Meissner is also the recipient of four PEN/NEA Syndicated Fiction Awards, and a 1989 Loft-McKnight Award of Distinction in Fiction.

OLDŘICH MIKULÁŠEK (1910-1985) was the author of many poems, known for their full-blooded, suggestive atmosphere they evoke, as well as their ability to convince through the inner intensity of the experience they describe.

CHARLOTTE NEKOLA was born in St. Louis in 1952. Her work has appeared in *New Letters, The Massachusetts Review, Calyx* and other publications. She has been the recipient of the Schweitzer Fellowship in Humanities at the State University of New York at Albany, a Major Hopwood Award in Poetry from the University of Michigan and a Fellowship in Poetry from the New Jersey Council on the Arts. Currently, she teaches creative writing and literature at William Paterson College.

DEBORAH O'HARRA (born Deborah Tobola) discovered in her early twenties that "bohunk" was an ethnic slur, instead of a term of endearment. "Bohunk Love" first appeared in the *Wisconsin Review*; the poem "Litost" appeared in *CutBank* and was twice nominated for a Pushcart Prize. O'Harra has just completed her first book, titled *The Trick of Forgiveness*. She lives in Anchorage, Alaska with her husband and two sons.

LAURA PAPPANO majored in English at Yale. Following graduation, she worked at Crown Publishers in New York City and is now a daily news reporter for *The Patriot Ledger* in Quincy, Massachusetts. She is also at work on an oral history of the past eighty years, as told by her Czech grandmother, Eleanore Svehla. She lives in Brookline, Massachusetts with her husband, Thomas J. Lynch, Jr. This is her first published story.

LILLI PARROTT is a Ph.D. student in Slavic Languages and Literatures at Harvard University. She has also translated poetry from Russian (Tsvetaeva and Mayakovsky) and French (Rimbaud and Mallarme).

IVA PEKÁRKOVÁ, New York taxi driver, recently went to Thailand to examine Cambodian refugee camps. Her first novel, *Feathers and Wings*, was published by Sixty-Eight Publishers of Toronto, in 1989. The book will appear in English next year.

JAMES RAGAN is currently the Director of the Professional Writing Program at the University of Southern California. He has been a Fulbright Professor of Poetry at the University of Ljubljana, Yugoslavia (1984) and at Beijing University, China (1989). His books of poetry include *In the Talking Hours* (Eden-Hall/London, 1979) and *Womb-Weary* (Carol Publishing, 1990). His poems have appeared in *Antioch Review, Poetry,* and elsewhere.

RONALD J. RINDO was born and raised in Muskego, Wisconsin, a suburb of Milwaukee. Rindo received his B. A. from Carroll College and his M. A. and Ph.D. from the University of Wisconsin-Milwaukee. His first collection of short stories, *Suburban Metaphysics* (New Rivers Press) won the 1988 Minnesota Voices Project, and appeared in 1989. He currently teaches at Birmingham-Southern College, in Birmingham, Alabama. Rindo's paternal grandmother was born in Pecovska Nova Ves, Slovakia, and speaks the languages of both the past and the present.

ZDENA SALIVAROVÁ was born in Prague in 1933. She is a singer, actress, publisher, and novelist. She performed with the Magic Lantern Theatre, the Pravan Theatre, and appeared in several Czech films of the New Wave. In 1966 she began to study at the Prague Film Academy, but was interrupted by the Soviet invasion, which prompted her to emigrate to Canada with her husband, novelist Josef Švorecký. They live in Toronto, where they are the publishers of Sixty-Eight Publishers. She has had three of her own books published, one of which received the prestigious Egon Hostovský Memorial Award for Best Czech Fiction in 1976. In 1990 she was awarded the Order of the White Lion by President Václav Havel for her publishing efforts.

JAROSLAV SEIFERT, born in 1901 in Prague, won the Nobel Prize for Literature in 1984. His *Selected Poems* appeared in 1986. Earlier collections (none, unfortunately, available in English), include *A City in Tears, The Nightingale Sings Off-Key, Clad in Light, Helmet of Clay, Mozart in Prague, As Long as It Doesn't Rain on Our Coffin, One More Spring,* and *She Is Loveliest When Mad.*

CHRIS SEMANSKY's work has appeared in numerous small press and literary magazines including *College English, Spoon River Quarterly, Haight-Ashbury Literary Journal, The Reaper,* and *Exquisite Corpse.* In 1983 and 1984 he received the Queens College Alumni Award for poetry for the chapbooks *Sarah Thustra* and *Bonemeal.* His poem included here first appeared in the April 1989 issue of *College English.* Semansky is a second generation Czech, whose grandparents came from a small village on the outskirts of Prague.

DANIEL SIMKO was born in Czechoslovakia, and came to this country shortly after the events of 1968. He received his education from the University of Cincinnati, Oberlin College, the University of Iowa, and Columbia University. His verse and translations have appeared in numerous national and international magazines and anthologies. He has held the Clair Woolrich and Tennessee Williams Fellowships in Poetry at Columbia University, a writing fellowship at the Fine Arts Work Center in Provincetown, and is presently an N.Y.F.A. fellow. He is also a member of S.V.U., the Czechoslovak Society of Arts and Sciences.

JAN SKÁCEL, born in 1922 near Straznice, studied philosophy in Brno and later worked as a factory hand and as a literary editor, both for Czechoslovak radio and for the literary monthly *Host do domu.* His collections of poetry (none currently available in the U.S.) include *How Many Opportunities Has A Rose, What's Left of the Angel, The Hour Between the Dog and the Wolf* and *We Got Lost.*

JOSEF ŠKVORECKÝ was born in 1924, in Náchod, and is a writer, translator, editor, and professor of English at the University of Toronto. He received his Ph.D. from Charles University in Prague, briefly taught school, and served in the tank corps of the Czechoslovak Army. His first novel was published in 1958, and was confiscated by the police. In 1969, after the Soviet invasion, he emigrated to Canada. With his wife, Zdena Salivarová, he founded Sixty-Eight Publishers, which publishes mostly books banned by the Communists in Prague. In May of 1990 Škvorecký was decorated with the Order of the White Lion by President Václav Havel.

LUDĚK ŠNEPP was born in Lńy in 1922 and he attended school in Prague. During World War II, he was forced to work in a Berlin factory. After two years, he escaped and returned to Prague. After the war, he settled in Děčín, and later in Cheb, where he studied literature and philosophy, and worked in a construction company. He began writing, and in 1959 won several state contests. In 1968, two months after the Soviet occupation, he escaped from Czechoslovakia, to Ontario, Canada, where he still resides. He continues to write, and after twenty years, his books are now back in Czech libraries.

JIŘÍ SÝKORA is a writer, actor, and journalist who was born in Prague. He is the author of a collection of short stories, a novel, and numerous scripts. Sýkora currently works as an announcer and writer for Voice of America and has just had a novel accepted for publication by Sixty-Eight Publishers.

OTTO ULČ was born in Pilsen in 1930. He studied at Charles University, Prague and Columbia University, where he received his M.A. and Ph.D. Ulč, a Professor of Political Science at the State University of New York-Binghampton, specializes in international law and politics. He has consulted with the Department of State, the Foreign Service Institute, and served as an advisor to the premier of the Cook Islands. Ulč has received many awards, including a Fulbright, and is the author of numerous articles.

BRONISLAVA VOLKOVÁ was born in Děčín. She studied Slavic linguistics at Charles University, Prague, where she received her Ph.D. In 1974 she left Czechoslovakia. After a two-year stay in West Germany, she emigrated to the United Staes, where she is currently an Associate Professor of Slavic Languages and Literatures at Indiana University, Bloomington. She is the author of three books of Czech poetry, all banned in Czechoslovakia. Two other books are forthcoming. In 1988, she was awarded the George Gall Memorial Award for her "significant contribution to modern poetry."

PHOTOGRAPHERS' NOTES

GEORGE ERML was born in 1945 in Brno, Moravia. He attended the Film and Television Academy of Fine Arts in Prague from 1964-68. After several exploratory trips he finally managed to take his whole family for a "vacation" to Yugoslavia in 1980. Before departing, he spent his last years in Czechoslovakia photographing the "normalized" population.

JAN FRANK was born in Plzeň, in southern Bohemia, in 1950. He worked as a photo-reporter and advertising photographer after graduating from technical school. He collaborated with his wife, a fashion designer for major Czechoslovak magazines. He emigrated to the United Staes in 1982.

BOHUMIL "BOB" KRČIL, born in 1952 in Prostejov, Moravia, studied in Brno to become a surveyor. In 1969 he did not return to Czechoslovakia after a trip to Austria. He studied Aesthetics at the University of Uppsala, and received a B.A. in photography at the School of Industry Arts in Stockholm. He has worked at any number of jobs, including roadmender, longshoreman, stagehand, treeplanter, barber, mason, translator – to support his photography and the travel connected with it.

JAN LUKAS was born in 1915, in the town of České Budějovice. His photographs started to appear in Czechoslovak magazines in 1932, when he was seventeen, and throughout Europe when he was nineteen. He studied graphic arts in Vienna, then worked as a photo-journalist in Prague. The Communist coup of 1948 left him without a job, since the magazines he once had worked for were suspended. He escaped with his family to Italy, via Yugoslavia, in 1965, and ten months later he emigrated to the United States.

ACKNOWLEDGEMENTS

"Loss of an Enemy" originally appeared in *The Minnesota Daily*; "For My Mother, Who Lives" originally appeared in *Elkhorn Review* and *Looking for Home: Women Writing about Exile* (Milkweed Editions); "Photograph of My Room," "On Returning to Detroit," and "Endurance" originally appeared in *The Country Between Us* (Harper and Row, 1981); "V. Nezval" and "An Abandoned Hothouse" are from *An American Baedeker*; "Elegy for the Burned" © Patricia Hampl (1978) from the book *Woman Before an Aquarium* published by University of Pittsburgh Press. Permission granted by the Rhoda Weyr Agency; Excerpts from *A Romantic Education* © Patricia Hampl (1981) from the book published by Houghton Mifflin Company. Permission granted by the Rhoda Weyr Agency; Excerpts from *Spillville* © Patricia Hampl (1987) from the book published by Milkweed Editions. Permission granted by the Rhoda Weyr Agency; "Cemetary in Dolni Dobrouc, Czechoslovakia" originally appeared in *Antioch Review*; "Altiplano" originally appeared in *The Chariton Review*, "The Gift of the Night" originally appeared in *The Embers and the Stars: A Philosophical Inquiry into the Moral Sense of Nature* (The University of Chicago Press); "Ma's Dictionary" is from *A Singular Education* (Editions Seghers, Paris); "Closing Distances" originally appeared in *South Coast Poetry Journal*; "Fainting" originally appeared in *Minnesota Monthly*; "Don't Read Those Stories" originally appeared in *The First Anthology of Missouri Women Writers* (University of Missouri Press); "Litost" originally appeared in *CutBank*; "Bohunk Love" originally appeared in the *Wisconsin Review*; "Feathers and Wings" was published by Sixty-Eight Publishers (Toronto); "Lawn Tennis," "Poet," "Love," "Solace," "Circus," and "History" originally appeared in *Na vinach TCF* (V. Petra, Praha); "The Map Is Not The Territory" originally appeared in *College English*; "Feminine Mystique" originally appeared in *Granta*; "Pittsburg" originally appeared in *The North Stone Review #9*; "To a Child Running" originally appeared in *The Milkweed Chronicle Vol. 3, #3*. Our thanks to the editors of these publications for allowing us to reprint these pieces here.

PG 5063 .B68 1991

The Boundaries of twilight
                    (91-986)